Just the Way You Are

A Wounded Warrior Legacy Novel

Nika Rhone

P9P | PARK NINE PUBLISHING

Book Cover Design by 100 Covers

Published by Park Nine Publishing

With deepest gratitude to the military and first responders who keep us safe, and run toward danger when duty calls.
Thank you for being on the wall.

And to those who raise and train guide, service, and therapy dogs, many thanks for everything you do for the wounded warriors who sometimes return from that wall in need of support.

"Stop hating yourself for everything you're not; start loving yourself for everything you are."

Ritu Ghatourey

Prologue

Today was going to be a first.

And possibly not in a good way.

"Are you sure this is a good idea, George?"

He gave his wife a wry grin. Twenty-two years of marriage meant they seemed to share a brain more often than he was comfortable with.

"I thought you told me I should agree to the Winchester's offer when I got the email, Dee?" It had been an unusual enough request that he'd asked her opinion even after he'd brought it to Dwayne, his friend and partner in their non-profit.

Neither had seen any problem with the offer of three purebred golden retriever puppies being donated to the service and guide dog foundation. Nor had he.

It was the *reason* they were being donated that had given him pause.

It still did.

But it was too late to change his mind now. The Winchesters were due any minute. Turning them away when they got here would likely be one cruel blow too many to a family already dealt more than any parents should have to handle.

Losing a child was never easy.

Delia brushed absently at a clump of fur stuck to her shirt like a badge of honor. Occupational hazard when working kennel duty. "I did. But now I'm worried they might be acting on impulse, driven by their pain. What if they change their minds in a few weeks and want the dogs back?"

"Then we'll deal with it." He reached across the metal table lined with the food bowls they'd been filling and squeezed her arm. "What do you always tell me? Don't borrow trouble, the interest is too high?"

She smiled and placed her hand over his. "So, you do listen to me once in a while."

A smart man always listened to what his wife was telling him. Even if she wasn't saying it in words.

He leaned across the table and kissed her. "Always."

"Oh, God, are you two getting smoochy in here? Do I need to cover my delicate ears?"

George snorted at the long-suffering tone and gave his wife another loud, smacking kiss Dwayne was sure to hear. "Every day, pal."

"And twice on Sundays." Delia added another loud kiss complete with obnoxious smoochy sounds before going back to portioning out the afternoon meal for the kennel. "Are you here to help, or just to play martyr because Janie's visiting her mother so you're not getting any and we are?"

"Yes, and yes." Dwayne moved into the room, one hand on the harness handle attached to the golden retriever at his side, white cane loosely grasped in the other. The dog led him unerringly to the worn metal table and stopped. "Do you want me to scoop or deliver?"

"You can take over delivering. I need to get out front and wait for the Winchesters."

"Oh, right." Dwayne gave a small frown. "I hope we did the right thing there."

Delia sighed. "That makes two of us."

Three of us.

The scent of the season's first grass mowing perfumed the air as George used one of the wide paths to cut across the campus to the building housing the foundation's business offices. A few of the newly arrived students who'd begin training Monday with the mobility service dogs they'd just been paired with wandered the grounds.

He greeted each by name as he passed. If memory served, this group included men and women from as close as New Jersey and as far away as Wyoming. That made thirty-seven states where they'd placed service dogs, all at zero cost to the recipients. Eventually, they'd hit all fifty. As long as the donations kept coming in, they'd keep expanding.

We did damn good here.

Pride at how far they'd come from the tiny one-building operation they'd started as never failed to put an extra bounce in his step.

Although his knees protested that bounce more and more lately. Just like they moaned and groaned about getting out of bed, standing up, and pretty much anything that involved walking, bending, or kneeling.

All of which, unfortunately, made up a large part of his work with the dogs in their various stages of training.

One of these days he was going to end up with replacement knees to match the titanium rods and plates the Army had put his shattered pelvis back together with after the explosion that took out his and Dwayne's Humvee thirty years ago.

"But not today," he muttered, flexing the misbehaving joints. He preferred to keep his original parts as long as possible. He was only fifty-five, for fuck's sake. Way too soon to turn into a damn Erector set.

After a quick stop inside to wash the gritty smell of kibble from his hands, he headed out front. Just in time to see the black Suburban pull into the long circular driveway and loop around to a stop in front of the building. He waited, hands in his pockets, as a man and woman in their mid-forties got out.

What he didn't expect was the teenage girl who slid out of the rear seat like a pale wraith. Blonde hair half hiding her face, dressed in jeans and a dark purple t-shirt emblazoned with a band logo he didn't recognize. She stood near her parents but still apart, looking lost, sad, and a little angry.

Oh, this could end up being even worse than he'd thought.

Suck it up, buttercup. You've faced down enemy fire and VA red tape. You can handle one moody teenager.

At least, he hoped so.

He walked toward them, hand extended in welcome. "I'm George Bassi. You must be the Winchesters."

"Yes." The middle-aged man dressed in neat khakis and a light blue polo shook his hand with a firm grip. "I'm David. This is my wife, Carol, and our daughter, Nicole."

"Nice to meet you folks." He and Carol shook, then he offered his hand to the teen. Which seemed to surprise her, judging by her brief hesitation before taking it. Her fingers were delicate in his, like a fragile bird's wings, so he took care not to crush them.

"Now, I understand you were interested in donating a few pups from your dog's litter to Another Step Forward for our service dog program. Is that right?"

"Yes. Three of them." David Winchester hooked a thumb over his shoulder toward the steadily increasing yapping coming from the rear of the vehicle. "Sadie's litter was eight total. The breeder was promised one as a stud fee. Three went to good homes. And we, uh, we decided we'd like to keep one for ourselves. So Sadie doesn't feel too lonely, since Mikey..." He ended on an uncomfortable shrug.

The girl, Nicole, spun on her heel and went to open the back of the Suburban without a word. But not before he saw the shimmer of tears she was trying to hide.

The concerns simmering in his gut flared to life again as he half-listened to her talking to the puppies, whose noise level immediately went way down. "Are you sure your daughter is okay with this?"

David nodded. "It was her idea, actually. These three were slated to be sold with the others, and half the money donated to the local animal shelters. That's the deal we made with Mikey. Our son. He was upset we chose a papered purebred over going to the shelter. So as a compromise, we agreed that if we ever bred Sadie, half the profits from her puppies would go to the local shelters to help other animals in need."

David's dry tone made sense. Golden retriever puppies with documented pedigrees went for a decent chunk of change. Their son must have been quite the negotiator for his father to give up half the extra income they'd probably bought the dog for in the first place.

Which raised the question.

"Not that we're not grateful, but then why are you giving three of them to us?" It seemed strange for them to go against what was essentially their late son's last wishes.

"Nicole—" Carol darted a glance toward the rear of the SUV and lowered her voice. "Nicole is having a hard time with Mikey's death."

From the catch in her words, her daughter wasn't the only one.

"She wanted to do something to honor his memory in a more meaningful way than a plaque on veteran's square or a street being named after him. Something that embodied who he was. How he lived, and why he...why he's not with us anymore."

"He was an Army medic." David's words were gruff. "He died saving his injured men after an ambush. Some of whom may very well have come home needing a service dog for their injuries."

Ah. Now the pieces were fitting together a little better.

But there was still one piece he wasn't sure would snap into place the way everyone was hoping. Himself included.

He tipped his head. "Would it be okay if I talked to Nicole alone for a minute?"

The couple exchanged one of those brain-sharing looks he and Dee did so well before David nodded. "Sure."

Not entirely certain how this would go, he took a slow stroll to the rear of the Suburban. Nicole had opened it and was sticking her fingers through the wire bars on the three carrier doors as she talked and cooed to the squirming puppies.

As soon as she noticed him, she jerked her hands back, wiping them on her jeans as though he'd caught her doing something wrong.

"They're cute," he observed.

"They're little teeth monsters. But," she added with a laugh, "they're adorable monsters." She picked at the remains of some purple polish on her thumbnail. "They'll make good service dogs, though. They're super smart. Just like Sadie."

"It's a very generous thing you're doing here."

She shrugged. "Not really."

"Yes, really. I don't think you'd be here if you didn't believe your gift would make a difference in someone's life. Three someones, actually. The veterans and first responders matched with our dogs are able to lead active, independent lives because of people like you and your parents, who care enough to help make it possible."

"It isn't about us. This is for Mikey."

The snap in her tone had him wanting to smile. So, the fragile dove had some steel in her, after all. That was a good sign.

He leaned a hip against the SUV. "Mikey's your brother, right?"

"He was. He's dead."

Ah. There was the pain and anger.

"He's still your brother," he said softly.

Her throat worked as she swallowed. She nodded. Tears shimmered again, but she blinked rapidly, not letting them spill over. "Thank you. Nobody else seems to think that. It's like he's become off-limits to even talk about."

"Then talk to me. Tell me about your brother."

It was like that simple request uncorked everything she'd kept bottled up inside for who knew how long. Her words, stumbling over themselves sometimes in her rush to say everything at once, painted a picture of not a saint, but a big brother she'd spent a lifetime looking up to and trying to emulate.

The boy who'd had a love of animals and taught himself how to care for any injured wildlife that showed up in their yard.

The teen who'd allowed his head to be shaved to help raise money for the St. Baldric's childhood cancer foundation every spring.

The high school senior who didn't take a date to prom, but instead organized a large group of friends to go together so no one felt left out.

The soldier who'd run out into a market in some tiny village whose name she couldn't pronounce under heavy enemy fire to try and help three of his wounded brothers.

How he'd saved their lives at the expense of his own.

How he'd missed coming home to them at the end of his enlistment by a mere twenty-seven days, and in doing so missed the birth of Sadie's puppies, his own twenty-first birthday, and everything he might have accomplished in what should have been a long life and a future full of possibilities.

She paused to take a breath.

When she spoke again, her tone was softer. More reflective. Hopeful.

"My brother always thought of others before himself. But he's gone now. He can't help anyone anymore. But since Sadie was pretty much his dog, having some of her puppies become service dogs is almost like he still is, you know?"

Some undefinable emotion squeezed inside his chest. What he'd first thought a sullen, angry girl-child had turned out to be a surprisingly empathetic young woman, inciteful beyond her years.

"It will be *exactly* like he still is," he said with quiet certainty. "It's an excellent way to honor his memory, Nicole, and I'm grateful you're entrusting us with your brother's legacy."

His words seemed to light a spark inside her.

"Legacy. Yes. Exactly. Thank you."

As they unhooked the straps holding the three plastic carriers in place, she spoke without looking at him. "Can I ask one small favor? Well, two, actually."

Uh-oh.

"Sure." He answered with the same wary caution she'd asked.

She tapped the blue painter's tape with a single word in black magic marker affixed to the tops of the carriers. "We already named them. After...after the men Mikey saved that day. I know we probably should have waited and let you do it, but...it kind of seemed right. You know?"

She shot him a quick look from the corner of her eye.

Clearly, this meant a lot to her. And though it was unusual, so was using dogs that hadn't come from their own breeding program, vetted or not.

"I understand." He read off the names on the labels. "Samson, Bailey, and Cooper." He grinned as the pups each yipped. "Those are good names. And it seems they already know them, so I don't see why they shouldn't keep them."

Her slight shoulders sagged with relief. "Thank you."

"And the second thing?"

She worried at her lip before meeting his gaze.

"If I give you a letter, three copies of a letter, would you give them to the people who eventually end up with the puppies? I don't want to intrude on their privacy or anything," she added hurriedly when he opened his mouth to say no. "I just want to tell them about Mikey. So they know who he was, and how these guys became service dogs because of him." She swallowed. "I don't want him to be forgotten."

Well, shit.

This request went right past unusual and dove straight off the cliffs of inadvisable into a sea of stupid.

She must have read his expression, because she blurted, "You can read them yourself, so you know I didn't write anything bad or ask them to keep in touch or invest in bitcoin or something."

Despite the weak joke, the plea in her gray eyes was unmistakable.

Damn it.

"Alright," he said slowly, second-guessing himself even as he said it. "As long as they look okay, and my partner agrees, I think we can do that. I can't guarantee they'll be read, but I can pass them on when the time comes."

"That's fine. Thank you, Mr. Bassi. You're the best."

No, he was a sucker for a clearly hurting kid looking for a way to make some sense of the loss of her big brother.

Dwayne is going to fucking kill me.

"I think your brother would be very proud of you, Nicole."

For the first time, the clouds lifted a little from her eyes. "Yeah?"

"Definitely." He paused. Should he?

What the fuck, why not.

"Would you like to tour part of the campus? See exactly what it is we do here?"

Her eyes brightened even further. "Sure! I mean, yes, please."

After depositing the pups in the kennels, he gave the family the nickel tour. The indoor arena, the classrooms set up for real-life situational training, the mock downtown for learning street and sidewalk navigation. The only place they didn't walk through was student housing, though he did explain its dorm-like setup, which provided both community and privacy as needed.

Some of their vets struggled with PTSD, and having a safe, quiet place to retreat to with their dogs was a must.

Nicole seemed to soak in every word and asked a thousand questions. After almost an hour, he thanked them again and finally waved them on their way.

Since today seemed to be the day for impulses, he went back to the kennel and leashed up one of the puppies at random. Samson, according to the nametag on his blue nylon collar. He did a pretty decent job of following basic commands on the way back to his office, only biting at the leash a few times and trying to dart off after a squirrel once. Otherwise, he trotted along at George's side like a little pro.

The kid hadn't lied. The pups were indeed smart.

The puppy he settled on the dog bed in his office with a new chew toy. The three envelopes from Nicole he laid on his desk with the respect normally given a bomb.

He sat and stared at them for a few long minutes. Cursing himself for agreeing to her request. Wondering what they could possibly say. Debating whether he should just toss them into the trash unread. It wasn't like she'd ever know.

But *he'd* know, damn it.

"Fuck."

The puppy yipped in response to the sharp curse. It studied him with bright eyes for a moment before deciding everything was okay and attacked the toy with renewed vigor.

Resigned to the repercussions of his own stupidity, he picked up the top envelope and slid out the single sheet of stationery filled with small, neat handwriting. Actual stationery. He didn't think people even used that anymore. And of course it was purple. That seemed to be Nicole's favorite color.

Okay, now he was just stalling.

With a sigh, he started reading.

Dear Serviceperson,

First, I want to thank you for your service. If you're reading this, it means that you were wounded in some way and are in need of a service dog, and for that I'm truly sorry. But if you're reading this, it also means that you're getting one of the dogs that was born to my brother Mikey's dog, Sadie, and for that I'm glad. You see, Mikey was a medic in the Army, and he was killed trying to help some wounded soldiers just a few weeks before he was supposed to come home.

I'm sorry to say I was really angry with my brother when I first heard what he'd done. I guess it's selfish of me to think he should have cared more about keeping himself safe than risking his life for other people. But the more I thought about it, the more I realized there was no way he could have done anything else. Mikey was always the kind of guy everyone could rely on. He was smart, and funny, and the best big brother anyone could ever have. I loved him lots, and I'm going to miss him even more, every single day of my life.

I'm not telling you any of this to make you sad. I just wanted to explain about my brother, and why the dog you're getting is so special. My brother spent the short time he had on this Earth helping others. I can't wish him back to life, but I can wish this: that his generous spirit live on in the love and comfort you receive from your service dog. Take each day you have together as a gift, and maybe once in a while think about Mikey. I know when I do, I'll be picturing him smiling down on you, knowing that his legacy, and Samson, are in good hands.

Wishing you a happy and fulfilling life,

Nicole

Well then.

Now he knew why she'd gotten that look when he'd used the term legacy.

Leaning back in his chair, he shook his head in amazement. Hard to believe a teenager had written that. Clearly, she had a lot more of her brother's maturity, compassion, and fortitude in her than she realized.

Than her parents likely realized, either.

Clearing his throat, he re-folded the letter and slipped it back into its envelope. A quick peek at the other two showed they were identical except for the dog's name at the end.

He tapped the small stack of envelopes on the desk. There was no reason not to give them to the people who ended up with Samson, Bailey, and Cooper. He'd still run it by Dwayne and Delia, but he was pretty sure they'd say the same thing once they read them. They were beautiful and thoughtful.

Of course, that was all kind of moot if the pups didn't have the basic skills after their foster period was over to actually make it into the program. Or to pass all the task-specific training after that. Not all dogs had the unique combination of ability and personality to make a good guide or service dog.

For Nicole's sake, though, he hoped hers did.

Of course, there was still the option of them becoming emotional support or therapy dogs if they flunked out of the program, though that would mean passing them off to someone else. They weren't set up to handle that particular training here.

Not yet, anyway.

He glanced over at Samson, who'd cued in on the sound of the envelopes tapping and was watching him closely, his chubby body poised with barely contained expectation. A smile came to his lips.

"You're a sharp one, aren't you, pal?"

Nothing was a guarantee. But after all these years he was a pretty good judge of dogs, and right now he had a good feeling about these three. One way or another, Michael Winchester's legacy of helping others would be carried on exactly the way his sister wanted.

Chapter 1

"Dude, why didn't you tell us your neighbor was so bangin' hot?"

Ben Murphy choke-snorted at the idiotic question.

Hot? His neighbor was a geriatric Attila the Hun who'd scared the snot out of him as a kid, despite being his gram's best friend.

He continued painting the bedroom wall without bothering to look toward the window his friend was staring through, opened wide to let the faint June breeze air out the room. "Maybe because I didn't know you had a thing for older women, Cody."

"If that's older, I have no problem with it." Cody's forehead thunked against the glass. "Sweet Jesus, I think I'm in love."

"And I think the paint fumes have finally gotten to you if you're drooling over Mrs. Roketzki."

"She's married?" Cody picked up his head with a sound of disappointment, leaving behind a sweaty smear. "Man, that's a damn waste. But hey, at least you can still enjoy the view."

"Would you watch it?" He hopped over the tray of pale cream paint they'd both been working out of and snatched the brush dangling forgotten from Cody's hand as he mooned out the window. "You're dripping all over the place."

"So what? You're redoing the floors anyway."

His teeth snapped shut over a crude retort. Yes, he'd be refinishing all the old hardwood in the place. And yes, his friends were supplying cheap labor in his ongoing renovation project in exchange for little more than free food and beer, so he couldn't really bitch too much. You got what you paid for.

But the closer they crept toward finally being done, the less it felt like just a reno project and the more it was feeling like an actual home.

His home.

And with that feeling came a strange new sense of possessive pride. One that made Cody's careless treatment of it itch like sand in his board shorts after a wipeout at the beach.

"Could you maybe finish cutting in the trim on that last wall instead of joking around? I'd like to get this done today."

Before he lost his free labor and had to finish it himself.

Cody and the other two guys he'd wrangled into playing Joe Painter for the day would head home right after he fed them the burgers and brats waiting in the cooler downstairs. All members of the same FDNY truck company, today was their last day off before their next tour started in the morning.

"Who's joking? You've been holding out on us, man."

Ignoring the hint of accusation, Ben held out the brush, bristles up.

After one last wistful look out the window, Cody took it and turned back to the wall he'd abandoned mid-stroke with a dramatic sigh.

Before returning to his own roller work, and despite knowing he was probably doing exactly what Cody and his sick sense of humor wanted, he couldn't resist one quick peek.

Ho-ly shit. That was *not* Mrs. Roketzki sunbathing in the yard next door.

Not even close.

Oh, no, the dark-haired woman stretched out on the striped lounger in Mrs. R's backyard was a young, nubile work of art clad only in a tiny black bikini.

On her stomach, face turned in the other direction, only her back half was visible. A long, straight line of sun-kissed light brown skin that ran from defined shoulders down to the cloth-covered mound of her delectable ass and ended with two long legs he had no problem imagining wrapped around his hips.

Or his neck.

Fuck. Me.

Kenoway was a quiet little hamlet of less than fifteen hundred people, and his new neighborhood seemed polarized between retirees and mommies pushing strollers. Opportunities for meeting attractive, single women his own age were thin on the ground.

Which was okay. Not shitting where you lived was a hard-learned lesson he had no interest in repeating.

But the sunbathing goddess next door...she didn't live there.

That made her fair game.

"Guess you're not as averse to older women as you thought, huh?"

Ignoring the snark in Cody's voice, he shook his head. "Trust me, if that was Mrs. Roketzki in a bikini, you'd be looking for eye bleach. Who that is"—he nodded toward the window—"is a mystery."

One he intended to solve before the day was over.

Tearing himself away from the view was tough. But he forced himself to focus on finishing the job at hand, giving it the same attention to detail as before he'd spotted all that intriguing deliciousness next door.

Easier said than done, of course.

A weakness for beautiful women was something he and Cody shared. During the four years they were roommates, they'd cut a wide swath through the single female population. Not only where they lived in Queens, but the other New York boroughs as well.

Between Cody's golden beach boy looks and his own dark hair and Irish green eyes, it wasn't vanity but fact that they did well with women. When they went out on the prowl together, they did even better. Add in their firefighter status, and getting dates was almost too easy.

Hell, he'd even picked up one woman—or been picked up, he still couldn't decide which—late one night while he'd still been soot-covered and smelling like the dumpster fire they'd just put out.

And that hadn't even been his strangest conquest.

Since they went out together so often, he and Cody had one simple rule to avoid potential problems: the first one to spot a woman had first claim on her. If he passed, the other could make a move. But if he tried and struck out, she was off limits.

No guy wanted his friend scoring with someone who'd found him lacking.

It was a system that worked well for them in the past.

Now, though, it presented a problem.

Cody had seen the backyard mystery goddess first. Technically, that made her his. And Ben wasn't okay with losing the chance to see if all that sun-kissed skin tasted as good as it looked.

Not even to his best friend.

"He threw at him on purpose!"

"You're outta your mind. It was a hundred fucking degrees. The ball slipped coming out of his hand!"

Cody shook his head at the raised voices from the bedroom at the other end of the upstairs hallway. "You knew it was going to happen eventually."

Yeah, he did.

Honestly, he'd expected it to happen a lot sooner.

Bryan Wong was a diehard Mets fan, while Dominic Russo bled Yankees blue. Usually, they could agree to disagree when they talked baseball. But the teams had played each other in a Subway Series over the weekend, so they'd been taking good-natured pot-shots at each other all day.

From the increased volume, it seemed their rivalry had hit its limit on friendly.

Time to pack it in before they started trading more than angry words. After six long months of reno work, the last thing he needed was anyone knocking holes in his brand-new sheetrock.

Once he sent Cody to grab the two knotheads and bring them down to wash up and get the grill started, he threw some plastic wrap over the paint tray with a sigh. Looked like he'd be knocking out whatever was left on his own after all. Though with luck, maybe Bryan and Dom had finished their room before getting on each other's last nerve.

But even if they hadn't, he was finishing this damn painting tonight, regardless of how tired he'd be for his commute down to the city in the morning. Not to mention sore. His right arm and back were already barking.

But it would all be worth it to come home after his tour in two days and have one more thing checked off of his never-ending to-do list.

Two more weeks.

If he stuck to his timetable, that's when he'd finally be able to stop living out of the tiny bedroom downstairs. Once his grandmother's crafting room, it had become his combination bedroom, living room, and kitchen.

If you could call a microwave and mini-fridge a kitchen.

Living in the middle of a construction zone sucked. It hadn't seemed like a big deal when he'd first decided to gut the entire house at once rather than break it into a bunch of smaller projects. After just a few weeks, though, he would have gladly moved back in with Cody if he hadn't already gotten a new roommate.

Before heading downstairs, he couldn't resist one more look out the window.

And damn near swallowed his tongue.

His mystery woman must have taken a quick dip in the inground pool to cool off. She was just reaching for the towel draped at the end of her lounger, water streaming from her lithe body.

And oh yes, her front side more than lived up to the promise her back half had made.

She slicked her short brown hair straight back against her skull, reminding him of the mythical Irish selkies his gram used to tell him stories about when he was a kid. Sleek, seductive, and not of this world, they ventured from the sea to ensnare unsuspecting human men.

Well, consider him caught.

After giving her wet body a brisk rub with the towel, one that got *his* nerve endings tingling, it appeared she was going to lie out in the sun some more.

Oh, yeah, do it, please!

A loud bang came from the back of his house as the screen door slammed. Bryan and Dom continued their argument over a hit batter as they went out onto the patio where the barbeque and a few chairs were set up.

That seemed to be the deciding factor for his pretty little sunbather.

Instead of lying down again, she wrapped the towel around herself and headed for the back door of Mrs. Roketzki's house, her steps precise and measured like a dancer. Or maybe a runway model.

She snapped her fingers and a large golden dog he hadn't noticed lying in the shade jumped to its feet, shook itself, and trotted obediently to her side. Letting the dog in first, she closed the screen door behind her. And then the inside door as well, judging by the loud thump.

Well, fuck.

Guess she wasn't coming back out anytime soon.

With no reason left to linger, he trotted downstairs to the one functioning bathroom to wash up. When he joined his friends, Bryan and Dom had thankfully traded baseball for beers, while Cody tinkered with the gas grill he'd coveted for the past two months.

As well he should. The thing was ginormous.

He probably shouldn't have splurged on it, what with the million other expenses drilling a bottomless pit in his bank account. But he knew he'd be without a functioning kitchen for several months. And he needed something to handle cooking for however many hungry firefighters he could get to come help out on their days off.

And they could eat a fucking *lot*.

Grabbing a Bud from the cooler, he twisted off the cap and dropped into one of the white plastic chairs from the dollar store. He downed several long, cold swallows before coming up for air. "God, I needed that."

"Your own fault for being such a goddamn slave driver." Dom tipped his own beer back and drained it, finishing with a belch. "No reason we had to get every friggin' room in the house painted in one day."

"Oh, so you were coming back our next day off to finish up, then?"

Dom's features fell into a look of comic surprise. "Fuck no!"

"Well, there ya go." Another long swallow, and the last cloying tang of paint coating his tongue all day finally washed away.

"At least it's cooler up here," Bryan said, garnering unanimous agreement. "It's fuck-all hot back in the city."

Ben grimaced at the reminder. Barely even summer, the hot, humid conditions that had gripped New York by the throat for the past week were bad enough. But add in sixty pounds of gear and a ripping three-alarm fire, and it could feel like your balls were going to boil in your own sweat.

Where they were stationed in Brooklyn was usually a good ten degrees cooler than in Manhattan. There, the heat and stale air collected in the maze of skyscrapers until you could choke on it. But this time, it felt like everything south of the Throgs Neck Bridge was in a slow cooker set on high.

Just one more reason buying his gram's house after she passed last year and moving north to the suburbs of Westchester County was a good idea.

Even if he did get a little nauseous when he made that mortgage payment every month. He'd paid a little under market value, since it was his dad and uncle selling it to him. But it was still a hefty chunk of change to someone who'd only ever rented before, even at New York prices.

But damn if it wouldn't be worth it in the end.

I hope, anyway.

The next hour was filled with talking, joking, and eating. Both he and Cody tapped out after one beer apiece. Cody because he was driving, and him because he didn't want his walls to end up looking like a drunken orangutan had finished them.

And because he was still trying to figure out who his little selkie next door was, and how he was going to get around their stupid first-dibs rule. Or how he could meet her without having to deal with Attila Roketzki.

It was doubtful she was one of Mrs. R's granddaughters. Not with that face and body. There was someone who came to check on the house over the winter while she was snowbirding in Florida with half the over-sixty population of New York State. But they didn't usually help themselves to the pool.

Plus, it was June. She should definitely be back already.

Now that he thought about it, he hadn't seen Mrs. R since he moved in. Not even to bitch at him about the noise. Maybe she was sick or something. Myrna Roketzki was fixed in his mind as an indestructible old harridan, but she was around his gram's age, so it was possible his selkie was a live-in nurse or caretaker of some kind.

He could work with that.

Nurses were very partial to firefighters.

After all the food and beer were gone, he helped Cody pour the other two men into the backseat of his shiny black Avalanche. "You sure you don't want to separate them?"

"Nah, they'll probably both be asleep before I hit the Hutch." Cody looked in through the still open door and added, "But if either of you starts any shit, I'm kicking both your asses out on the side of the parkway and you can walk home. Got it?"

After he slammed the door shut on their crude replies, he scrunched up his face as though having an internal debate before finally sighing. "You should go for it."

Mouth already open to persuade—okay, beg—his friend to give up his claim on their mystery woman, Ben closed it again, nonplussed. Did he mean...?

"Just to clarify, go for what, exactly?"

"Her." Cody jerked his head toward the two-story Cape Cod next door.

"Really?" Cody Moore was giving up dibs on a hot babe without a fight?

On *that* hot babe?

The world must be ending.

Not that he was complaining or anything. He was just surprised.

"Yeah. I know you want her, too. And I'm down in Queens, and you're here, so...yeah, she's yours."

Relief mixed with the thrill of anticipation already fizzing in his veins. "You don't have to sound so pissed about it."

"I am pissed. She was..." His hands outlined imaginary curves. "Fuck!"

Yeah, she was that.

After scrubbing the last remnants of paint from his hands with another round of Goo Gone, he sped through a thirty-second shower and threw on clothes he hadn't spent the day sweating through.

There'd been no car in the driveway next door, but he hadn't heard one leave while they'd been eating, either. Chances were fair to good his little selkie, whoever she was, was still there.

And he wasn't about to miss his chance.

Sitting at her kitchen table, Miranda Hernandez bit into the chicken leg she held. She groaned out loud as the array of spices from the crispy coating burst over her tongue in riotous abandon.

So. Good.

Definitely worth the extra effort of going to the small mom-and-pop grocery one town over for this week's shopping. This was so much better than the boring fried chicken they had at the local chain supermarket, even if they did deliver. In this case, taste definitely trumped convenience.

Damn. She'd have to tell Trixie she was right.

Even the knowledge of her friend's smug "I told you so" couldn't dampen the pleasure of the meal. The potato salad was fresh and tangy, and the jalapeño cornbread tasted like it could have come straight from her *abuela*'s kitchen. The icy, tart lemonade was the perfect thing to wash it all down with.

Foodie heaven.

The only thing that would have made the meal better was enjoying it out on the patio in the fresh air and waning sunshine like she'd planned. But that was before her noisy neighbor had destroyed the peace and quiet of the afternoon and driven her inside from the sanctuary of her backyard.

Again.

It had been going on practically from the first day she'd moved in. Long stretches of blissful silence broken by several days of power tools and hammers and lots of extremely loud people who didn't seem to understand the concept of volume control.

Or that voices actually travelled past property lines.

Or filters. Some of the language that drifted over the chain-link fence when they congregated outside was downright raw.

That wasn't the part that bothered her, though.

In fact, after her five years in the Marines, she'd found some of the more creative insults kind of amusing to listen to. And maybe a little nostalgic. One of her best friends in the Corps had been a champion of the foul mouth. No one could curse like Gator.

With that slow N'awlins drawl of his, he could make even the worst words sound downright sexy.

No, what bothered her was when she really just wanted to zen out in the quiet solitude of her yard, and couldn't. Kenoway was barely fifty miles north of NYC, but summer didn't last all that long here. She wanted to enjoy every nice day possible between now and when the cold and snow of winter eventually trapped her inside.

Unable to do that this evening, she focused on enjoying every bite of her meal instead. The carbs were a killer, but so worth it. She'd add an extra mile to her run tomorrow to make up for the indulgence. Life was too short to deny yourself the little things that made you happy.

A truism she was far too intimately acquainted with to ignore.

After she put her plate and fork in the dishwasher, she sat back down to enjoy the last of her lemonade. Before she took a single sip, though, there was a knock at the front door.

She frowned and checked her watch. Almost seven.

Anyone she knew who might stop by would have called first. And it was kind of late for any kids to be out selling something. Or maybe not. The sun didn't set until after eight this time of year.

Buying that tub of popcorn from the twins down the block to help support their scout troop had been a strategical error. Once word hit the neighborhood grapevine there was a sucker for a good cause in their midst, she'd have kids selling everything from cookies to wrapping paper on her doorstep.

No good deed goes unpunished.

She briefly considered ignoring the knock and pretending she wasn't home, then shook her head at the cowardly impulse. She'd faced down much scarier things than pint-sized peddlers, for God's sake. Hiding wasn't an option.

Besides, it might be Girl Scout cookies.

She'd run an extra *five* miles for a box of thin mints.

As she walked to the front door, her golden retriever Samson joined her, nails clicking lightly on the old hardwood floors. She stroked his head, fingers sliding through the soft silk of his fur without having to reach down too far. Though on the tallish side for a woman at five-eight, Sam was pretty big himself.

Which had its downsides. Especially when Sam decided he wanted a cuddle and crawled into her lap while she watched tv on the couch. An eighty-pound lapdog was damn heavy no matter how cute he might be.

And Sam was pretty darn cute.

"You're a handsome boy, aren't you, Sammy?" She used her mushy voice as she tugged lightly on one of his feathered ears. He rewarded her with a quick doggie kiss on the wrist that made her smile. "Yeah, and you know it, too, don't you? Shameless attention whore, that's what you are."

Sam sneezed as though in agreement.

She was laughing at that when she pulled the wooden inner door open. "Yes?"

"Oh, good, you *are* home. I was beginning to wonder if I'd missed you leaving or something."

The laughter drained from her like a pulled plug.

Not a neighborhood kid. A man.

One she didn't know.

Instantly, her instincts went from welcoming to suspicious. "Can I help you?"

There was a pause, probably the stranger wondering at her sudden brusque tone. "Um, sorry. I didn't mean to intrude. I'm Ben. Ben Murphy." Another pause before he added, "From next door."

Ah. Her noisy nemesis.

Some of her tension eased, but she felt no inclination to unlock the screen door separating them and invite him in. Just because he lived next door didn't mean anything.

If he was even who he said he was.

She hated being so distrustful. But it was a lot harder to take things at face value these days. Which sucked, but this was the reality of her new normal. If she was going to live independently, she'd have to learn to deal with this kind of thing.

Realizing the long silence was her cue to speak, she reluctantly said, "I'm Miranda Hernandez."

"Well, Miranda, it is *very* nice to meet you."

Oh. My.

Something about the low timber of his voice was like the stroke of crushed velvet against her skin. And a few other places.

It kind of irritated the hell out of her. Guys with a voice like that usually knew how to use it. And did. Shamelessly.

Case in point. One damn sentence, and he had her totally out of sorts.

Suck it up, Hernandez.

The familiar refrain from her old drill instructor helped stiffen her spine against the inner wobbles caused by that velvety stroke.

All she had to do was gut it out until he said whatever he'd come over to say and left.

Then she could melt into a gooey hormonal puddle.

"That's a good-looking dog. Is he a retriever?"

Her hand dropped to where Sam had planted himself at her side and stroked his head self-consciously. "A golden retriever, yes." She was used to questions about her dog, but they could still be uncomfortable.

"Cool. I like dogs." Pause. "What's his name?"

"Sam. Samson."

Another pause. When she didn't offer any other information, Ben cleared his throat, possibly realizing he'd strayed into unwelcome territory.

"So, ah, are you here visiting with Mrs. Roketzki?"

Interesting. Clearly, he didn't have an ear to the ground about what was going on in his own neighborhood.

If he really lived here.

Suspicion spiked again. "Mrs. Roketzki is in Florida."

"She is?" He sounded confused. "I thought she only snowbirded until around April or May." He paused. "It's June."

Thanks for clearing that up, Slick.

The retort nearly spilled from her mouth before she caught it back. Not everyone appreciated her sarcastic brand of humor.

Or so she'd been told.

Thankfully, he seemed to realize the idiocy of his words all on his own, because he chuckled. "Right. You know that, obviously. What I meant was, why is Mrs. R still in Florida this late? She always said Vero Beach in the summer was like the third ring of hell."

She debated a few seconds on whether to answer. It wasn't like the entire block didn't already know.

"She fell and broke her hip over the holidays. After she got out of the hospital she went to stay with her daughter in Miami while she goes through rehab."

"Oh, wow. That sucks. I hope she's going to be okay."

The fact he sounded genuinely concerned moved him up a notch on her measuring stick. He might not be attentive enough to notice Mrs. Roketzki was MIA the past few months, but at least he cared once he found out why.

"She should be fine, from what her grandson told me, but the rehab might take a while. Which is why she's staying in Florida for the rest of the year before deciding whether to come home in the spring or move there permanently."

And as much as she didn't wish the elderly woman any ill will, she secretly hoped she chose the latter.

It had only been a few months, but she was already in love with the house, the neighborhood, and the town. She was comfortable here. Something she hadn't been sure she could achieve, especially so fast. Moving and starting over somewhere else would be difficult as well as disappointing.

"So, while she's gone, you're...?"

"Renting."

"Really."

It was hard to tell from a single word, but he didn't sound thrilled she was his neighbor for the foreseeable future. The pinch of hurt that caused was surprising.

Well, too bad.

It wasn't like she was thrilled about living next to him, either. In fact, now would be the perfect time to bring up a few things that were eroding her own neighborly goodwill.

"So, I can hear you're doing some work on your place."

"Oh, yeah. A complete reno, right down to the studs. I reconfigured some rooms, added another bathroom up on the second floor, reworked the kitchen layout...it's been a huge job. It's almost done, though. Finally." He paused, and the animated enthusiasm in his voice changed to chagrin. "Damn, it's probably been pretty loud and annoying for you while I've been doing all that, hasn't it?"

Rather than blasting him with a resounding "Yes!" she found herself shrugging as if his renovations hadn't been as irritating as bivouacking in a field of poison ivy. "Sometimes, yeah, a little."

A little? Where had that come from?

Way to wimp out, Hernandez.

He made a sound of frustration. "I am *so* sorry about that. If I'd known you were living here, I would have come over and apologized sooner. But I swear the worst is over with. Well, the kitchen still needs to go in, and the floors need to be sanded and stained, but that's it on the big stuff. And we knocked out all the painting today. Well, mostly. I have one more wall to get through tonight—maybe two—and then it's done."

An unspoken *thank God* hung at the end of that statement.

The fact they'd been painting today explained both why she hadn't known they were working at the house until they'd invaded the backyard, and why the citrusy odor of Goo Gone was drifting through the screen door from him like some cheap cologne.

"I'm just curious. If you didn't know Mrs. Roketzki was still in Florida, why didn't you ever come over to apologize to *her* about the noise?"

"Honestly? Because she scares the crap out of me." There was laughter in his tone, but it was clear it was also the truth. "I figured I'd wait until she called over and complained before I bit that particular bullet."

"Seriously? You're afraid of her?" The woman had to be in her eighties.

"Have you ever met her?"

She shook her head. "I've only talked to her over the phone a few times. I dealt with her grandson, since he's local. And my realtor."

And now her landlord. Which had seemed a conflict of interests, but the price had been too good to care.

"Then don't judge. She's freaking terrifying."

She laughed. "Okay, I'll take your word for it."

"Thanks." There was another pause. "So, um, since the house is almost finished, maybe you'd want to come over for a 'welcome to the neighborhood' drink? You know, so we can get to know each other a little better."

Her breath caught at his words. He couldn't possibly mean...

Was he *flirting* with her?

"I could give you the grand tour, see what you think of the improvements I've made to the place. It started out with the same floor plan as this house, so you'll be able to compare them and appreciate the changes. Plus, maybe seeing what all the noise you had to put up with was for will help you forgive me faster," he added with a teasing chuckle.

All the tingly warmth that had shot through her body chilled to icy numbness.

Oh, God.

He didn't know.

And she'd been too lost in the moment of easy banter between them to consider the possibility. But if Ben didn't even know about Mrs. Roketzki, he probably didn't know about her, either, even though most everyone else on the block did.

Her hand curled around the doorjamb with punishing force, anchoring her as the hard smack of reality landed with painful clarity.

"I don't think that would be a good idea." Her mouth was so dry the words felt like sandpaper abrading her throat.

"Ah, come on. Why not?"

Because I'm not what you think I am.

But the words wouldn't come out, stuck someplace between her tongue and her pride. Instead, she swallowed hard and lied.

"I was actually in the middle of dinner when you knocked. Maybe...maybe another time."

Not that she really thought there'd be another invitation.

Not after he figured out the truth.

"Oh! Hey, I'm sorry, I didn't even think..." He gave a slightly self-deprecating laugh. "Wow, I'm making a mess of this, aren't I? Look, it was really nice to meet you, and I'm sorry again about the noise. And for interrupting your dinner. I'll be at work the next two days, so you'll have total peace and quiet, I swear. And maybe when I'm home again, we can give this another try. How does that sound?"

Like something that was never going to happen.

But she forced her lips into a polite smile anyway. "Sure. Sounds good."

"Good! Well, okay then." Another of those awkward pauses. "Well, goodnight."

"Goodnight." Spine so stiff it might snap if she wasn't careful, she stepped back and closed the door.

Only once that barrier was safely between her and the man outside did she allow herself to unleash all the curses Gator had taught her during those long nights on radio watch. Silently, of course. She *had* promised her mother she'd clean up her language when she got out of the Marines, after all.

As long as she didn't say them out loud, she wasn't technically breaking her word.

Once she completed the salty litany, she pushed away from the wall and stuck out her hand for Sam, who was immediately at her side. Together, they walked the familiar path to the living room couch.

Why not? he'd asked.

Simple.

Because her new neighbor with the sexy voice clearly had no idea she was blind.

Chapter 2

"Good morning, Miranda!"

"Morning, Gail." She used her free hand to send a wave in the direction of her neighbor's voice while keeping the other firmly on the handle of Sam's harness as she continued down the sidewalk. Gail and her husband, Frank, had been a godsend since she moved in next door. They were a super sweet couple anxiously expecting their first child, always eager to help but not pushy enough to make it seem intrusive.

Something my family needs a few lessons in.

No.

She wouldn't let the early morning phone call make her pissy for the rest of the day. Which was why she'd broken her routine and gone into town to see Trixie rather than do her usual five miles on the treadmill. Her friend was funny, irreverent, and knew exactly how to make her laugh even when she was rip-down-the-walls furious.

The fact she owned Trixie's Treats bakery was just a delicious bonus.

Willpower? Not a problem for her.

In most things.

But there was something about the lure of sugar and spice that tested her resolve like nothing had since training. The Crucible had nothing on trying to pass up one of Trixie's icing-oozing cinnamon buns.

Okay, maybe that was a slight exaggeration. The Crucible had been one of the most brutal, soul-sucking challenges of her life. But she'd made it through. Sometimes she looked back on the field-training exercise that was the culmination of Marine Corps boot camp and marveled she'd ever survived it.

At the time, she simply hadn't allowed herself the option of failure, no matter how often she wanted to quit. Instead, she'd pushed through the pain and kept moving in the only direction possible: forward.

Pain is weakness leaving the body.

That mantra was one of many that helped her make it through those grueling 54 hours of deprivation and misery to earn her Eagle, Globe, and Anchor. It had helped get her through the nightmare that stole that victory away just a few short years later. And it helped her get through every damn day since, finding her way forward in a world forever set at zero-dark thirty.

Caught up in her thoughts, she almost over-walked Sam when he stopped for the curb at the end of her block. Annoyed with herself, she gave him a pat and a quick ear rub.

"Good boy, Sam. At least one of us is paying attention."

And that someone should have been her.

After listening for any coming cars, she gave the forward command to cross the street. Sam was smart, but he was still just a dog. An extremely well trained one, but even he couldn't get them where she wanted to go safely without a little input from her.

Sam stopped to indicate another curb when they reached Main Street. One of the reasons she loved the house she was renting was it being a mere two blocks from the heart of town. And, bonus, she only had to cross one street to get there. Two, if the store she wanted was on the other side of Main.

Street crossing wasn't nearly as terrifying as it had been back when she'd first been learning how to navigate a world of darkness, but it still made her palms sweat, just a little bit. Once they left the sidewalk, too much of her and Sam's safety was out of her hands and in those of the drivers she couldn't see coming.

The bakery was halfway down the street on their right. She started to give Sam his command, then hesitated. He was totally in love with Trixie—and the organic doggie treats she made especially for him. He knew which yard to turn into when they hit their block and she said "find home." Maybe if she said "find Trixie" instead of "find the bakery" he'd still drag them right to her front door.

Curious to see if he could do it, she said, "Sam, find Trixie. Find Trixie, boy."

After a small pause at the new command, he tugged her to the right and got them walking at an enthusiastic pace. She grinned. Even if this little experiment didn't work, Main Street wasn't long enough for them to get too lost. Still, she ticked off the usual landmarks as they passed them.

Roses. The bush in front of the florist shop was in full bloom, perfuming the sidewalk with its heady bouquet.

Bacon. Coffee. Her stomach gave a little grumble at the mouthwatering aromas from the deli.

Squeal-clank. Someone dropping a letter into the mail slot in front of the tiny post office.

Every scent and sound was a marker her brain used to help track her progress. She knew what stores were on each side of Main, and the order they were laid out in. Robin, her mobility and orientation coach, had worked with her and Sam on getting to the ones she used with verbal commands, but she liked having the environmental markers as a mental backup.

Because unlike with the Marine Corps and the Borg, failure for her *was* still always an option.

Especially when a new store opened, and she tried to get there without dragging Robin out to help train Sam with the new location command. She'd tried to do it on her own, miscalculated, and ended up at the laundromat instead.

Not the end of the world, but frustrating nonetheless.

If she was going to prove to everyone—including her-self—she could live a normal life all on her own, she had to step up her game. But, she was learning, part of that was knowing when to admit she needed some help and asking for it. Some-thing the other visually impaired people in her online support group were quick to remind her of whenever she started bitch-ing about wanting to feel capable and self-sufficient.

Of course, they'd never been subjected to her family's smoth-ering form of help.

Lucky them.

Exactly where she thought they should, Sam turned them right and stopped for the door. She pulled it open and inhaled a lungful of amazing goodness that said they'd reached their proper destination.

Giving Sam a vigorous ear rub, she said, "Good boy, Sammy. Smart boy." Maybe next time she'd give the command as they left the house and see if he could replicate the result. The dog truly was scary smart.

The small bell overhead tinkled to announce their entrance.

"Be right with you." Trixie's call came from what sounded like the kitchen at the rear of the shop.

Miranda slipped her fingers over her watch and grimaced. She'd been so upset by the phone call she hadn't considered the time. The bakery did brisk early morning sales with the people heading to work. Trixie baked like a fiend during the after-rush lull to restock the cases for the afternoon crowd.

"No hurry. It's just me." Turning left, she navigated to the first of the three little tables tucked into the corner. Sam settled under the table at her feet.

Other than the faint music drifting from the radio, the shop was silent, so at least she didn't have to worry about feeling on display to other customers while she waited. Not that anyone meant to be rude. But people who didn't know her usually fell into one of two categories: the whisperers and the shouters.

The whisperers seemed to think because she couldn't see them, she couldn't hear them when they speculated amongst themselves about how she'd lost her vision or how horrible her life must be. The shouters talked at her like she was either hard of hearing as well as blind, or didn't understand the English language.

Both were frustrating. But neither was as bad as the few who fell into a third, much more annoying category: the touchers.

Usually, they had the best of intentions. But it had still amazed her when she first ventured out on her own, either with a cane or, later, with Sam, how many people seemed to think it was okay to just walk up and take hold of her arm in order to "help" her. The first time it happened, her military training had kicked in and she'd very nearly dislocated the Good Samaritan's elbow.

Lesson learned for them both.

"Miranda, sweetie!!" A fragrant cloud of sugar and spices announced Trixie's arrival a second before her arms closed around Miranda in a warm hug. "It's so good to see you."

Miranda returned the hug with a smile. "You, too." She gave Sam his release command, and his tail thumped against her ankle as he squirmed in pleasure at Trixie's attention.

"So, what brings you two out so early? Is everything okay?"

"Everything's fine. I had a craving for one of your pastries and a little company, if you've got the time."

"Well, you're in luck, because I happen to have both. What do you feel like today?"

"Surprise me." Picking a favorite from Trixie's bake case was like trying to pick a favorite child. Impossible, because she loved them all.

"Be right back."

She listened to her friend's footsteps as she went behind the counter, rummaged around a bit, and came back. Trixie had a distinctive tread, almost like she was dancing rather than walking.

Which was kind of funny, since she'd sucked at ballet for the year they'd both been forced to take lessons together as kids. Miranda had liked it more, but she'd insisted on quitting, too, when Trixie did. They'd been thick as thieves ever since, even after Miranda joined the Marines and Trixie moved to Kenoway to open her bakery.

Trixie slid a plate in front of Miranda before pulling out the chair across the table and taking a seat. "Coffee's at one o'clock."

Her hand slid over the edge of the table, found the plate, and carefully slid around it until her fingers touched the insulated cup. With that position fixed in her mind, she moved back to the plate. "So, what did you bring me?" Whatever it was, it smelled like heaven.

"A bear claw."

"From what, a real bear?" The pastry was huge, nearly filling the entire plate. God, she didn't even want to think about how many extra crunches this was going to cost her.

"Hey, when it comes to food, I don't skimp on size."

Or taste. There was no holding back the moan of pleasure that came with her first bite. Flaky dough and sweet almond flavor melted on her tongue along with the sugary icing.

"Oh my God. This is so good."

"Of course it is."

That was Trixie. Not a modest bone in her body.

Then again, when her pastries tasted like this, there was no reason to be.

She took a second bite, barely resisting another moan. "I think I'm in love."

Trixie snorted. "With me or the bear claw?"

"Could go either way. If I got to eat like this every day, I might consider switching teams."

"You're all alike. You only love me for my food."

Miranda paused. There was a thread of something in her friend's tone that wasn't entirely joking.

"Trix, is everything okay with you and Willa?"

Trixie sighed before replying. "Yeah, it's all good. We're just...working through some stuff. It'll be fine."

"Are you sure? If you want to talk about it..." She let the offer hang.

"No, no. It's not a big deal. Really. Besides," Trixie continued in a tone that said the subject was now closed, "we need to talk about what's bothering you. So?" The slight creak of her plastic chair and the soft click of the beads in her cornrowed hair signaled Trixie had shifted forward in her seat expectantly. "What gives? Your pops didn't bail on dinner at your place again, did he?"

Miranda shook her head and ate another bite of bear claw to fortify herself before answering. If this was about her dad, she'd need something a lot stronger than a pastry, no matter how awesome it was. "Isobel called this morning."

"Really? What does the little brat want now?"

Brat was probably the nicest thing Trixie ever called Miranda's spoiled baby sister. *Troublemaker* and *diva* were other favorites. Occasionally *bitch* would come into play, depending on Isobel's current transgression.

The sad thing was, every one of those labels was one hundred percent accurate.

"She wants to come stay with me."

The stunned silence that announcement caused was broken by Trixie's incredulous laugh. "You can't be serious?"

"That's what she said."

"Did she say why?"

"Because Mom and Dad are 'totally impossible' and she can't live under their 'ridiculous rules' anymore." There'd been a lot more whining and complaining, but that's what it all boiled down to. It seemed her parents had finally laid down the law with their youngest child, and she hadn't liked it one little bit.

"So, her solution is to move in with you?"

"Apparently."

"I hope you said no!"

"Do I look insane? Of course I said no."

"Thank God." The relief in Trixie's voice was genuine. She was the only person who knew the full extent of the animosity that had grown between Isobel and herself in the three years Miranda lived back in the family home after losing her sight.

She loved her friend dearly for the unwavering support, but she still felt a little guilty about sharing family dirt with her when her own mother wasn't even aware of all the problems Isobel had caused.

Bitch was being kind.

"How'd she take it when you told her no?"

She grimaced. "About as well as you'd expect. After she got finished calling me a mean, selfish *perra* who didn't care about my family and was only interested in myself and not in helping anyone else, she hung up."

"I think she kind of got the two of you mixed up, because that's Isobel to a T."

"Yeah, well, Izzy has always seen herself through a much kinder lens than everyone else does."

"That's one way of putting it," Trixie said with a laugh. "Another is she thinks the universe revolves around her and everyone should just fall in line with whatever she wants without question. I blame your parents for that."

So did she. Isobel was the youngest of the four Hernandez children, which would have guaranteed her a spot as most coddled child for that fact alone. But Izzy had been born six weeks early and incredibly tiny.

Oh, she'd become a perfectly happy, healthy baby long before her first birthday. But those first few weeks in the NICU had set the tone; everyone treated her like a fragile porcelain doll. Whatever Isobel wanted, she got, because she was the miracle baby and no one wanted to spit in fate's eye by denying her anything.

Isobel was still playing on that sentiment over twenty years later, and Miranda for one had had enough of it.

Savoring another bite of pastry, she considered not telling Trixie the rest. Then she sighed. "I think my mother might have put her up to it."

"Why would you say that?"

"Because she called about twenty minutes after Izzy hung up on me to say she thought it was a *wonderful* idea to have my sister come and live with me. That it would solve *everyone's* problems."

"Everyone's problems? I wasn't aware you were having any."

"To my mother, being blind and trying to live on my own is nothing but problems."

Trixie gasped. "You're *blind*? No!"

Laughing, she reached out to slap at her friend's arm. "Stop. It's not funny."

"No, it's not," Trixie said, voice sobering. "And you're not just trying to live on your own. You're doing it. And pretty damn well, I might add."

A big piece of self-doubt that had lodged in her chest like it always did after talking to her mother melted away at the conviction in her friend's words.

But not all of it.

"Thanks. I think so, too. But my parents…"

"Are worried about you. It's only natural." *After you nearly died.* The words didn't need to be spoken.

"I can't live my life in bubble wrap for them." She said it softly, because as true as it was, saying it still made her feel guilty. She knew how much her injuries had affected her family. The fear and uncertainty of survival. The long recovery. The final, devastating prognosis.

She might not be able to see them, but she could tell her parents had aged over the events of the past four years. All because she'd chosen a path neither one of them had wanted for her in the military.

"So then don't. You need to do you."

She gave a short laugh. "Yeah, like it's that easy. This is my mother we're talking about, remember?"

"Do you *want* your sister moving in with you?"

"God, no!" She'd rather go through the Crucible again. Twice. On her knees.

"Then you need to stick to your guns and not let your mom beat you down with that velvet whip of hers." A timer buzzed from the back of the shop. Trixie's chair scraped on the tiled floor. "I have to take the scones out. Be right back."

Eating the rest of her delicious gazillion-calorie pastry while she waited, she tried to take comfort in Trixie's steadfast support. Not letting Isobel move in was the right choice. But guilt and doubt had started nipping at her resolve from almost the second her mother had hung up with her. Despite the strain between her and her father, family was still everything in the Hernandez clan. She felt like she was failing them somehow by insisting on being independent and doing things her way.

Look what happened the last time she'd done that, enlisting against her father's wishes.

She pushed the empty plate away with a sigh and carefully wrapped her hands around her coffee. The truth was, there were a lot of reasons she didn't want Isobel to stay with her, but not all of them had to do with the fact they'd be at each other's throats within a few days.

No, the very first reason that popped into her head had nothing to do with clashing personalities, and everything to do with the sexy-voiced neighbor who'd somehow taken over more of her thoughts than he was entitled to.

Isobel was gorgeous. And despite knowing she'd likely never follow up on that hint of interest Ben had shown in her, it still just about killed her to think of all that sexy flirtation refocusing on her sister if he had the two of them to compare.

It felt too much like what had happened with Umberto, the occupational therapist who'd made all those extra visits to see her off the clock her first year living home after getting out of the rehab facility. She'd let herself spin fantasies then, too.

Only it hadn't been Miranda he'd wanted in the end. It was Isobel. And he'd gotten her, too, despite her sister knowing how she felt about him.

She'd sworn to never put herself in the position of having her heart shredded by either a man or her sister ever again.

She was still brooding over it when Trixie returned.

"What's got that brain of yours spinning now?"

"My neighbor." Realizing she probably shouldn't have answered quite so honestly, she added, "I was just wondering if you knew him, is all. He finally came over to introduce himself last night."

"Well, it's about damn time." Trixie sounded peeved on her behalf. "You've only been living there for what? Over four months now?"

"Yeah. But in his defense, he did say he didn't know Mrs. Roketzki never came back from Florida, so he didn't realize I even existed until yesterday."

"And what happened yesterday?"

"He must have finally noticed me out in the backyard."

In that stupid little bikini her sister Jules had goaded her into buying last week. She hoped the blush she felt warming her face didn't show. The only time she'd been outside the day before was to do laps in the pool and soak up a little sun on the lounger. When she'd realized that fact last night as she lay in bed, she'd discovered she still had enough vanity left to be glad she kept herself in good physical condition.

"And he made a beeline straight to your front door. Yeah, that sounds like Ben."

"So, you *do* know him."

"A little. I mean, he's come into the store a few times, so I've met him, but mostly I just know what Phil told me about him."

The local real estate agent as well as Mrs. Roketzki's grandson, Phil had been looking for a renter who wouldn't trash his *abuela*'s house. She'd been looking to rent something furnished, in a place easy to navigate by foot with Sam. One close enough to her family in Pawling for visits, yet far enough to discourage impulsive drop-overs.

Trixie had been the common denominator to point them in each other's direction. And even though she'd been thinking apartment, not a whole-ass house, once she saw the yard and pool and heard the very reasonable price, one she could totally manage on her disability pension from the Corps, she'd been sold.

It made sense Phil might know something about his grandmother's neighbors. But...

"Why would Phil tell you anything about Ben?"

"Because I asked." Trixie gave an exasperated huff. "Do you seriously think I'd suggest my best friend move into a place without making sure she wouldn't have some creepy serial killer wacko living next door first?"

"I appreciate you thinking about that." And it was true, despite the pinch to her pride that she'd had to.

Just accept the assist and move on, Hernandez.

"So, what else did Phil tell you about him? Other than he isn't a serial killer."

"Not much. He doesn't know him all that well, since Ben's family moved down to Long Island when they were kids. But since their grandparents were neighbors, they still ran into each other over the years. When old Mrs. Murphy died last year, Ben bought the house. Which kind of surprised Phil, since Ben's a fireman down in New York City and living here must be a hell of a commute. Personally, I think he was just ticked he didn't get a chance to grab the listing the first time around."

"The first time?"

"He seems to think Ben's fixing the place up to flip it and move back to the city with a tidy profit in his pocket. He's hoping for a shot at the commission when that happens."

Remembering the pride in Ben's voice when he talked about the renovations he'd been doing, she shook her head. "No, I don't think he plans to sell. He sounded...invested."

"Well, bad for Phil, but better for you if he stays. At least you know what you're getting with him as your neighbor. Plus, it doesn't hurt to have a fireman living next door in case there's an emergency."

She didn't see how, but didn't argue the point.

The bell over the door jangled. Miranda sipped her coffee while Trixie took care of her customer. She smiled into her cup at the way her friend patiently dealt with what sounded like an elderly woman, judging by the papery quaver of her voice and the tap of a cane as she'd come in. It seemed like she asked about every pastry in the bake case before finally making her choice.

After the door closed with another jangle, Trixie slid back into her seat with a grumpy sigh. "Every Tuesday, it's the same old thing. I swear, that woman lives to drive me crazy. Asks about everything, how fresh is it, what's it made with, blah blah blah. And then she buys an apple turnover, every single time."

"I think she's just lonely."

"She's a pain, is what she is." Trixie paused. "Lonely? Why would you say that?"

She shrugged. "Just something in her voice. She didn't sound like she was trying to be difficult. More like she wanted to stretch things out. Like she didn't have anywhere else to be or anyone else to talk to."

Wow, project much?

"Huh. I never considered…you know, now that I think about it, she used to come in all the time with her husband. Every Tuesday. And they'd buy two apple turnovers and coffees and sit here at the tables and eat them. They were the cutest little old couple. But I haven't seen him in months, though." Trixie's groan was etched with distress. "Oh, God. I am such a shitty person. How did I not put that together?"

"No, you're not."

"Yes, I am. I'm sitting here being bitchy about her taking up my *precious* time instead of wondering why she was all alone. I should have figured it out before you had to point it out."

Damn. She hadn't meant to make her friend feel guilty.

She shifted uncomfortably, causing Sam to stir at her feet. When she didn't get up, he settled back with a doggy sigh of patience, his chin on her foot.

"Oh, that reminds me! I have something for his furriness." Trixie's chair scraped back again. While she was gone, Miranda got out her wallet and took a few bills from their assigned slots, tucking them under the edge of her plate and, she hoped, out of sight.

"Oh no, you did not just do that."

Busted.

"We're not having this argument again." She closed her purse and slipped the long strap across her body before she stood, careful not to step on Sam's paws as she did. "I eat, I pay."

"I don't charge my friends." Indignation rang clear in her tone.

"And I don't mooch off of mine."

There were a few tense seconds of silence before Trixie sighed, breaking the stalemate of wills. "Fine."

Something inside her relaxed. "Good."

It was a stupid thing to fight over, but every single scrap of independence meant something to her. Paying her own way. Carrying her own weight. It was part of who she'd always been, and who she wanted—hoped—to become again.

Today it was paying her tab. Eventually, it would be living entirely on her own without being a burden to her family and friends.

That was the goal, anyway.

All it had taken was one phone call to remind her not everyone shared her optimism about her ability to make it actually happen.

She reached down for the handle on Sam's harness. "I'll let you get back to work. Thanks for the snack and the sympathetic ear."

"Anytime, you know that. Oh, wait. Here. Sam's treats."

There was a rustle of plastic and a light touch on her free hand. She took the shopping bag from her friend. It weighed a lot more than it should have, which meant Trixie had slipped in a few Miranda treats along with Sam's. No wonder she'd given in so easily about her paying for the bear claw.

"Trix..."

A buzzer sounded from the back. "Oops, Danishes are done. Gotta run. Take care, girl. Love you!" She gave Miranda's cheek a quick press with her own, her multitude of tiny braids soft against Miranda's skin, before she retreated to the safety of her kitchen, knowing Miranda wouldn't follow there with Sam.

She huffed out a laugh. Outmaneuvered by a civilian.

She briefly considered leaving more money on the table but decided to let Trixie win this one. With a shake of her head, she adjusted her grip on both the bag and the handle. "Okay, Sam, time to burn off some of those calories. Let's go home."

Home.

Funny how quickly she'd started to think of the rented house that way. In some ways, it already felt more like home to her than the house she'd spent most of her life in.

Not something she planned to ever mention to her mother, who already gnashed her teeth and lamented over her *pobre bebé* being so far from her watchful eye.

She didn't want to be anyone's poor baby. Or their problem. She just wanted to be herself again. Strong. Capable. Determined.

Which was why she needed to do everything in her power to keep her well-meaning family at arm's length. Before they undermined all she'd accomplished and turned her back into the mewling, pitiful creature who'd emerged from a coma into a new world of utter darkness and despair.

Chapter 3

"I DON'T BELIEVE IT. Mighty Murph actually struck out!"

Dom was laughing so hard as he leaned over from on top of the aerial truck he nearly lost his balance and dropped head-first to the truck bay's cement floor. He wasn't the only one, either. Each of Ben's friends was having a good chuckle over his failure to close the deal with his sexy neighbor.

Eavesdropping bastards.

Besides, it hadn't been a failure, merely a temporary delay. Timing just hadn't been on his side last night. The next time he approached his little selkie, he needed to make sure he had all day to coax her into coming out to play.

And she would. Of that he had no doubt. It wasn't like she'd been indifferent to his charms.

Okay, yeah, she'd been a little stiff and wary at first. Only natural, given she was a woman all alone and he was the random guy who'd knocked on her door out of the blue. But she'd loosened up once she knew who he was. He'd even made her laugh.

God, that laugh.

Soft and throaty, it had nearly done him in, then and there. That, together with the impact of seeing her up close for the first time—even through a screen door and dressed in shorts and a bright red tank instead of that devastating bikini—and he'd been embarrassingly close to springing wood.

Standing beside Ben as he waxed the firetruck's passenger-side cab door, Cody shook his head, a mournful expression on his face. "Dude, I handed you a gift, and you fumbled? What the fuck?"

"I didn't fumble. I was laying groundwork."

He *should* have been laying groundwork. What he'd actually done was make a rookie mistake, asking her back over to his place like a one-night bar hookup at last call instead of biding his time. Planning the long game.

His only excuse was that his brain had been lacking sufficient blood flow for rational thought. Too much of it had already drained south the second she opened the door.

"Did you get laid last night? No, you did not. That, my friend, is a fumble."

"Now, why would I want to rush and settle for one lousy touchdown, when if I play it right, I can score all season long?" He snapped Cody with his polishing rag, eliciting a yelp followed by a curse. "It's called finesse."

"Finesse my ass." Dom leaned even further over the side to reach a few stray spots of wax. "Oh, and thanks for not mentioning there was a hot babe next door and keeping her all for yourselves. Fuckwads."

"Yeah," Bryan chimed in. "No wonder you two 'volunteered' to paint the bigger bedroom, with a view like that."

Ben rolled his eyes skyward, seeking patience. "I didn't even know she was living there until last night."

"Yeah, sure you didn't," was Bryan's reply. Dom's was a lot cruder.

"Whatever." Arguing would be fruitless. His friends were determined to razz him, no matter the truth or the facts. It went on all the time. Today was his turn to be on the receiving end. Tomorrow they'd be riding Dom over still living with his mom, or Bryan about the cheesy mustache he'd been trying to grow after being told by one woman too many what a "sweet baby face" he had.

"Now I'm really sorry I couldn't make it yesterday." Working on the rear of the truck, Hector Salazar spoke up for the first time since the subject had been raised. Recently transferred in from one of the slower houses in Staten Island, he was still trying to find his place in the group.

"Don't be." Dom showed off both his rock-climbing skills and total disregard for personal safety by doing an acrobatic half-flip from the top of the aerial truck. He landed in a loose-kneed crouch like a cat. "It was a lot of boring, smelly work for a few lousy beers and some burned brats."

"I wouldn't bitch too loud about that if I were you," Cody said, "since you're the one who was supposed to be watching them and went off on another baseball rant instead." He got the finger in reply.

"Why weren't you there, Salazar?" Bryan asked.

Hector grimaced. "My little sister's car took a shit. I had to go deal with the mechanic trying to jerk her around about the repairs."

"Don't worry about it, man," Ben said to Hector. "I totally get the family obligation thing." He ignored the twinge of conscience that called him a hypocrite.

"Thanks. I swear, though, next time you need some help, I'm in."

"Appreciate it."

And he did. Any extra hands were welcome, especially now that he was in the home stretch. If it wasn't for the help-a-brother-out attitude of his friends in the department, he'd still be living in a half-finished shell trying to figure out how he was going to pay a contractor, the bank, *and* be able to eat all at the same time.

After they stored the cleaning supplies, they all headed for the kitchen, where lunch was close to being ready. The rich, spicy aroma of simmering chili had permeated every corner of the firehouse all morning. His stomach was more than ready for some follow-through on the hours-long palate tease.

Cody slid in beside him as they walked. "I only saw her back half, which was…" He bit his fist and groaned. "But I gotta know. How hot was she from the front?"

Five-alarm hot.

Sweat prickled along his skin whenever he brought up the picture of that sweetly shaped body in his mind. "She was okay." He laughed when Cody popped him in the back of the head. "Okay, okay, she was smokin'. She didn't have the bikini on anymore—"

"She was *naked*?" Cody grabbed his chest. "Fuck, just kill me now."

He gave him a shove. "No, she wasn't naked, you ass. She had on shorts and a top." And her feet were bare.

Why that tiny detail stuck with him, he couldn't say.

"She's in some hellacious shape, though. Those legs went on for *miles*." He liked tall women. At six-two, he'd found sex with much shorter women could sometimes be a little awkward.

Miranda had looked like she'd fit just right in his arms. And his bed. And anywhere else he could get her horizontal and naked.

Although horizontal wasn't necessarily a requirement.

Neither was naked.

Damn.

His body reacted predictably to the erotic image of taking his leggy neighbor up against the front door of her house, shorts around her ankles. Scowling, he reached for the coffee pot and forced his thoughts back into less dangerous territory.

What was it about this woman that continually set him off like a firecracker? She was cute and well-built, sure, but so were most of the women he'd had sex with. What made her so damn different?

It had to be the anticipation.

Usually when he zeroed in on a woman, they sealed the deal in bed the same night. With Miranda, he'd botched the whole thing and been left hanging. Literally. So, it must be simple unsatisfied lust making him horny as a tom cat, not anything special about her. The same thing would have happened with any woman he had to wait to have a taste of.

He was pretty sure, anyway.

He'd never had to wait before.

As he took his first sip of coffee, the speaker crackled to life to tone out both the engine and ladder. As Jackson's pack-a-day voice barked out information for a reported commercial structure fire, Ben scrambled back the way he'd just come, heading for his gear, all thoughts of Miranda and her strange effect on him forgotten as the rush of the job took over.

"How's the knee?"

Hurts like a motherfucker.

Ben shrugged at the roomful of curious eyes as he limped into the firehouse kitchen, tugging at his uniform shirt where the material stuck to his shower-dampened skin. "S'okay. The ER doc said it's nothing a little Icy Hot and a wrap won't fix."

Both of which were doing shit-all for it at the moment.

Cody gave him a look like he was going to call bullshit, then shook his head and finished putting his empty bowl on the counter with the others instead.

"Watch where you're going next time, would ya, Murph?" Dom slapped him on the shoulder as he walked by out of the room, making Ben wince. "It never looks good when we have to go in and save one of our own."

And they'd almost had to.

He bit back a grimace as he remembered the stomach-dropping sensation of his foot plunging through the roof of the burning warehouse. Thank God it had only been a small hole, and the whole damn roof hadn't collapsed underneath him. Somehow, he'd managed to throw himself backward before it could open wider and swallow him down into the blazing maw of the fiery beast steadily eating the inside of the two-story brick building.

But just barely.

Still, he'd strained his knee pretty good in the process. Not bad enough he couldn't finish his tour. But he'd be feeling it, and the bruises from landing on his SCBA tank, for the next couple of days.

Fun times.

Heading for the stove, he grabbed a clean bowl from the stack next to the steaming pot on the big six-burner range top. Their lunchtime chili had turned into an early dinner, but as long as it was hot and filling, no one cared. It was rare in the fire service when a meal was actually cooked, served, and eaten without interruption. You either got used to eating reheated leftovers, or you ate a shit-ton of sandwiches.

At this point, he was just glad there was any left.

After wasting two hours at the hospital getting his knee looked at, he'd fully expected to come back to an empty pot and a chorus of "you snooze, you lose." Only the fact the engine had gone on another call before they got their rig parked in the barn kept it from being a sandwich-for-dinner night for him.

Dropping into one of the scarred wooden chairs around the large table, he dug into his food like a starving wolf. Sweat popped out on his brow, but in a good way. Eva Boone made some damn fine chili.

As he was scraping up the last spoonful, the clatter of the bay doors opening signaled the return of the engine company. Still streaked with soot and wreaking of a hard day's work, they straggled into the kitchen to claim what was left in the pot.

Full bellies would always win out over getting clean.

Oliver Cartwright dropped his large frame into a chair at the far end of the table, chili slopping over the edge of his overfilled bowl. The chair creaked ominously. At six-five, two hundred fifty-plus pounds, he was a big man.

Unfortunately, very little of him was made up of any redeeming qualities.

"So, Murphy, heard you struck out last night."

Fucking great.

It would have been too much to ask for 192's resident troublemaker to not latch onto that tidbit. Or use it to torment Ben in every way he could.

But no. Cartwright was watching him with an expression that said he was ready and eager to stir some shit.

"You heard wrong, then, Hoss. Me and the lady got along just fine."

"Just fine?" Ignoring the hated Bonanza nickname he'd been saddled with, Cartwright shoveled a huge spoonful of chili into his mouth. "Just fine ain't getting laid."

Not interested in discussing his new neighbor with the man any more than he wanted to watch him talk through his half-chewed food, he shook his head and pushed back from the table. "I'm a man with a plan, don't you worry."

He ignored Cartwright's derisive snort and stacked his dirty bowl on the counter with the others, leaving the kitchen before the jackass could goad him any further.

Every house had that one guy who got under everyone's skin, but with Cartwright, it was a conscious choice to be a major dick. He was a hell of a fireman. Ben couldn't fault him on that. But as a human being, he was a total waste of DNA.

His phone vibrated in his pocket. Ben slipped it out, glad for the distraction. Until he saw who was calling. "Mom. Hi."

"Benjamin, sweetheart, how are you?"

"I'm good." He sat on the back bumper of the rig, wincing as much at the jolt of pain that lanced through his knee as he did at the white lie. "How are you? And Dad?"

"Are you sure? I saw on the news there was a big fire in Brooklyn today. Was that anywhere near you?"

"Yes, Mom, it was, and yes, I was there, and yes, I'm perfectly fine." Wow. Two lies in less than two minutes.

Or did it still only count as one since it was the same lie, just told twice?

"Well, all right, if you're sure."

"I'm sure."

There was a familiar gusty sigh in his ear. "You just know how much I worry about you."

And here it came. In three...two...one...

"If you'd only take a job that wasn't so dangerous, I wouldn't have to worry all the time."

His head thudded back against the truck. "Mom..."

"What, I'm not allowed to worry about my son?"

"Mom..."

"What kind of mother doesn't worry about a son who runs into burning buildings for a living?"

The kind that trusts their adult child to make his own life choices?

Okay, unfair and unkind. He sighed, knowing he needed to get off this well-trod subject before he said something he'd regret. "I'm good at my job, Mom."

She sniffed. "Of course you are. I wouldn't expect otherwise from any of my children."

The compliment would have meant more if she hadn't lumped him in with his highly successful siblings, but he'd take what he could get.

"Then trust me to not do anything stupid and get hurt."

Like step through a hole in the roof of a burning building.

Okay, maybe she had a *small* reason to worry.

Another sniff. "I will *always* worry about my baby."

"I'm not your baby, Mom. Caleb's the baby."

"You're all my babies, and I'll worry if I want to."

He grinned at the snap in her voice. It was a lot better than the guilt-inducing sniffles. His mother had a full repertoire of those kinds of noises, some with corresponding expressions, that he and his siblings had learned to interpret early on. As kids, scoldings could sometimes be delivered without the use of a single actual word.

And in Deborah Friedman Murphy's eyes, thirty wasn't too old to still deserve a good scold.

Using the one bait he knew his mother could never resist taking, he asked, "So, how are Abby and Caleb doing?"

"Abigail won another big case last week." The pride was so thick in her voice Ben thought he might choke on it.

"That's great. And Cay? He must be counting the days until school ends so he can enjoy the summer."

"Caleb was asked to teach an advanced trigonometry course to the accelerated class over the break."

Of course he had. His little brother was nothing less than brilliant when it came to numbers. But even a brainiac deserved some time off to recharge his circuits.

"I thought he turned them down?"

"He was asked to reconsider."

Meaning no one else wanted to do it, and Caleb was low man on the seniority pole. If he wanted to keep his very lucrative position at the university where he and their father both taught, he didn't really have a choice about saying yes.

"I bet he was thrilled about that."

"It will look good on his academic resumé." His mother's answer to everything.

"I guess. Look, I have to go. I have to take over the watch soon." In about an hour when his mutual shift started, but she didn't need to know that.

"You'll still be here for family dinner on Friday, won't you?"

The way she asked made it seem like he'd already agreed at some point to come, which he hadn't. But he was an expert at recognizing his mother's ambush techniques. "I don't know, Mom. I'll have to check my schedule and see what I'm working."

One huge advantage of his crazy-ass rotating twelve-hour shift cycle of two days on, two off, two on, three off, was how confusing it was to civilians. Add in the mutuals like he was working tonight, where they traded shifts with each other in order to work thirty-six or forty-eight hours straight and get more days off in a row, and no one could ever figure out if he was working or not.

"I already checked the app. You're definitely off."

Unless, it seemed, you were his mother.

Cursing whatever FDNY work calendar app she'd found, he rubbed between his eyebrows and thought fast. Nothing sprang to mind fast enough to not sound like he was making it up other than working on the house, and that was a sore subject he'd rather not poke at.

Damn. He was well and truly stuck.

"Then I guess I'll be there. What time?"

After he hung up, he glanced over at Cody, who had been shamelessly eavesdropping for the past few minutes. "Want to go to dinner Friday night?"

His friend pressed a hand to his chest in mock modesty. "As long as you know I don't put out on the first date." He grinned when Ben shot him the finger. "As much as I love your mom's brisket, I already have a better offer."

"Does this offer have a name?"

"Candy." Cody's eyes nearly rolled back in his head. "And man, is she ever sweet."

"Actress?"

"Model. She's in town for some fashion thing at the Javits Center."

Which made her Cody's perfect type. Gorgeous and temporary. Hell, that was his perfect type, too. But for some reason, the only envy he felt was that he knew Cody was going to have a good time Friday night, and he'd be in hell.

Okay, that was harsh.

He loved his family. But it would be a long-ass drive down from Kenoway and out to Long Island's south fork, all to listen to his mother spend three hours enthusing over his siblings' successes and making him feel like the loser child.

Not that she did it on purpose.

Or even realized she was doing it at all.

Abby and Caleb were simply shiny red apples that had fallen right under their parents' academically-minded trees, while he...wasn't. He was more of a pear, never quite fitting in with the rest of his brilliant family and their brilliant ambitions. They didn't know what to do with him any more than he knew how to deal with them.

"How long are you going to keep letting them get inside your head like this?"

He glanced up at Cody, startled out of the downward spiral of his thoughts by the sharp words. "What?"

"I know that look. So what if you weren't high school valedictorian, or didn't graduate from some fancy ivy league university with a bunch of letters after your name? That's them. You've got a college diploma and a job you love, and you're damn good at it. Tell them that. *Own* it."

He did own it. With attitude. There was no better job than being a firefighter. And he owned that shit right up to the front door of his parents' house.

But the second he crossed the threshold, he somehow went from a mature, confident thirty-year-old right back to that dense teen who'd had to be tutored through twelfth grade math by his little brother. Who never had anything of real value to contribute to the conversation around the dinner table.

Then *or* now.

"Did you tell them you're taking the lieutenant's test?"

The chili made an unpleasant gurgle as nerves twisted his gut into a tight ball. Written tests were not his friend.

"No. I don't want to jinx it." He scowled at the eye roll he got. "Fine, I chickened out, okay? I'll tell them. I will," he added when Cody shook his head at him.

"Believe it when I hear it."

"You know what, fu—"

The speakers crackled to life overhead. Just like that, his thoughts clicked over to all business. As he grabbed his gear, adrenaline sang through his veins.

This. This was what he was born to do.

He knew it in his gut every time that alarm sounded and the trucks roared out into the streets, lights and sirens blaring. What he did was important, damn it. Valuable.

A calling that took intelligence and ability.

He just needed to find a way to make his family see it that way, too.

Chapter 4

Leg muscles burned as Miranda's feet hit the treadmill in a steady rhythm to the accompaniment of the AC/DC song pumping out of the speaker. She would have loved to crank it up even louder to totally block out the godawful noise coming from next door, but at least *she* had some consideration for her neighbors.

Unlike other people, who had been at it since practically the crack of dawn this morning. The constant grinding buzz was enough to make her teeth ache.

She winced as the music faded between songs, allowing the annoying screech of whatever tool of torture the man was using to grind on her eardrums for several long seconds before the opening strains of Thunderstruck dulled it again to mere background noise.

"Jerk."

Wiping away a bead of sweat before it rolled off her nose, she wished she still had her earbuds. They'd always been a necessary part of her workout equipment in the past, like a good pair of sneakers.

With them, she'd been able to block out everything around her while she ran. Focus on putting one foot in front of the other. Listen to her body. Her muscles as they warmed and stretched. Her lungs as they expanded. Her heart as it found the steady beat that matched her feet against the ground.

It had been just her and the music.

Which was exactly why she couldn't use them anymore.

Back then, blocking one sense had still left her with another to keep her safe. But with the black curtain now drawn over her world, her hearing was her most important connection to what was going on around her.

Blocking that off made her feel much too vulnerable, even in her own home. The few attempts she'd made had left her twitchy and out of sorts, like a kid imagining the boogeyman was reaching up from under his bed because his foot was hanging over the edge.

So, the earbuds had been retired, and her sister Julietta had helped her create a variety of timed playlists she could use both on her phone and the Amazon Echo speakers throughout the house. A gift from her brother, the voice-activated AI had become her next best friend after Sam and Trixie.

When the final song on the current playlist started, she reached out and found the control panel, bringing the treadmill down to a cool-off walk. As the last strains of Who Made Who faded, she shut the machine off and grabbed the towel on the bar to her right to mop her face and neck. Then froze in shock.

Silence. Peaceful, blessed silence.

"Thank you, baby Jesus." Plucking the water bottle from the built-in cup holder, she drank down several greedy swallows before mopping her face again. Towel slung over one shoulder, she stepped down and made her way to the back door. With quiet restored, she was taking full advantage of the sunny afternoon after two straight days of rain.

"Sam, out?" she called back into the house.

There was a thump from upstairs as he jumped off her bed, and the soft patter of paws as he scrambled down the hallway to the stairs. Normally, he napped in the sunshine right outside the small room off the kitchen she'd converted to her gym while she ran. But today he'd retreated to the furthermost part of the house he could get from the noise next door.

Smart dog.

She reached down and rubbed his ears when he pressed against her leg. "I know, buddy. I hate it, too. But at least he's finished. I hope," she added, mentally crossing her fingers as she dropped into one of the wrought-iron chairs around the matching patio table.

The hammering and sawing she could take, annoying as they were. But whatever he was doing today was like going to the dentist without Novocain.

Sam burrowed against her legs and lavished a few kisses on her sweaty face before she laughingly pushed him away. "Ew, gross, Sam. Stop."

With a blowy sigh, he backed off and settled on the ground nearby, probably in a patch of sun. Scrubbing off the dog spit, she settled back, wishing not for the first time that the hard chairs had cushions on them.

Maybe she'd take a trip into Mt. Kisco and do some shopping. The furniture might belong to her landlady, but nobody said she couldn't spruce things up a bit and make it more comfortable. If she was going to be staying here through the end of the year—and hopefully longer—then maybe it was time to start adding the little finishing touches that would make it feel more like her home.

Some new pillows for the couch would be nice. Big, squishy ones. And maybe a super-soft throw for when she was curled up watching tv or listening to an audiobook. Oh, and some over-sized fluffy towels. What she had were fine, but that didn't mean she couldn't upgrade to something more decadent. Spa-like, even. Indulgent.

She deserved to treat herself, just a little, didn't she?

Excited by the idea, she went back inside. "Alexa, call Julietta."

She was totally in love with the Echo's AI virtual assistant program. The freedom it gave her sometimes let her forget the limitations blindness had imposed on her world.

Limitations that made it almost impossible to do anything spontaneous anymore. She'd once been the queen of spur-of-the-moment. Now, her life had become a series of well-planned, carefully thought out and coordinated actions that bordered on the monotonous.

Well, no more.

Beginning today, right now, she was going to start adding some life back into her life. Even if it was just buying some stupid towels and pillows.

Already writing a mental list of stores she wanted to visit, there was a hard pinch of disappointment when the call connected to her sister's voicemail. "Hey, Jules. It's me. What do you think about doing a shopping day? Today, if you get this soon, or maybe tomorrow? Give me a call. Love you, *chica*. Bye! Alexa, hang up."

Well, hell.

All the mounting enthusiasm leaked out of her like a Macy's balloon the day after Thanksgiving. It didn't matter that she understood her sister was busy with school and had a life of her own. It was just one more example of how even her spontaneity had to be planned.

Depressed, she went back outside. "Maybe we should go into town and see Trixie," she said to Sam. A memory popped into her head of the lonely old lady coming in and dithering over pastries because she had nowhere else to be.

"Or maybe not."

She grabbed her water bottle from the table and took a long swallow. No, using Trix as a crutch every time she was feeling lonely or out of sorts wasn't the answer. Or healthy for their friendship.

She should get online with her support group instead. Or even see if any of the local members felt like going to the mall, or a movie.

There was usually at least one playing that had audio description available. It would be a little pricey, but she could Uber and meet them there. None of the drivers in the area had a problem with letting Sam in their car.

There. Not exactly spontaneous, but it wasn't sitting around moping, either.

She took a self-congratulatory drink.

"Hey there, neighbor!"

The unexpected shout nearly made her choke on the water.

"Miranda, right?"

Damn.

That sexy voice did all kinds of things to her, making her name into a teasing caress.

Turning in the direction of his voice where the chain link fence separated their yards, she cleared her throat. "Mr. Murphy."

He laughed. "Ben, please. Mr. Murphy is my dad. Well, actually, he's Professor Murphy, but...anyway, you know what I mean. I'm just Ben."

There wasn't anything 'just' about him.

She really should have asked Trixie to describe him the other day when she'd brought him up. Building a picture in her mind of someone made it easier to talk to them. Kind of like having an avatar in a chatroom.

Hell, who was she kidding? She just wanted to know if the face was as intriguing as the sexy voice that went with it.

"Okay, then. Ben."

There was an awkward silence.

This time it was him who cleared his throat. "So, ah, it looks like I've caught you in the middle of your workout." He made it part question, part apology.

"No, actually I just finished my run." And was a hot, sweaty mess.

That inconvenient tug of vanity raised its head again, almost making her check her hair to see how bad it was. She could feel strands sticking to her sweat-dampened neck where they'd escaped the elastic band holding them. How wild and unruly the rest of it looked she tried not to think on too hard.

At least he wasn't near enough to smell her *eau de* sweat.

"Oh, good. Then I guess I'm not interrupting. Again," he added with a self-deprecating chuckle. She was confused for a second before she remembered the white lie about him interrupting her dinner the other night.

If she said he was, she had a feeling he'd back right off without a fuss. But for some reason she didn't want to send him packing just yet. "No, I'm done for the day."

"Great. That's great. So am I, actually. Finally. Wasn't sure I'd get all of the floors sanded down in one shot, but they were in pretty decent condition, considering their age and how many shoes have stomped on them over the years. If I can do the same with the stain and poly, I might be able to save myself a few days rental on the machine."

So that's what that hellish sound had been. A commercial sander.

"Well, I hope you can finish up early, then."

As much for her and Sam's sake as for his.

"Yeah, I'm sorry about all the noise. I tried keeping the windows closed to muffle it, but since I had to cover all the vents to keep the dust out, I couldn't use the a/c, and after a while it got kind of stifling."

So, he *had* tried to be considerate.

Knowing that made her like him a little better.

"I hope that's not what sent you out running. I'd hate to think I literally chased you out of your own home." He sounded like he was probably teasing her, but there was an edge of serious to his tone as well that said maybe he wasn't.

It also answered the question of whether or not he'd realized she was blind.

"No, I...ah...I run pretty much every day." She let his assumption about where she did that running stand without correction. Did it really matter?

He gave a low whistle. "Wow, that's some hard-core dedication."

No, determination. For a goal she had every intention of reaching, no matter how unrealistic anyone thought it might be.

She gave an uncomfortable shrug. "I like to stay in shape. Old habits die hard."

"Well, I'd say you're doing a fine job of it." There was a heavy dollop of appreciation in his tone.

There went that stupid vanity again, making her cheeks heat. She grabbed the end of the towel still slung over her shoulder to dab at her face and hide it. "Thank you."

"Sorry, I didn't mean to embarrass you."

"You didn't. It's fine." He had, but it was a good kind of embarrassed. The kind she hadn't felt in...well, a very long time.

"Okay. Good." He gave a low laugh. "Then maybe I didn't screw up my chance to ask if you'd like to share a pizza with me tonight? My treat."

No.

The refusal rose immediately inside her, but she stifled it. This was twice now he'd asked her to spend time with him. If she turned him down this time, he might never ask again.

Wait. Did she *want* him to ask again?

Maybe she did.

It was stupid, rash, and impulsive—and okay, maybe even a little selfish—but hadn't she just been whining she needed a little more spontaneity in her life? And having dinner with her bedroom-voiced neighbor was *way* better than dragging herself and Sam to a movie she didn't really care about seeing.

Of course, once Ben clued in to her blindness, things might get a little weird. Definitely awkward. Which was something she could get out of the way right now by just telling him. It was the right thing to do.

But "Hey, by the way, in case you didn't realize it, I'm blind" wasn't exactly an easy add to the conversation.

Still, she should do it.

Then again, he was sure to figure it out on his own, probably within a few minutes of walking through her door. That would be a lot less awkward for them both. And if he didn't...well, *then* she'd mention it.

But really, what were the chances of that happening?

Quickly, before either common sense or her conscience could take over, she gave him a wide smile. "I like my pizza plain. Does six o'clock work for you?"

"Six works just fine. See you then, Miranda." The way he said her name sent shivers through her tummy.

Oh boy. If she couldn't get her body's reactions to him under control before tonight, she might be in some real trouble here.

Still humming the song that had been on the radio, Ben grabbed the large pizza box out of the passenger seat of his Pathfinder with a grin despite the dull ache in his back, shoulders, and pretty much every other part of his body.

He'd definitely overdone it, pushing to finish sanding the entire house in a single day. But seeing all that beautiful fresh hardwood in every room made the pain worth it. Once the stain and polyurethane went on, they'd be spectacular.

His grin turned wry. He was pretty sure his new neighbor didn't share his enthusiasm for his marathon day of work. She'd been polite enough, but it had been easy to see on her face she'd been a little miffed about all the noise.

Not that he could blame her. Even with ear protection, it had felt like ice picks stabbing his eardrums by the time he was done. Not to mention the constant vibration rattling his body. When he'd finally finished the last room, he couldn't escape fast enough to the peace and quiet of his backyard with a beer.

And seen *her*.

A low rumble of appreciation escaped as he remembered looking over at the sound of a screen door slapping shut and watching Miranda up-end her sports bottle for a drink. He'd watched her throat work as she swallowed and had a fast flash of an image so incredibly erotic, he'd damn near dropped his beer.

Add in the spandex that hugged her body like a glove, and it was a wonder she hadn't taken one look at his face and run into the house and locked all the doors.

As it was, she'd been a little cool and distant at first. Kind of like the first time they'd talked, a bit aloof and stingy with the eye contact. Only this time she'd said yes. So, he was already one hundred percent ahead of where he'd been on Monday.

Proof that patience paid dividends.

Something to keep in mind during dinner. Slow and easy was clearly the way to go with her. And he would, no matter how hard it was. After all, he was the man with a plan.

Which almost went flying right out the window when Miranda answered the door.

She'd showered and changed, the spandex running shorts and sports bra exchanged for a pair of white hip-hugging capris and a blue tank top similar to the one she wore when they'd both stood in this exact spot before. Only this time he had an invitation inside.

Suck on that, Hoss.

"Half cheese, half pepperoni, as requested," he said, forcing his expression to something he hoped was neutral and not leering. But *damn*, the woman had legs that went on *forever*. Right down to feet that were once again adorably bare.

Who knew he had a secret foot fetish?

The golden retriever standing behind her gave him a not entirely friendly look, despite the breed's well-known easy temperament. Or maybe he was just projecting. The dog couldn't know what he was thinking. Could he?

"Mmm, smells delicious. Bring it into the kitchen, please." She stepped back to let him in.

It had been years since he'd been inside this house. Walking through, he saw many of the same pieces of heavy wooden furniture he remembered, but a lot less clutter. Gone were the handmade doilies covering every surface, and the hundreds of Hummel figurines he'd been terrified of accidentally breaking as a kid.

There were a few picture frames of various shapes and sizes on the hall table, mostly filled with people who looked like they were probably related to Miranda. Other than that, there weren't any knickknacks or tchotchkes laying around to give him any insight into the woman living here.

Although maybe the lack of excess crap was its own clue. She might be one of those minimalists who liked clean lines and less clutter. Or maybe she just hadn't finished unpacking all of her stuff yet.

"So, how long ago did you move in?"

He set the box on the kitchen table, where two place settings were already laid out with paper plates and napkins. The spot at the end had a half-empty bottle of beer beside it, marking it as hers.

Too bad. After being trapped inside breathing through a respirator all day, he'd kind of hoped they'd eat out on the patio since the temperature had started to dip along with the sun. But he was nothing if not adaptable.

"In March. What would you like to drink?" she asked, pulling open the refrigerator. "I have water, iced tea, and beer."

"A beer would be great, thanks."

March? He'd had this leggy goddess living right next door for almost four months and never noticed until this week?

Cody would never let him hear the end of it if he found out.

By the time Miranda set his beer on the table and took her seat, he'd plated them each a slice. "You did want cheese, not pepperoni, right?" he asked when she just sat there, biting her lower lip. He was positive that's what she'd said earlier.

Or maybe it was because he'd touched her food. Hell, he was so used to the family-style meals at the firehouse, it hadn't dawned on him she might not appreciate his fingers all over her pizza.

Her expression cleared. "Yes. Thanks."

Weird.

Cracking his beer open, he tipped it toward Miranda in salute, but she didn't notice. All her attention seemed to be focused on her food. And despite the rumble in his empty stomach, all of his attention was glued to her.

Her hand circled the edge of the plate until her thumb connected with the crust. Folding it with her right hand, her left skimmed along the bottom of the slice until her fingers came to rest under the drooping tip, holding it up.

Transfixed, he watched as she guided it to her mouth, where her lips closed gently around the end and she took a careful bite, followed by a small groan of pleasure.

Jesus.

That had to be the sexiest way to eat a slice of pizza he'd ever seen in his life. The way her hands had mimicked guiding something else to her mouth...she *had* to have done it on purpose. No way could that have been anything less than the opening salvo in the dance of seduction between them.

Okay, then. Looked like they were on the same page. Flirt. Tease. Arouse.

Then, when one of them finally broke under the pressure, they'd seal the deal, and everyone would be satisfied.

His body reacted as she ran a fingertip around the corner of her mouth, catching the sauce that lingered there. Oh, yeah. *So* satisfied.

Clearing his throat, he took another drink. "So, how do you like living in Kenoway so far?"

"I love it. Everyone is so friendly, and it's exactly the kind of quiet, laid-back place I was looking for." She gave him a quick side-eye glance, her lips quirking. "Well, most of the time it is, anyway."

He laughed and held up his hands in mock surrender. "I swear, I'm almost done. A few more weeks, and you won't hear another peep out of me."

She laughed with him, the sound soft and a little throaty. "Somehow I doubt that." She paused. "If you don't mind me asking, why is it taking you so long? Don't home renovations usually go quicker than yours?"

Watching her take another bite of pizza using the same seductive maneuver distracted him from the question for a second.

"Um, it depends. Usually, yeah, if you hire a contractor to do the whole thing in one shot. But I've been trying to do as much as I can on my own, and only bringing in professionals to help with the big stuff like plumbing and electric. A lot of guys I work with do that kind of thing on the side—legit, they're licensed and insured—so I get a really good price. But I also have to work around not only my schedule, but theirs, too, and sometimes it can take a few weeks to get something done when it should have taken a day."

"Sounds frustrating, even if you are saving money."

"It can be. But I really don't want to pay more than I have to. And I'm definitely not going to watch a few YouTube videos on wiring up a new electrical panel and think I can do it myself. Saving a little time and money isn't worth the risk of burning the place down."

"Probably something a firefighter worries about even more than most people, since you've seen the end result of faulty wiring, I imagine."

"Oh, so you've been checking up on me, huh?" Because he was pretty sure his line of work hadn't come up in their two very short conversations.

"No." She sounded annoyed and embarrassed, looking down at her plate rather than at him. "My friend Trixie mentioned it in passing the other day. In conversation."

"A conversation about me?" He gave her a wink and a grin. Neither of which she reacted to. Damn, she was tough to get a read on.

"A conversation about a lot of things, of which you were one small part." She drained the last of her beer.

Okay, she definitely sounded annoyed.

Backpedaling fast, he asked, "You know I'm teasing you, right?"

The long, deep breath she took did wonderful things to the breasts beneath that silky tank top.

"Sorry. I...I'm kind of out of practice at this."

"Eating?" He made sure the teasing was very clear this time. She laughed, so it must have worked.

"Being social. Having a...having dinner with someone I don't know and making small talk. Being able to tell when someone is teasing, for fu—um, Pete's sake. Because, well, it's just that I'm...I mean, you should know..." She floundered for a second before sighing. "I need another beer. Do you want one?"

From the way her gaze never seemed to focus directly on him as she spoke, he had to wonder how many she'd already had. "Sure, thanks. Want another slice?"

"Yes, please. It's really good."

Was the extra sway in her booty as she walked to the fridge for his benefit? Damn, he hoped so.

"It's from Delfino's." He slid the largest cheese slice in the box onto her plate. Maybe food would help counter the alcohol a little. The last thing he wanted was for her to be anything but one hundred percent aware when the time came to move things to the next level.

And he was really looking forward to getting there tonight.

"I don't think I've ever tried them before."

"It's over in Bedford Hills, but worth the extra drive." He reached out for the beer Miranda brought back, but rather than handing it to him, she retook her seat and placed both bottles on the table instead. He lowered his arm with a frown.

What the hell?

"Oh, that's probably why. I usually just walk up to the place on Main Street."

His frown remained as he watched her go through the same odd ritual of sliding her thumb around the edge of the plate, picking up and folding the slice, and guiding it to her mouth with her other hand.

What had been sexy a few minutes ago now struck him as a little odd and obsessive.

"Yeah, that's right, I didn't see a car in the driveway." Probably why he'd overlooked her presence for so long. "Is it in the shop?"

"No, I had to get rid of it. I can't, um..." Looking troubled, she put her head down and took another bite instead of finishing.

I can't...what?

Afford to keep one?

Oh, fuck. He was an ass.

Times were tough for everyone in different ways. There was no shame in that. But he'd gone and made her feel embarrassed about it. Hell, that was probably why she was renting in a small town like

Kenoway in the first place. There wasn't much of anything not in walking distance here.

Of course, if she couldn't afford a car, why would she be renting a house instead of a much more economical apartment? Sure, not all rentals were pet-friendly, but still.

Things weren't adding up.

Not my business.

That didn't stop him from asking, "So, you know what I do for a living. How about you?"

Miranda took her time chewing, then drew it out longer as she washed it down with a long swallow of beer. "Nothing right now, but I was a radio operator in the Marines."

"You're kidding."

Wow, way to sound like a sexist jerk, Murph.

"Sorry! I just meant, when I think of the Marines, I think of, you know, Stallone or Dwayne Johnson or something."

He swallowed a groan. Oh yeah, that was making it *much* better.

Miranda's lips quirked as she stared down at the beer cradled in her hands. "For the record, neither of them was ever a Marine, only played them in the movies, but I get your meaning. Marine equals big macho guy to most people. But trust me, there may not be a lot of women in the Corps, but we worked our asses off and made it through the same training the guys did, so we're just as much Marines as they are."

Great. First he embarrasses her, then he insults her. What happened to the smooth-talking man with the plan?

"Hey, I believe you. Women can be just as bad-ass as men. I mean, you're obviously in some hella good shape." He put his appreciation of that into his expression, his voice dropping to a velvety bass. "Must be all that running you do."

Her throat worked as she swallowed hard. "Thank you."

He hid his grin. That tone got them every time.

"I'd ask if you wanted some company the next time you go out, but I don't know if I could keep up with those legs of yours. You'd probably leave me in the dust."

"Oh! Um, I, ah, I don't..." She looked away, biting her lip. "I'm sure you're extremely fit. You know, with your job and all."

He could almost feel his ego shrivel two sizes.

Talk about damning with faint praise. Especially since she'd seen him with his shirt off just a little while ago while they kibitzed over the back fence. He wasn't vain or anything, but he knew he had a decent six-pack, and his glutes were rock hard.

I'm sure you're extremely fit? Who the hell was she comparing him to, Wolverine?

His ego growled.

Okay, so maybe he *was* a little vain.

Which meant he was going to run with this woman even if it killed him, just to prove how *fit* he actually was.

"Well, I'm up for the challenge if you are." He laid his hand over hers on the table, stroking his thumb over her soft skin. And tried not to read too much into her flinch at the contact. "So whadda ya say? Care to give me a try?"

Expressions chased across her face too quick to decipher, but the grim resolution that settled there at the end was less than encouraging. "Ben, believe me, I would love to go out running with you. But I *can't.*"

His fingers squeezed hers lightly, certain success was a few simple words of persuasion away. "Sure, you can." But even as he gave her his most seductive smile, he noticed again how her eyes didn't quite connect with his.

"No. I really can't." She gave her hand a small tug, but he held on, frowning.

Not won't.

Can't.

For the first time since he'd walked through the front door, he put aside all his preconceptions of how the evening was going to play out and really *looked* at the woman sitting at the table with him. Not her attractive face or the smoking hot body he'd been so intent on getting an all-access pass to, but the actual woman.

The one who had her home decluttered and organized to within an inch of its life.

The one who hadn't responded to a single one of his looks, not even the guaranteed panty-melters.

The one who still wouldn't meet his gaze.

No. Not wouldn't.

Couldn't.

Suddenly, everything began to make sense. The pre-set table. The strange eating ritual. The beer. Jesus, the *dog*. All the pieces finally gelled into one glaringly obvious fact he'd somehow missed.

His sexy new neighbor was blind.

Which was something he'd need a minute to unpack. Later.

Right now, what felt like a fist in his gut was that she'd *known* he didn't know, and just let him blunder on through the entire meal, completely oblivious. For what? To make a fool out of him? Play a mean little game of seeing how many stupid things he could manage to say before he finally caught on?

Whatever the reason, he was pretty sure she'd been laughing at him the entire time. And that was the cruelest blow of all.

Chapter 5

Miranda knew the exact second Ben figured out the truth.

The cozy atmosphere in the kitchen evaporated as his hand disappeared from hers like he'd been burned. She missed the touch immediately. Such a small thing, human contact. But it had sent a wave of warmth through her that awakened the tiny corner of her soul starved for it.

Losing her vision had left her isolated in more ways than the obvious.

Braced for the discomfort of the sympathy and, worse, pity, sure to come next, she was totally unprepared for what she actually got.

His bitterness.

"Did you think this was funny?"

The words had her blinking rapidly in confusion. "What?"

"Making me look like a dumbass. Was that the plan? See how long it would take the idiot next door to figure it out?"

The sullen accusations swirled in her brain as if in another language, not making any sense. "What are you talking about? There was no plan. And I certainly never meant to make you feel like an idiot."

"Then why didn't you just tell me?"

Her conscience cringed.

"It's not like I was hiding it." Not exactly, anyway. "It's just...I wasn't sure how to bring it up. I never had to actually *tell* anyone before."

He gave a harsh chuckle. "Great. So, I'm the only idiot who couldn't figure it out. Perfect." His chair screeched back on the tile, making her wince.

"Ben, no, that's not what I meant. Wait!" But his footsteps were already thudding toward the front door.

Shit.

Way to totally screw up, Hernandez.

Pushing her own chair back, she found the edge of the table with her hand and rushed around it after him. "Ben, please. It wasn't—"

She rammed into his chair, which she'd forgotten about in her haste to follow. Her knee hit the heavy wooden seat, her foot somehow getting tangled underneath and throwing her off balance. With a short cry, she pitched to the side and despite her best efforts to bring her hands up to protect herself, a sharp pain pierced her head as it connected with something solid.

Pain.

Blinding darkness.

The rush of her own heartbeat in her ears.

The sharp tang of blood on her tongue.

Air. Where was the air? She couldn't breathe.

Gasping on the floor, she struggled to push the old memories away. The pain in her head made it hard to focus, hard to catch her breath.

Glass exploding.

Metal crunching.

The heat of fire licking near her skin.

Trapped. Can't move. Can't escape. Going to die. Going to burn.

She was only distantly aware of Sam's warm tongue on her cheek, and then a pair of strong hands pushing the dog away. A voice that sounded like it was coming from a thousand miles away tried to penetrate the angry roar that filled her head.

"Miranda! Jesus, are you okay?"

"I..." She swallowed the sour bile at the back of her throat. "...don't know. Ow!" She turned her head and batted at the hand investigating her forehead, sending shards of agony lancing through her brain. "Stop that!"

"You gave yourself a hell of a knot there. I'm calling an ambulance."

Panic hit, swift and urgent, overwhelming the pain. "No! No ambulance. No hospital. I'm fine."

"You're not fine. You could have hurt your neck or have a concussion."

"I didn't. I don't."

"Are you dizzy? Nauseous?"

"I know what a concussion feels like. Trust me, I'm good."

"You should still go and—"

Reaching out, she snagged his shirt, clenching it tight in her fist. "No. Hospital."

Not only had she had more than enough of being in them to last her ten lifetimes. But the second her mother got wind of it, she'd have Miranda packed up and tucked back in her old childhood bedroom so fast her head would spin worse than it was doing now, with no hope of ever escaping that velvet prison again.

"Okay, okay." He patted her fisted hand, his voice changing, becoming soft and a little patronizing. "Let's get you up off the floor, and then we can reevaluate, okay?"

Reevaluate her ass.

But getting off the floor sounded like an excellent plan.

She didn't argue when Ben helped her first into a sitting position, then to her feet, because honestly, she was pretty sure she would have gone right back down again if he hadn't been supporting her. She might not have hit her head hard enough for a concussion, but from the way it was throbbing in time with her heartbeat, it was a near thing.

"Okay?"

"Mmhmm," was the best she could do through clenched teeth. She sucked in a deep breath, willing away the vertigo, and got a lungful of the warm, masculine scent that had been teasing at the edge of her senses since she opened the door for him.

Hot. Smoky. Sexy. Like a drug, it distracted her from the drum solo in her skull, making her want to lean in and take another whiff.

"Put your arms around my neck."

She pulled back. "What? Why?" Was he seriously hitting on her right now?

Oh God, had he caught her sniffing him? Wouldn't *that* be humiliating.

"Because I'm going to carry you to the couch."

She bristled. "I'm perfectly capable of walking." Probably. With a little help.

His chest rose and fell as he took a deep breath. "One of the beer bottles broke when it hit the floor, and you don't have any shoes on."

"Oh." Indignation deflated, she started to do as he said, then pulled back. "Wait. Sam. Where's Sam?"

"Under the table."

"He didn't step on any glass, did he?" She'd hate herself if he was hurt because of her stupid clumsiness.

"I don't think so. I don't see blood anywhere."

"Thank God." She reached out, finding the edge of the table to orient herself. "Sam." There was a soft whine before a tongue laved her fingertips. She stroked over his nose and rubbed between his eyes the way he liked. "Sam, stay." She added the hand signal to reinforce the command. "Good boy. Stay."

"Ready now?"

Not really. But insisting he go get her a pair of shoes instead of carrying her a few lousy steps seemed a little ridiculous.

Not to mention there was a tiny part of her that wanted this.

She slid her arms around his neck and swallowed a soft gasp as he carefully scooped her up and started moving with long, steady strides, as though she weighed nothing. It was only for a few seconds, but her body drank in the sensation of his strong arms around her, his hard chest, the soft hair on his nape against the inside of her arm, his broad shoulders.

Oh yeah, he definitely had the body to back up that sexy, bedroom voice.

Grateful when he lowered her to her feet rather than putting her on the couch like some stupid damsel in distress, she found the edge of the cushion with her leg and sat. She hated feeling helpless. *Hated* it.

The only thing she hated more was people *witnessing* her helplessness.

She heard his footsteps head back to the kitchen, the open and close of a few drawers, the soft thud of the freezer door, and then he was back, pressing a dish towel filled with ice into her hand. "Put this on your head."

Too grateful for the impromptu ice pack to feel annoyed at either his bossy tone or the invasion of her kitchen space, she did as he instructed. Hissing at the pain, she wished she'd never made her mother that stupid promise about cleaning up her language. If ever there was a time for some of the salty phrases she'd learned from her teammates, it was now.

From where he was still crouching beside her, Ben asked, "Hurts, huh?"

"No, not at all," she replied through clenched teeth.

"I still think—"

"No."

He stood, muttering "stubborn woman" under his breath as he did. "So, is your dog going to bite me if I try to pick him up?"

"Pick him up? He's, like, eighty pounds. You can't carry him!"

"I carried you, didn't I?" He sucked in a breath she could only interpret as horrified. What? Did he think she'd be insulted by a vague reference to her weight? Then again, she supposed some women might be.

"I just meant I'm trained to carry people who weigh a lot more than you do out of burning buildings. Trust me, carrying the dog won't be a problem."

Not unless Sam decided it was some new kind of game and tried to drown Ben with happy doggy kisses like he did to the vet techs during his checkups. She wanted to laugh at the image, but it would only make her head hurt worse than it already did.

"No, he should be fine with you. Guide dogs are trained to be non-aggressive, even with strangers, in case their handlers are incapacitated and need help."

There was a moment of silence as they both absorbed the obvious irony.

Then Ben's footsteps receded toward the kitchen. "Hey, Sam. Nice doggie. Come here. Come on, boy."

"He won't move until I release him from the stay command." She changed to the upbeat tone she used when giving the dog direction. "Sam, break. It's okay, go visit. Go visit Ben."

"Go visit" was the okay to interact with other people while he was in harness. Though while inside the house he was technically off-duty and could do whatever he wanted, under the circumstances it might be a good idea to reinforce her approval to go to Ben and not try to run straight to her.

There was a soft *oomph*, a few heavy footsteps, and finally Sam's nails on the hardwood as he galloped over to her, shoving his cold nose under her free hand.

She immediately dropped the icepack on the cushion and ran her hands down his body, checking each paw carefully for damage. Her fingers came away wet on the last one, making her heart thud until she put her fingers to her nose and sniffed.

Beer.

She let out a sigh of relief. "I think he's okay, but can you please double-check for me?"

A few seconds later, Ben said, "He's fine. Not a scratch."

Thank God.

The throb in her head was nothing compared to the knot in her gut at the thought of Sam being hurt, even just a little.

The dog you're getting today is special. That had been in the handwritten letter she'd received the day she graduated with Samson, written by the young girl whose family had donated him to the service and guide dog foundation. And it was absolutely true. Sam was such a vital part of her life she couldn't imagine being where she was without him.

He was more than her eyes. He was a part of her heart.

"Ben, thank you. I just…" She swallowed the stupid thickness in her throat as her hand twisted in the fur on Sam's neck. "Thank you."

"You're welcome." The gruffness of the words hinted he was as uncomfortable receiving her gratitude as she'd been giving it. "Put the ice back on that bump."

She bit back the snotty reply that rose to her lips, though she did mumble, "Bossy much?" as she followed his order.

"All the time."

She grinned despite her annoyance at the cocky reply. Sighing, her head sank back onto the cushion, ice pack balanced where it would put the least amount of pressure on the knot growing out of her temple like a newly emerging island from the sea.

The throbbing was a steady beat now, in time with her heartbeat, and her right elbow was starting to ache. She must have whacked it somewhere during her graceless swan dive. Other aches and pains would no doubt show themselves in the next little while, too. But for now, it was her head that took center stage.

Ben was right. She probably should go and have it looked at.

But she was ninety-nine percent certain she hadn't given herself a concussion. The vertigo and nausea had been minimal, and only right after it happened. Now there was just normal pain. Nothing like the last time.

And yes, the doctors had warned her about any future head injuries. As in, to avoid them at all costs. But at this point, what more could really happen? The damage was already done, and life wasn't a made-for-tv movie where blindness was suddenly "cured" by a second bump on the head. Blind was forever.

For her, at least.

No, there was no good reason to spend the night in the emergency room. All it would do was stir all the old nightmares back to the surface again, and she could really live without that, fuck you very much. The ones that still hit randomly were already bad enough.

But damn it, her head freaking *hurt*.

Pulling herself back from the depressing swirl of thoughts, she considered swallowing her pride to ask Ben to get her some aspirin. Only to realize he wasn't in the room with her anymore.

She stiffened.

He hadn't just left, had he? Sure, he'd been upset before, but he wouldn't go without at least saying something. Would he?

The tinkling of glass and the thunk of her garbage pail lid answered that question.

Her first reaction was relief he was still there. Then came a pinch of annoyance at his presumption to poke through her cabinets looking for the broom and dustpan. Then came even more annoyance, this time directed at herself.

The man was *helping*. She had to stop getting so defensive every time someone did something for her she could no longer do for herself.

Easier said than done when she heard the water running in the sink. "You don't need to do that, you know."

Whatever it was he was doing.

In her kitchen.

Without asking.

Okay, maybe she was entitled to be a *little* annoyed.

"I want to do a quick damp-mop to make sure I get any little slivers up."

Pride warred with practicality for all of about two seconds. "Okay, fine." Realizing how bitchy she sounded, she added, "Thank you."

Let it go, Hernandez. You can't control everything. Just let it go.

Listening to him bang around in her kitchen, filling the bucket and moving chairs around as he mopped, brought on a strange sensation. Irritation, yes. But something else. Something almost...cozy.

Which was stupid, considering her neighbor was only still there because he felt sorry for her. As soon as he finished his good deed—because that's what people like him did—he'd be out the door like a shot and that would be the last she heard from him.

And maybe that was for the best.

Needing to assert a little independence, and because her head really was killing her, she put down the ice pack and got up, pleased when the world didn't wobble around her. Sam automatically got out of her way, although he stuck close as she made her way toward the small main level bathroom.

She reached down and ruffled his soft ears. Poor pooch. He probably had no idea what the hell was going on. But he must have sensed she was hurt, and he wasn't leaving her side anytime soon.

"What are you doing?"

The gruff question made her jump, which annoyed her as much as being questioned in her own home did. "Getting some aspirin."

"You should have asked me. I'll get it. Just tell me where."

Ignoring the fact she'd intended to ask him to do just that before he started mopping her floor, she said, "I'm perfectly capable of getting it myself."

"Jesus, stubborn much?"

She gave him his own answer back with a smirk. "All the time."

There was a short hallway to the downstairs bathroom, across from the miniscule bedroom that housed her treadmill. From the medicine cabinet there she took out the bottle on the left side of the bottom shelf, automatically double-checking the Braille label before popping two tablets into her mouth and washing them down with some cool water from the sink.

Her stomach gurgled, but thankfully didn't object.

Ben stayed silent as she made her way back to the couch, but she could practically feel his eyes burning into her the entire time. With exaggerated care, she sat and resumed her former position, head back on the cushion with the towel-wrapped ice balanced strategically on her forehead.

That seemed to satisfy him, because a few seconds later she heard the sound of the mop being squeezed into the bucket again as he got back to work.

Bossy, pushy, annoying man.

The combination of aspirin and ice was just starting to numb the worst edges of the pain by the time Ben came back to the living room.

"I think I got everything, but you probably shouldn't go barefoot in there until you mop a couple more times." He hesitated before adding awkwardly, "Or, um, maybe you could have someone else do it. There were a lot of little slivers."

"Thank you." The awkwardness she ignored. He was right. She could mop just fine on her own. Normally. But she couldn't be sure she got up what she couldn't see. For that, she'd have to rely on someone else.

Just one of the million adjustments to her independence she was learning to make. And trying hard not to resent.

The floorboards creaked slightly as he shifted his weight. "You should probably replace the mop head, too. In case there's any glass in it."

"Right."

"Okay then." Another creak. "If you need anything else..."

"There is something." Since he seemed a few heartbeats away from bolting, and no matter how dented her pride might be, she had to say this. "I need you to know I wasn't trying to make you look foolish. I'd never do that."

He made a small sound in his throat, suggesting she'd surprised him with the change in topic. "But you knew I had no idea you were..."

"Blind." Her lips tipped up in a half-smile with no humor to it. "It's okay to say the word." Too many people danced around it, using stupid euphemisms instead, or just avoided the topic altogether.

Like she didn't know what she was.

"Okay, fine. You knew I had no idea you were blind."

"True."

"And yet you didn't do anything to clue me in. You just let me fumble through dinner like an idiot. Why didn't you just tell me?"

Was that hurt she could hear in his voice?

Her conscience gave her a kick in the rear, which made her a little defensive.

"What was I supposed to do, meet you at the front door with my white cane and dark glasses? I knew you'd figure it out on your own." Okay, maybe she'd more *hoped* he would, so she wouldn't have to actually say it. But evidently, she'd gotten a little too good at being comfortable in her own home to throw him any obvious clues.

"So, you were what, waiting to see how long it would take? To see how stupid I am?"

"No!" She bristled when he snorted. "Wow, you have some serious chip on your shoulder about that, don't you? Okay, yes, maybe I should have said something sooner. I almost did, when I mentioned being out of practice at small talk, and when you asked about my not having a car. But..."

"But?"

"I chickened out, okay?" Which made everything that happened tonight her fault. "I'm sorry. I was about to set you straight there at the end but you got there on your own first. Before that, though, I guess I held off because it was just...nice. Having an evening like everyone else. Being talked to like a regular person for a change. Not a disabled person. Not a blind person. Just...a person."

Just a woman.

She shrugged, hating the heat of embarrassment that stung her cheeks. "I was being selfish. And I ended up making you feel bad, so, yeah. I'm sorry."

"No," he said after a lengthy silence. "I'm sorry. I might have overreacted a little. It was just, when you kind of threw it out there about everyone besides me knowing without you having to tell them, and it took me so long to figure it out..."

She wanted to smack herself.

"Because everyone else has seen me out walking around with Sam wearing his full working harness. You've only ever seen him—and me—here at home."

"Oh." There was a thoughtful pause, hopefully as he used that information to readjust his take on her words. "Okay. So, you don't need him all the time, then."

"Not in places I'm comfortable. At home he's just a regular dog, since I know my space well enough to navigate without bumping into things." Her fingers rose to her forehead but fell away before touching the throbbing lump. She gave a wry grin. "Well, most of the time, anyway."

"Damn, that's my fault. I left the chair out—"

"And I knew it was there and still ran into it, because I acted before I thought about my surroundings. It's not the first bruise I've gotten, and it won't be the last. Trust me, this being blind thing is a constant work in progress."

"I'd still feel better if you let me take you to the hospital."

"That's guilt talking."

"If you could see what your forehead looks like right now, you'd be saying the same thing I am." There was another of those uncomfortable pauses. "Damn. I didn't mean..."

A little piece of her soul cringed.

"And that's exactly what I was talking about. Don't apologize for saying something normal. You don't have to edit your vocabulary because you think it might upset me to hear you say 'see' or 'look' or 'watch.' I still watch tv. I tell people I'll see them later. Figures of speech don't hurt me. Being treated like helpless, damaged goods does."

Something her family had yet to understand.

"Okay. Got it. So...hospital?"

She had to give him points for persistence. "So...no?"

He let out a sigh that sounded closer to a growl. "Then will you at least go see your own doctor tomorrow?"

"I can absolutely promise I'll see a medical professional tomorrow." It wasn't really a lie. Her sister, who was currently studying to sit for her nursing NCLEX exam, was coming over for their shopping trip in the morning. That made her sort of a medical professional. "Good enough?"

"Okay, yeah, I guess." *Creak.* "So." *Creak.*

Annnd...they were back to being ready to bolt again.

She huffed out an impatient breath. "You know what? How about we forget tonight ever happened and start over?"

The moment before he answered seemed to last a lifetime.

"I like that idea. But I have an even better one. What if we just forget the second half of the night instead? I kind of enjoyed the first part."

"Yeah, me too." Probably more than she should have. "Okay." She dropped the ice pack to the cushion beside her and stuck out her hand. "Hi. I'm Miranda Hernandez, your new neighbor, and this is my trusty guide dog, Sam. It's nice to meet you. I hope we can be friends."

Ben's large hand enveloped hers, sending a delicious shiver through her body.

"It's very nice to meet you, Miranda. I'm Ben Murphy, the very noisy guy next door. I'm looking forward to getting to know you."

Oh, if only that were true.

But based on her experience, now that he knew the truth about her blindness, it was only a matter of time before her sexy-voiced neighbor ghosted right out of her life as though he'd never been there at all.

Chapter 6

Blind.

How the hell had he missed that important little detail?

Ben flicked his directional on and eased over into the left lane of the Long Island Expressway. Simple. He'd been too busy picturing ways to get her naked in the least amount of time, that's how. That, and she was really, really good at pretending.

No, not pretending. There hadn't been any attempt to be something she wasn't. As she'd said, she was just that comfortable in her own home that she was able to function like a normal person.

He winced. Bad choice of words.

So were the ones when he'd accused her of trying to make him look like an idiot. The truth was, that was entirely on him. If he'd been thinking with anything other than his dick, he wouldn't have ignored all the little warning signs something was off from the time he first met her right through to his belated epiphany.

The way she looked at him but didn't truly focus on his eyes when they were talking.

The lack of reaction to his winks and smiles.

The damn beer she didn't hand him. That more than any-thing should have clued him in to what was going on. But no. He'd been too distracted by her sweet strawberry/vanilla scent and her lush mouth and, yeah, her ridiculously adorable naked feet, hell if he knew why.

Then he'd gone and let his old insecurities rise up and overtake common sense. All those times he was called stupid as a kid came welling up inside. For a second, it felt like middle school all over again, getting lured in by one of the cool girls he'd been crushing on only to end up laughed at and humiliated by her and her friends. Like *Carrie* but without the pig's blood and high body count.

Miranda didn't try to embarrass him, though. She hadn't even lied to him, unless you counted omission. But she'd unknowingly punched one of his major buttons, and ended up hurt thanks to the evidently unresolved issues of his inner fourteen-year-old.

"I am such an asshole," he muttered, switching to the center lane to get around an old pickup truck loaded with landscaping equipment belching noxious black fumes from its exhaust pipe. Dude was in serious need of an oil change.

A glance at the time showed he was going to be late for dinner. Again.

Getting back into the left lane, he increased his speed a little, but the summer traffic heading east on the Island had the expressway clogged. One of the many reasons going to Friday night family dinner at his parents' house was on his list of least favorite things to do.

And yes, he could have avoided the worst of the tourist traffic by leaving earlier in the day. But he'd wasted too much time today thinking about Miranda as he laid down the stain on his freshly sanded floors. Arguing with himself over going to check on her.

He'd actually started over there twice before better judgement hauled him back to his side of the property line.

It wasn't like he didn't know she was okay. She had called him first thing this morning as she'd promised after adding his number to her contacts—at his request—to have for emergencies.

He shook his head and grinned. Yeah, he probably should have put a little more thought into what "first thing" might mean to an ex-Marine. The phone had startled him out of a deep sleep at six a.m. sharp.

He'd been distracted again about midmorning when a tired little Jetta pulled into her driveway. The woman who'd gotten out and gone into the house looked too much like Miranda not to be a relative. She appeared a few years younger, with long, dark hair tied up in a ponytail that went halfway down her back, bouncing above a nicely rounded booty that usually would have been the stuff of his fantasies.

Today, all he'd thought was how glad he was Miranda wasn't alone anymore.

Then he continued to play creepy peeper by watching Miranda and her...sister, maybe?...walking to the car about a half hour later. The sight of her holding the handle of the sturdy leather harness attached to Sam had punched him in the gut.

She really was blind.

And yeah, he'd already accepted that fact. But seeing her with Sam cemented it in his brain in a way nothing else had. She was right. If he'd seen her like that first, instead of rocking a bikini and walking around her backyard, it would have been obvious, even to a slow learner like him.

The dog had hopped into the back seat like it was old hat. Miranda then got into the passenger seat, laughing at something loudly enough for the sound to carry across the yard and through the open windows. Relief and something else had filled him at the sound.

Relief that if she could laugh like that, she was probably okay.

The something else he ignored. It was going to take a while before his body got the message Miranda was off-limits.

It had taken a surprising amount of effort to let go of her hand the night before. He'd felt the little shudder she tried to hide. With any other woman he wanted to get into bed, he'd pounce on that sign of sexual awareness and leverage it to the next level. A smile.

A look. A quick caress. He had a whole repertoire in his bag of seduction techniques. But Miranda...

Miranda was blind, and that changed the rules.

At least, he thought it did.

Hell, shouldn't it?

It felt...*wrong* to be thinking about getting into her pants. Well, about *just* getting into her pants. And sex was really all he had to offer. He didn't do serious relationships, and he made sure the women he was with knew it.

Miranda had a natural sensuality she wore like a second skin, consciously or not. But would someone in as vulnerable a position as she was be into that kind of sex-only association? He certainly didn't want to be the asshole who took advantage of her, pressing for something that might hurt her in the end.

Not to mention she was currently sporting the mother of all knots on her forehead, a fact that burned in his gut like a bowl of Boone's chili. His job was to help and protect. Being the cause of her injury left him drowning in all kinds of unwanted guilt.

By the time he pulled up to his parents' two-story brick Colonial, he'd argued himself in circles about whether to proceed with caution on the Miranda front, or concentrate on working on his house and forget all about her and her sexy little feet.

It was clear he needed to give the whole situation a very long, careful think before he decided anything. And in the meantime, maybe he'd just keep an eye on her. Quietly. Like any good neighbor would.

He let himself into the house and called, "Sorry I'm late. Traffic."

Which on a summer weekend in the Hamptons excused pretty much anything, since half the population of New York City and western Long Island seemed to migrate to the east end every Friday afternoon. They'd take advantage of the beaches and vineyards for the weekend, then pack up and slog their way west again Sunday night.

It was a wonder the whole island didn't tip right over.

"Traffic you could have avoided if you'd planned a little better."

Wow. Five seconds in the door and his sister was already pointing out his failings. A new record. "I do have a two-and-a-half-hour drive to get here from home, you know, even with clear roads."

Not that a little fact like that would matter to Abby. As far as he knew, her life was so tightly scheduled and spreadsheeted out, she'd never been late for a thing in her entire life, starting the day she was born. Right on time, with no fuss or muss.

Unlike him, who'd been two weeks late and breech. It had been a sign of exactly what roles the two of them would play out in the Murphy family dynamic in years to come.

"You should have bought a house closer to home, then," his mother said, coming from the kitchen as she wiped her hands on her apron. "I told you that old place would cause you nothing but problems."

The only problem was it not being even further away.

He dutifully leaned down to kiss her cheek, flushed from the heat of the oven. "Hi, Mom. Good to see you, too."

She sniffed. "If that were true, I wouldn't need to guilt you into spending time with your family."

He didn't say anything, because she was kind of right. He loved his family. He just loved them better from a distance.

"I'm also late because I stopped and got this." He offered her two white bakery boxes tied with string. "Macaroons and rugelach."

"From Zimmerman's?"

"Where else?"

"Well, I guess tardiness can be excused for good rugelach." She patted his cheek before heading back to the kitchen. "Wash up, Benjamin. Dinner will be on the table in a minute."

The familiar childhood refrain did little to help him hold on to his determination this dinner was going to be different. Cody was right. He needed to stop letting his family get inside his head and doubt his own accomplishments. So what if he wasn't a doctor, or a lawyer, or a teacher? Those were their strengths. His was being a kick-ass firefighter.

Fucking own it, Murphy.

Walking into the dining room a few minutes later, he greeted his brother with a handshake, which Caleb turned into a one-armed guy hug.

"Late again, huh?"

Two years Ben's junior, he'd resented his gifted younger brother for a large chunk of his teenage years. Now, he could admire the brilliance of Cay's brain without wanting to shove him into a locker.

"Perfect timing, you mean," he said with a laugh.

"Yeah well, I was kind of hoping you'd get here sooner. I, uh, I need to ask your opinion about something."

The awkward admission piqued his interest. "My opinion? Wow, that's a first. You're the one who always has all the answers."

Okay, so maybe he wasn't as over the resentment as he thought.

"Don't be a dick."

"Sorry, sorry. So, what do you need help with? No, let me guess. It's a woman, right?"

Caleb snorted. "Like I'd need your help with that."

"Cay, come on. You may be brilliant, but even you have to admit women are my expertise."

"Women, yes. Relationships with women, no."

Well, he had him there.

"I appreciate the offer, but that's not what I wanted to talk about. Do you think we could—" Caleb broke off as their mother and sister came in carrying platters of delicious smelling food, a chagrined look on his face before he managed to blank it.

"Benjamin, please go and get the bread from the kitchen," his mother instructed. "Caleb, please pry your father out of his study. And don't take 'I'll be right there' as an answer. He said that half an hour ago."

Curious what his brother had been about to ask, Ben made a mental note to corner him again before the evening was over. There hadn't been a lot of times in their lives he'd been able to do something for Cay, other than getting the assholes on the football team to stop picking on the nerdy little brainiac back in high school. If he could help him out with something now, he would.

He just couldn't figure out what that could be.

Conversation over dinner followed the usual pattern.

"Abigail, dear, your bosses must have been very pleased you won that big case for them last week," his mother said. "Have they mentioned anything more about making you a junior partner yet?"

Ben nearly choked on his pot roast. "Junior partner? Holy sh—crap, Abby. That's huge."

"It's just talk right now. Nothing definite."

Brandishing her fork, his mother pointed at Abby. "If they have any brains in their heads, they'll offer it to you before you get snapped up by some other firm."

"We'll see."

His sister was wearing her serene lawyer face, making it seem like she wasn't worried one way or the other about it. But Ben knew how to see around the edges of her mask and could tell she was excited. And maybe a little nervous.

He caught her eye across the table and gave a wink. "Way to go, sis."

The mask cracked for just a second as she rolled her eyes at him, before putting her attention fully back on her food.

From the other end of the table, his father said, "Caleb, your mother told me you changed your mind about teaching the summer advanced program. That was an excellent decision. You can never have too many extracurriculars on your academic resumé."

Looking like he wanted to argue that statement, Caleb cut into his meat with a little too much aggression, knife screeching on the plate. "I'm still considering it."

"What?" His mother looked shocked. "I thought you said it was all settled."

"It is. It was. But..." Caleb stabbed the pot roast with his fork. "I haven't given them my final answer yet, that's all."

"Well, if you want Tanner's seat when he retires in a few years, you need to start showing them *now* that you're willing to put in the extra effort."

Ben looked from his frowning father to his grimly chewing brother and back. "What's Tanner's seat?"

"Mitchell Tanner, head of the mathematics department at Whitman."

"Who's older than dirt and isn't going to give up that spot until he keels over dead at his desk. Not that anyone would notice right away," Caleb added under his breath, only loud enough for Ben to hear.

His father gave Caleb the look he'd perfected in his classroom for dealing with a student who'd disappointed him. Or in Ben's case, a son. It was a little disconcerting to see it used on one of his always-perfect siblings for a change.

"Mitchell Tanner is a respected educator who's dedicated his life to academia. You'd do well to emulate him, rather than mock him."

Looking duly chastened, Caleb sighed. "You're right, sir. I'm sorry."

Adjusting his silver-framed glasses in what Ben always thought of as his "professor's pose," his father nodded. "Trust me. Play your cards right, and you'll become the youngest department head Whitman University has ever had."

He might have been wrong, but it didn't seem like Caleb shared their father's certainty. Or enthusiasm. His brother merely nodded and shoveled another forkful of food into his mouth, ending the conversation.

Dread tightened his gut as the wheel of inquisition turned his way.

"Benjamin, the junior high school is looking for a new athletics coach for the fall."

The non sequitur left him confused. "Okay?"

"You were always so brilliant in sports, dear. You should give them a call."

Familiar frustration soured his appetite as her meaning clicked. "Mom, I already have a job."

"You need a different job. One that's not so dangerous."

"It's not *that* dangerous."

"You said you weren't hurt at that fire the other day. Why were you limping when you came into the house, then?"

Damn her super mom eyes. They saw *everything*.

"I twisted my knee a little. Nothing a little rest won't fix."

Which he hadn't given it, choosing instead to spend the last two days doing all of the sanding and staining so the floors would be prepped and ready for the polyurethane top coats he planned to start applying first thing tomorrow.

Not to mention picking up and carrying his neighbor last night, *and* her squirmy-ass dog who tried to French him the whole time he'd had the mutt in his arms.

If only it had been Miranda kissing him in gratitude.

He struck the errant thought away. Hadn't he already decided she was off-limits until he thought things through?

"Are you sure you're all right?" His mother's sharp gaze ran over him as though he might be hiding a gaping wound beneath his clothes somewhere.

"I'm fine, Mom. I just stepped in a hole." In a burning roof. "No big deal."

Unimpressed by his reassurances, she tilted her head and looked down her nose at him. Before she could launch into another chorus of "you need a safer job," he beat her to the punch. "Did I mention I'm going to be taking the lieutenant's test next month?"

"Oh, Ben, do you really think you should do that?"

It shouldn't have surprised him. But his mother's unenthusiastic response still felt like a hot knife of betrayal in his gut.

"Why wouldn't I? Advancement is the goal in any job, right?" Hadn't they just been throwing praise at Caleb and Abby for that very thing?

"But don't you have to score extremely well on those tests for that to happen?"

The knife sunk deeper.

"The written test is only half the overall score. The rest comes from my seniority and awards."

"But the test..." His mother exchanged a look with his father, passing the verbal baton.

"We just don't want you to be disappointed, Son. That's all."

Too late.

"Well, I wasn't too stupid to pass the entrance exam and get into the department." He fought his temper, which was wriggling to get free as hard as Sam had done in his arms the night before.

He'd studied almost a whole year for that test, signing up for every prep course he could find, and somehow managed to wrangle his poor test-taking skills under control long enough to do a pretty good job. Better than he'd hoped, actually. Enough to make it into a class before the list of candidates expired.

Something a lot of other people *hadn't* done.

His mother's voice turned sharp. "Nobody said you were stupid. You can do anything you put your mind to."

"Except do well on the lieutenant's test, you mean." Bunching up his napkin, he dropped it onto the table next to his half-eaten meal.

"Don't speak to your mother in that tone," his father warned.

"Benjamin, please." Eyes pleading, his mother leaned forward in her seat. "I just don't want to see you disappointed when things don't go the way you expect them to. Like when you went to get your learner's permit with all your friends."

And didn't. Because he'd been the only one to fail the test everyone else had boasted was so easy. He'd had to go back and take it again the next week, *and* still only barely squeaked out a passing grade. Just one in a multitude of similarly humiliating moments from his past.

One he could have done without being reminded of yet again.

He looked around the table at his family. His smart, successful family, all looking back at him with varying degrees of concern and pity. Who never had to worry about being disappointed about their choices because they were each capable enough, *intelligent* enough, to reach whatever goals they set for themselves, no matter how high.

And then there was him.

The mental dud.

The one who shouldn't ever aim too high, because he was sure to fail.

Fuck this.

He pushed his chair back. "Thanks for the meal, Mom, but I better be going. I have a long drive home."

She looked stricken as he stood. "Oh, but...I thought you were staying the night."

That had been the plan. Another two-plus hour drive was going to suck.

But since he wasn't sure he could keep a lid on the bubbling pit of resentment growing inside him, staying was no longer an option.

"I have a lot of work to do still at home. Better I get an early start on it." He bent and kissed her cheek before she could object further. "Love you."

"Oh, Benjamin." Her hand on his arm halted his retreat. "I love you, too. I just want what's best for you."

Too bad they never seemed to agree on what that was.

Swallowing words he knew he'd regret, he managed a pained smile. "I know, Mom."

After quick goodbyes to everyone else while pretending not to see his father's disapproving scowl, he made his escape. Only to remember after he was safely in his SUV that Caleb had wanted to ask him something.

"Damn it."

Going back inside wasn't an option. Instead, he pulled out his phone and shot off a quick text to his brother, telling him to call tomorrow if he still wanted to talk.

Taunts from his childhood chased him all the way back to the expressway like the banshees from his Granny Murphy's bedtime stories of Irish ghosts and ghoulies. *Moron. Idiot. Stupid retard.* Kids could be particularly brutal to one of their own once they found a weakness to exploit. Being the one who always needed to stay for additional help, who always had to do extra credit to bump up a C to a B minus made his painfully obvious.

What had really exasperated him was the fact he *knew* the material. At least, he'd thought he did. But the second that test paper hit his desk, it was all just...gone. Lost in a jumbled swirl inside his thick, useless head.

If it wasn't for the growth spurt between eighth and ninth grade, the "stupid" label might have followed him into high school. Instead, he'd discovered the two things he could excel at: sports, and girls. Things with the other kids had gotten easier after that.

But the schoolwork hadn't.

Eventually, he'd accepted he was never going to be as good at any of his classes as his brother and sister were, and stopped trying so hard. But while the taunts in the classroom had changed to cheers on the football field, they still rang loud and clear inside his own head.

Glancing down at the speedometer, he cursed and let off the gas. It didn't matter how fast he went, there were just some things he'd never be able to outrun.

His own inadequacies topped the list.

By the time he made it to the Nassau/Queens border, the combined weight of mental and physical exhaustion was starting to drag at him. He could either keep driving for another hour plus to get home, which was doable but would suck. Or he could crash at his old apartment, which was less than ten minutes away.

Switching lanes in rapid succession, he took the next exit.

A night on Cody's couch would probably play havoc with his sketchy knee, but it was still the better option. At least it seemed that way until he walked into the four-story apartment building he'd once called home.

"Benny!"

"Son of a bitch." He growled the curse under his breath as the squealing woman rushed toward him across the small lobby, blonde hair and big boobs bouncing with every step. Christ. What bad karmic juju was hanging over his head tonight? First his parents' emasculating "concern," and now this.

"Hey, Val." He expected her to stop, but she ran into him at full speed, wrapping her arms around him in an octopus-tight embrace. His knee groaned as he was forced back a step to absorb the impact, barely keeping them both upright

"Benny, Benny, Benny!" The squeal had him wincing. "I'm so happy to see you!"

"That's...great."

No, it wasn't. But what was he supposed to say? You're the nightmare I moved to get away from and I wish you'd stay the hell out of my life?

Too cruel, even if it was the truth.

Trying not to sneeze from the overpowering cloud of perfume she always doused herself with, he gently peeled her arms away and took a step back, gaining some much-needed personal space.

Which Val immediately stepped forward into, hands on his chest as she blinked up at him with those huge, blue anime-sized eyes of hers.

"I heard you were hurt the other day, at that big fire on Stillwell. Are you okay?"

He stepped back out of touching range again. "Where did you hear that?" Because he knew his name hadn't been anywhere in the news. If it had, his mother would have been the first to let him know about it.

Loudly.

With a secret smile, she twirled a piece of hair around her finger. "Oh, a nice little birdie at the station told me all about it."

More like a loud-mouthed turkey named Cartwright.

"Listen, Valerie, you have to stop coming to the firehouse asking about me. We're not seeing each other anymore. You need to let it go, okay? Please."

"But we're still friends, right? I mean, we were together for three whole months. That's got to mean something, right?"

"Together" wasn't exactly what he'd call it.

More like a bunch of scattered days where the mood and their schedules aligned. And they certainly hadn't been exclusive. Distilled down to the actual time they'd been in each other's company, it was probably less than ten days total.

Ninety-nine percent of which had been spent having sex. And mostly because they only lived a few floors apart. A neighbors-with-benefits situation.

Not that she'd appreciate hearing such a cold breakdown of the facts. Val had always been a bit of a romantic dreamer. And a clinger. Which was part of the reason he was having such a problem getting her to face reality without having to resort to being brutally honest.

He tried a different tack.

"Look, you don't want to get me in trouble with my boss, do you? Because that's going to happen if you keep showing up at the firehouse all the time." Silence. "Well, do you?"

"No." The word sounded like it was being dragged from her mouth.

"So, you'll stop?"

She shifted as if she wanted to stamp her foot. "But I like visiting there. All the guys are nice to me, and…" The rest of the words were a mumble.

"What?"

"I thought maybe you'd get a little jealous of them."

"Jesus, Val, that's…" Crazy. Maybe even a little stalkerish. "That's wrong, okay? And it's not going to happen, so please, just stop."

Her mulish expression told him that wasn't likely.

He sighed. "Look, I'm sorry you don't want to accept it, but it's over. It's been over. And if you don't learn to back off and respect that, then there won't even be a way for us to be friends."

"But…I miss you."

Christ, were those tears?

"I'm sorry." He put as much finality into his tone as he could and prayed the threatening sheen in her eyes stayed put.

"You were always so good to me. You made me feel safe."

It took every ounce of willpower he had, but he didn't let the lost tone of her voice sway him. Hell, he was nobody's safe harbor. This was why he didn't do relationships. People started expecting more from him than he had to give.

When it became clear he wasn't going to say anything, Val laid a trembling hand on his chest again. "Can we at least be together tonight? For old time's sake?"

It was tempting. Oh, so tempting. After the shit night he'd had, losing himself in some between-the-sheets therapy might be just the thing.

He looked down at her. She was pretty in a regular kind of way, with those blue eyes and pink-tinted mouth, and a full set of curves that had once been enough to entice him into a few hours of sweaty, meaningless sex at any time, no matter how tired he might be. But this time, he felt...nothing.

No, not true. He felt ashamed, for thinking about using her to escape his troubles the way he would a bottle of Jack Daniels.

Which was why he carefully removed her hand from his chest and gave it a gentle squeeze before releasing it. "That wouldn't be fair to you. I'm sorry, but I have to say no."

Her chin wobbled a little as she nodded, blinking rapidly. "Okay. I...I guess I should be going, then."

"Sure. I really am sorry," he added, feeling like a piece of crap despite the fact he hadn't done anything wrong.

"Me, too. Bye, Benny." With a sniffle, she turned on her high heels and hurried toward the elevator.

Fuck. Fuckfuckfuck.

Crashing with Cody was out of the question now. Val may have seemed to accept his no as a final answer. But he had a feeling it would only be a matter of time before she came knocking on his door, trying to persuade him to change his no to a yes.

And, being a weak-willed bastard led by his dick, he was afraid she just might succeed.

She had before.

After stopping by the bodega on the corner for a Red Bull, he got back on the road. The drive home was definitely the lesser of two evils. The last thing he needed was to give Val false hope. Relationships weren't something he knew how to do.

And even if he did, he wouldn't want to.

To have anything more meaningful with a woman than a few hours in the sack meant having to get past the sex and the bodies and give her something more. Something real. The true him, underneath the shiny outer surface he showed the world.

Problem was, he'd learned a long time ago there wasn't much there worth giving.

Chapter 7

It had been too much to hope Julietta wouldn't mention the bump on her head to their mother.

Early Saturday morning, the steamroller that was Inez Hernandez descended on Miranda without any more warning than a phone call to say she was pulling into the driveway. Having just finished her post-run shower, she hurried through getting dressed, knowing she wouldn't beat her mother to the door, but trying anyway. Such a small thing, but she knew it would set the tone for the rest of the visit.

As if she didn't already know how *that* was going to go.

The front door opened as she got to the bottom of the stairs. They really needed a refresher on what, exactly, her emergency key was supposed to be used for.

She swallowed a groan when she heard not one set of footsteps, but two, enter the house. Too light and clacky to be either her father or brother, unless one of them had suddenly developed an affinity for sling-back sandals. Knowing Julietta had work today, that left only one other person it could be.

Freaking wonderful.

Well, as her friend Sergeant Gerry "Gator" Cormier would say in that lazy Cajun drawl of his, *laissez les bons temps roule.* Let the good times roll.

"Miranda?"

Rubbing Sam's ears as he leaned his comforting weight against her leg, she pasted on a neutral expression at the inquiring call from the front of the house. "Hi, Mom." She listened to the footsteps advance down the hall toward her. "This is a surprise." It was as close as she could get to a rebuke for the unannounced visit.

"Did you honestly think I wouldn't come after I heard?" Strong arms engulfed her in a smothering embrace.

The scent of the lavender sachets her mother kept tucked in her dresser drawers teased at her senses, filling Miranda with a nostalgic pang. "It was just a bump."

"Just a bump?" Her mother pulled back abruptly and clucked her tongue. "Half of your forehead is black and blue. Why didn't you call and tell me you'd been hurt?"

Because she'd known she would rush right over and make more of it than it needed to be. Kind of like she was doing now.

"Trust me, it looks way worse than it is." Julietta had described the rainbow of sickly shades she'd been sporting the day before. It had sounded gruesome enough that she'd allowed her sister to slap some concealer on her face before they'd gone out shopping. "Really, it barely even bothered me this morning during my run."

Her mother made another of her many sounds of annoyance. "Always with the running, ever since you were a girl. You can't stop for one day to let yourself get better?"

"I did skip yesterday." Something she'd hated doing. It threw off her entire training regimen. If she was going to be ready by October, she needed to step up her game, not coddle her aches and pains. But even she wasn't stubborn enough to push her body past its limits, and yesterday, it had told her *no freaking way*.

"Wow, the big, bad Marine admits she isn't super woman. Let's have a parade."

Turning her head toward her sister's voice, Miranda replied in the same snarky tone, "That's Wonder Woman to you, brat."

"Isobel, be nice to your sister." Their mother's chastisement was met by a grumble that might or might not have been agreement.

Miranda was betting on not.

"Izzy, don't you have work today?" Hopefully?

She worked at an upscale clothing boutique in the new mall up in Shenandoah. She loved the clothes, but hated the customers, the hours, and her coworkers.

Not an easy person to please, her sister.

"It's my day off." Her sulky tone said it all. Checking in on Miranda wasn't how she'd planned to spend her free Saturday. Fair enough. Miranda hadn't planned on hers being invaded by her family, well-meaning as they might be.

"Which means we can both spend the whole day with you, *mija*."

A flash of panic hit at her mother's pronouncement. Oh, hell no. A few hours were bad enough. But the whole day?

"Oh, Mom, no. You don't have to do that. *Really*. I'm fine."

"Are you hungry?"

As always when it didn't suit her, it seemed her mother was going to ignore Miranda's objections.

Okay, then. New plan. Maybe she could at least get them out of the house. Neutral territory was always safer. "Actually, yes. I didn't have breakfast yet."

"Perfect. I'll make us something."

"Well, I usually just have fruit or cereal, so there's not much else in the fridge. There's this great little diner in town that has the most amazing food, though. Why don't we go there?"

"No need. We stopped at the grocery store on the way. Isobel, go and get the bags from the car, please." More muttering and clack-ety-clacking of her sister's sandals followed her retreat, punctuated by the slap of the screen door.

"Come." Her mother's arm wrapped around her waist to guide her as they walked, much to Miranda's weary exasperation. "You can keep me company while I cook and tell me about this man who left you all alone after you were hurt, instead of taking you to the hospital like anyone with half a brain would do."

Jules and her big mouth again.

"He wanted to take me," she said, settling into the chair her mother led her to even though it wasn't where she usually sat. She'd learned to pick her battles. "I was the one who said I didn't need to go."

"Miranda."

She winced at the chiding tone. "You know how much I hate hospitals."

More like pathologically feared them.

Her mother clucked her tongue. "He still should have made you go."

"Maybe he trusted my judgement." Which had been a nice change of pace. Usually, everyone just rolled right over her with their good intentions.

Although she had a feeling if Ben had *really* thought her injury was more serious than she was letting on, he wouldn't have hesitated to force the issue.

"Hmph." Water ran in the sink, followed by the rattle of the kettle on the stove. Despite the perfectly good Keurig on the counter, her mother still preferred her tea the old-fashioned way. "So, tell me more."

Trying not to cringe as she listened to the contents of her cabinets being ransacked and moved around as her mother hunted up the pans she wanted—the ones she could have given her the exact location of, if only she'd bothered to ask—she said, "His name is Ben. He's fixing up the house next door."

"Oh? If he's one of those flip people, you should give him your father's card."

Mention of her father sent a familiar pang of mixed emotion through her chest. "Isn't he already all booked up with jobs for the summer?"

"He could probably fit in another small renovation. Especially if it's a neighbor of yours."

So he could grill Ben to within an inch of his life? Ha! They might not be able to hold a civil conversation most days, but that didn't mean her dad wouldn't go all Rottweiler on her behalf at the drop of a hat.

Complicated didn't begin to describe their relationship.

"No, he's not a flipper. And he's been doing the work himself, with the help of some friends." Her mother's *hmph* told her what she thought of that. "Besides, I think he's just about done, anyway. At least, that's what he said."

"And what does this Ben person do? Aside from taking money out of the pockets of legitimate contractors."

Her lips twitched. Her mother was nothing if not loyal to the family business. All those DIY home shows had cut into their customer base, and their bottom line. "He's a firefighter down in New York City."

"Who's a firefighter?" Isobel asked.

Miranda cursed silently. Of course, her sister would walk in on that juicy bit of information.

"Miranda's neighbor." Bags crinkled as they were emptied onto the counter.

"Oh? You mean the hot, hunky, stud-muffin I just saw getting into his SUV next door?" There was an undercurrent of feminine interest to her words Miranda didn't like one little bit. "He seemed super nice. Waved hello and everything."

"Yeah, Ben's a really nice guy." Who was evidently also a hot, hunky stud-muffin. Who waved to her gorgeous younger sister.

And didn't that just grind up in her gut like broken glass.

"Ben." The dreamy way Izzy said his name tightened Miranda's insides even more. "Hey, you know, maybe I should go invite him to come join us for breakfast. Since he's your neighbor and all."

Over my dead body.

Tamping down that vicious bite of jealousy, she asked, "Didn't you just say he was leaving?"

"Oh, right." Isobel sounded disappointed, but Miranda was relieved.

Which was pathetic and uncalled for.

But she still was.

"Where do you keep your butter?" From the sound of it, her mother was rooting around in the refrigerator looking for it and making an absolute mess of things.

Her hands curled into fists in her lap, nails biting into her palms with sharp little stings as she listened to the utter destruction of her methodical organization. "On the door, second shelf down." Right where it always was. "What are you making, anyway?"

"*Huveos rancheros.*"

Oh, yum. For her mother's *huevos rancheros* she'd put up with having to reorganize her entire kitchen.

Enthusiasm rising for the first time since the phone had rung, she stood. "Sounds good. What do you want me to do?"

There was a brief lull in the clatter of food preparation.

"You sit back down and rest, *mija*, and we'll take care of everything."

Her mother's patronizing tone rankled. "I'll set the table."

"Your sister can do that. You just—"

"I can set the damn table, Mom." She winced. "Sorry. I didn't mean to be rude. But I don't need to rest, and I don't need to be waited on. What I need is to stop being told what I can't do, and start being allowed to show you what I can."

There was a pregnant pause.

"Then you should do what you want, of course. This is your home, after all. It's not my place to tell you what to do."

Oh, if only that were true.

Her mother *lived* to tell her children what to do. But after Miranda lost her sight, it had gone from loving quirk to compulsive smothering.

With a sigh, she started to walk around the table, then stopped. "Is there anything on the floor between me and the cabinets?" Because her sister had a penchant for leaving things laying around for her to trip over, no matter how many times Miranda reminded her not to.

Not that she thought Isobel did it on purpose, but...sometimes she kinda thought maybe she did.

"No, there's nothing." Her mother sounded anxious. "Do you want me to—"

"No, Mom. I've got this." Knowing her every move was being watched made the skin between her shoulder blades itch the way it had when her Marine unit was under surveillance by hostiles.

She went to the cabinets, checked the numbered Braille label next to the pull to make sure it was the right one, and took down three of the dishes Trixie helped her pick out when she'd first moved in. They were pretty, white with little blue swirls around the edge, and supposed to be close to indestructible.

So far, they'd lived up to their claim.

After putting them on the table, she went back and got silverware from the drawer next to the sink. Then mugs from another cabinet. She finished each place setting off with a napkin before finally taking her seat again, feeling pleased with herself. She was still perfectly capable of participating in the family ritual of meal preparation.

In some small way, at least.

"Oh, that was wonderful!" Her mother clapped her hands together twice in excitement. "Very nicely done, *mija*. Didn't she do a good job, Isobel?"

Every drop of satisfaction filling her drained even before her sister's grudging agreement. With one well-meaning comment, her flawless act of self-sufficiency had been reduced to a skill no better than a dog balancing a ball on its nose.

A familiar sense of depression pressed in on her as she sat listening to her mother and sister preparing the meal together in nimble harmony. Why did she even bother to try? No matter what she accomplished, no matter how independent she became, her mother was always going to see her as her blind daughter. Her *pobre bebé*. The one everyone needed to take care of, look out for, and worry about.

Why couldn't she see that she was so much more than her disability?

She barely tasted the food put in front of her. Listening to her sister gush about the pair of Jimmy Choos she'd gotten for a steal on clearance, she methodically chewed her way through enough of the egg dish that her mother wouldn't comment on her lack of appetite and start in again about her head.

When she couldn't force down another bite, she sat back, cradling her cup of coffee, and let the conversation swirl around her. She didn't think either of them noticed she never said a word.

Even with her family, it seemed her blindness could render her virtually invisible.

When the time came to clear the table, she didn't even bother offering to help. What would be the point?

She was perfectly capable of stacking things in the dishwasher, a feat she managed every single day with no problem. But her mother would probably clap her hands again at what a wonderful job she'd done of such a simple task.

And she didn't think she could handle that lowering experience for a second time quite so soon.

The clatter of the bucket and mop being dragged from the utility closet by the basement stairs broke her out of her morbid introspection. "Mom, you don't have to do that. Jules already made sure the kitchen was clear of any glass slivers yesterday."

"Well, since we're here, we might as well give the whole house a thorough scrubbing."

"The house is fine, Mom."

It felt perfectly clean to her. It even smelled clean. Between her own daily efforts, the Roombas that ran every night to chase after Sam's fur, and Trixie's niece who earned a few extra bucks by coming over to do a deep cleaning twice a month, she thought she was managing pretty damn well.

Her mother's standards, however, were on par with a clean-room-in-a-computer-chip-factory level of cleanliness.

So, like with the cooking, she was reduced to listening to the frenzy of vacuuming and mopping coming from every room of her home while she sat curled in her favorite corner of the couch, Sam next to her, his big head on her lap. She stroked his ears and tried hard to smother the resentment burning in her belly as every shred of privacy she had was scrubbed out of existence.

"She only does it because she loves me," she reminded herself.

A familiar refrain.

The flat New England accent of her therapist stole into her mind with another one.

"There's a fine line between loving and enabling. You'll have to decide where to draw it, and what you're going to do when it gets crossed."

What she'd done about it was move out on her own. A huge step forward, in Dr. Harding's opinion. A huge mistake in her mother's.

But the doc had been exactly right. The longer she stayed holed up in the same house where she grew up, sleeping in the same little bed, having her mother treat her like an invalid incapable of doing the simplest task for herself, the easier it became to accept that version of herself. To believe she *needed* to be taken care of for the rest of her life.

Moving out had given her back her independence.

And her backbone.

Needless to say, her mother was not her therapist's biggest fan.

"Doc would be very disappointed in me," she told Sam, who merely groaned and pressed his head into her hand harder as she rubbed. "I'm falling right back into old patterns." Something she'd warned Miranda could happen at their last monthly session.

Sometimes the path of least resistance was very appealing. Especially when it came to dealing with well-meaning loved ones.

She owed her family so much. They'd been there when her world fell apart, and helped put the pieces back together afterward. She hated to ever seem ungrateful when they offered to help. But if she was going to maintain the control over her life that she'd just gotten back, she needed to stop being a wuss and just say *no*.

Making her mother hear that no might be a little trickier to manage.

Thanks to the old house's creaky floors, she was able to track her mother's and sister's progress from room to room overhead. There shouldn't be anything for them to do in the two unused bedrooms at the end of the hall except maybe dust. But from the sound of it, they were spending a lot more time in the room directly over the living room than they should.

Alarm bells started to jangle in her brain.

What were they up to?

Kicking her inner wuss to the side, she got up to see what was going on. Sam huffed a doggy sigh at the loss of his ear rub and jumped off the couch to follow her. "No, Sam. Go to your spot."

He didn't need to be upstairs with all the fumes from the cleansers her mother had no doubt scoured every available surface with. Miranda only bought products with the mildest scents possible, but she had a feeling that wouldn't matter with her mother's heavy-handed idea of cleaning.

Just as she passed the front door to head for the stairs, there was a push on her leg as Sam squeezed by and planted his body in front of her in a blocking stance.

She stopped immediately.

To have disobeyed his spot command, Sam had to have a very good reason. And if he was blocking, that reason was somewhere right in front of her.

With cautious hands, she reached past Sam. They connected with the large solid object by the door that she'd been about to walk into.

What the hell?

Obviously, something her mother or sister had brought with them. But what?

"Good job, Sammy! Good job." She squatted down and gave him a quick rub and a hug. He squirmed under the praise, his tail fanning in rapid arcs that made his entire rear end dance. "You're such a good boy. Extra biscuits for you later."

Job done, Sam let her shoo him out of the way so she could examine the mystery item. It didn't take her long to figure it out.

"Son of a bitch."

Her annoyance at almost face-planting for the second time in a week was quickly surpassed by the implication of the suitcase that had nearly done the deed.

The very *big* suitcase.

"Son of a *bitch*," she repeated with feeling.

Leaving it where it was, because no way was it coming any further into her house, she continued to the bottom of the stairs. "Mom, can you come down here for a minute, please?"

"I'll be right there, *mija*."

Fuming as she waited, she forced herself to think of any other logical reasons there would be a suitcase sitting in her front hall. Anything other than the conclusion that had her ready to use all of those salty words her mother hated so much.

She came up empty.

"What is it, sweetheart?"

Miranda took firm hold of her temper. "We need to talk."

"Of course. Let me get these clothes into the washing machine and we can sit and have a nice chat."

"Forget the clothes, Mom." Which had been sorted for washing exactly the way she wanted them. Now? Who knew. "I want to talk about *that*." She pointed behind her.

"That?" her mother repeated in a vague, *what are you talking about?* tone.

"The suitcase, Mom."

"Oh, that."

She rolled her eyes. "Yeah. That. What's going on?"

Her mother cleared her throat, a nervous tic Miranda became well acquainted with in the months following her accident. "Let me make some more tea and we can sit down to—"

"No tea. Just talk. Why did Izzy bring a suitcase with her?"

"How did you...*hmph*. Fine, yes. We thought it would be a good idea for your sister to spend the weekend with you after this latest accident of yours, that's all."

Way to make it sound like she was tripping over her own feet and walking into walls on a regular basis. Other than a few stubbed toes here and there, and one wickedly banged elbow, her header into the kitchen table was the first major damage she'd done to herself since moving out on her own.

Refusing to let her mother distract her with guilt, she asked, "Don't you think you should have asked before assuming I'd be okay with it?"

"I knew you'd come up with a lot of excuses to say no."

And yet she'd done it anyway.

"So, what? You figured you'd just dump Izzy and her suitcase off and call it a done deal?"

"You have so much room here," her mother said, ignoring both the question and the sarcasm. "The bedroom at the opposite end of the hall from yours is perfect. It will give you both plenty of privacy."

No wonder they'd spent so much time cleaning up there.

"Didn't I already say no to this idea when both of you called me the other day?"

"That was before your accident."

"I tripped, Mom. That doesn't mean I need a keeper." Least of all Isobel. Miranda had tripped over her carelessly discarded shoes and purses more times than she could count. "The answer is still no."

"It's only for the weekend. What can two little days hurt? And it would make me feel so much better knowing there was someone here with you when your poor head looks like that."

The extra heaping of guilt almost concealed the stench of bullshit in that statement.

"There's a lot more than two days' worth of stuff in that bag."

"You know how your sister always overpacks for everything. She's a bit of a clothes horse."

She had to grin at her mother's words, spoken as though revealing some huge secret. "A bit?"

"Let her stay for the weekend, *mija*. You two don't spend enough time together anymore."

With good reason. But since she'd never told their mother about the Umberto betrayal, or exactly how intolerable Isobel had gotten in those last few months before she moved out, she couldn't very well point it out now.

"Doesn't she have to work tomorrow, anyway?"

"But she'll be able to spend the evening with you. And tonight, too." Her voice softened. "You need your family, *chiquita*. This will be a good thing."

No. No it wouldn't.

But if Izzy was working tomorrow, that severely limited how much time she'd have to deal with her before she could reclaim her space. And, more important, her privacy. Wasn't two nights of torment worth making her mother happy?

"Okay, fine. She can stay for the weekend. Just the weekend," she emphasized even as she heard a small voice in her head—one that sounded an awful lot like Trixie—calling her an idiot. So much for not wussing out anymore.

But it was only two days. How bad could it be?

Stupid, stupid question.

Four months away from Isobel's narcissistic company had dulled the memory of just how annoying it was to share a living space with her little sister. Their mother hadn't been gone two whole hours before Izzy had taken over the upstairs bathroom. Walking into the steamy room after her sister's thirty-minute shower was like entering a jasmine-scented rain forest.

Nose wrinkling, she tried mouth-breathing to lessen the intensity, but that only made it worse as the heavy floral scent settled on her tongue.

Disgusting.

A quick check of the sink vanity confirmed her worst suspicions. The entire countertop was filled with Izzy's stuff. Cosmetics, blow dryer, creams, lotions, and who knew what else were scattered about in her sister's usual brand of casual chaos.

Her own few things—toothbrush, toothpaste, face cream and cleanser—she found pushed aside into a small heap.

She took a slow, measured breath.

Two days was going to be a freaking nightmare.

If she didn't nip this in the bud right now, it would only spiral out of control until she lost her shit entirely. She knocked on the closed door to the bedroom Isobel had claimed as her own. The second it opened, she knew she had an even bigger problem on her hand than just a messy bathroom.

"Are you smoking in there?"

"What? No. Why would you even ask that?"

She didn't need Izzy's guilty tone to know she was lying. "Because I can smell it."

"No, you can't!"

Yeah, she could. Even past the heavily perfumed bath lotion and scented candle she caught a whiff of, which were probably enough to mask the odor from their mother.

"You do realize you just admitted it, right?"

There was a pause, probably as Izzy replayed their exchange in her head. "No, I didn't."

Miranda sighed. "Whatever. I'm telling you right now, knock it off. No smoking while you're here."

"I'm an adult, so it's legal. You can't tell me what to do. And anyway, it's just vaping. It's not like it's pot or anything."

Good thing, because then she'd have to kick her baby sister's ass that much harder.

"You may be twenty-one—barely—but this is my house, and I don't want smoking in it of any kind."

"Fine."

"That goes for outside, too."

"Oh, come on, that's not fair! It's only flavored liquid. It's not bad for you. And you can hardly even smell it."

She didn't bother pointing out—again—that she *did* smell it. Or that sucking aerosolized chemicals into your lungs was most definitely bad. No, she had to pick her battles. Getting through the weekend came first. Her sister's vape habit was a skirmish for another day.

"My house, my rules."

Isobel huffed. "Whatever."

"And while we're on the subject, you need to remember that while you're here we're sharing a bathroom, and *you're* the guest. You don't just move my stuff around to make space for your own."

"I put everything in one place where you could find it."

"Where I could find it was where I left it."

"God, what's the big deal?"

She gave a short laugh of disbelief. "Uh, you do remember I can't see, right?"

"Like I could ever forget it," Isobel muttered.

"What's that supposed to mean?"

"Nothing. Forget it. Look, I'm sorry I touched your precious things. It won't happen again. I'll move my stuff out of your way when I get home, okay?"

"Get home?" Those alarm bells started blaring again. "Where are you going?"

"Out with my friends for a little while. It *is* my day off, you know."

"Did Mom know you had these plans? Because I thought you staying here this weekend was so we could spend more time together."

"Oh, my God," Isobel groaned. "Do you really want to sit around all night singing kumbaya and doing sisterly bonding shit?"

Good point. Why was she arguing?

"Have fun. Be careful." As she started down the hallway she added over her shoulder, "And be sure you're home by eleven."

"You have *got* to be kidding!"

"My house, my rules."

She couldn't contain the smirk that blossomed at Izzy's shriek of annoyance behind her. If her sister thought moving in with her was going to be an escape from rules and responsibility, she had another think coming. She wouldn't be getting away with half the things their parents let slide.

Isobel banged out the front door a half hour later without bothering to say goodbye. Miranda grinned from her seat at the kitchen table, where she was taking a break from putting everything back to where it should be. With any luck at all, by the time Monday rolled around, Izzy wouldn't need any extra persuasion to pack her bags and leave.

She raised her glass of iced tea toward the front door in mock salute. *"Laissez les bons temps roule."*

Chapter 8

The Monday morning clouds finally cooperated and broke long enough to let some glorious sunshine peek through by afternoon. And for once, there was no hammering or sanding or any other obnoxious noises coming from next door to chase her inside.

Miranda headed out to the pool to take advantage of both the sun and quiet while they lasted. Whatever Ben was working on today, it was something blessedly silent. She hadn't heard a peep from his place since he'd pulled into his driveway shortly before nine.

Not that she'd been listening for him or anything.

Okay, that was a big, fat lie. But only because other than that wave and hello to Izzy Saturday morning, there hadn't been any sign of him all weekend. It was like he'd dropped off the planet. At least her tiny corner of it, anyway.

She'd known deep down the man would probably ghost her after that disastrous dinner despite their agreement to ignore the disaster part and start over fresh.

It was still disappointing to be proven right.

And yet, she'd put on the stupid bikini on the off-chance he might be around to see her in it. Because he should know exactly what he was missing out on.

Setting the portable Bluetooth speaker on the table, she raised the volume to where it could be heard from the inground pool but no further and started one of her longer playlists. She needed to put her neighbor out of her mind and concentrate on training. He was a distraction she didn't need. Or want.

Another lie.

She'd replayed the sensation of being cradled in his arms over and over for the past four nights as she lay in bed, dissecting every tiny detail she could recall.

The flex of muscles in his back as he lifted her.

The softness of his hair brushing her arm around his neck.

The prickly five-o'clock shadow against her cheek.

The masculine scent of beer and pepperoni, with a hint of sawdust and sweat.

And even after she was finally claimed by sleep, every night he'd followed her into her dreams as well.

Hot, erotic, holy-shit-I-need-me-some-of-that dreams.

Okay, so she wanted him. At least, her body did. But she didn't *want* to want him. He'd proven himself to be just as douchey as every other man she'd encountered in the past four years. Too freaked out by the *blind* part of the blind woman equation to bother sticking around to find out more about the *woman* part of it.

Besides, she rationalized as she shed her cover-up and walked to the edge of the pool. It wasn't like she knew all that much about him. They'd shared some pizza and beer, and a little meaningless conversation.

Just because he had strong arms and smelled good didn't mean he was someone worth getting to know better. No matter what her lady bits thought.

No. She was going to put him right out of her mind and concentrate on her training. Gator's suggestion to work on her lung volume in the pool was already showing benefits on the treadmill, but it still wasn't good enough.

She only had four more months to try and erase what four years away from running had done to her stamina. There was no room for any might-have-beens with her hot jerk of a neighbor.

Her dreams, though, were going to be a lot harder to corral than her thoughts.

The woman was trying to kill him.

She had to be.

Why else would she be parading around in her backyard in that scrap of a bathing suit again, flashing all of that gorgeous tanned skin for him to see? Of course, it was her yard. And he wouldn't be seeing her if he wasn't staring out his upstairs bedroom window playing pervy peeper. Again. But still…

Killing. Him.

Because as much as his dick liked looking at her, that was all he was going to be doing with her. Oh, there would probably be some neighborly "hellos" and "isn't it a nice days" when he couldn't avoid running into her. But those plans of long, sweaty nights curled up around his leggy selkie until her lease was up and Mrs. R came home?

Those were dead and buried.

He'd made that difficult decision after several erotic dreams so vivid he woke up questioning if he'd really been alone in his bed. His body clearly knew what it wanted. His conscience, on the other hand, kept flashing him images of Miranda sprawled on the floor with that nasty knot on her forehead.

His fault.

The embarrassment that his little hissy fit had caused her harm might have been surmountable, if it hadn't been for his run-in with Val. Nothing like some clingy negative reinforcement to remember why getting into bed with your neighbor could turn out to be a colossal mistake.

But even that reminder didn't seem to be enough to stop tormenting himself, staring at what he couldn't have. He'd been measuring the windows for blinds and curtain rods when he saw her come outside, and just like that, he'd been snared.

Part of him was impressed by the easy way she moved across the patio, as though she weren't blind at all. But part of him—the sulky embarrassed part—was still kind of pissy about the same thing.

He knew he'd overreacted the other night. Miranda had accused him of having a serious chip on his shoulder, and she wasn't wrong. A childhood spent feeling like the butt of every "stupid" joke had primed the pump for the giant leap he made that she'd been playing nasty games with him to make him look like an idiot.

"Why didn't you just tell me?"

If he could go back and redo any part of that evening, it would be to ask that one simple question *before* storming away from the table.

Okay, more like running away.

"It was just...nice. Having an evening like everyone else. Being talked to like a regular person for a change. Not a disabled person. Not a blind person. Just...a person."

Remembering her explanation only made him feel worse.

He hadn't been there as a good neighbor, to have a friendly chat over pizza and beer. He'd been there to try and get her naked and wet. Preferably with her legs wrapped around his hips.

Those long, long legs.

Which were eating up the length of the pool as she did laps, back and forth, at a pace that told him she wasn't doing it for fun. The woman had a serious workout going on.

The fact she was in the water, alone and blind, made him fidgety, but he pushed it aside and went back to his measurements. She was a freaking Marine. She was clearly capable of swimming on her own.

Not a blind person. Just...a person.

But damn it, she *was* blind. And the only one there to see if she got into trouble was the damn dog.

"None of my business," he muttered, moving to the last window, which took him out of sight of the pool and the aggravating woman in it. "She's probably been in the pool every freaking day without me noticing and been fine. She knows what she's doing."

And yet the image of that lump on her head kept coming back to haunt him. Because accidents, by their nature, happened when you least expected.

After jotting the measurements on the small notepad, he crammed it into the pocket of his cargo shorts and took a look around the room. What had once been small, dark, and dated was finally starting to live up to his vision. The expanded footprint and new attached bath made it almost luxurious. The bigger windows and fresh paint made it bright and clean, while the newly refinished hardwood floors and thick crown molding kept that small touch of the original craftsmanship.

A sense of satisfied pride settled into his bones.

After months of sleeping on a fold-out couch in a tiny broom closet of a room in the middle of a construction zone, eating nothing but microwaved meals and takeout, the finish line was finally in sight. There would still be tons of detail work to take care of. But he could do that in much smaller bites, spread out over the fall and even into the winter.

God knew he was going to need something to do once the weather turned and he didn't have a bikini-clad Miranda to spy on anymore.

There were two more bedrooms to measure for curtains, but glutton for punishment that he was, he couldn't resist one more peek out the window first.

Disappointment filled him. No sexy selkie doing laps.

She must have finished up and gone inside while he wasn't looking. Probably for the best, anyway. Just because she couldn't see him peeping at her didn't make it any less pervy. Actually, it might just make it worse.

Except...

He stopped and went back to the window.

Her coverup was still on the end of the lounger. And there weren't any wet footprints on the patio blocks by the inground pool's steps to show she'd gotten out. Plus, the dog was still lying in the same spot.

Wouldn't he have followed Miranda if she'd gone inside?

Heart thundering, he looked at the pool again, but the sun glinting off the water made it impossible to see beneath the surface.

"Fuck."

Pounding down the stairs, he tried to convince himself he was wrong. There had to be any number of explanations that didn't involve Miranda misjudging the edge of the pool on a turn, knocking herself out, and drowning.

The sun had dried her wet footprints. She'd told the dog to stay outside while she went in to get a drink or pee or whatever.

Something. Anything.

He hit the back door and jogged across his own neglected yard to the fence, scanning for her as he went. But she hadn't miraculously reappeared in the last ten seconds. Without slowing, he hopped the chain-link in one easy movement.

"Miranda!" The dog lifted its head at his shout, but there was no answering call from inside the house. *"Miranda!"*

On its feet now, the dog watched him, but he didn't spare it a thought. Stopping at the edge of the pool, his worst fears were suddenly right in front of him. A dark shape floated still and lifeless near the bottom of the pool's deep end.

He dove in, not wasting any precious seconds to shuck his work boots first. The chlorine burned his eyes, but he never took his gaze off his target. He snagged an arm around Miranda's middle and kicked upward in one motion.

The second he touched her, she jerked and struggled, sending a wave of relief through him despite the sharp elbow he took to the ribs. As they broke the surface, both sputtering and coughing, he shifted his grip to the hold he'd learned during his summers lifeguarding at the beach and towed her to the edge of the pool.

All the time, he kept repeating, "It's okay. I have you. Just hang on to me."

The struggling and coughing continued all the way, but he was okay with both since they meant she was alive. He could still taste the sour bitterness of terror in his mouth. Along with the coppery tang of blood from where her head had connected with his lip during her flailing.

A fat lip for a life was a tradeoff he'd take any day.

Shifting his hold as they got to the edge, he asked, "Do you think you can grab onto the side to get out?"

Still coughing, she nodded, reaching out to find the concrete coping surrounding the pool. He gave her a quick boost, trying to ignore the fact his hands were on her gloriously almost-naked ass, and helped her out of the water before following.

Landing beside her with the grace of a beached whale, he sent a prayer of thanks up to whatever guardian angel had been on his shoulder today that made him look out the window one more time.

"You...you..." She couldn't seem to get the words out past her gasping breaths. He rolled onto his side to face her and gave her arm a comforting pat.

"It's okay. You're welcome."

"You...*idiot*!"

He froze mid-pat. "Excuse me?"

"You almost drowned me!"

What in the actual fuck?

"Maybe the lack of oxygen has you a little confused. I just *saved* you."

She let out a sputtering laugh and swiped at the wet hair plastered to her face. "Saved me? From what? I was perfectly fine until you grabbed me and scared the ever-loving *fuck* out of me. *That's* what almost drowned me!" She pushed the dog away from where it was nosing at her face with concerned whines. "It's okay, Sam. I'm okay."

Ben stared at her tight expression in confusion. Maybe he was the one with lack of oxygen to the brain, because nothing she was saying made any sense.

"You were under the water, for like, over a minute at least."

"Two minutes, seven seconds. I was shooting for two and a half." Her frown darkened. "I probably would have made it this time, too."

"You would..." The feeling he might have just jumped to yet another incorrect conclusion about his neighbor was starting to creep in. "That was on purpose?"

"Yes! What else...oh. Shit." The scowl faded. "You thought I was drowning."

"Of course, I thought you were drowning! That maybe you hit your head again or had a relapse or something. What else was I supposed to think when you were laying at the bottom of the goddamn pool?" He didn't care he was yelling. She'd scared the ever-loving hell out of him.

"I was training."

"Training? For what, deep sea diving?"

"Don't be ridiculous."

"*I'm* being ridiculous?"

"Yes!"

It wasn't until the dog whined that he realized they were *both* yelling now. He swiped a hand over his face and flopped onto his back with a squelch of wet clothes. "Shit."

As Miranda pushed into a sitting position, he tried not to notice the precarious hold the material of her bikini top had on breasts glistening with beads of water. But as one of the drops took a long, leisurely glide down over her collarbone and into her cleavage, he found he couldn't look away.

He swallowed hard.

Damn, what he wouldn't give to be that drop of water.

Forcing his eyes from dangerous territory, he noticed for the first time the scattering of scars that broke up the perfection of all that beautiful skin on display. The worst one was below her left breast, horizontal along her ribcage. Thick and pale, several inches long, it spoke of something horrible that had happened.

The same thing that caused her blindness, maybe?

Had it been while she was in the military? Or later, after she was home? How awful would it be to have survived years in a job that would put her in harm's way, only to come back to where she should be safe—or at least safer—and suffer some traumatic injury?

Suddenly, examining her scars seemed even more invasive than staring at her boobs. He cut his eyes away to look back up at the late afternoon sky, squinting against the sun.

"I'm sorry I scared you like that," he said finally, all of the anger draining out of him. "I honestly thought you were in trouble."

"No, I'm sorry. I shouldn't have snapped at you when all you were doing was trying to save my life." She gave a wry grin. "Thank you for that, by the way."

He shrugged before remembering she couldn't see the motion.

"I'm just glad you didn't actually need it." His skin prickled with goosebumps as some of the clouds slowly refilling the sky crossed in front of the sun. "We might want to get inside. Those clouds look like they're moving in to stay."

Miranda sighed as they got to their feet. "I'm, um, a little turned around as to where we are, exactly. Could you help me back to the lounger? I can get my bearings from there."

"Oh, sure." He started to reach for her arm, then hesitated. "How should I..."

"If you give me your arm, it's easier for me to follow your lead." She extended her left hand out to her side.

Sounded easy enough. He moved closer until her fingers brushed his right forearm.

She wrapped surprisingly strong fingers around his elbow. "Lead on, Macduff."

"Lay on."

"What?"

Cursing his wayward tongue, he started them moving toward the house. "It's actually 'lay on,' not 'lead on.' Doesn't matter."

"Huh. What does it mean, then?"

"Hell if I know." He concentrated on keeping the path in front of her hazard-free. Thankfully, the dog seemed to know enough not to get in the way, following at their heels like a nervous aunt instead. "I've heard my father correct people so many times, it popped right out of my mouth."

And wasn't that a scary thought, sounding like his stodgy old man?

"And your father just goes around randomly correcting people's Shakespearean mistakes because...?"

"He's an English professor, so he feels it's his solemn duty. He doesn't think twice about lecturing complete strangers like they're his students." Which was embarrassing as hell, especially when he was a kid. "He's kind of a pretentious ass about it."

Miranda laughed. The sound shivered through him like a breeze on his wet skin, only the goosebumps were on the inside this time.

She brought her free hand up to pat his shoulder. "Well, I'm sure he—" She broke off with a small gasp as her fingers touched the sleeve of his wet t-shirt. "Oh, my God, I didn't even think. You jumped in with all of your clothes on, didn't you?"

"I didn't exactly have time to strip."

"But...your phone! And your wallet!"

"Both safe at home. The only thing I had in my pocket was..." He groaned.

"Was what?"

"Just a notepad. It's no big deal."

"That wasn't a no-big-deal sound."

"It just has a bunch of measurements in it." For almost every freaking window in the house. Which he now had to go back and measure all over again.

Fuck.

He stopped walking. "Okay, we're here. The end of the lounger is to your right by about a foot." He felt the loss of her touch as soon as she let go to reach down and feel for it. Which was damn stupid. He'd been her temporary eyes, nothing more.

"Perfect." She picked up her coverup and slid it on. "Excellent job. Most people walk me into at least one thing their first time out. It's not as easy as it looks."

Funny, he hadn't had any problem at all.

Which might have something to do with how hyper-aware he seemed right now about every little thing that had to do with her.

Like how her nose had a tiny bump on the bridge.

And that the yellowish-green bruise on her forehead was already disappearing.

And her right ear was double-pierced, but her left one had a third stud up top where it must have hurt like hell to get.

And how that cover-up fell short of doing what its name implied, stopping just below the v of her thighs, taunting him with flashes of black cloth every time she moved. God, it would be so easy to reach right under it, strip that bikini bottom away, and bury his face against a slice of heaven.

"Let me have it."

He nearly choked on the drool starting to pool in his mouth from the dirty daydream. "What?" Had he said any of that out loud?

Kill me now.

"The pad. Let me see if I can at least salvage your measurements. A hairdryer might do the trick."

"Right. The notebook." Relief she hadn't been responding to his sudden, irrational desire to go down on her warred with a ridiculous sense of disappointment about the same thing. What the fuck was *wrong* with him?

Wrapping her long fingers around the soggy notepad he handed her, she said, "I'm going to take a quick shower and change. Why don't you do the same and come back over in, say, twenty minutes?"

He had a flash of them taking that shower together, her fingers wrapped around something a lot more interesting than a notepad, before he pummeled his pervy brain into submission.

"You know, you really don't have to go to the trouble. I can just let it air dry. Or put it in the microwave or something."

Because the smart thing would be to stay away from her until he could figure out how to get his brain to shut off the porn channel it seemed to be tuned into.

With Miranda in the starring role.

"As a fireman, do you really think the microwave's a good idea?" She held up the notepad and ran a finger along the metal spiral holding it together. "Besides, you tried to save me. The least I can do is try to save this for you."

He meant to say no. Honest to God, that was his intent when he opened his mouth.

But when she picked her arm up, the coverup went with it, flashing him another peek at the promised land, and he heard himself saying, "Twenty minutes sounds good."

Well, shit.

No one had ever accused him of being smart.

Why the hell should that change now?

Chapter 9

He was either a masochist or an idiot.

Probably both.

Nothing good could come from spending more time in the company of his neighbor and her mile-high legs and ass made for biting. Even a quick jerk in the shower to try and get his short-circuiting sex drive back under control hadn't helped.

The fact it had been Miranda he was picturing on her knees doing the honors was probably to blame.

Okay, was totally to blame.

But here he was, walking up to her front door with a six-pack under his arm and a semi in his shorts, trying to remember all the reasons this was a bad idea. Every single one of which floated away the instant she opened the door and smiled at him.

I am in serious trouble here.

Miranda's smile faltered, her body going from relaxed to tensed in a split second. "Ben?"

Say something so she knows it's you, idiot.

"Yeah, sorry I'm a few minutes late. I was, uh..."

Jerking off to thoughts of those rosy lips.

He coughed. "I lost track of time in the shower."

Relief and something else chased across her face as her body loosened again. "Don't be silly. I just got out of the shower myself. Come on in."

Fighting images of her all naked and wet, he followed her through the house to the kitchen, the same as he'd done the last time he was here.

Except this time, he knew she was blind.

And no matter how closely he watched her, he still couldn't tell. Not until she got to the counter and ran her hands along it until she found the soggy notepad, which was sitting next to a hairdryer, plugged in but off.

"I didn't want to start drying it without asking about the ink first. It didn't run or bleed through the pages, did it? Because it's a waste of time if you can't read anything."

"I used a ballpoint pen, so it should be fine." He put the six-pack on the counter and gingerly opened the soggy cover. "Nope. Looks good. Well, not good, but legible, anyway." He put it back next to the hairdryer.

Miranda had cocked her head slightly. "Was that...beer?"

He stared at her in surprise until he realized she must have heard the bottles clink. Her expression was so hopeful, he couldn't resist teasing her a little. "Maybe. Or it could be root beer."

"Now that would just be cruel."

Her faux pout made him shift weight to make room in his suddenly tight shorts. One little twist of her lips, and his dick reacted in a way all of Valerie's blatant invitations hadn't been able to achieve.

"Yeah, cruel." Tearing his gaze away, he grabbed a bottle from the cardboard container and gave the top a vicious twist. "I hope you like pale ale, it's all I had in the fridge. I thought maybe we could both use a drink."

God knew he definitely needed one right now.

Several, in fact.

"You thought exactly right." She held out her hand.

He passed it to her, gritting his teeth as their fingers brushed. He tried to look away as she put her mouth around the end of the bottle, but it was impossible. As she took several long swallows, he felt every one like a tug on his aching dick, which was now fully awake again and hungry for some attention.

The small pop as she broke the suction of her mouth from the bottle nearly did him in.

"Ah," she sighed, "I needed that."

Not sure he could form actual words at the moment, he grabbed a beer and drained half of it. Miranda carefully placed her bottle against the back of the counter near the wall before locating both the notepad and then the hairdryer with gracefully questing hands.

It was hard to resist the urge to make it easier and just hand her both, but also satisfying to watch her so effortlessly do it herself.

Dryer on low, she laid it on the granite countertop and positioned the notepad a few inches in front of it. After testing the heat with her fingers, she moved the pad another inch away and tested again before she seemed satisfied.

"There. That should start the drying-out process without setting anything on fire."

"Well, lucky for you, there's a trained professional on the premises." She rolled her eyes at his purposefully boastful tone, making him grin before he got serious. "And, don't take this the wrong way, but do you have a fire extinguisher handy? Because every kitchen should have one."

"Under the sink."

He had no expectations of having to use it, but habit made him check to see that it was the proper type for kitchen fires (it was), and hadn't expired (it hadn't). While he was under there, he couldn't help but notice every bottle, from dish soap to disinfectant spray, was lined up in orderly precision.

Something else caught his eye. He picked up the hand soap refill bottle, running his thumb over the stuck-on clear label with raised bumps on it.

What the...?

Then it hit him.

"Is this Braille?" As soon as he asked, he realized she wouldn't know what he was talking about. "The labels on the bottles."

In the middle of raising her beer to her lips, Miranda stilled for a second before nodding and took a long swallow. "The shape of the containers helps me tell them apart, and I keep everything in the same place so I know what's where. But sometimes I need the labels to be sure." She made a face. "Household tip: don't put dish soap in the dishwasher by mistake. You'll be cleaning that shit up for days."

He laughed. "Yeah, we had a probie do it last year at the station. That's a probationary firefighter," he explained when she cocked her head in question. "It looked like someone opened up a foam truck on the kitchen."

Diggs still hadn't lived it down.

Standing, he noticed for the first time the small clear labels on the corner of each cabinet near the handle. He ran a finger over one. What was it like for her? Even with labels and neatly ordered cabinets and the dog who was snoring away on his bed, just getting through a normal day had to be nearly impossible. "Can I ask you something?"

"Sure."

"Isn't it hard, living on your own? I mean, wouldn't it be easier if you had someone who could, you know..."

"Take care of me?"

He hated the bitterness that saturated her words. "Help you."

Miranda lifted one shoulder. "Same thing."

"No, not really."

"Tell that to my family," she muttered, taking another long swig. When she put the bottle down again, it was empty.

Ben could sympathize. His family made him want to drink sometimes, too. "Care to elaborate?"

She laughed. "No, not really." Sliding her hand along the counter, she found the six-pack, put her empty into one of the open slots, and took out a fresh one. "You ready for another?"

Swallowing down the last few gulps, he held the empty out before remembering he needed to actually use his words with her.

"Yeah, thanks." He took the full bottle from her hand and replaced it with the empty, which she neatly deposited with the other dead soldier. "You're good at that," he said without thinking.

"At drinking?" She grinned. "Marine, remember?"

He did, though it was still something he was having trouble wrapping his head around. "No, at doing things for yourself and making it look easy."

"Back to that again," she said with a sigh. "We may as well sit if we're going to have 'the talk.' Check your pad first, though. Make sure it's not getting crispy."

He watched as she walked toward the refrigerator, touching it with her hand as though to orient herself before turning left and walking straight a few steps until she came to the same chair at the head of the table she'd sat in during their ill-fated dinner.

Okay, that answered some questions right there.

After he turned the notepad so the lukewarm air was hitting the other side, he joined her, taking the seat to her left. "The talk?"

"You know. 'You're blind, so you shouldn't be trusted with sharp objects or open flames.'" She wrinkled her nose, making her look too freaking adorable. "Although I might have to agree with that one, seeing as I did set a potholder on fire on my mother's gas range once when I was heating up some soup."

He shot a quick glance toward the stove.

"Don't worry, this one's electric."

He started. "How did you…? Damn, that's creepy."

She laughed into her beer. "Yeah, I get that a lot."

Despite the laughter, it seemed he'd touched on a sore spot. "I didn't mean anything by it."

"I know." She rolled the bottle between her hands. "But getting back to your question about living on my own. I love it, I wouldn't change it, but yes, it can be hard sometimes. There was a pretty big learning curve at the beginning. I mean, really big. And scary, even after knowing how to function on my own in my parents' home before making the move. But like anything new, it gets easier with time and repetition."

That made sense.

"I guess it's kind of like fire training in a way. The first time searching for victims in a burning room where you can't see squat is a total freak-out. After you've done it a few dozen times, it's mostly muscle memory."

"Exactly. After I walked through the house enough times, my body knew where each door frame and piece of furniture was. And without anyone here to move things on me, I eventually stopped banging around like a pinball." She gave a wry grin. "My knees and elbows were grateful."

"But what about the other stuff? Like cooking and grocery shopping and picking out what clothes to wear?" Or the hundred other little things he was just now realizing he did every day that for her were probably not so little.

Might, in fact, be a major hurdle.

"Most of my clothes are matchy-matchy, so they can go with anything. But they also have small labels sewn in so I know what color they are. For groceries, most of the time I have them delivered, but sometimes I walk to town to pick up a few things. And I cook like anyone else, only slower, and I have a few specialized tools to help me. Plus, there's all the pre-cooked meals my mom loads my fridge up with," she added with a tight jaw. "Because I'm clearly not capable of staying alive all by myself."

And that sounded like she wasn't just talking about her mother.

"Listen, about what happened before in the pool—"

"I know you might not think so, but I'm perfectly capable of swimming without someone there to *supervise* me."

The amount of contempt she jammed into the word made him consider what he said next very carefully.

"Actually, it wasn't the swimming part that freaked me out so much as the drop-like-a-rock-to-the-bottom part." Mentioning that seeing her in the pool alone *had* been his first concern no longer seemed relevant. Or prudent.

Having a sister had taught him *some* sense of self-preservation.

"I told you, I had it perfectly under control. I've stayed underwater for a lot longer than that, under much worse conditions. My drill instructors were nothing if not thorough in teaching us water survival skills."

"Yeah, but I bet they never walked away and left you on your own while you were training, though, did they?" Her annoyed silence was answer enough. "Look, I'm not saying it's dangerous to do on your own just because you're blind. It would be stupid for *anyone* to push themselves underwater like that without some kind of safety protocol in place."

"Stupid?" There was an ominous softness in her tone.

"Yeah, Legs. Stupid." Damned if he was going to back off on this. How could he go through the rest of the summer wondering if today was the day he'd find her at the bottom of the pool for real?

Miranda looked stunned before sputtering, "Did you just call me *Legs*?"

Well, shit. He had.

Blame it on the rapid alcohol consumption with an empty stomach.

"You have to admit, you've got a helluva nice pair of them."

"I, uh...thank you. I think." She shook her head. "You are so weird."

He had to laugh at her bemused reaction. "That's us, weird and creepy." He took a sip of beer as several expressions he couldn't interpret chased across her face. "And I'm sorry. I shouldn't have used the word stupid. You're obviously far from that."

And especially not when it was one of his own hot buttons.

"No, you're right, it *was* stupid." She scowled down at the beer in her hand. "If one of my instructors caught me doing underwater drills alone, he'd kick my ass from here to Parris Island and back. Hell, if Gator knew, he'd come up here and do the same."

"Gator?"

"Sergeant Gerry Cormier, one of my old unit buddies."

He didn't particularly like the affectionate undertone her words carried. Which made no fucking sense at all. "Gator, huh? Interesting nickname."

If she noticed his clipped tone, she didn't comment.

"Well, we also called him the Cajun Heartbreaker, because he was a player of the first order. Looks to die for, and a voice that could melt butter and panties with equal ease." Her lips quirked. "You know, now that I think about it, you remind me an awful lot of him."

"I'm not sure if I should feel honored or insulted."

"Go with honored," she said with a laugh. "Gator's the best of guys."

There went another of those unpleasant flares of annoyance.

God, he couldn't actually be *jealous*, could he? No. That would be ridiculous. How could he when he'd already decided to keep his distance from her?

Yeah, and look how well *that* plan was going.

"So, why would this Gator want to kick your ass?"

"Because he's the one who suggested I use the pool to increase my lung volume."

"Then shouldn't it be his ass that needs kicking?" Something he'd be at the front of the line to volunteer for. What the hell had that asshole been thinking?

She sighed. "No, because he was very clear when he brought it up that I needed a spotter. Mine is the only ass in trouble here."

It didn't make him like the guy any better. He'd still put the idea in her head. "If you knew the risk, then why do it?"

"I told you before, I'm training."

He waited. When she didn't elaborate, he asked the obvious. "Training for what?"

Rather than answer, she got up and carried her beer to the counter, finished it off, and came back with the last two bottles. She put his on the table and pushed it in his direction like she had the night of the pizza disaster before opening her own and taking a long swallow.

"Look, if you don't want to tell me—"

"The Marine Corps Marathon."

"Seriously? No, don't get pissed," he added quickly when storm clouds darkened her expression. "I didn't mean that to sound condescending. I just meant marathons are grueling. That's a pretty ambitious plan."

"For a blind person, you mean."

"Now who has the chip on their shoulder?"

Neither agreeing nor denying, she said, "I know exactly how intense a marathon can be. I used to run them all the time."

The unspoken *before I was blind* hung between them.

He side-stepped that landmine. "What was your best finish?"

"Two hours, twenty-four minutes."

He whistled. "That's damn good. The best I ever did was three nineteen."

"You've run marathons?"

Not sure if he should be offended or not by the surprise in her voice, he shrugged. "A few. Mostly in New York. But I did go with a bunch of other firefighters and cops to run in Boston the year after the marathon bombing there. To show our support."

"That must have been intense."

"It was." In a gut-wrenching, horrible déjà vu kind of way. Seeing the still shell-shocked and grieving faces of the people there had been too much like walking through the streets of Manhattan in the months, and even years, after 9/11.

He'd only been a teenager when it happened, but he still remembered the long, agonizing hours before they'd gotten word his Uncle Sean, a captain with the FDNY at the time, hadn't been in either of the towers when they came down. But most of the guys who'd joined them for the Boston run had lost family, friends, and colleagues that day.

And some would say a bit of themselves as well.

"It was a little triggering for some of the guys, but it meant a lot for them to do it. To show our support. Solidarity in tragedy, you know?"

Miranda nodded. "That's exactly why this year's marathon is so important to me. We lost someone from my old unit a few months ago to a nighttime missile attack on their base. Jason was my run buddy. He ran the Marine Corps Marathon every year he was INCONUS." She pressed her lips together until they lost all color, as though trying to hold back whatever emotion was threatening to leak out.

Hoping to distract her, he asked, "What's INCONUS?"

She tipped him a small smile as though she knew exactly what he was doing. "Sorry. Inside the continental US." Clearing her throat, she went on. "Anyway, they're supposed to rotate off deployment by the end of summer, so everyone's planning to do the marathon this year in his honor. For him, and all the other guys we've lost. I want to be a part of that. I *have* to be a part of it."

The words held such fierce need he could practically taste it peppering the air.

"Then you'll do it."

"If only it were that simple." Her finger swirled around the rim of her bottle, catching and holding his attention so he almost missed her next words. "I only have until October, and I'm totally out of shape."

He snorted. "Don't take this the wrong way, Legs, but in what freaking universe are you out of shape?" Any other woman he knew would have preened at the compliment.

Miranda just shook her head.

"My muscles are almost where they need to be, but my stamina is for shit. That's why I was trying to increase my lung volume. We'll be running as a unit, which makes us only as good as our weakest link. I don't want to be the one who holds everybody back. I might never run elite again, but I know I can do better than I am now."

No way was he getting into another argument about the damn pool. "How does that work?"

"How does what work?"

"How do you, you know, run? With Sam?"

"No, he's not trained for that. And I wouldn't make him run that far, even if he was." She gave an affectionate look in the direction of a particularly loud doggy snore. "Not that he wouldn't give it all he had. That dog is all heart. And fur," she added with a grin. "But mostly heart."

He glanced at the golden retriever, whose paws were currently twitching as though already running in his dreams. "Then how?"

"Robin said she'd show me how to run with a human guide, but she's crazy busy getting ready for her wedding right now."

"Robin?"

"My orientation and mobility coach. She's the one who helped me learn to function out in the world again. Without her, I'd still be stuck living in my old bedroom at my parents' house, too afraid to even try at having a life of my own."

For the confidence in Miranda's voice alone, he already liked this coach. "From what I've seen, I'd have to say she's damn good at her job."

And *that* was what earned a blush.

Not the compliment about her body. The one about her ability to take care of herself.

The woman continued to defy expectations.

"She's good because she truly cares about the people she helps, about making their lives better."

"Well, if she loves her job so much, you should let her do it."

Miranda shrugged. "I can wait until after the wedding. It's not like I have anyone to practice with, anyway."

"None of your friends would help you out?"

"Of course they would. But there's not a runner in the bunch."

"None in your family, either?"

"My brother, Tino, but..." Reluctance was written all over her face.

"But?" He watched her upend the bottle, which was answer enough. "Let me guess. You haven't told them about your plans to run in the marathon."

She gave a bittersweet smirk. "Oh, I told them. They just don't believe it's ever going to happen. In their minds, there's no way a blind person can manage something like that. As far as they're concerned, I'm kidding myself. Pretending I can still do the things I used to do, and they won't have anything to do with supporting my refusal to accept my limitations." She air-quoted the last word with a grimace.

Disbelief stirred a bubble of annoyance in his chest.

Did these people even know her? He'd been in her company a total of three times, four if you counted that first brief conversation at her front door, and he already had zero doubts she could accomplish just about any damn thing she put her stubborn mind to.

Well, you know what? Fuck them.

"I'll train with you."

"You'll...what?"

"Train with you. Practice doing...whatever it is a guide does."

"Wow. That's...wow. Thank you." She looked a little stunned.

Which was fair. He felt a little stunned himself as the ramifications sunk in. He'd just committed himself to countless hours of one-on-one time with a woman who looked like sin personified in her workout clothes, but had promised himself not to touch.

Murphy, you are one stupid motherfucker.

"Not that I'm not grateful for the offer, but why?"

"Because no one deserves to have their dreams crapped on. Especially by their own family." He should know. His had the shit stains to prove it.

"That's..." She sagged back into her chair. "You really get it. Thank you."

He shrugged in response before remembering. Words. "No problem."

"If you're sure, I can call Robin in a few weeks to—"

"Tomorrow."

"What?"

"Call her tomorrow and set up a time we can all meet so she can show us the ropes. Surely, she can spare you half an hour if she loves her job as much as you say."

"A whole half hour, huh? Pretty sure of yourself."

"How hard could it be? I did pretty good guiding you earlier today. You said so yourself."

She grinned. "We walked about twenty feet on level pavers. Running on the open road is an entirely different animal." She reached over, and after one near miss, gave his arm an awkward pat. "Don't get too cocky. Remember, we'll be tethered together somehow. If I go down, we both eat dirt."

His horny brain rearranged a few of those words into a picture that had him shifting uncomfortably in his chair.

Damn pervy brain.

This could be a huge problem. Guiding her probably meant touching her. And touching her meant he'd have more than just her sexy ass in spandex to deal with when it came to resisting temptation. He'd have his own traitorous body to contend with as well.

Definitely a stupid motherfucker.

"I know you're still working on your house," Miranda was saying as he shook his head at himself, "so we can do this totally around when you have any free time."

"Other than the kitchen going in tomorrow, almost everything else is down to finish work, so I'll have more time for other things." An idea popped into his head. "Since we're doing this, can I ask a favor in return?"

"Of course," she replied without hesitation.

"Don't do any more underwater training crap without letting me know first?" He saw the second her stubborn started to show. "Do I need to track down this Gator guy to, what was it? Kick your ass to Parris Island and back?"

It could have gone either way, but thankfully, she laughed.

"Okay. You're right. I won't do it alone anymore." She got up and walked to the fridge, touched it, and turned to walk to where the hair dryer was still pumping out warm air onto the notepad.

He didn't miss that her promise wasn't exactly what he'd asked for, but it was close enough. He had a feeling once Miranda gave her word, she didn't go back on it.

"It feels mostly dry." She fanned the pages, touching a few. "What do you think? Did we save it?"

He went over and took the small pad from her. The pages were swollen and misshapen, but none of them had torn or disintegrated from the dunking. "It's good enough to get what I need from it. Thanks."

As he crammed the pad into his shorts pocket, he watched her unplug the hair dryer and meticulously wrap the cord around the handle before setting it on the counter, once again toward the back, out of the way.

With his reason for being there now gone, an awkward silence fell before they both spoke at the same time.

"I guess I should—"

"Would you like to—"

They both laughed and, like a soap bubble, the awkwardness broke.

"You first."

She looked like she might argue, then said, "I was going to ask if you wanted to stay for dinner." She jerked a thumb over her shoulder. "My mother crammed enough food for a month into my fridge and freezer when she was here the other day. It wouldn't take more than thirty minutes or so to heat up one of her casseroles. Which, I hate to admit, taste a lot better than anything I could ever make, even before." She gestured vaguely toward her face.

The impulse to say "no thanks" and run for safety was strong. He was already in far too deep.

But when he thought of going home to his empty house and eating another microwaved potpie while he sat alone in front of the tv, he found himself saying, "Okay, yeah. That would be great. Thanks."

Her smile said she was as surprised as he was at the answer. "Okay. Good. Great." Going to the refrigerator, she asked, "You don't have any food allergies, do you?"

"Nope."

"And how do you feel about spicy?"

He had to grin. "Bring it on. The hotter the better."

"Hmm. That sounded like a challenge." She pulled out a glass casserole dish. "I'll have to make you some *chilate de pollo* one of these days and see if you can live up to your own hype."

"Hey, fireman, remember?" His entire body twitched as he watched her, fighting back the instinct to jump in and take over the meal prep.

She snorted as she put the aluminum foil-covered dish into the oven with unerring precision. "You guys get way too much credit for making some chili that's a little spicy." Her fingers slid over the temperature controls to set them.

Now that he was looking for them, he could see the raised dots that guided her, and she seemed to be counting the audible beeps for each increment of temperature adjustment. The whole process impressed the hell out of him.

That didn't mean he'd stand for her talking smack about firehouse chili, though.

"A little spicy? I'll have to cook you a pot of Boone's Hellfire chili and see what you say about it then. If you can still talk, that is."

That shit had been known to make grown men cry.

"Deal." She stuck out her hand.

"Deal."

The second his hand closed over hers, he knew he'd been kidding himself.

There was no way he could be around this woman and not want her. Not when just that small touch awakened every nerve ending in his body and kicked his heart rate up to a steady jog.

Worse, the same quickened beat thrummed in her wrist as he swept his thumb over the tender skin there before letting her go.

Which was a lot harder to do than it should have been.

The meal turned out to be as good as she said it would be. He ate every last bite on his plate, even when his stomach sent up the white flag on space. Food like this shouldn't go to waste. He might have to roll himself out the door, but it would be with a smile on his face and a mouth full of happy taste buds.

"You were right," he said, patting his belly. "Your mother deserves her own cooking show."

"Please don't give her any ideas. *Papí* would be lost if she wasn't there to keep things running smoothly for him with his construction company."

Because of the cloudy skies, twilight was already starting to fill the kitchen, giving it a cozy, almost intimate feel. The second the thought entered his head, he knew it was time to leave.

He popped to his feet and grabbed both of their plates. "Let me get these into the dishwasher for you."

"You don't have to do that."

"Firehouse rules," he joked as he went to the sink. "You cooked, so I clean up." He had the first dish under the water to rinse when she came up beside him and picked up the second plate from the counter.

"This isn't the firehouse, though. You're my guest, and guests don't do dishes."

If he wasn't mistaken, she sounded a little more annoyed than the situation warranted. It didn't take a genius—something he'd never claimed to be—to figure out why.

"I know you're perfectly capable of doing it yourself. More than. But firehouse rules aside, my mother would beat me with a shoe for not doing my part in clearing the table."

"And mine would give me endless grief for letting a guest lift a finger."

Ben shut off the water and wiped his hand dry on his shorts. "How about this? Since neither of our mothers are here, why don't we stop worrying about what they'd do and just be us instead?" He took hold of the dish she'd reclaimed. "How about, whoever didn't cook cleans. Okay?" It took a small tug to get her to release her grip.

"But that's still not fair. If you cook, I won't be able to—" She bit her lip and turned her head away. "Never mind."

She wouldn't be able to clean, because she wouldn't know his kitchen the way she knew her own.

Shit.

"Okay. New plan." He set the dish in the sink. "Whoever owns the kitchen makes the rules. If you want to handle cleanup tonight, it's all yours. I won't object." No matter how wrong it felt. "But you need to do the same when the shoe is on the other foot. Although, you might be too busy putting out the fire in your mouth to worry about anything else," he couldn't resist adding.

As he hoped, the teasing brought a spark back to her eyes as she turned to face him.

"Bring it on, chili boy."

Damn, he enjoyed that sass.

"So, your kitchen, your rules. My kitchen, my rules. Deal?"

"Deal." She stuck out her hand again.

But this time when he took it, he didn't just get a buzz from the skin-to-skin contact. It also came from the fact she was standing less than a foot away, close enough he could smell the berry-scented body wash she'd used.

Close enough to feel the heat she gave off.

Close enough to make him want to reach out and draw her even closer, until he could feel every delicious inch of her body against his. Which was so attuned to the rocketing rhythm of her heartbeat and the quickening of her breath that it wanted to howl in triumph.

She was his for the taking.

All he had to do was lean down and take her lips, and she was—

"Manda, did you make dinner without waiting for me? It smells so good, I don't even care about the calories. I hope you left me some, I'm absolutely *starving*. And why can't you ever remember to turn the lights on? It's like a cave in here. I swear, it's as if you—"

The stream of words cut off in a startled gasp as the kitchen light snapped on, blinding Ben with the sudden brightness.

Busted.

Chapter 10

It was a good thing she had another sister, because she was going to kill this one.

Normally she would have heard the car pull into the driveway. Or the front door open. Or at the very least, Isobel's heels clicking as she made her way to the kitchen.

But she'd been so wrapped up in the sensual spell Ben had been weaving she missed every bit of advance warning she might have had, and now she was standing here like a kid caught with her hand in the cookie jar.

Or, rather, on the man her sister had repeatedly referred to as "that gorgeous god next door I'd like to climb like a tree."

Gag.

"Izzy. I wasn't expecting you home so early."

Translation: your timing sucks.

Her sister gave a little snort. "I can tell. And it isn't early. It's after six."

"It is?" How had that happened? "I guess I lost track of the time."

"Yeah, can't imagine why." Her sister's voice changed, lowering in pitch to almost a purr. "Hi. I'm Manda's sister, Isobel. We met the other day."

"We did?" There was uncertainty in Ben's tone. Like he honestly couldn't remember.

Miranda didn't buy it for a second. *Nobody* forgot Isobel. Especially when she made a point to be noticed.

Which, with a good-looking man, was always.

"Yes." Izzy covered the sharpness of the word with a laugh. "On Saturday morning. Remember? My mother and I came over to help poor Manda take care of things since she's all alone here, and we ran into each other outside. By the cars." When he still didn't acknowledge the memory, her voice turned sharp again. "You said good morning."

Help poor Manda take care of things?

She bristled. Bad enough Izzy was flirting with Ben right in front of her. But to make it sound like she wasn't capable of taking care of herself?

Her entire body stiffened in outrage.

It wasn't until Ben's fingers smoothed over her wrist in a soothing caress that she realized he was still holding her hand. Or maybe she was still holding his. She tried to pull away, but he tightened his grip, running his thumb over and over the pulse-point, distracting her from her anger.

"Oh, right." He didn't sound convinced. "That was you?"

"Yes, it was me."

Miranda had trouble holding back a smirk at her sister's incredibly put-out tone. Ben had to be messing with her. But it didn't mean she couldn't enjoy seeing Isobel taken down a peg or two.

The fact Ben's thumb was still doing delicious things to the sensitive skin of her inner wrist was just an extra bonus.

"Oh. Well, in that case, it's nice to meet you. Again." To Miranda, he said, "I should probably be going."

"Oh, no! Stay!" Isobel's words echoed Miranda's thoughts exactly.

"No, I lost track of the time myself. That's what happens when you're having a good time."

"A good time?" Izzy sounded confused. "With Manda?"

"Walk me to the door?" He gave her hand a small tug to get her moving. "Have a good night, Izzy."

"But…"

Ben didn't give her sister the chance to say more as he led her out of the kitchen. Not that she needed to be led, not in her own space. And Ben knew it. Which meant he wasn't trying to guide her. He was simply holding her hand.

Because he wanted to?

Or was he putting on a show for Isobel's sake?

Not that it mattered. She was content to enjoy the sensation of his large hand over hers, the ridge of callouses along the bottom of each finger a reminder that this was a man who both worked and played hard.

It likely wouldn't happen, but she couldn't help wondering what it would feel like to have those hands all over her body. If he could coax her long-dormant libido back to life with just his thumb, what pleasures could he arouse with some full-body contact?

She was so focused on her thoughts she wasn't ready for when Ben made an abrupt halt. Her body stayed in motion for another second, pushing her up against him, her breast smooshing into his arm before she could correct her balance and pull back. "Sorry."

He cleared his throat. "I, ah, guess I should have said something before stopping. My fault. I didn't want you to trip." She could tell from the change in pressure on her hand he'd bent down, and there was the sound of something being moved on the floor in front of them. Something small, with a familiar clickety sound. "They're against the wall now."

"Let me guess. My sister's shoes."

No matter how many times she reminded her, Izzy never seemed to understand why she couldn't just kick them off wherever she felt like it around the house. At least now she knew why she hadn't heard her click-clacking toward the kitchen.

"Yeah, about your sister."

And here it came.

Your sister is so beautiful. Tell me all about her. You don't mind if I ask her out, do you? Do you think you could put in a good word for me?

She'd heard every possible variation.

"Why do you let her treat you like that?"

Except that one.

"What do you mean?"

"Come on. 'Manda'? I could feel you cringe every time she said it."

She made a face, because he was right. "It's a nickname from when we were kids. She always called me Manda Panda. Which is cute when you're eight, but at twenty-eight, it's just embarrassing."

"And she knows it."

Of course she did. But it felt disloyal to agree out loud.

"So, uh, is she staying with you now?"

"God, no! I mean, she stayed for the weekend, but she's going back to my parents' tonight." At least, that was the plan. *Her* plan, anyway. She had a bad feeling her sister's wasn't quite the same.

Especially now.

"Oh, okay. Good."

It was difficult to read the nuances of emotion that colored his words. Was he disappointed he wouldn't have Isobel right next door? Relieved? Would it be easier for him to pursue her without Miranda being around to make things awkward?

"She's single, you know," she said grudgingly.

"Who, your sister?"

"Yeah. She dumped her last boyfriend a few weeks ago, so she's totally available." If you could call Rodrigo a boyfriend. More like a vanity accessory. Isobel was in constant need of being surrounded by people to tell her how beautiful she was.

"Okay. And you're telling me this...why?"

She shrugged, the motion jerky and uncomfortable. "In case you were, you know, interested."

"In your *sister*?"

Okay, that time it was easier to read the emotion in his voice, and it wasn't relief. It sounded closer to disbelief, spiced with a healthy dose of annoyance.

"She's gorgeous, so yeah, I thought you'd want to know."

"Okay, yeah, she's pretty. She's also, what? All of about eighteen?"

"Twenty-one."

Ben made a low sound in his throat she took for a sign of displeasure. Disappointment that Izzy was too young for him?

"Do you always try to push guys in your sister's direction?"

"I'm not—"

"Or are you just trying to head off what you see as the inevitable happening? That now I've met your sister, I'll look right past you to her?"

Her back stiffened as his words scored a direct hit. "Of course not. It's just that Izzy is young, she's pretty, fun—"

"And she can see."

The words made it hard to breathe. "Yes."

"So what?"

"What do you mean, so what?"

"I came over to see you, didn't I?"

"You came over because of your wet notepad."

"Okay. But I didn't stay for dinner because of it."

"Why did you stay?" Because she'd never thought in a million years he'd say yes when the impulsive invitation had popped out of her mouth. She hadn't been thinking about all the reasons it was stupid to ask. All she'd known was that for the first time in a long, long time, she wasn't lonely, and she hadn't wanted it to end.

"Because I liked talking with you," Ben answered after a long moment. He sounded surprised by his own words.

"I liked that, too." She hadn't shared such a comfortable meal with someone outside her close-knit circle in years. If you didn't count the constant hum of sexual awareness that had been crackling just below the surface of her skin the entire time. But even that hadn't been uncomfortable. More like a pleasant surprise.

Four years was a long time to wonder if you'd ever feel like a whole woman again.

The clatter of silverware against a dish from the kitchen reminded her if her little sister wasn't already eavesdropping, she soon would be. "We should..."

"Yeah, I should go." Tugging on the hand he'd never released, he walked them the remaining few steps to the door and opened it. "My kitchen is being installed tomorrow. Cabinets in the morning, countertops in the afternoon. So, I'm going to apologize in advance for any noise. It's the last big day of work, I swear."

She loved how adorably earnest he sounded. "I'm sure I'll survive."

"Okay, then. Thanks again for dinner."

"Thanks again for trying to save my life."

It was an impulse. One of those things she should have thought better of, but at the time it seemed the right thing to do.

Using her hand in his as a guide for where he was standing, she leaned in and up. But either she misjudged, or he turned his head at the last second, because somehow, the thank-you kiss she'd intended for his cheek landed on his lips instead.

She should have pulled back immediately and apologized.

He didn't give her the chance.

With exquisite gentleness, his mouth pressed against hers, his lips soft but firm as he coaxed a response from her. Which she gave along with a small sigh.

Heaven.

All too soon, he pulled back and rested his forehead against hers. "I probably shouldn't have done that."

Her breath hitched. "Are you sorry you did?"

"Fuck no."

She smiled at his vehemence. "Me neither."

"Thank Christ." With a soft groan, he swooped in and took her mouth again. Not as chaste as the first kiss, this one brought teeth and tongue to the party, tasting like pale beer and dark desire.

Their mouths were still the only things other than their hands that touched, much to the disappointment of her lady bits, which were more than ready to join in. But being focused on that one point of contact somehow made the kiss seem bigger. Hotter. All consuming.

The loud bang of a kitchen drawer slamming broke them reluctantly apart.

"So."

"So," she echoed.

"I'll, ah, see you tomorrow." It was half-question, half-statement.

"If you want."

"Legs, you have no idea what I want." Like a precision strike, he swooped in for a last hard kiss before making a strategic retreat.

After the screen door closed with a soft thump behind him, she sagged against the wall, one hand on her lips, the other pressing against her belly where a tidal wave of insane lust had been about two seconds from breaking all over her unsuspecting neighbor.

"Oh, I think I do, Slick. At least, I really hope I do."

A nudge against her leg broke her from thoughts of hot, naked bodies and dragged her back to reality. Dropping her hand onto Sam's head, she gave a soft laugh at herself.

"One kiss, and I'm thinking about sweaty nights in bed with him. That man is a menace." The dog leaned into the caress and groaned. "You're just as bad, you know. You can totally be had for an ear rub and a rawhide."

At the word, Sam jerked away with a hopeful *woof*.

She grinned. "Yeah, I know. I said it, you get it. At least one of us will be getting a bone tonight," she added under her breath.

The sound of bottles clinking reminded her of why, exactly, she wasn't getting hers.

Feeling the tiniest bit spiteful, she searched along the floor with her bare foot until she found her sister's shoes. She held one of the sling-backs out at doggy level.

"Sam, carry." Dutifully, the dog took the shoe in his mouth and waited for the next command. "Sam, kitchen."

Since Ben hadn't mentioned any other potential hazards littering the hallway, she followed the sound of Sam's nails against the hardwood with more confidence than she usually had when her sister was in the house. She was almost there when she heard Izzy's shriek of outrage.

"*Miranda*!"

Not bothering to contain her grin, she entered the kitchen. "Problem?"

"Your *dog* is *eating* my *shoe*!"

"He's carrying it, not eating it. Although," she added, tapping her chin, "come to think of it, I did promise him a rawhide, and your shoes are made of leather, so..." She bit her lip at the wail her teasing provoked. "Sam, release."

"Oh my God, if he ruined it, you're *so* paying for a new pair. Do you have any idea how much these cost?"

Miranda held up the other shoe. "Probably too much to leave them lying around on the floor where I can trip over them."

"They were right by the door," Isobel said as she snatched it from her hand.

"Where I could trip over them," she repeated.

"Fine. I'll put them away." Isobel stomped from the room, only to return less than ten seconds later.

"You better not have just put them on the stairs. *Where I can trip over them.*"

Isobel made a strangled noise and stomped back out, this time continuing the stomping all the way upstairs and down the hall. Miranda shook her head. She knew her sister was a self-absorbed little snot, but sometimes it felt like she did this shit on purpose.

As Sam trotted off with his promised rawhide, the microwave reheating Izzy's plate of food beeped. She pulled in a deep breath, trying to find some sense of calm in the familiar aroma of her mother's cooking.

Instead, all she could think about was the taste of her mole sauce on Ben's tongue.

Down girl.

By the time Izzy clomped her way back downstairs, Miranda had loaded hers and Ben's dishes into the dishwasher and was at the counter filling a glass with iced tea. Willing to offer the first olive branch, she asked, "Do you want some?"

"I'd rather have a beer. Oh, wait, you didn't leave me any."

So much for declaring a cease-fire. Still, she hung onto her calm. One of them being a sarcastic bitch was already one too many.

"Okay, first off, you drank all of my beer yesterday."

Bottles rattled together. "Hello? Beer."

"Ben brought those for us, not you. And besides, you're driving home after you eat, so you shouldn't be drinking, anyway." There was a telling silence. "Izzy, swear to God, you are not pulling this crap right now. I agreed you could stay for the weekend. Period. It's Monday, and you're going home tonight like you promised."

"Why are you being such a bitch?"

Miranda recoiled as though slapped. "*I'm* the bitch?"

"All I wanted was to stay here so you wouldn't be alone, and you keep acting like I'm some kind of...of...leech or something."

A tiny squiggle of guilt tried to worm its way in, but she flicked it aside.

"You know, that pouty poor-me act would be a lot more convincing if you hadn't spent three-quarters of your time since getting here either at work or out with your friends"—*and never once thought to invite me along*—"and the other quarter messing up my house or hogging the bathroom. When, exactly, was it you were keeping me company? I must have blinked and missed it."

"I do not hog the bathroom."

It figured that would be the thing she took the most offense to.

"You do, but that's not the issue here. Did you think I forgot about you calling me last week, wanting to get out from under Mom's rules by moving in with me? I'm blind, not stupid, Iz. You being here is all about you, not me."

"You have no idea how hard it is living there. Without you to fuss over, *Mamí* is sticking her nose all up in *my* business now, always checking up on me, asking where I'm going, who I'll be with, what we're doing. And *Papí* is even worse! The last time Rodrigo came to pick me up, he actually asked what his intentions were. Can you believe it? His *intentions*? Do you know how humiliating that was?"

"Parents worry about their kids. It's normal."

"*You* moved out to get away from them."

"Staying at the house while I recuperated was always meant to be temporary, just until I got my life back on track and could manage to live on my own again."

Putting distance between her and her parents—and Isobel—had simply been the impetus to finally get her out the door. Her mother had done more than fuss over her. She'd damn near suffocated her. And her father...

Well, they had the opposite problem.

"I meant the first time you left home."

Ah. When she'd enlisted in the Marines.

"That was about wanting to be the first woman in our family to get a college degree. Joining the military was the only way I could do it without drowning in student loan debt the rest of my life. It had nothing to do with getting away from anyone."

A partial lie. Breaking free *had* been a small part of it.

Okay, a pretty big part.

She'd known long before she put her name on that contract with the U.S. government there was no way she could live the very traditional life her parents wanted for her. Marry, settle down, have lots of babies. Take a job with the family business, like her brother had after the Army. The next generation taking the helm of Hernandez Construction, just because they were the oldest.

That might have been fine for Tino. He wanted to inherit the business. Building things with his bare hands made him happy.

But she'd wanted more than to merely step into her mother's shoes, doing the books and answering the phone. She'd wanted an education. A choice. A life that would make her feel independent, valued, and fulfilled.

What she hadn't expected was to find all of those things in the Corps.

"Yeah, well, I didn't have that option, did I?" Isobel said with a snap. "Not after what happened to you."

The accusation stung because it was partially true.

Their parents would have lost their minds if Izzy or Julietta even considered going the GI Bill route like Miranda and Tino had. Of course, Isobel had never once shown any interest in following in her siblings' footsteps, to either college or the service.

If ever there was a woman ill-suited to the rigors and regimentation of military life, it was Izzy. It didn't keep her from throwing it in Miranda's face whenever the subject of dead-end jobs and leaving home came up, though.

And like a fool, she always felt guilty even when she knew she shouldn't.

"Look, if you want to move out on your own so bad, nothing's stopping you. You have a decent paying job. Find yourself an apartment and move."

"But it would be so much easier if you'd just let me stay here."

Of course it would. There wouldn't be any rent, or utility bills, or any other form of actual responsibility for Isobel to worry her pretty little head over. And no real way for Miranda to enforce any rules she might lay down. She could practically hear Trixie screaming not to fall into the guilt trap her sister set so well.

"Sorry, sis. You're going to have to handle leaving the nest all on your own."

"But Manda..."

Her strained veneer of calm developed another crack.

"I've told you a million times, stop calling me that." She took her glass to the table and sat, sipping the sweetened tea to keep from saying anything else.

"Fine."

She wasn't sure what her sister was agreeing to. But she had a feeling they weren't done yet. She waited out the silence as Izzy plunked her dish on the other end of the table.

"I know the real reason you don't want me staying here."

You moving things without telling me? Using all the hot water? Drinking my beer without replacing it?

"And what's that?"

"You don't want anyone knowing you're doing the nasty with your neighbor."

She sucked in a breath. "That's..." *Wishful thinking.* "You've got a dirty mind."

Evidently, they both did.

"I saw what I saw."

"You saw him holding my hand."

"*And* kissing you."

Her glass thudded down on the table, splashing a little onto her hand. "So, you *were* spying!"

"And he probably would have been doing a lot more than that if I hadn't been here, too." As usual, Isobel ignored the parts that reflected badly on her. "So much for telling *Mami* he'd only been over here the one time for dinner."

"Not like it's any of your business, but no, I'm not 'doing the nasty' with Ben, and no, I wasn't lying when I said I'd only met him last week."

"Then why was he here?"

"Because—" She caught her words back just in time. Mentioning anything about what happened in the pool would be adding more ammunition to her sister's arsenal. "Because we were talking earlier when I was in the yard, and I invited him." It wasn't a lie, exactly. More of an edited truth.

"And he just said yes."

"Obviously."

"And all you did was talk."

"And eat, yes."

"And he had a good time?"

The incredulity in her tone drove another crack through Miranda's weakening grip on her temper. "Difficult as it might be for you to believe, yes, he did."

"Fine, whatever." Isobel paused. "You know, I can stay out of your way whenever you want to, ah, *talk* with Ben. You already told me how I'm hardly ever home anyway, right? So, it won't be hard."

Leave it to Izzy to turn a criticism into a virtue.

"Sorry, but no. You living here just wouldn't be a good thing, for either of us. And it has nothing to do with Ben."

Well, maybe a little.

Her sister's fork clattered against her plate. "Fine. You want to play slut bunny with the neighbor? Go ahead. But I'm telling *Mami*."

As threats went, it was a pretty good one.

Just not good enough.

"And I'll tell her about how many times you snuck boys into your bedroom over the past few years while she and *Papi* were over at the Garcias' house playing Conquian. Do you think she'll ever leave you home alone on a Saturday night again?"

She might be blind, but the wall between their bedrooms wasn't nearly as thick as Isobel seemed to believe.

Isobel's angry screech was followed by a rapid diatribe in Spanish as she stormed upstairs. A door slammed, but she could still hear her voice, if not her words, which had all been about Miranda being a mean, selfish bitch, an awful sister, and pretty much a rotten human being in general.

The usual when she didn't get her way.

She sighed. She loved her sister, she truly did. But *Dios*, sometimes she really didn't like her all that much.

Forcing herself to stay at the table and sip her iced tea, she listened as there was some more banging and door slamming, then the sound of luggage being dragged down the stairs. She winced at each thud, hoping the carpet runner was enough to protect the wooden treads from any damage.

The suitcase hit the floor, and the wheels hummed rapidly in the direction of the front door, which also got a slam.

Having mentally prepared for some nasty parting shot, she almost felt let down.

When Izzy's car pulled out of the driveway, tires chirping on the street, she slumped forward and cradled her pounding head in her hands. What a disaster.

And it wasn't over yet.

The second Isobel got home and started whining, their mother would be on the phone with another round of "blood is thicker than water" with a chaser of "you shouldn't be living all alone."

Deciding to head that problem off by striking first, she called her mother. She kept it short, just telling her Izzy was all packed up and on her way home after her weekend sleepover. As agreed.

Her mother tried, but Miranda didn't let her get a word in edgewise. After she hung up, it felt like she'd taken back a bit of control over her life.

True, her mother was frustrated with her and her sister hated her guts, but otherwise, everything was great.

She shook her head at herself. It was her own damn fault for caving in the first place. If she'd just stood firm, she wouldn't have the beginnings of a migraine pecking away at her brain right now. And Ben wouldn't have left after just a few kisses.

Maybe. Probably.

Their lip contact might have been an accident the first time, but those other kisses...those had held nothing but pure carnal purpose. Thinking about it made her entire mouth tingle. The man sure could kiss, she'd give him that.

But the big question was, did she *want* him kissing her? Really?

Yes. Yes, she did.

All of her body parts were in complete agreement about that, even if the jury was still out on the wisdom of taking things any further.

It probably wasn't smart, and it definitely didn't make sense when she barely knew him. But for the first time since she'd woken to a world of darkness, there was a small bright spot on the horizon.

And its name was Ben.

Chapter 11

Hands on his hips, Ben surveyed the kitchen with its newly installed cabinets and appliances with a glowing sense of pride. It had been one thing to see the layout in a 3-D computer program. Seeing it for real made him feel like a kid on Christmas morning. Once the granite went in, it would be perfect.

This was definitely the crown jewel in his entire renovation project. He couldn't wait to show it off when it was done.

He checked his watch. Time to grab a quick lunch before the stone installers were due to arrive. And while normally he could eat just about anything, anywhere, last night's home-made casserole had ruined him for the crappy dorm room-style fare in his mini-fridge. Maybe he could go beg something off of Miranda.

Then maybe beg a few more kisses as well. Or more.

He had almost an hour to kill. He could do a lot with fifty minutes. Hell, they didn't even have to get naked. He'd be happy cuddling with her on the couch and touching her any way she'd let him, even if it was just holding her hand again.

That stopped his brain like he'd been clocked upside the head with a Halligan bar.

Cuddling? Holding her hand? Since when did Ben Murphy think about holding fucking hands with a woman?

Damn, he had it bad.

Which was why he threw a nasty frozen burrito in the microwave and forced himself to choke it down when what he really wanted was a simple fence-hop away.

Not even that.

Sometime in the past, either his grandmother or Mrs. Roketzki had installed a gate between their two backyards, probably to make it easier to visit each other kitchen-to-kitchen for their little afternoon coffee klatches. He'd forgotten all about it yesterday in his panic over Miranda's pool misadventure.

Now, it was all he could think about.

Such easy, tempting access to the equally tempting woman on the other side.

He was close to caving when the rumble of a truck pulling into the driveway made the decision for him. More disappointed than relieved they were early, he went out to meet the stone installers, knowing it was only a temporary reprieve from where his urges were leading him.

When they were gone, he stood in his kitchen and once more got that deep inner burn of possessive satisfaction. This was his. The gleaming stainless-steel appliances tucked in against the dark cabinets and light gray granite was everything he'd envisioned. And yet...

Not being able to share the moment took some of the shine off it.

Miranda came to the top of his thoughts again. She was right next door. It would take two minutes to go and get her.

The urge was disconcertingly strong. So much so, he pushed it away. Again.

No, there were plenty of other people he could share this accomplishment with. Safer people. Like his parents. Although his mom had pretty much hated the house since he bought it. Or Cody. Not that he'd ever shown much interest in the renovations past the post-work barbeque and beer.

Damn.

Okay, there was his sister, Abby. She probably had close to a thousand inspiration pictures on her "dream house" Pinterest board. He could text her some shots she'd drool over, and he could gloat when she got all jealous and bitchy. Yeah, that would work.

He didn't even reach for his phone.

Who the hell was he kidding? He didn't want to call any of them.

He wanted to share this sense of triumph with Miranda.

This inexplicable need to see her had been growing inside him since he opened his eyes this morning, stiff as a board and two seconds from having to change his sheets. He didn't understand it, but he finally accepted it wasn't going away.

Bowing to the inevitable, he walked across their front yards to her door with perhaps a little too much enthusiasm in his step. Relieved her sister's car wasn't in the driveway, he knocked and waited.

It still irritated him Miranda thought he'd be the slightest bit interested in Isobel. Yes, she was a looker, there was no denying it. But she also had all the tell-tale signs of being a spoiled little diva, and no amount of pretty could make up for that.

And that wasn't even taking into account the fact Isobel wasn't the one who made his skin buzz like an electric current was in the air whenever she was around. Who'd left him hard and aching after that kiss. Who—

—was wearing another of those stretchy tank tops and a pair of clingy running shorts, showing off those legs that had played such a large role in his erotic dreams.

"God, you look good enough to eat." Horror that the words had slipped out was mitigated by her soft laughter.

"Why, thank you. And who are you?"

The smile that teased at her lips had him playing along. "Can't you tell?"

"Hmm. The mailman?"

"Nope."

"Too bad. I've heard he's kind of dreamy."

Doubtful. Horace Duffy was pushing sixty, with a drinker's nose that made him look like he should be pulling a sleigh rather than driving a mail truck.

"Any more guesses?"

"Let's see." She leaned against the doorjamb and cocked her head in a thoughtful gesture. "Candygram?"

He stepped closer. "No, but I can certainly give you something sweet if you want." He was close enough to hear her breath hitch, which made him step even closer, his lips hovering mere inches from hers. "Do you?" he murmured, inhaling the delicious scent of her that seemed to rise from skin quickly flushing with arousal. "Want something sweet?"

"Oh, yes." The tip of her tongue came out to moisten her lips. "I want."

The soft words snapped the tenuous leash he'd had on his straining urges.

Surging forward, he pressed his mouth to hers, his tongue tracing the same path hers had taken over her lips. She groaned and opened to him, arms twining around his neck, her tongue clashing with his as the kiss went from zero to a hundred in nothing flat.

Thank God he had enough functioning brain cells to remember they were on her front step, in full view of anyone who cared to look. And with this neighborhood's high percentage of retirees with nothing better to do than snoop out windows, there was almost certainly at least one set of eyeballs on them right now.

Which was the only reason his hands stayed on her back instead of going on a side trip down to explore her magnificent ass.

It wasn't the only thing he wanted to explore, either.

For right now, though, everything except her luscious mouth and nimble tongue were off-limits. Which only made the rest of her harder to resist.

But for once in his life, he was doing something other than simply acting on his sexual impulses. This was Miranda, and she deserved more. More than a quick, public grope. More than a meaningless afternoon tumble.

More than he was used to giving a woman.

Or had ever thought about giving.

But terrifying as it was, he was thinking it now.

Gentling the kiss, he stroked her back, enjoying the flex of the muscles he could feel there. Her legs might be in spectacular shape, but the rest of her was no slouch, either. Of course, she probably had a lot of time on her hands with nothing to do other than work out.

His stroking fingers froze.

Son of a bitch.

He'd totally forgotten. Forgotten that maybe being blind made her a little extra vulnerable. That even easing into this, whatever this was between them, might still be the wrong thing to do.

For them both.

Because he was him, and his track record with women was nothing but a laundry list of short-term failures. Which was why he didn't even try for anything more. And why starting something up with Miranda might be a worse mistake than Val.

Because unlike his former neighbor, he thought he'd actually like being friends with this new one.

He jerked from the sharp pinch she gave to his side. "Hey! What was that for?"

"For thinking too hard."

God, it was scary sometimes, the way she seemed to be able to see inside his head. "So, what, you're a mind reader now?"

"Body language reader." She leaned back against the doorjamb, arms crossed. "And you just pokered up big time in the middle of what I have to say was a pretty mind-blowing kiss. Which means either Sam stuck his nose up your butt in a very over-friendly way, or you suddenly thought of some reason why kissing me was a bad idea."

"I..." No way could he say what he was thinking. "I just don't want to rush you into anything you're not ready for."

"Was I complaining?"

Her disgruntled tone had him grinning. "No. No complaints."

"Then what the hell, Slick?"

That earned a laugh. "Slick?"

"You call me Legs."

"You're right. I do." He ran his hands over her arms in a light caress, because not touching her was too damn hard. "So, *Legs*, I was thinking that entertaining the neighbors by making out on your front step might not be the best impression either of us could make."

That much was true, at least.

Miranda's mouth dropped open before she slapped a hand over it. A muffled squeak of laughter escaped. "Oh, my God. I didn't even..." Another squeak.

"Yeah, me neither." He moved his head closer to hers. "You do that to me. Make me stop thinking."

And forget why he shouldn't be standing so close.

The laughter stopped. Her hand dropped from her mouth, which was slightly swollen from the kiss. The sight brought out a primal sense of satisfaction in him.

"Same goes. I'm usually hyper aware of my surroundings. It's so easy to forget that just because you can't see other people doesn't mean they can't see you. But with you..." She gave a helpless shrug. "I seem to forget everything else."

"Good to know." Because he was totally floundering here, out of his comfort zone and not sure of how to proceed. Not being alone in the confusion at least made it a little easier to swallow.

"So, um, do you want to come in?"

The innocent question didn't feel quite so innocent, not with the way she was tugging on her lower lip with her teeth, cheeks flushed with either nerves or excitement.

Or both.

He wanted nothing more than to say yes and get her behind closed doors and drawn curtains, away from prying eyes and out of those workout clothes. But that wasn't what he'd come over here for.

Not the only thing, anyway.

"Actually, I was wondering if you wanted to go out."

"Out?" She looked adorably confused. "Where?"

Some of the proud excitement that had taken a backseat to the insta-lust of seeing her bubbled back to the surface.

"To my place. I want to show you the kitchen, now that it's finished. And then I believe it's my turn to provide dinner. Although," he added with a grimace, "it'll have to be takeout, since the cupboards are literally bare."

He needed to dig out the boxes of kitchen stuff from the garage, then go to the market. But he could do all of that tomorrow. Right now, all he was interested in was spending time with Miranda.

Who had a strange look on her face.

"Unless you don't want to." He mentally replayed his words, wondering what he'd said wrong.

"No, I do! I want to." The smile she gave him lit up her whole face. "Thank you for asking me. I'd love to go see your new kitchen. Just, ah, give me a minute to get changed and grab Sam, okay? Come on in and have a seat."

"Sure. Take your time."

In his experience, when a woman said it would take them "a minute" to get ready, it usually meant at least twenty. It was like new math or a different time continuum or something. But to his surprise, Miranda was back in the living room in under five.

She'd changed into a pair of light blue capri pants and a short-sleeved white top that showed off her toned arms and made her tanned brown skin practically gleam in contrast. The extra coverage did nothing to lessen her allure. If anything, it made him think wicked thoughts about peeling every single layer of clothing off her enticing body and licking each bit of skin as he exposed it.

His dick twitched.

Fuck, Murph, keep it in your damn pants for once.

He cleared his throat. "You look nice."

With a smile that bordered on embarrassed, she ducked her head as she reached down to stroke the dog's head, her hair falling forward to hide her expression. "Thanks."

"Ready?"

"Almost."

That was when he noticed the leash and harness in her other hand and reality swooped back in to smack him in the face.

Again.

"Oh, right. Take your time."

"It'll only take a second. We're old hat at this, aren't we, Sam?" She gave the dog another good ear rub before snapping the leash to his harness.

When she held up the harness by the rigid handle, he almost asked if he could help. But even before he could remind himself she definitely didn't need it, she said, "Sam, harness," and the dog simply stepped forward into the contraption.

It took only a few seconds for her to find the dangling straps and secure them under Sam's chest and belly. When she was done, she used that mushy tone he was coming to recognize as her "atta boy" voice as she praised the dog, slipping him a small treat from her pocket as a reward.

"Okay." She stood, adjusting the harness handle and leash into her left hand. "We're good to go."

"Would it be insulting to say that was pretty impressive?"

She ducked her head again. "No. But it's Sam who does the hard parts."

He didn't agree, but kept it to himself as they went outside, Miranda pausing to lock the door before following him down the walk to the sidewalk.

Where he hesitated. "Uh, how should I...should I let you go first, or should I go, or..."

"You can walk next to me if the sidewalk is wide enough for all three of us. Sam will steer me around any obstacles, but he'll stop us if there's not enough room. If that happens, keep walking ahead until we catch up."

It was just as easy as it sounded. Even when Sam moved Miranda around a section of sidewalk that heaved slightly upward from a tree root burrowing underneath, walking beside her didn't feel any different than walking with anyone else.

Right up until he forgot to tell her when they got to his walkway. He turned right, and she kept going straight.

"Oh, shit, sorry! I didn't...I was supposed to tell you when to turn, wasn't I?" He smacked himself in the forehead as he hurried back to her side. "Idiot. Some running guide I'll be. I can't even get you as far as one house safely."

At this rate, he'd steer her right into a ditch their first time out.

"Don't worry about it. It takes a little getting used to, that's all." She put her hand on his arm and gave it a squeeze before they started up the walkway. "You're making the effort to do it right, and you have no idea how much that means to me. A lot of people would have grabbed my arm and tried to turn me, which is not only rude, but dangerous."

"Dangerous? For you or Sam?"

"More for them, actually." She gave him a smile full of teeth as he opened the front door for her. "Combat swimming isn't the only thing I was good at."

He wasn't sure if she was joking or not. "Duly noted."

Once they were inside, Miranda hesitated. "You don't mind Sam coming in, do you? I know you just redid all your floors and everything."

"Nah, there's enough poly down to protect the wood from a herd of elephants. He's fine." He glanced at the dog standing patiently at her side. "But I didn't get a chance to do a really good sweep in the kitchen after the installers were done. I wouldn't want him to get hurt on some sliver of stone or stray screw or anything."

"Good thinking. Sam, you'd better stay here." She patted his head. "Good boy. Lay down and stay." With a gusty sigh, the dog sank to the ground and put his nose on his paws. Ben noticed his gaze never left Miranda, though.

I get it, pal. I can't keep my eyes off her, either.

Remembering her directions from the previous day, he said, "If you'd like to take my arm..." As soon as she reached for it, he moved closer, enjoying the way her fingers curled around his biceps instead of his elbow this time.

He barely refrained from flexing and making a true idiot out of himself.

Mentally rolling his eyes, he walked her straight through to the kitchen, trying not to overdose on the delicious scent of her as he went.

"Does your kitchen have the same layout as mine?"

"It did, but since I stripped everything down to the studs, I took the opportunity to move some things around to make it flow a little better. Plus, I added in an island for extra prep space and seating." He'd worried it might overpower the room, but the end result proved well worth the risk.

At her prompting, he described the handcrafted cabinets made by the brother of one of his fellow firefighters; the rubbed-bronze pulls he'd hunted through a dozen different antique stores to find; the granite with a soft veining of gold running through its white and gray depths.

Miranda ran her hands over each as he spoke, as though absorbing every possible detail. He'd never been jealous of an inanimate object before. But that almost changed when she fondled the deep country style sink and fancy detachable faucet with a throaty sound of approval.

Damn, the woman could tie him up in knots without even trying.

When she slid her hand further down the counter to the smooth surface of the stove, she stopped and turned toward him. "Huh. I gotta be honest, I was expecting one of those huge gas ranges with a hundred burners, not electric."

"Actually, it's induction."

"What's the difference?"

"The burner generates a magnetic field that converts to heat only when something metal comes in contact with it. So, if you accidentally touch it, or drop, say, a potholder on it, nothing happens."

Even as he teased her about her confessed mishap, it dawned on him how perfect that kind of stove would be for her. From the way she ran a covetous hand over the smooth cooktop and controls, it was clear she was thinking the same thing.

Great, now he was jealous of the stove, too.

Pathetic.

It only got worse. By the time she'd examined the huge French-door stainless steel refrigerator with water and multi-option ice dispenser, the sounds of appreciation she made had him as hard as the granite she'd just finished feeling up.

"God, you have all the best toys."

He let out a choking laugh. "Do I detect a hint of kitchen envy?"

"Yeah, I think you do." She smiled as she reached out and located the edge of the island before following it around to where he was standing. "You did an amazing job, Ben. There was a lot of thought and planning put into every little detail, and it shows."

"Thanks." Her praise fizzed through him like seltzer bubbles.

"No, thank you."

"For what?"

"For showing it to me."

This close, it was impossible to miss the shimmer of tears in her eyes.

Panic hit. "It was no big deal. Really."

"No, it really was. You invited me to come see something you were proud of, just like you would anyone else. That's a hella big deal." She put her hand lightly on his chest and went up on her toes, bringing her face closer to his. "Thank you." With that, she pressed an exquisitely tender kiss to his lips.

As she pulled back, his hand circled the back of her neck gently, stopping her retreat. "Well then, you're very welcome." His kiss wasn't nearly as chaste, but he forced himself to keep it light and quick.

When it ended, she snuggled in against him, wrapping her arms around his waist with a contented sigh. "Maybe we should skip the takeout and go back to my place to eat. As nice as your kitchen is, unless you forgot to mention it, it's still missing one very important thing."

"What's that?"

"Someplace to sit down."

Well...shit.

"How do you know I don't have furniture in another room we could use?" The image of his rumpled fold-out sofa bed mere yards down the hall leapt to mind, but he bit his tongue.

They were discussing dinner, not dessert.

"You mean besides the incredible echo?" He could feel her smile against his chest. "We didn't have to walk around anything from the time we came through the front door. And new furniture smells funny. Kind of like a new car does. Like chemicals and plastic."

She was good.

And right.

"I do have some furniture on order, but it's mostly bedroom stuff. I still need to go shopping for the rest." Escaping the cramped room he was living out of had been priority one. He'd probably need to pick up some extra shifts to help pay for everything, but he didn't plan on skimping with bargain store stuff now. He'd start with the bare necessities and go from there, a little at a time.

A place to sit and eat with Miranda had just jumped to the top of the list.

He eased back from the embrace. "So. Food." He cleared his throat. "Pizza okay?"

She made a face. "Or I could just make us something."

"Nope, it's my turn." He named a few other fast-food options nearby. "Or we could go to the diner."

After a few seconds of thought, she said slowly, "That would be nice. If you're sure?"

"Why not? The food is good there, trust me."

"No. I mean, I know, I've eaten there before."

Puzzled, he asked, "Then what?"

She smiled and shook her head. "Nothing. Nothing at all. The diner sounds great."

They decided to walk. Determined to put himself in her shoes, he paid extra attention to their surroundings. He noted things along the sidewalk he'd subconsciously always overlooked, but now realized would be a problem for someone who couldn't see them.

Garbage cans. A pair of hastily abandoned kids' bikes. A sprinkler overshooting the lawn. Low-hanging branches.

It was a surprisingly daunting task. At least, it seemed so to him.

Especially when it came to crossing the streets. The first cross-street had no traffic when they went over it, but Main Street was another story. The diner was on the other side, so the only way there was to go across.

As they stood on the corner waiting for the light to change, an unfamiliar sense of anxiety tightened his chest. How did she do it? It could be dangerous enough for a sighted person to cross a main road.

For Miranda, it had to be absolutely terrifying.

"Training," she said when he asked. "And lots of practice. Sam knows to stop at the curb. These," she scuffed her foot over the raised bumps on the curb-cut leading to the crosswalk, "tell me I'm in the right place to cross."

"But how do you know when to go?" As good as Sam was trained, he was pretty sure he couldn't tell when the light changed.

"I listen for the traffic in front of me to stop and the parallel traffic to go. And…" The crossing signal began to emit a beeping tone. "…for that. Sam, forward." By the time they made it to the other side, the tone had started to pulse faster. "That's the warning the signal's about to change. You do *not* want to still be in the street when it stops."

Like some dangerous game of musical chairs.

It shamed him to admit it, but he'd crossed that street a hundred times and never once thought about what the sound was for.

"What do you do at the corners without an audible signal? Or a light?"

She shrugged. "Rely on my ears and Sam's eyes. Which, with all the electric cars these days, are extra important since I can't hear them as well. If I tried to cross when a car's coming, Sam would stop me. It's called intelligent disobedience."

The level of confidence in her voice struck him as both admirable and dangerous. The dog was insanely smart, yes. But he could be the next Stephen Hawking and that still couldn't keep a car from running a light and taking them both out in a deadly instant.

A gut-churning image that haunted him all the way down the block.

The diner was starting to fill with the dinner hour crowd. As they waited to be seated, Ben caught the curious glances being thrown their way. Some people looked from Sam to Miranda with a hint of pity on their faces. But there were one or two who held a pinched look of disapproval at seeing Sam in an eating establishment, despite his obvious guide dog status.

Jerks.

He wanted to snarl at all of them. Miranda wouldn't want their pity, and she certainly didn't deserve their attitude. She was handling a major life-altering event with more dignity and courage than he—or they—ever could.

A waitress with long red hair headed their way, a wide smile on her face. He cursed to himself as he tried to remember the name of the woman who'd flirted so heavily with him the last few times he'd been in. Kandy? Kenya? Kiki?

Shit, it was something with a K. Wasn't it?

Just before she reached them, the waitress—Kimmy?—noticed Miranda. Her smile underwent a subtle change, going from hungry to curious to genuine in the matter of a few seconds. "Miranda! It's so nice to see you."

"Kasey, hi," Miranda said with a smile of her own, honest pleasure in her voice. "Do you know Ben?"

With a wry grin and what might have been regret in her eyes as she looked at him, Kasey replied, "I've seen him in here a few times." Her attention moved back to Miranda. "Come on, let me take you to your table."

She led them to a booth in the corner, where there would be plenty of room for Sam to lay down under the table on one side out the way. That meant Ben and Miranda ended up sitting next to each other, which suited him just fine.

As he listened with half an ear to Kasey rattling off the day's specials, he noticed she'd only laid one menu on the table. He almost mentioned the oversight before his brain caught up with the facts.

One menu, because only he could use it. Like crossing the street, it was such a simple, everyday thing he'd never given a second thought to.

Until now.

By the time they finished their meal, his admiration for the ease with which Miranda navigated her unsighted version of the world had risen exponentially. After describing the layout of the food on her plate, which was so precisely set at ten, two, and six he knew Kasey had informed the cook who it was for, Miranda had handled the rest.

Most surprising of all was that Kasey hadn't so much as given him a wink or a jiggle the entire meal, even knowing Miranda wouldn't be able to see her doing it. For that he was grateful. And relieved.

He might have been interested in what she was offering before. But not anymore.

Not since he'd met Miranda.

Which probably should have worried him.

The fact it didn't should have worried him even more.

The two women chatted enthusiastically about some show they both were following about Scottish Highlanders and time traveling women as Kasey cleared their plates. He knew the one they were discussing. Some of the guys watched it at the firehouse when there was nothing else on. They said it was for the battle scenes, but it was more likely for the occasional naked boob or ass.

What could he say? Men were nothing more than horny twelve-year-old boys at heart.

After using the restroom, he was headed back to their table when Kasey moved in on a determined intercept course.

Crap.

He steeled himself for the expected flirting she'd held off on before, but was surprised when she merely said with a touch of resignation, "So. You and Miranda, huh?"

What?

"No, it's not like that. We're just..." What, exactly? "Friends." Getting there, anyway.

"Right. Friends." Kasey shook her head, as though she knew something he didn't. Hell, maybe she did. "Well, if I had to lose out to anybody, at least it was her." Her expression sharpened. "You treat her right, y'hear? She's not a player like you and me. She's good people. She deserves to be treated that way."

Not sure if he was more surprised by the way she was surrendering the field without a fight or her fierce defense of Miranda, he said, "I'll treat her right. Believe me, I have no plans to hurt her."

Kasey offered a sad smile. "That's just it, Ben. Guys like you never mean to. But you can't help doing it anyway."

Chapter 12

Something had changed.

She couldn't put her finger on it, but Miranda could sense the difference in Ben. He was still walking right beside her, and yet it felt like he was on the other side of the street, distant and untouchable. The closer they got to home, the more she worried accepting his invitation to eat out had been a huge mistake.

The casual request had caught her off-guard. Just as being asked to go and "see" his new kitchen had. At the time, she'd been thrilled about both. It had seemed like he actually got it, her hunger to be treated as a regular person and not someone in need of constant coddling and supervision. That to him, she was just Miranda.

But now...

Somehow, something had backfired, but she didn't have a clue what it was, or how she could fix it.

The short walk from the sidewalk to her front door felt like a countdown to the end. And she didn't want this—whatever this was with him—to end. She'd never been one to shrink from a challenge.

God knew she'd never have made it through boot camp if she was.

That thought bolstered her courage. If she could make it through thirteen weeks at Parris Island, she could handle anything one suddenly broody fireman could throw at her.

Sam stopped, which meant they'd reached the front step.

Now or never.

"I haven't had a chance to restock my beer, but I do have some pretty good coffee. Want to come in for a cup?"

"Oh, I, um, I don't—"

She didn't give him time to finish the stammered rejection.

Stepping toward his voice, she reached out and put a hand on his chest to orient herself so she wasn't talking to his ear. "Unless you'd rather kiss me out here on my front step. You said you didn't want to give the neighbors a show, but hell, I'm game if you are."

She let her fingers smooth across his chest, where his breath hitched and his heart rate sped up beneath the soft cotton of his tee.

She grinned to herself.

That answered one question at least. He still wanted her.

Now she just had to figure out why he didn't *want* to want her anymore.

"Miranda, I should probably—"

"Come inside and stop being an ass?"

The laugh he gave had very little humor in it. "That's what I'm trying to do by *not* coming in."

"I don't understand." She really didn't. "Did we or did we not come within an inch of making out right here in this very spot not a few hours back? Because if that wasn't you, I've got a whole different problem on my hands."

The weak attempt to ease the tension earned a small sigh.

"Okay, yeah, we did." His voice might have been laced with reluctance, but she could feel the muscles across his chest tighten as his body responded to the memory.

"Then what changed?" She drew back, breaking contact with him as a horrible thought plowed into her like a runaway bus. "It was me, wasn't it? You were embarrassed to be seen out with me."

"What? No! God, no. It's nothing like that, I swear."

Only the sincere shock in his voice staved off the nausea trying to crawl up her throat. "Then what, Ben? What *is* it like? Because I'm coming up with all kinds of horrible things over here inside my head."

He blew out a sigh. "Shit. It's me, okay? I'm what's wrong. And no," he added before she could say it, "that wasn't an 'it's not you, it's me' cop-out. I mean I'm really not good for you."

"That makes no sense."

"Look—"

"No." Her hand shot up to silence him. "We're talking about this, but we're damn well not doing it out here. You're coming in, I'm making coffee, and we're going to get to the bottom of this sudden asinine theory of yours."

She slipped her key out of the small purse slung over her shoulder and opened the door, hoping the tiny tremor in her hand wasn't visible. Stepping inside, she turned back, head up, spine straight. "You coming?" It was a clear challenge.

One that Ben thankfully accepted, following her into the house.

Refusing to let her relief show, she snapped, "Have a seat in the living room. I'll go get the coffee started."

"Yes, ma'am."

The little-boy meekness of the response made her want to grin, but she held it back. She wouldn't let him smooth talk his way out of this discussion. They were getting to the bottom of this crazy idea of his even if she had to tie him to the couch to do it.

That thought brought another urge to grin, one she gave in to since she was out of his sight in the kitchen. After turning on the Keurig, she took care of unhooking Sam from his harness and gave him a quick hug and a few of his favorite treats.

He thanked her with a wiggle and a liver-scented kiss.

She'd been reluctant to switch from her cane to a guide dog when her mobility coach first floated the idea to her. A dog meant more training, and more importantly, being responsible for another living being's care and well-being at a time when she was still adjusting to taking care of herself.

Now, she couldn't imagine her life without Sam in it.

He really was something special. Just as the letter that came with him had said.

And like it or not, she was already starting to feel the same way about Ben. It was a slippery slope, but she didn't know how to change it, even if she wanted to.

The handy thing about using the Keurig was that it automatically dispensed a set amount of coffee, so she didn't have to use either the liquid probe or the old finger-in-the-cup method to know when to stop pouring. Something she only used for herself because sticking your finger in your guest's drink was rude, and didn't use at all for hot drinks because, hot.

The machine filled her oversized mugs only about three-quarters of the way, leaving plenty of sloshing space for when she brought her coffee to another room. Transporting *two* mugs was a slightly different proposition. One that entailed a tray to catch spills, and plenty of napkins. Just in case.

"How do you take your coffee?" she called.

"Black is fine."

Adding a splash of milk to hers, she carried the tray to the living room. Knowing Ben was watching had her hyperaware of every step, every movement. But she made it to the coffee table without mishap and carefully put the tray down, feeling for the edge to make sure it was far enough away to be secure.

"Thank you."

Well, at least he didn't clap like her mother.

His voice let her know which side of the couch he was sitting on, so she lowered herself to the other. Not too far away, but not as close as she'd like to be, either. She had a feeling they might need a bit of distance to get through this conversation. "Okay. Let's hear it."

"You don't cut a guy any slack, do you?"

"Not when it matters."

There was a long moment of silence. "This matters to you?"

The quiet yearning in his question made her heart hurt. "Of course, it does. We matter. *You* matter. I wouldn't have kissed you otherwise."

"See, that's the problem. I would have."

She recoiled. "Excuse me?"

"No, no, no! Fuck me, I'm saying this all wrong again." He let out a frustrated sound, and the vibration in the couch told her he'd probably smacked it with his fist. "You matter. No matter how badly I screw up this explanation, remember, you matter. Okay?"

"Okay." She drew in a steadying breath and let it out. "Go on."

"Okay. Well, you know I'm a fireman, right?"

She nodded.

"And, well, there are a lot of women who really...*like* firemen."

From the way he said it, she knew exactly what he meant.

"Right. Like tag chasers. Groupies looking to hook-up with someone because they're in the military." God knew she'd seen it happen a hundred times at the bars outside the bases she'd been at. Women—and men—trolling for someone, anyone, with dog tags to add to their scorecard.

For a lot of them, it was a competition. For others, an obsession. And for a very few, a desperate attempt to land a military spouse and the PX card and base housing that came with them.

"Tag chasers, huh? Never heard that one. Well, for us and the cops it's badge bunnies and hose honeys."

She snorted at the raunchy moniker. "Of course it is."

"Hey, I didn't come up with them."

"Right. So, what? You're telling me you date a lot of your *hose honeys*?"

"Yes. But, no."

"Well, that clears everything right up."

"Yes, I've hooked up with a lot of them. But no, I didn't date them. Mostly it was just a one-time deal."

"A one-time deal," she repeated, starting to get the picture. "So, just sex. No strings, no commitments, no promises."

"Yeah."

Not the worst thing for a single guy to do, especially if fire department groupies were as aggressive on the hunt as the tag chasers she'd seen in action. But still, a man didn't need to catch every coochie thrown his way, either. "And by a lot, you mean..."

"A lot."

She had no right to the flash of jealousy that zapped through her like a lightning strike. That didn't mean it didn't still hurt. "What about girlfriends? Lots of those, too?"

"Not really. Nothing long-term, anyway." He gave a short laugh. "I'm just not very good boyfriend material."

Was he serious?

"Um, did it ever occur to you that maybe you were with women who weren't good girlfriend material?"

"Yeah, no, I don't think they were the problem." He honestly sounded like he believed that, which made her wonder where someone with Ben's looks and talents had developed such a low sense of self-esteem.

"Okay, putting that aside, what does any of this have to do with us?"

"I don't want to hurt you."

"Okay." She waited, but that seemed to be the whole explanation. "So, don't hurt me."

"You make it sound so simple."

"It *is* simple."

"You don't get it." He shifted position, but at least he didn't get up and walk out. "I don't know how to do this."

"This?"

"Us. Whatever it is we're doing."

"I don't know, I thought it was going pretty well, myself." Right up until about twenty minutes ago, anyway.

"So did I. But then Kasey said...never mind."

"Kasey? The waitress at the diner?" Another flash of jealousy burst through her, extra painful because she knew and actually liked the woman who caused it. "Is she one of the women who's honeyed your hose?"

Ben let out a choking laugh. "Jesus. And no, we've never hooked up." He paused. "We did flirt a few times, but that's it, I swear. Nothing happened."

"But it might."

"No. Definitely not. She knows I'm not interested."

"You're not." She couldn't help but sound skeptical, because face it, she was.

"Not anymore. I haven't been interested in even looking at another woman since I met you."

She almost made a sarcastic comment on how a whole week of abstinence must have been so hard for him. But there was something about his voice, something a little vulnerable and unsure, that held back the impulse.

Needing to buy some time to process everything he'd said, she identified her coffee by the unique curve of its handle and took a few slow sips, hands wrapped around the mug to absorb the comforting heat as she thought.

"Is it the challenge?" she asked finally. "Is your interest in me because I didn't fall into bed with you first thing?"

"No. Absolutely not." But there was still a hint of uncertainty in his declaration that she shared.

"Well, there's one way to be sure about that." She put her mug down.

"Oh?" He sounded wary.

"Yup." She slid closer to him. "If you're holding your coffee, I suggest you get rid of it."

"I'm...not. Miranda, you don't have to—"

"But I want to." Moving closer still, her leg touched his. With one hand, she traced over his knee and up his thigh, marveling at the rock-hard muscles that quivered beneath her caress. "Do *you* want to?"

His breath rushed out like a bellows emptying. "Yes. Hell yes." He dragged her into his lap with a swiftness that surprised a squeak out of her. He froze at the sound. "Sorry."

"Don't be sorry." She put her hand on his shoulder, followed it to his neck and cupped his cheek, giving her the exact location of his mouth. "Just be sure."

She waited a heartbeat, two, three. When he didn't object, she leaned in and pressed her mouth to his. Her tongue begged entrance, and he gave it with a groan she could feel everywhere her body touched his, sending sparks to all the parts that were eager to join the party.

Ben's fingers tangled in her hair, anchoring her head as he met her kiss for kiss in what felt like a contest for domination. His other hand cupped her hip before sliding under her top and softly caressing her skin in tantalizing little circles.

But no matter how much she squirmed, trying to urge his touch up to her aching breasts, he didn't take the hint. He just teased at her stomach, circling her belly button, stroking over her ribs, before coming back and doing it all over again. It was driving her crazy.

Which was probably the point.

Finally, she broke away from the kiss with a growl. "What are you waiting for?"

"For you to set the pace, sweetheart." He nuzzled against her neck. "Your kitchen, your rules, remember?"

It was a ridiculous analogy, but she understood what he meant. Part of her resented even that small reminder he was being extra cautious with her, no doubt because of her blindness. But another part of her rose up to accept the challenge and show him exactly what she was capable of with the control he'd just handed her.

Careful to not accidentally geld him with her knee, she swung her legs around so she straddled his lap facing him. Before any doubts could creep in, she whisked her top up over her head and let it drop to the cushion beside them. "Touch me."

"Where?"

The word was a harsh rasp, spiking her confidence.

"Anywhere." She ran her hands over her covered breasts and down her belly. "Everywhere."

"*Christ.*" His hands started at her shoulders, then moved downward with reverent slowness, following the exact path hers had.

Goosebumps broke out along her sensitized skin. Her nipples hardened to painful points. By the time he reached her waistband, arousal had flushed her entire body so hot she thought she'd come with just one more touch.

She didn't expect the soft press of his lips to her breastbone in a gentle kiss, or his arms coming around her body, hugging her close to him, his face buried at her neck. If it weren't for the hard press of his erection nestled between her legs, she'd wonder if he somehow found her lacking. "Ben?"

"You are so beautiful." She felt the words against her neck as he spoke them, his breath warm and smelling faintly of the apple pie they'd shared for dessert. "I don't want to mess this up."

Probably impossible, with all the practice he'd evidently had over the years. But she had a feeling he was talking about more than just the sex.

She ran her fingers through his soft hair, reveling in the small intimacy and how he pressed into the caress like Sam did, taking pleasure in her touch. "Then we won't."

She included herself in the vow because honestly, chances were about fifty-fifty that Ben wouldn't be the one to ruin things between them.

She would.

The kiss to seal that promise was hungry and urgent. Ben's teeth tugged at her lower lip before soothing it with his tongue. The sharp little pain radiated like an electroshock straight down to her breasts. Already hard nipples rasped against her bra, making them ache, and she wanted it gone, wanting nothing between her skin and his.

She reached between them and ran her hands down his chest. When she found the hem of his tee, she gave it a tug. "Off."

With one quick flex of his arms, it was over his head and gone.

Putting her original intent on hold for the moment, she took the opportunity to explore this newly discovered territory. She smoothed her hands along the muscles and planes of his lightly haired chest, finding his hardened nipples and teasing them with her thumbs until he shuddered before continuing on.

His shoulders were broad, but he didn't have the over-pumped feel of a weight lifter. Instead, he was sleek and toned and very, very warm.

The need to feel all that delicious skin against hers came back in a rush, and she reached behind herself to unhook her bra. Ben sucked in a hard breath as she slid the straps down her arms, letting them dangle there for a moment before peeling the cups away and baring herself to him.

The dark sound of appreciation he made kept her from feeling too exposed.

"Beautiful." His hands covered her breasts with a gentle caress. "So damn beautiful."

She bit her lip and arched into his touch, which pressed her even tighter against the bulge straining beneath his zipper. They both groaned.

"Maybe," she panted, "we should bring this upstairs?"

Ben's hands stilled. "Are you sure?"

In reply, she slid from his lap and stood, holding out her hand. The swiftness with which he took it was gratifying. Lacing her fingers with his, she led him to the stairs, up them, and into her bedroom, bumping into the doorframe in her haste.

Every silent step ratcheted the tension between them. By the time she finally released him, steam practically rose from her exposed skin, while the rest of her body was all achy and confined and in desperate need of release from more than just her clothes.

"I really hope you were a Boy Scout, Slick." Her fingers felt thick and clumsy as she undid the button on her capris.

He gave a strangled laugh. "Be prepared?"

"Yeah." The zipper went down with a loud rasp. "So?" Her pants slid down her legs to puddle at her feet, leaving her in nothing but her panties. "Are you?"

"Let's see...on my honor, I'll do my duty"—there was the sound of shoes hitting the ground in quick succession—"to God and country"—a zipper hissed—"to help other people"—gentle hands came around her waist—"and keep myself physically strong"— she went sailing through the air and landed on the bed with a laughing shriek, Ben's large, almost naked body next to her, pressed tight—"mentally awake, and morally straight."

Still laughing, she said, "I'll take that as a yes."

"Yes, ma'am."

"Good."

The scorching kiss he gave her burned away all traces of humor, reigniting the desperate nerve endings in her breasts and between her legs. Rolling closer to deepen the kiss, her breasts pressed to his chest, the hair there teasing at her nipples and making her moan into his mouth at the sensation. But it wasn't enough.

She needed to touch him, feel him.

All of him.

With her mouth and hands, she took her time learning every inch of him, from his calloused fingertips to his crooked little toe.

Everything, from the texture of the hair on his legs to the defined cut of his Adonis belt right above the band of his boxer briefs, was stored away to play over and over in her head later on when she was alone again.

The lure of what lay beneath the snug cotton finally became too much to ignore. She slid her fingers under the waistband. "Yes?"

"God, yes." He sounded desperate, which made her admire his restraint in letting her play all the more.

With great care, she eased the briefs over his erection and down his legs, then ran her hands back up them to his hipbones before moving inward, trapping his rigid penis between her palms. They both sucked in a startled breath, his from her touch, hers at the hard heat of him.

It had been a long time since she'd gotten naked with a man. She'd forgotten the intoxicating beauty of all that male virility focused into one small piece of anatomy.

Her hand closed around him, making his erection pulse.

Well, maybe not so small.

He groaned, placing his hand over hers. "Sweetheart, I'm about to ruin the rest of the evening for us both if you keep touching me." He groaned again, a pained, desperate sound. "Christ. Please, baby."

Reluctantly, she gave in to the urging of his hand and released her hold on him. "But I like touching you."

"And I obviously like you touching me a little too much. Besides..." His hands cupped her breasts as he laid a gentle kiss on each. "I think it's my turn to explore, don't you?"

Moisture pooled between her legs at the heated intent in his words.

She shivered. "I guess that's only fair."

"Lay down."

She did, feeling like a pagan offering as he delicately traced his fingers across her collarbones and down the sides of her breasts before circling up over the aching tips, giving each a quick pinch that almost sent her over the edge.

The low, dark chuckle he gave told her he knew it, too. But he didn't repeat the caress, instead moving on to touch and kiss each and every other inch of exposed skin he could find, just as she'd done to him.

It nearly drove her insane.

Every touch, every caress, was ten times more intense than she could ever remember before. It went beyond four years of abstinence. Without her sight, all of her focus was narrowed down to tactile sensation alone. To the physical connection where his skin met hers.

Nothing else existed outside that point of contact.

Finally, his palm settled over her panty-clad mound. The warmth and pressure of his hand made her twitch, and she knew he had to feel how saturated the material was, how aroused he'd made her with all his teasing.

Or maybe it wasn't teasing. Maybe he was learning her the same way she'd been learning him.

And that possibility just aroused her all the more. What man had ever taken that much time to discover the secrets her body had to reveal? Where she liked to be touched, where she was ticklish, what made her squirm with anticipation or sigh with pleasure?

None. Not until Ben.

Realizing what he was waiting for, she whispered, "Yes."

It took only a heartbeat for her panties to disappear, so fast she wondered if he'd ripped them off. He cupped her again, one finger sliding through her curls and unerringly finding her clit. Her body bucked at the touch. "God, stop. You're going to make me come."

"That's the plan."

"No. I want you inside me."

He let out a velvety chuckle. "Oh, I'll be inside you, sweetheart, trust me. But this first time is just for you. To take the edge off."

"But I've never been able to…" She bit her lip and finished in an almost-whisper. "Come twice." And she didn't want to waste her only orgasm on foreplay. She wanted the whole soul-shaking, pounding-deep-inside-till-I-scream orgasm she'd been having dreams about the past few nights.

Especially if this might end up being their one and only time together.

"You couldn't, or the jerks you've been with haven't cared enough to take care of you right?"

"Um…" How could she think with his finger playing with her in small circles like that?

He leaned in and kissed her. "Let me take care of you the way you deserve."

"I…" Brain about to short-circuit, she let out a moan. "Yesss." With a mind of their own, her hips swiveled under the increased pressure he used with his thumb as one long finger teased at her entrance.

She was so wet, he didn't have any problem sliding it right into her. When he added a second, her hips did another shimmy as a sound of need and pleasure erupted from her throat. He pumped his fingers once, twice, and on the third stroke she went off like a rocket-launched grenade.

By the time her body stopped shaking and twitching, she was back in her head enough to start feeling self-conscious. It would be so much easier if she could see his expression right now. To know if he'd taken enjoyment from giving her pleasure, or if it had just been the *quid pro* to her *quo*.

"I'm going to go out on a limb here and say you enjoyed that."

She had to grin at the smugness in his voice. "It was nice."

"Nice?" A warm hand closed over her left breast in a soft caress. "I guess I'll have to work a little harder next time."

She shuddered, her body still sensitized to the point of pleasure-pain. "I want that next time to be with you inside me. Please." She wanted him bad enough right now she'd beg if she had to.

Lucky for her, Ben didn't seem to plan on tormenting her any further.

She felt him leave the bed for a minute, heard the crinkle and rip of the condom wrapper, and he was back. After a deep, lingering kiss, he came over her, his knees nudging hers apart. Swollen and sensitive from her first orgasm, she could feel every inch of him as he pressed inside with maddening slowness.

Just when she didn't think she could take it anymore, he stopped and let out a shaky breath. "Are you okay?"

"God, yes." She drew her knees up, bringing him in even deeper and making her moan. "You feel so good."

"Baby, we're just getting started."

He wasn't lying.

By the time he'd given her that second orgasm she didn't think she could have, they were both slick with sweat and breathing like two thoroughbreds straining for the finish line at Belmont. His guttural groan quickly followed hers, and he collapsed half-on, half-off her, his face pressed to her neck as he struggled to catch his breath.

Normally, being held down to any degree was a trigger. Too many bad memories of the crash and waking up unable to see, unable to breathe, pinned beneath the wreckage as flames crackled terrifyingly close.

But with Ben's heart pounding in time with hers, she didn't feel more than a mild twinge of anxiety before it disappeared, smothered beneath the lethargy of having been wrung both physically and emotionally dry.

"So," he said between pants, "did I manage better than just 'nice'?"

With a huffing laugh, she stroked his damp back and squeezed him closer. "Slick, I'd say we can easily score that as outstanding." Superb. Amazing. Incredible. The list went on and on. Clearly, she'd been missing out on something extraordinary all these years with her one-and-done orgasms. "You are *really* good at this."

"Yeah, well, when you're born with looks instead of brains, you learn to make the most of what you've got." The joking tone might have worked if she hadn't been holding him so close. The fine line of tension that invaded his body gave him away.

She drew back and scowled. "And what the hell is that supposed to mean?"

Chapter 13

The outrage in Miranda's voice helped soothe the familiar sting of knowing one of the few places he'd excelled in his adult life was in the bedroom. The question was, why had he brought it up in the first place?

Unless...he *wanted* her asking questions?

It seemed absurd, but maybe he needed to be sure what she felt for him wasn't based only on good sex.

Okay, outstanding sex.

But that was the measuring stick other women used with him. For whatever reason, he wanted Miranda's regard to be for *him*, not his incredibly talented dick.

She poked a finger into his chest. "Ben, what's that mean? Looks instead of brains?"

"It means..." He let out a sigh, feeling stupid. As usual. "It means my mouth engaged before my brain recovered from extreme blood deprivation." Which was partly true. He would have never said what he did without being under the influence of all those post-orgasm endorphins. He didn't think, anyway. "Just forget I said it, okay?"

From the stubborn look on her face, she wasn't buying it.

"Not okay. It obviously meant something to you. Why would you think you're not smart? Yes, from what I've heard, you're very handsome. And yes, you're pretty amazing in bed. But you also happen to be an intelligent, successful man who has an important and difficult job. So, why would you ever think you were lacking in brains?"

"If you met my family, you wouldn't be asking that question. They're all brilliant. Me? I had to take three SAT prep courses in high school—*three*—just to score a nine-fifty."

"That's not a bad score."

"But not a great one, either." *Average* was the nicest thing he'd heard from anyone. "My sister? She got a fifteen hundred without taking a single prep. And my little brother, Caleb? Perfect eight hundred on the math section. Compared to them, I'm the freaking Scarecrow with straw for brains."

"Why compare yourself to them at all?" Miranda shook her head. "Look, I get the whole family jealousy thing. My little sister is in nursing school on a full scholarship. She's got, like, Big Bang Theory level brains, but without all the nerdiness. But her being smart doesn't mean I'm stupid."

Having one smart sibling wasn't the same as sitting around the dinner table listening to conversations that flew entirely over your head night after night. Conversations he only got to join in when someone remembered to bring the level down to a topic he actually knew something about, like sports or cars.

Which had only made him feel even stupider.

Dumb jock had been a little too spot on a description.

"It's not just about them. I always had a hard time in school. Borderline ADHD, short attention span, whatever you want to call it." *Lack of ambition* had been a favorite opinion of some of his teachers. *Lazy* had been another. "And I absolutely sucked at taking tests. All of them, not just the SAT. My sixth-grade teacher, Mr. Zimmer, used to drag my desk up next to his to 'help me concentrate better' whenever he gave one."

A low sound of sympathy accompanied the comforting stroke on his arm. "That was mean. And probably made you do even worse."

He shrugged. "He thought he was helping, but yeah, it did."

It also opened him up to the ridicule of his classmates.

"But when I hit high school, I finally found sports. Football, mostly, and some track. I didn't need to take tests for those, and suddenly I was good at something. Really good. My test scores were still mediocre, but as long as I made my mark as a jock it didn't seem to matter so much anymore."

Plus, sports were the one thing he could do that his brilliant brother couldn't.

"But that's not what you meant with that comment, is it? You said *looks* over brains, not muscles."

Damn her keen perception. And damn his wayward mouth.

"Sports only lasted me through high school. But by senior year I'd discovered something else I excelled at."

"Sex," Miranda guessed.

"Sex. High school is a smorgasbord of horny teenage girls looking to experiment with their budding sexuality and raging hormones. And college was more of the same, although I had to try a little harder since I didn't have the letterman jacket working it for me anymore."

"Poor baby." The wry words told him she was amused rather than put off by his admission of being an oversexed horndog.

So far, anyway.

"Yeah, well, we already discussed the whole hose honey thing, so you know how things went in that department after college."

"Still waiting for the looks over brains explanation."

He hesitated. There really wasn't any good way to say this without sounding like a vain ass. "Women like having sex with me. So...I give them what they want."

Her expression impossible to read, Miranda stayed silent. The only promising sign was that she kept playing her hand back and forth over his arm in distracting strokes. She wouldn't still be touching him if she was disgusted, right?

"Miranda?"

"You seriously think your looks and sex are the only reason women want you?"

"Well, yeah. It's not like I have much of anything else to offer."

"You know what? The really sad thing is I think you honestly believe that." Wrapping her hand around the back of his neck, she brought him down for a kiss. It was soft and sweet and filled with aching need. Hugging him tight, she said almost too softly for him to hear, "Give me a little time. Bet I can prove you wrong."

It was a sucker bet.

Ben knew what he was and what he wasn't. Most of all, he knew the more time he spent with Miranda, the faster she'd know it, too.

"Two minutes, twenty seconds."

Hanging onto the side of the pool, Miranda gulped air in huge swallows. Even with the water running down her face, it was easy to see her frustration at his announcement. She'd been shooting for two and a half minutes underwater for the past week now, and had been stuck at ten seconds short of her goal for just as long.

"One more time," she panted, swiping her hair back, slicking it to her skull. "I know I can do better."

And he knew she'd keep trying until she totally exhausted herself.

Again.

"How about we stop for lunch and pick this up again later?"

She reached over to where his legs were dangling into the pool and ran her hand around his calf in a sensual caress. "One more time now, then lunch, then we'll do whatever you want this afternoon."

"Whatever I want, hmm?" He slipped off the edge into the deep water, one hand anchoring him to the side as the other slid down to her amazing ass and squeezed. "That covers an awful lot of territory, Legs. Think you can live up to your promises?"

He let out a grunt as those legs he admired so much wrapped around his waist, pulling his burgeoning erection into direct contact with its new favorite place in the entire universe.

"Have I given you any reason to believe I can't?"

She hadn't.

In between working on his house, shopping for furniture, and meeting with Miranda's mobility coach, Robin, to learn the art of running as Miranda's guide, they'd still found the time to get naked and crazy at least once a day when he was off.

Usually more.

On the days he was stuck at work, especially on his overnight shifts, he discovered just how intimate talking on the phone could be. And not only the phone sex, which should have seemed juvenile but instead had been incredibly erotic, despite the lack of privacy in a firehouse filled with nosy assholes.

No, most of the time they just spent hours talking about everything and nothing. Stupid stuff, whatever came to mind about their pasts.

She told him about all the outdoorsy things she'd done as a kid, camping and white-water rafting in the Adirondacks whenever her father could clear a spot in his busy work schedule to take her and her brother.

He confessed to secretly enjoying the trip his family took to see the museums in D.C. when he was ten, even though he'd complained long and loud about it at the time because he wanted to go to Disney and been outvoted by his siblings.

She told him about the nightmares that still sometimes chased her in the night about the accident where she'd lost her sight, although she never went into detail about what had actually happened.

He told her about the nightmares he'd had after the twin towers had come down, and the certainty which had grown in the years following that being a firefighter was what he was meant to do, despite that hard proof of the danger the job held.

It surprised him when he realized how personal some of the things he was sharing with her were. But it never felt awkward or forced. The distance of talking over the phone, with only her voice in his ear, somehow made it easier to open up about things he'd never told anyone before.

Some of them not even to Cody.

Like how he'd hadn't spent the hours in a motel room after junior prom getting between Barbara Franchetti's legs like everyone assumed. Instead, he'd let her cry on his shoulder about the scummy ex-boyfriend who dumped her the week before prom so he could take the girl he'd been cheating on her with since Christmas break in her place.

Or when he'd given all his treasured football gear from his all-star senior season to a teen whose apartment went up in flames a few years ago. His single mom didn't have the money to replace what had been destroyed in time for the game the following day, where he'd be seen by scouts from colleges as well as the pros.

In some weird way, the hours he and Miranda had spent on the phone were almost more intimate than the ones they spent in bed.

And yet, with all that talking, all that intimacy, he somehow still hadn't gotten around to mentioning his trips down to Queens weren't just to hang out with Cody. That they were actually doing prep work for the lieutenant's test.

An oversight he wasn't in any hurry to correct.

Telling her he was a slow learner was way different from having it shoved in her face.

"So?" She ground herself against him and gave a sharp nip on his lower lip, dragging his attention back to her and her question. "One more time?"

Fuck.

He knew when he was beat.

"Just once more. Then"—he returned the nip, with interest—"you're all mine."

She smiled and unwrapped her legs with a slow slide of skin that left him gritting his teeth. "Deal."

He waited while she went through the now-familiar routine of deep breathing to expand her lungs. When she nodded she was ready, he held his finger over the button on his watch, pressing it to start the stopwatch feature the second she slipped beneath the surface.

He understood why running in the Marine Corps Marathon was so important to her. But he had to wonder why she was pushing so damn hard to hit the seemingly arbitrary two-and-a-half-minute mark underwater. Was it to prove she was doing everything she could to honor the memory of her friends who had died?

Or to punish herself because she hadn't died with them?

Like him, there were some things she still kept to herself.

Miranda broke the surface with a gasp. He stopped the timer and knew she wasn't going to like what he told her.

"Two nineteen."

"What?" Wheezing, she shook her head. "No way."

"Yes way." He caught her arm. "Come on, you're exhausted. Tomorrow's another day."

"But..." Her shoulders slumped as she tipped her head back with a sigh. "Okay, okay. A promise is a promise."

"That's right. And I have your promise you'll do whatever I want." He took her arm and tugged her out into the center of the pool, where he brought her between his legs and leaned back, making a raft of himself for her to float on as he slowly moved them toward the shallow end with his hands.

"I think the promise was that *we'd* do whatever you want." She tried to look stern, but there was laughter in her voice.

"Same thing. I'm pretty sure whatever I want, you'll want, too." He swung his legs down now that he could touch bottom, pulling her wet body even closer to his. "Right?"

"Hmm." She made a face like she had to think about it. "We'll see."

"We'll see, huh?" With a growl he bent, put his shoulder to her middle, and swung her up over his shoulder in a fireman's carry, eliciting a laughing shriek as he sloshed through the shallow water and up the stairs to the pool deck.

She squirmed and protested between laughs, shrieking again when he brought his hand down on her upturned ass with a wet smack. "How about we see what you think about how loud I can make you—"

He stumbled to both a physical and verbal stop.

"Fuck." He whispered the word under his breath as he stared at the three people clustered in Miranda's open kitchen door. Two of them were wide-eyed, with mouths open in identical *ohs* of surprise.

The third looked ready to murder him where he stood.

Breaking free of his shock, he gently put Miranda back on her feet, whispering against her ear as he did, "You have company. Family, I think," he added, recognizing the younger woman as the one who'd taken Miranda and Sam away in her car the day after their disastrous first dinner together. Her sister Julietta, the nursing student.

Which meant the older woman was probably her mother. The man glaring daggers at him was too young to be her father, so that had to make him her big brother, Santino.

He was seriously fucked.

Miranda whispered *shit* before asking, "Where?"

"Kitchen door. Jules, and maybe your mom and brother." He applied light pressure to her shoulders to turn her so she was facing the right direction. And, conveniently, blocking his body with her own.

His board shorts might be baggy enough to hide the erection Miranda had teased to life, but better safe than sorry until the stupid bastard went back down again.

"Miranda! *¿Que pasando aqui?*"

"Mom." There was a distinct hint of panic in her voice. "I wasn't expecting you today."

Although, Ben realized, they probably should have.

Her sister Isobel had stopped by unannounced the night before on the pretext of looking for something she thought she'd forgotten when she packed. She hadn't stayed long, but it was clear she'd been annoyed to find them in a state of rumpled disarray on Miranda's couch.

No clothes had started coming off—yet—but it had been pretty obvious what they'd been up to. She must have gone right home and tattled to their mother about what she'd seen. After having met her only twice, he had no trouble believing she'd stir the shit pot out of spite after Miranda basically kicked her out.

And confiscated her key.

Mrs. Hernandez let loose with a bout of rapid Spanish. From the way Miranda tensed, it wasn't anything good.

"Mom," she said loudly, cutting her off mid-rant, "English, please. You always told us it was rude to talk about someone in a language they can't understand."

Reprimanding her mother must have been a big no-no, judging by how Julietta's eyes rounded as she slapped a hand over her mouth.

Her brother's eyes went the opposite direction, narrowing under his dark brows. "Is that how you speak to your mother?"

"Tino, what are you doing here?"

"Is there a reason I shouldn't be?" He crossed his arms, lethal gaze directed at Ben as he asked it.

"Since it's Thursday and you should be at work with *Papí*, yeah." She hesitated. "He didn't come, too, did he?"

"No, he's too busy. We're in the middle of a huge project."

If Ben wasn't mistaken, she deflated a little, rather than seeming relieved. "And yet, here *you* are."

"One of us had to take care of family business. Just be glad it was me."

She cocked her head. "And I'm the *business* that needs taking care of?"

Her brother might not have, but Ben clearly recognized the warning signs of temper in her cool words. Hoping to head off full-out warfare, he put his arm around Miranda's shoulders and walked with her to the lounger. "Why don't we go inside and talk." No need to give the neighbors an earful of family drama.

He picked up Miranda's coverup and handed it to her before slipping his t-shirt on. It clung uncomfortably to the wet skin he hadn't bothered to towel off first.

"*We* can go inside," Tino said. "You can leave."

He wanted to argue, but it wasn't his fight. Or his decision. "Miranda?"

"Ben stays." She laced her fingers through his.

"*El no es familia,*" Tino snarled.

"No, he's not family, but he was invited, which is more than I can say for you." She reached out and touched the lounger with her free hand to orient herself. "Sam, house."

The dog, who had learned to stay far away from the pool when they were in it or risk a surprise dousing as they splashed, trotted behind them as they walked toward the kitchen door. The two women stepped back, but her brother refused to give ground so easily.

"*Estas haciendo la ridicula.*"

"*No, tu eres.*" Miranda kept walking as she spat out the words. At the last second before she'd collide with him, Tino moved aside, letting them both pass. Although not without a promise of retribution in his eyes when he caught Ben's gaze.

"What did he say?" he murmured to Miranda.

She didn't bother whispering her reply. "That I was making a fool of myself. And I told him that no, he was. Which is the truth," she said, angling the words over her shoulder toward her brother.

He almost groaned out loud. Jesus, didn't she know not to poke a bear when it was already growling?

It was her sister who came to the rescue.

She moved to Miranda's other side and looped their arms together. "Miranda, why don't we go upstairs so you can rinse off and get changed? Then we can all sit down and have a nice, cool drink and talk. Politely." That last seemed directed at Tino even though she never looked his way.

Miranda's fingers tightened on his. "But Ben—"

"Can take care of himself for two minutes," Julietta said. The look she tossed him dared him to admit any different.

Okay, it seemed she wasn't a fan of his either. Great.

"I'll be fine." He brought their still-linked hands up so he could press a kiss to her fingers. "But you might want to actually introduce me to everyone first."

She laughed. "Yeah, that might help, huh?" She turned, forcing her sister to let go. His hand, he noted with satisfaction, she kept hold of. "Mom, Jules, Tino." Her mouth curled on his name. "This is Ben Murphy. He lives next door. Ben, my mother, Inez Hernandez, my sister Julietta, and my brother, Santino, who seems to forget he's not my father."

"I'm your brother, which is as good as, since he isn't here," he snapped.

"Okay, clothes, then talk." Julietta all but yanked her sister from the room, cutting off whatever reply Miranda was about to give.

Which left Ben standing there being eyed with a combination of distrust and anger. Fair enough. They'd just caught him manhandling Miranda, not to mention slapping her ass.

Fuck, he *really* hoped they hadn't heard what they'd been talking about.

That would be…beyond awkward.

Taking the proactive approach, he did what he did best. With a smile set at charming, he said, "Mrs. Hernandez, it's very nice to meet you. Can I get you a glass of lemonade, or maybe some coffee?"

She sniffed, clearly unimpressed. "It's my daughter's kitchen. I think I can get my own drink, thank you."

"You seem to have made yourself pretty at home." Tino scowled as he dropped into the chair at the head of the table where Miranda usually sat. "Don't get used to it."

It was true. He did feel at home here. Since he still only had a few pieces of furniture scattered around his house, Miranda's place was their primary hangout.

And despite his brand-new bedroom set being delivered a few days ago—and well christened by them many times since—her bed had become his default place to spend the night. Something he normally didn't do.

He'd never actually *slept* with any of the women he slept with.

Until now.

Not the kind of thing he should be thinking about, which he realized when he saw Tino's scowl darken. "Miranda makes it easy to feel at home around her."

"Easy to take advantage of her, you mean."

He barely bit back a snort. "If you believe that, you don't know your sister as well as you think you do."

Tino sat forward and thumped his fist on the table, rattling the salt and pepper shakers in their metal stand. "Don't tell me I don't know my own sister. I know what you're doing. You saw a girl who was blind and alone, and decided she'd be easy pickings."

Only the fact he was looking out for Miranda's welfare kept his temper in check. "First of all, she's not a girl. She's a woman." Tino bristled at the implication, so he hurried on. "And second, your sister is nobody's fool. She knows how to take care of herself."

"Maybe before." He murmured *gracias* to his mother as she put a glass of lemonade in front of him. Ben didn't miss that she hadn't offered to pour one for him. "But without her sight, she's dependent on everyone around her for everything. How can she tell the difference between, say, a helpful neighbor and a predator?"

"The same way I can tell the difference between an overprotective brother and a jackass," Miranda answered as she walked into the room. "I use my brain."

From the disgruntled and slightly abashed look on her brother's face, he hadn't expected her to rejoin the conversation so fast.

Neither had he, although he was grateful for her quick-change act. Judging by the haphazard way her wet hair was still pulled back into an off-kilter ponytail, she'd done nothing more than strip off her bathing suit and throw on some shorts and a top.

Which was clinging to parts of her damp body in places he really didn't need to be thinking about at the moment.

"Miranda, language."

"I'm sorry, Mom, but he is. Tino, leave Ben alone. He isn't a predator, for God's sake."

"Then why was he playing grabby hands with you in the pool?"

"Santino! *Dios mio*, how did I raise such children?" Mrs. Hernandez hustled over to Miranda and took her by the elbow. "*Mija*, sit and rest. I'll get you a nice glass of lemonade and some cookies."

He held his breath, waiting for the explosion sure to come, both from the arm-grabbing and the patronizing tone. To his surprise,

Miranda went meekly with her mother and sat in the chair she directed her to on the far side of the table. Where, he realized after a second, she'd be out of the way.

Where was the anger? The spark of indignation at being treated like a helpless child?

Where was his Miranda?

As Mrs. Hernandez bustled around the kitchen, opening cabinets and shifting things as she looked for cookies—which were in the cabinet closest to the fridge, if she'd bothered to ask—Ben could finally see the smolder of temper in Miranda, although she was keeping it tightly banked. By the time her mother deposited the glass and a napkin with several chocolate chip cookies on it in front of her like she was five, he was surprised the top of her head hadn't blown completely off.

"Here's your snack, *mija*."

"Thanks, Mom." She touched the edge of the table, but before she could even try to locate the glass, her mother slid it closer and pressed Miranda's hand around it. Her lips tightened into a hard line before she loosened them into a weak smile. "Thanks."

He shook his head. What the hell was wrong with everyone?

"Actually," he said, walking to where Miranda sat and putting his hand on her shoulder where she grabbed it like a lifeline, "we were about to come in for lunch when you got here." Snuck in uninvited was more accurate, but he didn't point that out. "Would you all like to join us?"

"We don't need you to invite us to eat in my sister's house," Tino snapped.

"I think that's a wonderful idea," Julietta said, stepping into the breach before the next angry volley could be launched. "I'm sure there's something in the fridge Mom and I can throw together for everyone."

The slump in Miranda's shoulders had him wanting to kick each and every member of her family in the ass. "No, that's okay. Miranda and I can handle it." He gave her hand a squeeze.

"Yes." She pushed her chair back and stood. "Jules, you and Mom sit and rest. We've got this."

From the quick grin on Julietta's face, she hadn't missed Miranda turning her mother's own words back on her. "Sounds good to me." She took a seat and gave Ben a speculative look that was at least a little friendlier than the one she'd aimed his way earlier. "I'm starving."

Her mother wasn't going to be as easy to vanquish.

"Miranda, you shouldn't have to—"

"Mrs. Hernandez, please, it would be my pleasure to help make you lunch as thanks for all of the wonderful food you've made that Miranda's been kind enough to share with me." He smiled broadly, pouring on the charm as he held out the chair at the opposite end of the table from her son. No woman had ever been able to resist when he resorted to using what Cody referred to as his "Five-Alarm Panty Dropper."

Of course, the only thing he wanted Mrs. Hernandez to drop was the overprotective mother routine.

"Oh, but..." She wrung her hands, glancing at Miranda, who already had the refrigerator open. A glance at Julietta brought her no support. With a loud unhappy sigh of resignation, she took her seat.

Ben joined Miranda at the counter, where she'd deposited cold cuts and bread. They constructed sandwiches to the deafening silence coming from the table behind them. He didn't need to look to know they were the sole focus of everyone's rapt attention.

It felt like being a probie on his first day again, being silently judged, weighed, and measured. Only he wasn't as certain he'd win the respect and acceptance of Miranda's family as easily as he'd done with the men and women he worked with.

The thought stopped him cold.

Did he want their respect and acceptance? Why would that matter? What he wanted was for them to respect Miranda. To see her for who she really was, and not the helpless invalid they insisted on treating her as. What they thought about him didn't matter a damn bit.

Okay, maybe it mattered a little.

He carried the platter of sandwiches to the table while Miranda got out paper plates and napkins. Tino eyed the food with suspicion, but didn't hesitate to grab one and wolf down a bite. "You should use whole wheat," he said as he chewed.

"Ben and I prefer multigrain." She offered him a napkin. "And don't talk with your mouth full. It's disgusting."

Tino froze with the same look of "that was creepy" on his face Ben had felt a time or two himself.

As Miranda started to circle around the table to where her mother had put her, Ben reached out and touched her arm. "Hold on a sec." To Tino he said, "You're in your sister's seat."

"What?"

Miranda shook her head. "Ben, it doesn't matter."

"Of course, it matters. That's where you always sit."

"What's the big deal?" Tino demanded.

"The big deal is she knows exactly where everything in the kitchen is relative to *that* spot. By making her sit someplace else, you're making her life more difficult. And I know you don't want to do that."

He left the *unless you're an asshole* part unspoken.

Annoyance flashed through Tino's expression, but he pushed himself to his feet. "Fine. Whatever." He slid his plate and glass to the left and took the empty seat next to Julietta. "Happy?"

"Thrilled." He moved Miranda's glass to the seat at the head of the table and took the chair to her right. After a second's hesitation, Miranda sat. She looked flustered, but oddly pleased.

As Ben passed the platter of sandwiches to Mrs. Hernandez, he caught the same glint of speculation in her eyes as Julietta had had.

"So." Tino ripped off a huge bite of roast beef and Swiss, forcing them to wait while he took his time to chew and swallow in an obvious poke at Miranda's scolding comment. "You've made yourself at home in my sister's house. You're eating her food. Swimming in her pool. So, I have to wonder, *good neighbor Ben*." He put an ugly twist on the words as he stared him dead in the eyes.

"Exactly what else have you been helping yourself to while you're over here with nobody keeping tabs on you?"

Chapter 14

Miranda froze at her brother's words, the bite of sandwich she'd been swallowing getting stuck halfway down. Had he seriously just asked that question? In front of her?

In front of their *mother*?

Furious but still unable to talk past the lump of meat and bread clogging her throat, she resorted to old habits. She swung her foot out under the table and connected with his shin, earning a faint grunt.

"What was that for?"

The jackass had the nerve to sound like he really didn't know.

Jules piped up. "What my idiot brother meant to say, Ben, is that it's nice to see Miranda has a neighbor who's so friendly and around a lot. We worry about her being all alone. And it's not only because of your condition, sweetie."

That last was clearly aimed at her. Miranda swallowed hard and cleared the blockage. "Being blind doesn't mean I can't make friends, Jules. Or keep myself from being taken advantage of," she added for Tino.

"Oh, so now he's not just your neighbor, but your *friend*?" Tino scoffed. "The same guy who left you bleeding on the floor a couple of weeks ago instead of taking you to the hospital? Some friend."

She groaned silently. Sweet baby Jesus. Was no one ever going to let that stupid night go?

"Stop being such a fu—freaking jerk. I wasn't bleeding, I wasn't on the floor, and I was the one who refused to go to the hospital."

"Listen to yourself. You were hurt, and yet you're defending him. And you wonder why we're worried?"

"Tino. Let it go. I mean it."

He didn't. But he did change tactics.

"If he's just your friend, *hermanita*, then why did he have his hand on your ass a little while ago? Ow!" His grunt held more pain this time. Probably because Jules was wearing shoes and was able to inflict more damage than she had with her bare foot.

She made a mental note to thank her sister later.

"I know you're her brother," Ben said, his voice firmer than she'd ever heard it before, "but that doesn't give you the right to talk to her that way."

"It was a fair question."

"It was rude," her mother said.

"But *Mamá*—"

"Enough, *mijo*."

Bowing to the motherly authority in her tone, Tino subsided with a final mutter. Not that his silence would last for long. Her brother was rarely able to contain his opinion when he was sure he was right.

Which was always.

Ben, bless him, jumped on the live grenade her brother had left lying on the table.

"Mrs. Hernandez, I want you to know I mean your daughter no harm, and certainly no disrespect. What you saw was, well, two consenting adults being affectionate when they believed themselves to be alone."

Her mother made a humming sound that was neither agreement nor disagreement. "You understand why we might be concerned about this sudden...affection, considering you and my daughter have known each other for such a short time."

"You can learn a lot about a person in just a few weeks," Ben replied. "The important things, anyway." His hand suddenly closed over hers where it lay on the table. "The rest we'll figure out as we go."

Another hum from her mother. "So, you're saying, what? You have serious intentions toward my daughter?"

Feeling the tension that made Ben's fingers flinch on hers, Miranda's heart wilted a little. She summoned up a lighthearted laugh. "Mom, please. There's nothing serious. Like Ben said, we're just figuring it out as we go. Right, Ben?"

"Yeah. Right. Exactly." He gave her hand a quick squeeze before withdrawing.

And it was more than just his touch he removed. For the rest of the meal, it seemed like he'd stepped behind a mask. He was charming to her mother and sister, cautiously polite to her brother, and to her...he was the perfect friendly neighbor.

It was stupid for that to hurt, because that's all he was. She knew Ben didn't have serious relationships, even if she didn't agree with his reasoning. But if the sudden ache in her chest was anything to go by, some part of her had been considering it anyway. Thinking they might be inching closer to the possibility.

Only, judging by Ben's flinch and subsequent withdrawal, she'd been the only one making that mistake.

Lunch seemed to drag on forever, especially with Tino taking potshots at Ben whenever the conversation gave him the chance. To his credit, Ben remained civil, but she could sense a subtle tension building in him.

Sooner or later, he was going to shoot back.

Desperate to head off that possibility, she started clearing the table the second the last sandwich was consumed. Several chairs scraped back as soon as she did.

"*Mija*, let me—"

"I've got it, Mom."

"Then I'll make coffee."

"No!" Her family would linger at the table for hours if that happened. "What I mean is, lunch was nice, but Ben and I both need to take showers, and I'm sure the three of you have much more important things to do than sit around waiting on us."

"Nope," Tino said. "Not a thing."

Wishing she was still sitting so she could kick him again, she gave a tight smile. "Well, did you ever think maybe *we* had other things to do?"

"And what kind of things would that be?"

From his tone she knew his mind had gone right to the gutter. "Nothing that's any of your business." She ignored the *pfft* he gave in commentary and was about to give everyone another push toward the door when Ben spoke.

"Actually, a shower and a change of clothes sounds pretty good. I think I'll leave you folks to your coffee and head home."

"Oh." Nonplussed, she struggled for a reason to make him stay. "Are you sure? You could..." Well, no. Offering to let him use her shower probably wasn't smart. Not with Tino just waiting to pounce. "If you're sure you won't stay?"

She tried to put as much pleading in her voice as she could without sounding desperate, but he either didn't hear, or chose to ignore it.

"Yeah, well, I have some things to work on over at the house I've been neglecting, so I should get back to them."

"That's right," her mother said, "Miranda mentioned you were renovating your house. By yourself." No one could miss what she thought of that.

Ben laughed. "Not entirely by myself, no. I'm nowhere near that talented. But I'm lucky enough to know some people who are."

"They truly are," Miranda said, remembering the clean lines of the hand-made cabinets. "You should see his new kitchen. It's absolutely gorgeous!"

Silence followed her words.

"How would you…" Tino stopped himself before he completed the question.

"You really need to stop underestimating your sister," Ben said quietly into the silence.

Tino didn't reply, but that was a promising sign. Her brother sometimes had trouble operating his mouth and his brain at the same time. If he wasn't talking, maybe it meant he was actually thinking about what Ben had said.

Would miracles never cease?

"It was very nice to meet you all." Ben brushed her arm with his hand before it fell away. "I'll see you later, okay?"

That was encouraging, at least.

"Okay. Bye." She summoned up a smile for him when all she wanted to do was follow him out the kitchen door and all the way over to his place, and find out why it suddenly felt like he was a million miles away.

"Why the hell is he going out the back?" Tino demanded as the screen door bumped closed.

And the miracle was over.

"Because it's shorter going than going out and around the front." She decided mentioning the gate between their backyards wasn't necessary. Or smart.

"I like him," Jules said as Miranda continued picking up the used paper plates from the table. "I didn't think I would, but…he's actually kind of sweet. And hot," she added, earning a growl from Tino. "No wonder Izzy was pissed at you."

Outrage flared, swift and furious.

"I *knew* it! I knew she was the reason you all showed up here today. What did she say? That the 'studmuffin' next door was showing interest in me, so of course it had to mean he was up to no good? Because why else would a nice, decent, good-looking man be interested in me rather than her?"

Which he was. A fact that still gave her a very unsisterly jolt of smug pleasure every time she thought about it.

Isobel might have gotten Umberto, but she wasn't getting Ben.

Of course, after today, she might not either.

"She was worried about you." But from her mother's tone, it sounded like she was beginning to have some doubts about the true nature of Isobel's supposed concern.

"She walked in on us kissing last night and pitched a fit." Using the key Miranda had forgotten to get back from her when she kicked her out the first time. An oversight she'd immediately corrected.

If only she could take back her mother's key as easily.

"The only thing she was worried about was not getting what she wanted."

"Meaning Ben." Jules was well acquainted with their sister's pathological need to be the center of attention, since they'd shared a room growing up. Miranda had no idea how they both survived to adulthood.

"Well, I still don't trust him."

She sighed and shook her head at her brother's stubborn tone. "Tino, I love you to death, but it doesn't really matter what you think. I'm an adult. I get to have a relationship with a man without having to run it by the family first."

"Now it's a relationship? A second ago you were both saying it was just casual."

"Because no man wants to be ganged up on and put on the spot by a woman's family about how serious his intentions are, especially after only a few weeks."

"Oh, *mija*, I'm sorry," her mother sighed.

"No, Mom, it's okay. I know you all came here today out of love and concern for me. But honestly, you don't need to worry so much. I'm doing just fine taking care of myself."

No, it wouldn't always be easy, and sometimes she'd stumble and make mistakes. Probably some big ones. But she was doing it, living her life again, on her own terms.

Even better, she was *happy*.

And a big part of that happiness had just walked himself out of her house to go take a shower she wanted nothing more than to be sharing with him.

"Look. I love you all, but you need to leave now."

"What about my coffee?"

It was tough, but she refrained from rolling her eyes at Tino's petulant demand to be waited on. And from smacking him. "You have coffee at home. Go make it there."

"We should go," her mother said.

Tino sputtered. "But...we haven't settled anything yet."

"Yes, I think we have." A few soft footsteps, then her mother touched her cheek in a motherly caress that almost brought tears to her eyes.

"I'm still not sure how I feel about this young man, but I can see you like him, and the way he looks at you...well. I'll try to keep an open mind, *mija*. And to remember you're an adult who can have a relationship without needing our approval," she added, echoing Miranda's words back to her with a hint of apology.

She desperately wanted to ask how, exactly, Ben had looked at her. But settled for wrapping her arms around her mother in a grateful hug. "Thanks, *Mami*. That means a lot."

"I will always worry about you, though," her mother whispered against her ear. "So will your father, even if he's still too stubborn to leave your disagreement in the past. No matter how strong and brave you think you always have to be, you're still our little girl, and we would move mountains for you."

And that was enough to finally breach the dam on her tears.

Breathing in the familiar clean scent of Ivory soap and lavender, she spent a few minutes just absorbing the comfort of her mother's arms. For the first time since losing her sight, it didn't feel like they were smothering her.

They felt like home.

Five minutes later, she was waving her family off from the front step. Tino tapped the horn as they drove away. When the growl of the engine rounded the corner and disappeared, she reached down and gave Sam's ear a tug.

"Come on, Sammy. Let's go find our guy."

There's nothing serious.

Miranda's words chased after Ben as he stalked across her backyard toward the gate connecting their properties. Retreated, was more like it. But what else could he have done? Stick around for her family to ask more questions he clearly didn't know the answers to?

There's nothing serious.

She was right. There wasn't.

So why had hearing her say it cut so sharply?

Yes, they saw each other or talked almost every day. And had incendiary sex that all but scorched the sheets. So what? Proximity and chemistry, that's all it was.

But neither accounted for why, whenever they were apart, he felt a little lost. A little less. Or why he always knew how many hours it would be until he was with her again.

What the hell was that if not serious?

Slamming into his kitchen, he grabbed a beer from the fridge and drained half in a few brain-freezing gulps. No, damn it. It wasn't serious. It couldn't be. What they had was no different from any other woman he got involved with. Just simple, mutually satisfying sex that would eventually wind down and fizzle out, just like every other time.

So why did it upset him so much to hear Miranda call it *nothing serious*?

He hung his head and gave a bitter laugh at his own expense.

With all the phone calls and late-night conversations, the soul baring on both sides, in some stupid corner of his brain he'd been spinning some kind of idiotic thoughts about their relationship becoming something more. Something deeper. Something he'd never managed to have before.

Clearly, he'd been mistaken.

Because really, what would a woman like Miranda want with a dumb schmuck like him? Sure, he was good for helping her train and giving her a few dozen orgasms. All that made him was a personal trainer with benefits.

But what if he could be more?

What if he *wanted* to be more?

What if she didn't?

For the first time, he felt empathy with the women like Val who'd hinted they might want more than a few nights of sheet-ripping sex. Was this how he'd made them feel when he brushed them off, reminding them he never promised anything more than he'd given?

If so, he owed every one of them an apology, because this feeling *sucked*.

Banging on the front door jarred him from his maudlin thoughts. Probably Tino, come to give him more grief over touching his sister. Great, just what he needed.

Bolting down another gulp of beer as he stalked through the house to the door, he yanked it open and barked, "What?"

Only it wasn't Tino on the other side.

Miranda flinched slightly at the gruff demand, making him feel like an ass. "Shit. Sorry. I didn't know it was you."

She managed a wan smile. "Well, that's encouraging, I guess." After a pause she asked, "Can I come in?"

Despite the urge to say no, he shrugged and stepped back to make room for her and Sam to pass. "Sure, why not." After closing the door behind them, he leaned against it and stared at her with an unhealthy mixture of anger and longing. "So, what's up?"

"Got another one of those? I could really use it."

He didn't bother to ask how she knew he was holding a beer. The woman was like a damn bloodhound. "Don't you have to get back to your family?"

"Nope."

Which told him exactly nothing. He sighed. "Fine."

It wasn't until he'd grabbed another Heineken from the fridge that he realized only Sam had followed him to the kitchen. The dog nosed at the lower cupboard where Ben kept a box of the same organic dog treats Miranda gave him. He sat and looked up with an expectant doggy grin, tail fanning the wood floor like a furry dust mop.

He transferred both bottle necks to one hand and rubbed down Sam's soft back, now devoid of the harness rig he'd been wearing a minute ago. That signal he was "off duty" was the only time he was allowed to directly interact with him without Miranda's okay.

"I guess this means you're both planning to stay a while."

He wasn't sure how he felt about that.

Hell, he wasn't sure how he felt about anything right now.

He gave Sam's ears a scratch the way he liked before offering him one of the treats, which the dog trotted off to devour in the corner. With no excuses left to delay, he went in search of Miranda.

He found her in the living room, seated at one end of the sectional that had been delivered earlier. "Here." He placed the bottle in the hand she held out, but stayed standing.

"Thanks." She took a sip, then ran her free hand over the cushion with an expression of pleasure. "It's so soft. But I thought you were getting the leather."

So had he.

When he'd asked her to go furniture shopping with him, he'd been thinking complete man-cave set-up: oversized couch, massive screen 4K tv, heated leather recliners with built-in cup holders and massage. Stuff he and the guys would be comfortable hanging out on while watching the game, but not be able to do too much damage to.

The recliners ended up being too pricey, so he'd settled on the biggest leather sectional that would fit in the living room and still leave space to walk.

He shrugged. "I changed my mind." All because he couldn't get the look on her face out of his head when she'd sat on the sample in the showroom and petted it like it was her new favorite thing. The same look she'd had just now. Pure tactile gratification.

For that, he'd been willing to give up the leather for microsuede. *Idiot.*

He glanced toward the door with a sense of trepidation. "You sure your family isn't going to miss you? Or come banging on my door to kick my ass?"

Miranda groaned. "I am so sorry about them putting you through the third degree. And there will be no ass kickings, I promise. I sent them home."

That surprised him. "And they went?"

"I know, right? It kind of shocked me, too." Her lips rose in a shy grin. "I think it was because we gave them something to think about. Thank you for that."

"I didn't do anything."

"That's bull and you know it. You being there helped me finally open their eyes and see me as a capable human being who can function on my own without their constant interference. That's something I've never been able to do before." She grimaced. "As if you couldn't tell by the way I slipped right back into old patterns and let my mother manage me. Thank you for reminding them—and me—I'm not helpless anymore."

He shrugged away the zing of pleasure her words caused. "Sure. Glad to help."

The smile faded. "Are you still upset about what my mother said? I know she really put you on the spot asking about your intentions, but I swear, I'm not expecting anything more than you want to give."

"And what if I want to give more than you're expecting?"

Miranda froze. "What?"

Yeah, what?

He sealed his mouth over the beer bottle and drained it to keep from saying anything else stupid. Like talking about his *feelings*. What the fuck was wrong with him?

"Ben?"

"Forget it."

"Like hell." She put her beer down on the floor against the sofa and stood to face him. "Everything was fine between us until my mother asked that question. Then, it was like you were only half there, with one foot already out the door."

"No, things were fine until you made it clear you don't consider anything about us to be serious. So, I just gave you what you wanted."

"What I wanted?" She shook her head, looking confused. "No, that's what *you* wanted."

"Did I say that?"

"Yes! You said we were just taking things one day at a time."

"No, I said we were figuring things out as we go. I also said we'd already figured out the important stuff." He huffed out an unamused laugh. "Guess I was wrong about that, too."

"No. No, no, no. You flinched from the question. I felt it."

He had. But not for the reason she obviously thought.

"I've never been asked that question before," he admitted. "How was I supposed to answer her when we've never even talked about it ourselves?"

"So, let's talk about it." She reached out and found his chest, his arm, then his hand, and gave it a tug toward the couch. When he didn't budge, she added softly, "Please?"

Fuck.

It looked like they were going to talk about feelings after all.

"This is starting to become a habit for us," he grumbled as he dropped onto the couch.

She sat next to him, one leg under her so she was partially facing him. "Talking things out?"

"And you being bossy about it."

Her lips quirked. "I thought you liked it when I got bossy."

Yeah, he did. But now wasn't the time to admit it.

"Look, I'm sorry I flaked out back at your place. I've never been interrogated by a woman's family before." He tipped his head thoughtfully. "Well, except for Lily Estrada's dad, although that wasn't so much an interrogation as a warning."

"Oh?" There was a tinge of jealousy in the word that suddenly made him feel better than he had since he'd escaped from her kitchen.

"Yeah. Graduation. I didn't get her home till almost dawn from the after-party, and her dad was waiting on the front porch with a cup of coffee and his twelve gauge."

She sucked in a sharp breath. "He threatened you with a shotgun?"

"He didn't have to. It was just there, leaning against the house next to his chair. He never even said a word, but I got the message." The choice of getting between Lily's sweet thighs again or keeping his balls had been a surprisingly simple one to make.

"Jesus."

"Yeah, it was an experience not worth repeating. Good thing I don't have to worry about your dad threatening to shoot my junk off for touching you." He was going for levity, but the pensive crease on her forehead gave him pause. "Or do I?"

"Probably not."

"You don't sound as sure about that as I'd like." Not even close. "For the record, I'm particularly fond of my penis."

"For the record, so am I." Miranda paused. "But that's not why I like you. Or why I enjoy spending time with you."

"My penis is disappointed to hear that."

She smacked his arm. "Stop that. I'm being serious."

Which was exactly why he'd tried to make a joke out of it. Serious never turned out well for him. In fact, serious usually screwed everything the fuck up. Time to put his best weapon to use before that happened.

He took the hand she'd hit him with and drew his tongue across her knuckles. "You know, Legs, why don't we—"

"Are we dating?"

"Uh..." He blinked. "What?"

"I asked, are we dating? Because as far as I can tell, we probably are."

"We're, um..." Just like in school when a teacher called on him with an unexpected question, his brain went into scramble mode, words jumbling and tumbling out of control. Only this time, he had a feeling the consequences of a wrong answer would be much worse than looking stupid in front of his classmates.

Which only made everything in his head spin faster.

Miranda didn't seem to notice. "I mean, we spend just about every night together. We go out places, do stuff together. There's nobody else either of us is seeing...is there?"

"No!" Thank Christ, he finally managed to bitch-slap his thoughts into order. "I told you. I haven't looked at another woman since we met."

A relieved smile flickered across her face. "Good."

"What about you?" he felt compelled to ask.

"Me?" She snorted. "Right."

"Yeah, you. Guys look at you all the time." A fact that made him want to snarl every time it happened.

"Yeah, because I'm blind. It's the weird factor, like staring at a car wreck on the side of the road as you drive by. They can't help themselves."

"No, it's because you're beautiful. And smart, and caring, and sexy as hell." And a dozen more things. But he knew her well enough now to see the faint rise in color on her cheeks that hinted at her embarrassment, so he left it at that.

The woman really didn't take compliments well at all.

"Four years."

He barely heard the softly spoken words. "What?"

"It's been four years since a man has treated me like a regular, desirable woman. Well, except one, but he ended up wanting Isobel, so he doesn't count."

The undertone of hurt with a pinch of loneliness caused an ache deep in his chest. No wonder she'd been so certain he'd push her aside to chase after her sister. "Men are idiots." Why else would they have overlooked everything this woman had to offer for so long? "Especially that one."

Miranda gave a suspiciously watery laugh. "Yeah, they are. Except for you, it seems." She closed her other hand over both of theirs. "So, with that in mind, and since we seem to agree we're already dating without realizing that's what we were doing, let's make this official. Ben, would you like to be my boyfriend?"

Chapter 15

"Boyfriend?" The word tasted foreign on his tongue.

And terrifying.

But also good. Really, really good.

Almost as good as hearing Miranda say it.

"I know, it sounds kind of juvenile, so you can call it something else, but..." Her grip on his hand tightened. "You were right. What you said to my mother. You can learn a lot about a person in just a couple of weeks. And I've learned that, whatever term we use to define it, you're the kind of man I would be proud to call mine. So...what do you think?" She swallowed hard, waiting for an answer.

Proud to call mine.

The words bounced around his chaotic brain a few times, before they finally settled into place like a comforting balm over the rising panic. But they couldn't wipe it out entirely. There was too much history. Too many painful examples of failure.

"You know I don't know how to be a good boyfriend."

"Is that a no?"

"No, damn it, it's not a no. It's an 'I don't want to fuck this up.'" He pulled free of her hold and gently cradled her face in his hands. "I promise I'll do my best not to, but this is me we're talking about. I'm bound to fuck up at least once or twice along the way. Hell, probably a lot more than that. Please promise you won't give up on me when I do."

Because he *would* fuck it up.

It's what he did. What he'd always done with women, until he'd finally accepted he wasn't capable of being good enough for any of them to stick around for, and gave up trying. Since then, he'd soothed all the old hurts with mind-blowing sex, satisfying every woman who came to his bed until their eyes rolled back in unsurpassed satiation.

Then *he'd* been the one to leave.

If he put his heart—and okay, ego—on the line again, if he tried to be something he'd never managed to be for anyone else, he wasn't sure he'd survive failing this time. Because that meant having Miranda walk away like all the rest.

But he was so far in with her already, he didn't think he had a choice anymore.

Miranda put one hand lightly over his. "I'll promise, if you promise me the same thing. You're not the only one who's bound to screw up, you know."

"But I'll be the one to do it first."

She gave a small laugh, just as he'd hoped. "It's not a competition."

"Good, because I'd totally win." Of that he had no doubt.

Before she could protest that assertion, he swooped in and took her mouth in a gentle but possessive kiss. Her sweet lips softened beneath his, parting under the persuasive prodding of his tongue and welcoming him in with eager enthusiasm.

Normally, they would play and tease for however long they could stand it. Tantric kissing, she'd jokingly called it.

But right now, he had none of his usual control.

No finesse. No composure.

Only the blind need to get her naked and take her as many times as he could, branding her as his before she realized what a poor bargain she'd just made.

Laying her gently back on the couch, he stripped off her top and bra, peppering frantic kisses across her breasts and stomach as his fingers made quick work of the button and zipper on her shorts. Those disappeared down her long legs along with her panties.

He looked down at her, sprawled in naked abandon on the dark blue sectional, and felt the kind of possessive hunger he'd often teased his friends about when they'd talk about their wives or girlfriends.

An incredible sense of *mine* surged through him.

He yanked his tee off over his head, but when his hand gripped the waistband of his board shorts, common sense kicked in. Bathing suit meant no wallet. And no protection.

"Shit." The last thing he wanted to do was stop, but he had no choice.

"What?" Miranda rose up on her elbows. "What's wrong?"

"No condom. Stay just like that, and I'll be back in less than thirty seconds." His rigid dick twitched at the picture she made. "Maybe twenty."

To his surprise, she smiled. "Check my pockets."

Scooping up her discarded shorts, he grinned as he pulled two foil wrappers from the back pocket. "Looks like I'm not the only scout in the room." He yanked down his board shorts and ripped the corner of one package with his teeth.

"Never a scout, but a Marine is always ready for anything. Oh, God, *yesss*." The word came out in a satisfied hiss as he pressed inside her.

His mouth worshiped at her breasts. The sounds of her pleasure made him want to go slow, to make it even better for her, but the hot grasp of her body made that impossible. Too soon, the sensation of his looming orgasm shot up his spine like a runaway train, with no way for him to slow it down.

Bending to the inevitable, he reached between them and found the rigid nub where they were joined. If he was going over, so was she.

Which she did with a gasp and a scream, closely followed by his own groan as his hips continued to milk every last sensation out of them both. Finally spent, he collapsed as far as his elbows over her, breathing hard, careful to avoid making her feel confined, which he knew she hated but not why.

"Oorah," she panted.

"That good, huh?"

"Outstanding." She kissed him but had to break off to pant for more air.

"This was just the opening round. The rest of the afternoon is going to be all about taking my time giving you pleasure."

She raised a brow. "The rest of the afternoon? Isn't that a little ambitious?"

"We did agree we'd do whatever I wanted." He leaned closer and nipped her lower lip. "And what I want is to drive you absolutely crazy." He could feel the shiver run through her at his words.

"Can I make a request?"

"That depends. Does it involve multiple orgasms?"

Another shiver. "That...sounds amazing."

"It will be." He nuzzled her neck.

"Um..." She squirmed under the distraction of his mouth's exploration. "I, ah, was actually going to ask if I could take a shower first. I still smell like chlorine."

He thought she smelled like raspberries.

But since he wouldn't mind rinsing off himself, he pulled back and reluctantly withdrew from her still gently pulsating body. After taking a second to grab a tissue and dispose of the condom, they went up to the en suite bath he'd added to the reconfigured master bedroom.

Sleek and jam-packed with all the latest gadgets, from heated tile floor to a lighted showerhead that let you know when the water was the right temperature, it was quickly becoming his favorite room in the house.

And, he was starting to suspect, Miranda's as well.

Determined not to come in second place to a multi-jetted shower, he drew her into the glass enclosure and under the warm water falling from the giant rain shower fixture, soaking them both. With gentle care, he lathered her body, making her moan as he drew the pouf over her sensitive nipples and down her belly.

One soapy hand dipped between her legs and caressed her swollen folds, a finger slipping inside and making her moan. Ignoring her mewl of protest, he withdrew and gave the same gentle ministration to her back, ass and legs.

On the way back up, he reached out and changed the controls on the wall, sending water pulsing from the six body spray jets on the walls, making Miranda gasp.

Or maybe that was because he'd slipped his hand back between her sweet thighs. A second finger joined the first, and his thumb set up a firm rhythm on her clit as he kept her back tight against his front, his already resurrected erection tucked against her ass cheeks.

"Ben, I'm—" She didn't get to finish saying it before it happened. Her body convulsed around his fingers, head pressed back against his shoulder and hands clutching at his arms as she rode out the orgasm with frantic little moans, finally sagging in his hold when she was wrung dry.

After a quick rinse for them both under the rain shower, he turned off the water and grabbed one of the towels from the warming rack. He knew Miranda had to be spent by the way she stood quiet and compliant under his ministration. As he passed it, he took care to press a kiss to the scar beneath her left breast.

"Why do you always do that?" The words were slurry, like she'd had a few shots of Jack.

"What?"

"Kiss my scar." She covered it with her hand. "It's ugly."

"It's a part of you." He pushed her fingers aside. The pale, thumb-sized twist of scar tissue stood out in stark contrast to her light brown skin tone. "Part of what happened to you. What you survived." He kissed it one more time before handing her a smaller towel to dry her hair with. "One of these days, you'll tell me about it. When you're ready."

He left it at that, not wanting to push.

After giving himself a brisk toweling off, he followed Miranda out of the bathroom and to the large bed, letting her navigate on her own while staying mindful of potential hazards. He'd gotten into the habit of making sure nothing was left out in the middle of the floor, but there had still been a few stubbed toes and bruised knees and elbows as she memorized the revised layout of the rooms every time new furniture was added.

Developing the muscle memory to avoid walking into things seemed to come with a painful learning curve.

Miranda crawled onto the king-size mattress and collapsed with a sigh. "If you're hell-bent on doing this all afternoon, I think I need a nap first."

He liked the way she looked in his bed, sprawled and sexy and flushed from her shower orgasm. "I think we can both use a little recharge time." His heavy erection bobbed as though in disagreement as he climbed in beside her.

He ignored it.

Instead, he settled on his side, one arm under his head so he could watch her while he used his other hand to lightly caress from her collarbone to her hipbone and back in lazy lines. He might be willing to let her rest, but he planned to keep her body just as hungry for him as his was for her in the meantime.

Judging by the way she started to squirm and twitch under his touch like a thoroughbred jonesing in the starting gate, it was working.

On a groan, she rolled toward him. "What part of 'nap' did you not understand?"

"What? I wasn't making a sound." He grinned at the face she made.

"You're a menace." The laughter in her voice negated the condemnation.

"I'll be good." No, he wouldn't.

"No, you won't." With her fingertips, she started tracing lines over his shoulder and down his arm in an obvious imitation of what he'd been doing to her. "I think that deserves a forfeit."

"A forfeit?"

"Mmmhmm." Her finger dipped down along his ribs to his hipbone, making his dick bob in anticipation, only to be disappointed when she reversed course.

Fine. If she wanted to play, he'd play. "What did you have in mind?"

She grinned, making him wonder what he'd just agreed to.

"Do you have a bandana? Or better yet, a sweatband?" She wrinkled her nose. "Preferably clean."

Not what he'd been expecting. "Yeah, I think so. Why?"

"Just get it, and you'll find out." When he didn't move, she leaned closer and whispered against his ear, "I promise it'll be worth it."

Intrigued, he dug a sweatband emblazoned with the Yankees logo from one of their giveaway nights out of his dresser drawer. But when he tried to give it to her, she shook her head. "Put it on."

"Okay, this is getting a little weird." He slipped the elastic terrycloth band around his head. "Unless you expect me to work up enough of a sweat that I'll need this with whatever you're planning. In which case, I'm totally onboard."

She grinned. "You'll see. Just lay on your back, Slick." When he did, she swung her leg over him and straddled his waist. Then she leaned over him, breasts swaying enticingly as she slid her hands up his chest, to his face, up his cheeks...and tugged the sweatband down until it covered his eyes.

Ben stilled at the sudden loss of sight. "What—"

Her hands petted his chest. "Trust me?"

He did. At least, he thought he did. But it still took a lot for him to nod and say, "Yeah."

"Then just...enjoy."

He was going to ask what was so enjoyable about not being able to see her when she leaned down and pressed her lips to his in a teasing caress.

Before he could capture her mouth and deepen the kiss, she drifted away, nuzzling his cheek and closing her teeth around the lobe of his ear. He hissed at the unexpected sting, which she laved away with her tongue.

"Relax," she murmured, kissing from one side of his neck to the other. "You're always so focused on making it good for me. This time, shut off your brain and let me do the same for you."

Easier said than done.

As Miranda kissed and licked and nipped her way down his chest, he struggled against the urge to rip off the flimsy blindfold. If she was heading where he thought she was, he wanted to be able to watch. With every sensation she caused, every tremor of pleasure, his mind fought for the visual information that went along with it.

But finally, somewhere around the time she set her teeth to the ridge of muscle above his hipbone, his body started to overrule his brain. Instead of fighting for the one sense it had been deprived of, the others became more acutely focused than they'd ever been before during sex.

The feel of her soft inner thighs as she shifted lower on his legs, teasing the hairs there and sending tiny goosebumps of reaction along his skin.

The scent of the strawberry body wash he'd bought to keep in his shower for her rising from her heated skin, mixing with the sweet hint of her arousal as it perfumed the air and sent his own hunger soaring even higher.

The loud rasp of her breath—or was it his?—no longer steady, but coming in broken, uneven pants.

Individually, they intensified the experience profoundly, breaking the whole into concentrated slices of pure sensation. But when Miranda took his erection into her mouth without the visual cue to warn him, it was almost too much. His entire focus was pulled to that one point of connection.

The warmth of her mouth, the softness of her lips, the sharp edge of her teeth... Everything the same, and yet so different.

So much *more*.

Sensation whipped through him, lashing him with an intensity that would have been enough to scare him if he hadn't gone over the edge between one heartbeat and the next without warning.

Fire crawled up his spine as Miranda's mouth stayed sealed over him, drawing him deeper. Encouraging him without words to feel every last ounce of satisfaction she could coax from his body.

Blood rushed through his ears in time with his pounding heart. He knew he should apologize for not giving her any warning when he was about to come, but it didn't seem as though control had been ceded back to his brain yet.

All he could do was lay there, gulping in great lungfuls of air as Miranda slid her body up along his like a cat, her nipples hard against his sensitized skin.

"Keep your eyes closed," she said softly before removing the sweatband he'd at some point forgotten all about from his head.

She snuggled in against his side, one arm draped possessively over his chest. "Good?"

Was she serious?

Choosing her word from earlier, he panted, "Outstanding."

Her smile tickled against his neck. As he lay there, struggling to sort through the things he wanted to say once he regained the ability for more than single-word speech, her body went lax against his as sleep claimed her. He held her closer, listening to her breathe until exhaustion finally dragged him into unconsciousness as well.

"It was a helicopter crash."

Miranda spoke in a low, even voice, despite the fact her heart was already trying to crawl up her throat to escape along with the words. She focused on the warmth and security of being held in Ben's arms, in his bed, both of them still languid and a little dopey from too much sex and not enough rest.

They had woken earlier to growling bellies, which they'd filled with cold meatball subs scrounged from his fridge, feeding Sam the leftovers before letting him out to do his business and get in a bit of chase-the-ball. Then they'd ended up right back in Ben's bed for another round of mind-blowing sex.

Beyond mind-blowing.

Maybe even soul-searing.

She'd never felt this close to someone before. Or this safe. Not since the incident that had cost her her sight.

Which was why she'd decided it was time to finally talk about it.

Because he was right. Just like the scar, the crash was a part of her. And if she was going to ask him to be in her life, to be in a relationship that was about more than sex, then he needed to know it all.

"We were doing drug interdiction in Central America. Bilingual radio operators are in high demand for those types of deployments, so it was my third time there. The first two, the worst thing anyone came back with were a few infected mosquito bites."

Which had made what happened the last time so much worse.

"It was only our second day there. We'd been out doing night maneuvers in the helos, training the local troops on our techniques. Infil, exfil, touch and goes. Everything was going smoothly. Too smooth. Gator even joked how we needed something to go wrong just for a little excitement."

Words she knew her friend had regretted every day since.

"And something did?"

She nodded, tightening her hold on him, needing an anchor for the riptide of memories she was about to unpack from where they'd been safely stored.

"Someone—could have been the cartels, or just some *puto pendejo* wanting to make a name for himself by taking out some American troops, we never found out for sure—ambushed us with an RPG as we were heading back to base. One second, we were cruising along, everything five by five, and the next we were hit and spinning down toward the trees."

That instant of vertigo as they rocked under the force of the blast and started to plummet still twisted her gut as if it were yesterday.

Taking a deep breath only partially calmed the nauseating sensation.

"I can't recall much about the actual crash. I remember the warning lights, the smoke, hearing the pilot through the headset giving a mayday, bracing for impact, but then..." She shook her head. No matter how many times she talked about it, either for the review board or with her therapist, she'd never been able to retrieve the memory of the exact moment they hit the ground.

A gap for which she was profoundly grateful.

"After that, it's all choppy bits and pieces. The first thing I remember was hearing someone screaming. I thought it might have been me, until I realized I could barely breathe, much less manage to scream."

"Jesus." His arm tightened around her.

"I'd been thrown out of the chopper on impact, which was a good thing, because it was on fire. I could smell it, hear it. Feel it." Some nights she still woke up thinking she could taste the acrid bitterness of burning plastic and human flesh.

"The downside was the impact had done a lot of damage, including collapsing one of my lungs." Her hand drifted to the scar under her breast. "After they pried off the piece of wreckage that landed on top of me, the Corpsman had to do emergency field surgery and put in a chest tube to reinflate it. No time for neat and tidy, which is why it's so ugly."

No time for anesthetic, either.

Something she unfortunately *did* remember, in excruciating detail.

"Not ugly." Ben caressed the thickened skin with tender care. "It saved your life."

She took a breath to steady herself, forcing down the emotions threatening to creep into her clinical recitation of events. If that happened, she'd never get through to the end.

"The next thing I remember is waking up ten days later in the hospital from a medically induced coma."

No emotion, damn it.

"Besides the collapsed lung and bruising to a bunch of other organs, there'd been a 'significant impact' to my head, which caused my brain to swell and have several small bleeds. They kept me under so they could monitor them, in case I needed surgery. Which, thankfully, I didn't."

"Christ." Ben drew a sharp breath and said again, louder this time, "*Christ*! No wonder everyone was ready to kick my ass for not taking you to the hospital after you hit your head! If you'd told me you already had a brain injury—"

"I still wouldn't have let you take me." Her word rang with cutting finality. "I've spent too much time in hospitals as it is." Long, horrible months that continued to haunt her in nightmares. "It would take a major miracle to get me to voluntarily walk into one again. For any reason."

"But—"

"Do you want to hear the rest of this or not? Because I'm not going to talk about it again." She didn't even want to continue talking about it now. But she'd started this. She needed to finish it.

Then she could pack it all back up and store it away, never to see the light of day again.

Just like her.

No. Emotion.

"Yes, of course I do." He pressed a warm kiss to her temple and pulled her close.

She swallowed. Then swallowed again. Damn the man. He was turning her into a freaking teary-eyed wuss when she needed to be the tough-as-nails Marine.

Because this was the part that really sucked.

"It wasn't until I woke up and couldn't see that they realized there had been more damage to the optic nerves than they thought."

Opening her eyes to absolute nothingness had been the single most terrifying moment of her life. Followed by each and every moment afterward that grew more and more terrifying as the possibility that darkness might be permanent slowly sank in.

The Marine Corps had taught her to handle adversity and pain. It had never prepared her for the gut-wrenching sensation of isolation and vulnerability blindness brought with it.

"At first the doctors were optimistic that once the swelling went down, I might get at least partial vision back. I think they even believed it themselves for a while." A cruel hope dangled in front of her for weeks that only made the final truth all the more painful to accept when it came.

His arms tightened around her, as though protecting her from what couldn't be changed. She drew on that offered strength to go on.

"Every time they came to my room, I was so sure that would be the day they told me I was finally starting to get better. That the tests showed some tiny bit of improvement."

And every time they'd left, another piece of her soul was crushed under the mounting weight of despair.

"I spent a lot of nights talking to God in that hospital bed. Begging. Pleading. Bargaining. So, when there were a few times I was positive I saw flashes of light, I thought maybe...maybe he'd answered my prayers."

They'd looked like shooting stars against the night sky her world had become. She'd been so excited as she described them to the doctors, certain it was a good sign. Proof she was getting better.

Only to be told it was her brain playing tricks on her.

Their words had devastated her. It had taken her some time to accept them as true. But once she had, she'd lashed out. Blaming them. Blaming God for ignoring her prayers. Her mother had let her vent, then held her as she wept, saying softly, "God answers every prayer he gets, *mija*. It's just sometimes the answer is 'no.'"

"They ran all the tests they could think of, waited some more, then ran them again. But eventually, we had to face the facts. The damage was irreversible. My blindness was complete and permanent."

The anguish that had threatened to drag her under and drown her when she'd been given the final prognosis welled up for a split second as though it were fresh. For the first time in a long time, her ability to stuff her emotions away failed her, and a shudder ran through her body, a precursor to the sob she was struggling to hang on to.

Seeming to sense how close she was to the brink, Ben ran a comforting hand down her back, the way you'd soothe a child. "That was the prognosis then. But there's stuff in the news all the time these days about the advances being made in things like stem cell research. Maybe there's still hope."

"Maybe someday." It was something she tried not to think about too hard. False hope was worse than no hope, and she'd already lived through that particular hell. "But right now? Like it or not, you're stuck with me just the way I am."

As soon as the words were out, she regretted them. She groaned and pressed her forehead to his chest. "Shit. I'm sorry. That was totally uncalled for."

"It's okay. And for the record, I like you just fine the way you are. Besides," he added with a teasing lilt, "you come with a pretty cool dog who poops on command instead of leaving little bombs all around the yard. Why would I want to give that up?"

She laughed because he meant for her to.

But there was still a sore spot deep inside where all her fears and doubts hid that wasn't buying it. He might not care about her blindness now. But eventually, she knew it could end up being the thing that drove them apart.

Chapter 16

SHE KNEW IT WAS a dream because she could see.

The hospital corridor she stood in was long, white, sterile, the tile floor cold against her bare feet. Shivering, she started walking toward the only bit of color anywhere, the bright red door at the end of the hallway.

There were other doors along the way, but she ignored them. Knowing, somehow, she needed to go through *that* door.

Needed to see the truth on the other side.

Pushing through the door which felt as hot as its color, a blanket of stifling heat engulfed her, stopping her breath for a long, suffocating moment. Four hospital beds filled the room before her. Two were empty. Because Greenburg and Singh were dead. They'd never made it out of the chopper.

Never had a chance.

She knew who one of the injured was even before she walked to the first occupied bed. The man's lower body was hidden under a tented sheet, the rest of his torso and his remaining arm wrapped in white gauze to protect the burned skin beneath. Only his face remained mercifully untouched by the flames, pale and perfect beneath the mask of the ventilator breathing for him with a soft whoosh and puff.

"Jonesy. God." She looked away, horrified.

Jonesy was even younger than her, only twenty-two. He'd proposed to his high school sweetheart right before they deployed. It was so new they hadn't even had time to pick a date yet. They were supposed to have a lifetime together.

Now, he might not even *have* a life.

He didn't deserve this.

The bed across from his held what remained of another teammate. As she approached him, dread built in her gut with every reluctant step. His entire body was wrapped in sterile gauze, from his feet to his head, but he didn't look like a mummy.

He looked like a man who'd had his future seared away along with his flesh.

The only bits of him that showed, around his eyes and mouth, were red and raw, a horrifying hint at the rest. Standing at his bedside, there was nothing left of him to tell her who he was if she hadn't already known.

"*Madre de Dios.*" She crossed herself. "I'm so sorry this happened to you. I'm so damn sorry."

With snakelike speed, one of the bandaged hands reached up and clamped over her wrist as his eyes opened to glare up at her in dark-brown accusation. "It should have been you."

Jolting awake with a startled gasp, she lay in her bed, heart pounding a frantic beat against her breastbone like a prisoner trying to escape his cell. It took a moment for reality to reform enough to think past the sharp taste of fear coating her tongue.

A dream. It was just a dream.

And yet...not.

She really had walked that long corridor. Pushed into that unbearably hot room on the burn ward. Stood beside the beds of two of her teammates.

And died a little bit inside while she'd done it.

But the rest was all her mind's doing, pictures painted based on what she'd been told of their conditions by the reluctant nurse who'd escorted her that day to be her eyes.

Eyes currently leaking hot, salty tears down her temples. From the dampness on her pillow, she'd been crying for a while. "Damn."

She scrubbed at the tears, erasing them, but it seemed she wasn't done leaking yet because more followed in their place. With a sniffle, she let them come.

Out of all the dreams that haunted her, she hated this one the most. It brought back all the pain, all the doubts, all the *guilt*.

Why her?

Why had she survived and others hadn't? Why had she gotten off relatively unscathed, while Greenberg and Singh died, Cash lost his leg, Jonesy succumbed to his burns not long after her visit, and Gator—

"No." Forcing herself from that line of thought, she pushed herself upright in the bed. The worst thing she could do was let herself fall down that rabbit hole again. Survivor's guilt, her therapist had told her, was a real bitch.

It had taken a very, very long time to accept her being alive had absolutely no bearing on others who weren't. For her to walk forward without constantly looking back to wonder "what if?"

Sometimes, though, she still stumbled.

Sam's large head was suddenly there in her lap, a small whine signaling his worry at her distress. With a sniffle, she rubbed his soft fur, grateful for the way he always seemed to know her moods and be there when she needed him even though it wasn't part of his training as a guide dog.

"It's okay, Sammy. The bad dream is gone now." If only all the emotions it dredged up had disappeared with it.

The mattress dipped under the weight of his paws as the dog inched his upper body closer. She laughed, knowing exactly what he was doing. The big sneak.

"Okay, yes. You can come up. But only because you're out of sorts." She patted the bed beside her to reinforce the permission, ignoring the fact she was the one who required a little extra comfort right now, not Sam.

A girl needed a few illusions.

Like pretending self-doubt and insecurity didn't nibble at her almost daily despite the brave face she showed the world. Or, more important lately, she showed Ben.

Ben.

God, she wished he was here. Wished he was the one pressed against her side, so he could wrap her in his strong arms and hold her until the tremors of guilt and grief passed. But since she couldn't have that, she'd settle for the next best thing.

She grabbed her phone from the charging dock on the nightstand and used Siri to send a short text to Ben, asking if he was awake.

The phone rang a minute later. Smiling, she answered. "Hey."

"Hey, yourself." The low, intimate rumble of his voice in her ear made it almost feel like he was right there in bed with her.

Almost.

She still could have used those arms of his, though.

"Is everything okay?" he asked. "You're not usually up this late."

She checked the time and cursed. It was after two. "I'm sorry. I didn't mean to wake you up."

"You didn't. We just got back from a run. A tractor trailer jack-knifed near the Verrazano and took out a bunch of cars. One caught fire. Multiple pin jobs. It was a total freaking mess. The bridge was shut down for hours until we were done."

A shiver ran through her at his words, trying not to imagine anyone caught in one of the burning cars. It hit far too close to home.

"All the more reason I should let you get to bed."

"Nah, I'm too wired. I'm in the kitchen right now heating up some milk."

There was no stopping the grin that crept across her face at the thought of her studly fireman with a glass of warm milk to help him sleep. "God, you're adorable."

"Please promise you'll never call me that in front of the guys," he begged, making her chuckle. "Now. What's wrong?"

Suddenly, wanting to whine about a nightmare seemed foolish after hearing about the night he'd had. "I just had a bad dream. It's stupid. I shouldn't have called."

"It's not stupid, and of course you should have." She could hear the faint sound of liquid being poured, then a heavy mug being set on a table and a chair screeching against the floor as it was pulled out. "Okay, tell me."

"I was at the hospital. The burn ward." Thank God, it was one of the nightmares she'd already had when he was with her, so she was spared having to elaborate.

Ben swore softly. "I'm sorry I wasn't there to hold you when you woke up, baby."

Me too.

"Hearing your voice helps." And it did. She could already feel her nerves starting to settle into place like an upset porcupine's quills slowly going flat. "Now, let's talk about something else, so I can forget about it."

"Okay. How did things go with having your family over for dinner?"

And just like that, the settled feeling was gone.

"It went all right."

"Really?"

She scrunched her face up at his doubtful tone. "Yes." Then she sighed. "Right up until I got into an argument with my father"—again—"and he stormed out before the food even came off the grill." Not an unusual ending for the rare times her mother managed to get them together in the same spot for more than five minutes.

"Babe." The word conveyed both sympathy and exasperation.

"I know, I know. But I really did try this time."

They both had.

The strained politeness had been excruciating. But she and her father were way too alike in temperament. And stubbornness. It was all but inevitable they'd eventually bump heads, just like they had their whole lives.

Growing up in suburban America with a Mexican father holding onto deeply traditional and patriarchal ideals had been a constant contest of wills.

Ben let out a gusty sigh. "I can't claim to know the man, since I haven't met him yet, but I don't see why he's holding such a big grudge about you moving into your own place. Your mother doesn't like it, either, but she still comes over to see you without giving you grief. Well, too much of it, anyway."

"It actually goes back further than that. We had a huge blowout when I first told him I wanted to go into the military, so I could go to college for free like Tino did. I wanted to be the first woman in our family to get a degree."

"Why would he get mad about that? It's a good plan."

His support warmed her.

"He didn't think so. He's too old-fashioned in his beliefs on a lot of things. So, his response was to yell and stomp and say that no daughter of his was going to act like a man and join the Army."

"He seriously didn't want you to join because you're a woman?"

"He actually used the words 'I forbid it.'" The memory still rankled.

There was a moment of silence.

"Right. So, you went and joined the Marines instead. That's some passive-aggressive brilliance right there." The hint of appreciative irony in his voice made her smile despite the topic.

He totally got her.

"A little childish, I know. But I don't regret doing it. Not even after the hell of boot camp and the Crucible and...everything else. Being a Marine gave my life a sense of order and purpose I never realized was missing until then."

"I know exactly what you mean. I felt that way after I became a fireman. Everything just clicked, like it was what I was always meant to do."

"Exactly." He really did get it, which was why she felt comfortable sharing some of her family's dysfunction with him, when normally she kept it all wrapped up tight inside, trying to ignore how much her father's attitude hurt. This was stuff she'd never talked to anyone about before besides her therapist.

But with Ben, it just felt like it was okay to vent.

"I guess the only thing I really regret is the rift the decision caused between me and my parents. Which only got worse after I decided I wanted to make the Corps my career and signed on for a second enlistment." That conversation had been a battle of epic proportions.

And had been the last time she'd spoken to her father before waking up in the hospital a little over a year later, with him at her bedside.

Crying.

"Hmm."

"Hmm, what?"

"I just...look, I'm the last person who should be giving advice about parents, but...is it possible your dad is feeling guilty?"

"Guilty?"

Her father? The man who was always right about everything?

"About what?"

"Maybe he feels like it's his fault you enlisted, because of the way he told you that you couldn't?"

"I would have joined anyway, regardless of what he said."

"You know that, but maybe he doesn't." She could almost sense him shrug. "I could also be a hundred percent wrong. Like I said, I'm the farthest thing there is from an expert on relationships, parental or otherwise. It's just maybe something to consider."

They talked for a little while longer before she heard the exhaustion dragging at his words and sent him off to his lonely bed with a smacking kiss.

Snuggled back under her own covers, Sam a warm weight against her legs, she considered Ben's theory that her father's prickly distance from her all these years was caused by a sense of guilt rather than anger. It had some merit. She had, after all, gone down to the recruitment office the very next day after their argument to enlist.

The only problem with that was the one thing she hadn't told Ben. The bits and pieces of whispered conversation between her parents late one night in her hospital room when they thought she was asleep.

"What if her sight never comes back? What will she do?"

"She'll get better." Her mother had believed that right up to the end.

"But if she doesn't? What kind of life can she have? There will be no husband, no babies, no home of her own. She'll be all alone."

"She'll always have her family. We'll take care of her. And after us, Santino, or Julietta."

"And how is it fair to expect them to take on the burden of caring for a sister who can't see?"

A burden. That was how her father saw her. Someone without a purpose or a future.

Useless.

It was the way she'd seen herself, too, when she'd first been released from the hospital and moved back into the family home. She'd let her father's words smother her in doubt and self-pity for far too long before she pulled her head out of her own butt and decided to prove him wrong.

Prove *herself* wrong.

She was so glad Ben had never witnessed her acting like that. A weak, mewling mess so steeped in misery there had been stretches where for days she hadn't even gotten out of bed. He thought of her as this strong, capable person. Brave. He'd said as much to her, and proved it to her family when they'd made and served them lunch together just like anybody else would.

A tiny worm of doubt wriggled into her brain.

No, he'd never once acted like she was any kind of burden. But he'd only ever seen her doing things she'd already mastered. Living her life like it was almost normal. He thought she could handle anything that came her way, that her being blind wouldn't make any difference to the relationship she'd so selfishly asked him for.

She pulled the covers up to her chin, the peace she'd found from their conversation seeping away along with some of her confidence. Yes, he might think all that about her now. But what would happen if—no, *when*—he witnessed her fail big for the first time?

How capable and brave would he find her then?

"This seemed a lot easier when Robin was showing us how to do it."

Sitting on the grass beside the high school running track, Ben took a long swallow from his water bottle as he considered how to respond to Miranda's disheartened comment. Because she was right. It *had* seemed easier when her mobility coach had taken them to this very spot and gone over the basics of guiding a blind runner.

Robin had even commented on how well the two of them worked together right from the start, like they were naturals at it.

She certainly wouldn't think that today.

Knowing he had to say something, he tried to make it encouraging. "We probably got a little cocky after our first time out. She did tell us there'd be a learning curve."

"I guess."

Hating the apathy in her voice, he patted her nylon-covered knee. It was already hot enough out that even the lightweight sweats they both wore were uncomfortable. But with the real possibility of road rash if they tripped each other up, it had been the lesser evil.

"Come on, let's give it another try."

With a lot less enthusiasm than she'd shown for conquering her breath training in the pool, she got to her feet and held out her left hand for her end of the elastic cord that would tether them together. After slipping the loop over her wrist, she put her hand on his and followed him back onto the track. "Any other people I need to know about?"

"Nope, we've got the place to ourselves for now."

He'd picked midmorning in hopes of missing both the early-morning runners and the lunchtime walkers who used the track most weekdays during the summer. There had been only one other person there when they started their first circuit around the oval, but he'd finished up and left a short time ago.

Maybe it was simple self-consciousness making her so stiff and awkward. A few days ago, she'd been loping along like a long-legged gazelle.

His end of the tether went over his right wrist, putting him at Miranda's left side, just like Sam. It felt a little weird to be there, and maybe a touch ironic. "Ready?"

"I guess."

The continued lack of enthusiasm even though they were now alone was concerning. So, it wasn't the thought of being watched bothering her. What was it, then?

"Are you sure you want to do this? Because we can always pack it in and come back another day."

His offer seemed to stiffen her spine. "No. We're here. Let's do this."

"Okay, then."

He let her start them at an easy pace down the straight leg of the track, using the slight tension on the elastic tether to keep her going straight the way Robin had shown him. As they approached the end of the straightaway, he called it out. "Starting to curve to the left in about twenty feet."

Miranda reached over and took hold of his wrist, keeping hold until they'd passed through the curve and were back on the straightaway. Then she released him and let the tether take over again.

As her confidence increased, so did her speed. Matching his stride to hers, an enormous sense of pride tugged at his chest. There she was. The woman who fearlessly faced down crossing busy streets and obnoxious big brothers without a flinch. Whatever had been bothering her, it seemed she was working through it.

When he called out the second curve at the opposite end of the track, she started to reach for his wrist again, then hesitated. A look of steely determination crossed her face, and she dropped her hand, choosing to rely on the tether instead.

Knowing it was her decision didn't make it any easier watching her struggle to keep their spacing. Focused on letting her take the chance, he forgot to watch his own footing for a few, crucial seconds.

One step they were fine. The next, Miranda's foot was somehow tangled with his. Or maybe his with hers. Either way, they both stumbled. Quick reflexes had him reaching for her to steady them both. Which might have worked if it hadn't been for the tether, which made his arm jerk hers at an awkward angle, throwing them even further off-balance.

They both ended up on their asses. Which was at least preferable to their faces.

"Are you okay?"

Rather than answer, she shouted a heartfelt "Damn it!" to the sky.

"Miranda?" He yanked the tether from his wrist and ran his hands over her legs in a quick inspection for injuries, which she batted away.

"I'm fine. I'm just…" She gave a wordless growl of frustration.

He understood all about frustration. He'd spend years trying to make his brain work the same as his brother's and sister's did, only to come to the conclusion he was wired differently than them. They absorbed knowledge like plants soaking up sunshine, while he needed to pound every nugget in with a shovel.

"It's okay. It's going to take more practice, that's all. You're good at a lot of stuff, Legs, but even you can't master everything in a day."

"Or ever," she muttered.

"What?"

She shook her head. "Nothing. Are you okay? You didn't get hurt when we went down, did you?"

"I'm fine. What do you mean, 'or ever'?" When she didn't answer, he said, "You need to cut yourself a little slack here. You'll get this. Just like you get everything."

"Not everything." She gave a short laugh full of unhappiness. "There are so many things I'm not going to be able to do, no matter how hard I try. Things you'll want to do that I can't."

Not sure where this was coming from, he said slowly, "And there are probably things you'll want to do that I won't. So what?"

"Don't *want* to do, not *can't* do."

"I'm not seeing the difference."

"Ben..." She drew in a deep breath and let it out on a sigh. "Okay. You mentioned the other day a group from your firehouse was talking about doing a whitewater rafting trip in the spring, right?"

"Yeah, it's a blast. We did it this year, too. Total adrenaline rush. Well, you know, you said you've gone before, too. You'll love it."

"Yeah, I would have. Before this." She gestured roughly toward her face. "I don't know if I'll ever feel confident enough to try it again now."

Way to be an insensitive ass, Murphy.

"Okay, so, we don't have to go. No big deal."

"It is a big deal! I don't want you to not have fun with your friends because of me."

For the first time since he'd met her, it felt like he was walking through a minefield with no safe pathway through it. That no matter what he did or said, eventually he was going to step on one and set it off. Almost like she *wanted* him to.

And he had no idea why.

"So, what? You *do* want me to go on the trip?"

"Yes."

"Without you."

"Yes."

"Then how come your face doesn't match your answer?" Because she looked like she was about to cry.

"I'm...God, I don't know what I'm saying." She drew her knees up toward her body, hugging them tight. "I'm being stupid. Let's just forget it."

He scooted himself closer so the long line of their bodies touched. "No, and no. This is obviously something that's bugging you, so talk. What's going on inside that head of yours?" When she didn't answer he rocked his shoulder into hers. "You know I'm not going to stop asking until you tell me, right?"

She gave a watery laugh. "You can be such a pain."

"But I'm your pain," he replied with a grin and another shoulder nudge.

"Yeah, you are. And I guess that's what I've been thinking about. That I trapped you into this relationship before you really understood what kind of limitations my blindness might put on the things we can do together. The things you like to do. The rafting trip is just the tip of the iceberg."

Of all the things he'd expected her to be upset about, this hadn't even hit the radar.

"Okay, first of all, you didn't trap me into anything, the decision was completely mine. I went in with eyes wide open." He winced at his choice of words, but didn't apologize for them, knowing she'd hate it.

"And second, I could give a shit about some rafting trip. I know, I know, it's not really about that," he said when she started to protest. "What I'm saying is, all relationships are based on compromise."

"And if one of us is doing all the compromising and starts to resent it?"

"Then we talk it through and figure it out. Hey." He slipped his arm around her shoulders, breathing in the subtle scent of berries the sun was teasing from her skin. "We've only been at this relationship thing for a little while. You're not giving up on us already, are you?"

Because the possibility was like a knife twisting in his belly.

"No, of course not! I...this is so stupid. When I had that bad dream the other night, it kind of got me thinking about...other things. How I might not realize how much of a burden I am to the people around me sometimes." She shrugged as though it wasn't a big deal when it so obviously was.

"Listen to me. You are not a burden." He tucked his finger under her chin and turned her head to face him. From this close, her eyes had no place else to focus but on his, giving the illusion she was seeing him.

But she never would.

Which didn't matter to him. Clearly, though, she still needed some convincing.

He rested his forehead against hers. "I'll say it as many times as it takes to sink in, Legs. Not. A. Burden."

She took a shuddery breath. "Okay."

The word was a mere whisper against his lips before she kissed them. A simple press that deepened between one breath and the next to something more desperate, more needy, for both of them.

The slam of a car door from the nearby parking lot broke them apart with an embarrassed laugh. "I think we'd better get back to running."

"Actually, I think I'd rather go home and finish this instead." Miranda leaned in and kissed him again, hard and a little bit dirty.

"Okay, home it is." He got to his feet, keeping her hand to help her up with an impatient tug. "See, compromising already."

She laughed as she brushed herself off. "You're so full of shit. You'd pick sex over running in a heartbeat. How is that a compromise?"

He leaned in and said softly against her mouth, "Because I'm willing to wait until we get home and not just take you in the parking lot up against the car like I want to right this second." His lips brushed hers in the merest promise of a kiss. "Compromise."

"God." She grabbed his arm. "Home. Now."

The short drive was spent telling her all the things he planned to do to her, each more sensual and erotic than the last, keeping them both teetering on the edge of arousal and impatience. By the time they hit her front step, he didn't think he could wait any longer.

It was clear she couldn't, either.

The second the door slammed shut she pushed him against the wall and started stripping his tee from his body with shaking hands. He helped get them both naked, then reversed their positions before remembering the condom.

With a frustrated curse, he fumbled it out of his wallet from the pile of clothes and somehow got it on without tearing it. Pressing her to the wall, he kissed her hard. "Last chance to move to the couch."

"Here," she panted, reaching down to circle him with one hand. "Like this. Like you wanted to do against the car."

The knowledge she was fulfilling his fantasy—in a way that wouldn't get them arrested for public indecency—send a jolt of fierce pleasure through him. Nearly on fire with need, he thrust into her body with a long, slow push.

It was the last thing that was slow.

Everything else was fast and wild and over much too soon. Although from the limp way she collapsed against him, still entirely satisfying.

After they'd caught their breath, he took care of the condom while Miranda soothed Sam, who seemed agitated and unusually clingy. "He was confused, I think," she said as they cuddled on the couch after redressing. "He might have thought you were hurting me."

Ben looked at the dog, who was watching him with a seriously disgruntled expression. "I guess I'm lucky he didn't bite me in the ass, then." Miranda laughed, but he was only half joking.

Trained not to be aggressive or possessive or not, he'd be paying a little more attention to Sam's whereabouts the next time they decided to have spontaneous non-bedroom sex and all his naked bits were exposed.

Lying with her head against his chest, Miranda stroked her fingers in slow circles across his cotton-clad abs, which contracted under her light touch. "How about we spend the rest of the day being lazy by the pool, then after dinner we can do that again. Only this time longer and slower. Maybe even all night long."

Unbelievably, his penis twitched in interest.

Insatiable bastard.

"I think it sounds like a great idea." Then he groaned. "Except I have to go to Queens tonight."

She echoed the groan. "Again? Do you really have to?"

"Yeah, unfortunately, I do." He sucked in a breath as her fingers slipped past the waistband of his sweats and found him. "But damn, you make it hard."

"I can make it harder."

"I have no doubt." He savored her touch a few seconds longer before reluctantly removing her hand from his semi. "Sweetheart, if it was anything other than studying for this test, I'd blow it off in a heartbeat to stay in bed with you. You're way more fun than Cody."

"Well, I should hope so." Sighing in defeat, she went back to drawing circles on his stomach. "So, what test are you taking? I don't think you ever mentioned it before."

Well, shit. He hadn't meant to say that, since he purposefully *hadn't* told her anything about the test. Although, maybe now was the perfect time.

"It's, um…"

His brain stuttered, clogged with all of the negative reactions he'd gotten from people about his plans—the horrified pity from his parents, the vicious laughter from that fucking asshat Cartwright. Even his little brother had shown his lack of faith when he texted to offer his tutoring skills if Ben "was determined to go through with it."

He didn't think he could take that kind of bad reaction from Miranda as well.

"It's for promotion to lieutenant. But I'm, um…I'm helping Cody study. He's taking it."

Way to wimp the fuck out, Murphy.

At least it was more of an evasion than an outright lie. He *was* helping Cody study. He was just glossing over the part about Cody helping him study, too.

And about him taking the test.

And another prep course on top of their self-study program.

But this way, if he did lousy, he'd never even have to tell her. Never need to feel stupid in front of this woman whose opinion was coming to mean more to him than almost anyone else's.

Of course, if he did well, he'd kind of screwed himself.

But really, what were the odds of *that* happening?

Miranda hummed against his chest as her fingers meandered lower again. "Okay. I guess we'll have to be hedonists tomorrow night instead. Put it in your calendar, Slick. You and me, naked and sweaty in a bed."

He cleared his throat because damn, he *really* wanted that. Except...

"Actually, I have to go down tomorrow night, too."

Her wandering fingers stopped abruptly. "Oh, come on, seriously? How much studying does he have to do to pass a stupid test?"

Her words struck right at the heart of his insecurities.

And his worst fears of what she'd think of him.

Then she sighed. "Sorry, forget I said that. You made a commitment to your friend, and I shouldn't be all pissy about it just because I get to spend a little less time with you this week. Compromise, right?"

Having her say that when he didn't have the balls to tell her the whole truth only made him feel guiltier. Especially when this wasn't the only week he'd be schlepping back and forth to Queens on his days off.

Between the studying he'd been doing with Cody at his apartment the past month, and the official prep course that started tomorrow, he'd now be losing *two* nights a week with her until the test was given at the end of July.

The frustration of her initial reaction worried him despite her backtracking. The last thing he wanted was for Miranda to dislike his best friend before they even met. Especially since the situation was for his benefit as well as Cody's.

His mind scrambled for a way to deflect her annoyance.

"Tomorrow's not for Cody. It's, um, for Dom. He's, ah, redoing one of the bathrooms in his mother's house and asked me to help."

It wasn't bad for a spur-of-the-moment excuse. But he didn't like that he'd officially crossed the line from mild evasion to flat-out lie.

Guilt sat even heavier in his gut.

"And because he helped you with your house, you have to return the favor. I guess that's only fair." She sighed. "How long do you think it'll take?"

"A couple of weeks, probably. Maybe a little more." Like six.

"That must be one hell of a bathroom."

He winced at the thick sarcasm in her voice. "It's, um, a mold issue. Total gut job down to the studs, remediation, the whole nine yards." The deeper he dug himself into the lie, the more certain he was he'd end up paying for it down the line. "Plus, he has to rely on when people can work him into their schedules, like I did. That can drag it out. A lot."

"Yeah, I remember. Boy, do I remember." She smirked when he groaned at the reminder. "So, how late do you think you'll get back?"

"I dunno. Depends on the traffic, but it could be pretty late. You probably shouldn't wait up for me." Spending a few nights exiled from her bed seemed fitting penance.

After a few silent moments of idle finger circles that were coming dangerously close to his waistband again, she asked, "What if I gave you a key, so it didn't matter what time you got back?"

He stilled. "Are you serious?"

A key? She was willing to trust him with a *key*?

"Why not? That way you get to help your friends, and I still get to have you, too. Win-win." She snuggled closer. "It's kind of selfish, actually, since you'll be all tired and wanting to sleep, and I'll be wanting to ravage you all night long." Her teeth nipped at his nipple through his t-shirt.

"*Fuck.*" He cleared his throat. "I mean, yes. I mean, no, it's not selfish. Ravaging sounds...awesome. But yes, I'll take the key. Thank you." It was an incredibly monumental moment.

And an equally terrifying one.

She was offering him total access to her home. As gestures went, they didn't get much bigger than that. He needed something, anything, to offer her that would put them back on equal relationship footing. Just asking her to take a key to his place in return wouldn't cut it. It needed to be something *big*.

There was only one thing he could think of. He'd been avoiding it, dreading it, actually. But now he needed it.

He had no choice.

"So, um, I was thinking, maybe you might want to come with me to my parents' for dinner next Friday?" As soon as the words were out, he wanted a do-over.

Could you have sounded any lamer, dickhead?

"Oh. Uh, sure, maybe. Can I let you know?"

Her less than enthusiastic response left him a little stymied.

"Of course." Because, what else could he say? He'd just asked a woman to have dinner with his family for the first time, ever, and all he gets is "maybe"?

Then again, it had been a pretty lukewarm invitation at best. What he should have said was something like, *I'd love for you to come with me to dinner next week and meet my family, because I'm dying to introduce you to them.*

Damn. He needed to say that. Now.

Before he could, Miranda's nimble fingers finally danced their way back down to his erection and distracted him. "So, how much time do we have before you have to leave for Cody's, and what can we do with it?"

"Too soon, and not enough, damn it." He groaned as she stroked him, then again when she stopped.

"Sorry, that was mean. I know you have to go." She gave a long, resigned sigh. "You're a good friend, Slick."

Her admiration sliced deeper than any criticism ever could.

He pulled her closer, glad for the first time she couldn't see his face. "I'll make it up to you. I promise." And he would. For lying. For the lousy dinner invitation. For being a fucking coward.

For everything.

Chapter 17

"So, what do you think?"

"I think that was incredible." Miranda gave a happy hum as she licked each finger clean. "Mmmm. Give me more."

Ben stifled a groan as he handed her a napkin. "Yeah, one deep-fried Twinkie is probably more than enough."

Because if he had to watch her eat another with the same amount of lust-inducing enthusiasm as she had the first, he was going to be forced to do something drastic. Like drag her behind one of the street vendor's tents and give her a different reason to make those happy noises.

"Do I even want to know how many calories I just put in my mouth?"

He ignored his dick as it twitched at the image her words evoked. "Probably not. But we're not counting calories today, remember?"

Today was all about showing Miranda a little fun outside of her usual comfort zone of Kenoway. To try and counter her worry about being a burden on their relationship because her blindness might keep them from doing things.

A concern that seemed to have cropped up out of nowhere, but that he was taking dead seriously. Because he was taking *them* seriously. Which was still strange and new and a little bit scary for him, so maybe it was for her, too. She'd said he was the first man in her life since she lost her sight.

Well, besides that Umberto asshat. Who he might have wanted to track down and kick his ass for what he did to her, if not for the fact he'd ended up with Isobel. Which, in his opinion, was its own form of punishment.

He'd spent the last week trying in subtle ways to reinforce to Miranda that she was in no way, shape, or form a burden to him or their budding relationship. He wasn't sure words were enough, so he'd decided to prove it with actions instead. It had taken a bit of convincing for her to agree to come to the street fair in his old Queens neighborhood, but so far, she seemed to be enjoying herself.

So was he, though mostly because she was.

And right now, she was looking like she was still jonesing for another Twinkie.

He wrapped an arm around her shoulders and nuzzled her ear. "Eat whatever you want, babe. We'll just work it all off later, anyway." The shudder that ran through her made him smile against her hair.

"Then it's okay if I have another one."

He straightened with a chuckle. The woman had a one-track mind when it came to something she wanted. And since he seemed to be one of those things, he was grateful for her tenacity.

"I thought you might want to try some other stuff. But hey, if you'd rather have this than chocolate..."

As expected, her eyes lit up. "Chocolate?"

He laughed. "God, you're easy."

He pressed a kiss to her pouty mouth before moving them and Sam through the crowd toward the vendor booth with artisan chocolates. Run by a brother and sister team who had grown up in the neighborhood, Creatively Cacao was starting to become a recognizable name for their daring and often unusual confections.

Before they got there, a woman with flawless black skin and short natural hair saw him and changed direction to intercept, the red sundress she wore rippling high on her thighs as she walked. "Ben Murphy, hi!"

"Hey, um…" What the hell was her name? "Nancy. Hi. Enjoying the fair?"

"More now than I was a minute ago." Her gaze drifted over his body with such possessive intent it made him want to squirm. "How's that knee of yours doing?"

"Fine, thanks." To Miranda he said, "Nancy was one of the nurses in the ER when I was brought in a few weeks ago after I twisted my knee at a fire."

"Well, thank you for taking such good care of him," Miranda said.

"Are you kidding? Getting this man out of his pants was the highlight of my entire shift."

Normally, he would have laughed at the slightly inappropriate joke. But Miranda's fingers clenched around his, so he knew she didn't find the remark the least bit funny. He tightened his grip on her hand to ensure she didn't try to pull away.

"Well, it was nice to see you again, Nancy. Have fun."

"Yeah, you too. Hey, want to get a drink later?"

He froze in disbelief. "You do see I'm with someone, right?"

Nancy's gaze drifted over Miranda and Sam, where it lingered on the working harness and rigid handle in Miranda's grasp that marked him as a guide dog. Pity showed in her expression before she looked back at him with something close to admiration.

"Of course, you should definitely finish doing the fair with your friend first. We can meet up at Calhoun's later. Or better yet, you can come by my place, and we'll see about getting you out of those pants again. I promise you'll have a lot more fun this time."

"You've got to be kidding." Had she really said that? Had she seriously just dismissed Miranda as competition, as a *woman*, because she was blind?

Son of a bitch. She had.

"Aw, come on. No need to be bashful. You know what the hospital grapevine is like." She stepped closer to his side opposite Miranda and lowered her voice. "I just want a chance to see if all the talk from the other nurses is true or not."

"Talk?"

"You know." She glanced at his crotch and licked her lips. "About how the Mighty Murphy always delivers."

Before he could even begin to form a reply to that outrageous comment, Miranda spoke up, her voice oddly pleasant. Almost casual.

"See, I was going to give you a pass on asking my boyfriend out for a drink with me standing right here, because I know how freaking adorable he is, and women can't seem to help themselves around him."

Nancy reared back as though slapped. "Boyfriend?

"But then you had to go and cross the skank line, and that's not okay, no matter how low you *think* you're talking." Her expression took on a hard cast. "And even if he wasn't taken, which he is, I'd tell you the same thing. Back. Off. He's not some piece of meat for you to use and compare notes with your friends about."

"I didn't—"

"You did."

"Look, I'm sorry. I didn't know you two were together like that." She looked pissed and confused at the same time. "I mean, come on, he's him, and you're b—" Her lips clamped over the word.

"I'm what?" Miranda's tone dared her to answer.

Nancy had the grace to look embarrassed. "Nothing. Forget it. It doesn't matter. I obviously made a mistake. I'm sorry. Let's just pretend none of this ever happened, okay?" With a last regretful glance in Ben's direction, she turned and hurried away.

He didn't bother to watch her go. All of his attention was focused on Miranda. "I swear to God, I never slept with her." To his surprise, she laughed.

"Yeah, I think that was the problem."

"I'm sorry."

"For what? You don't have any control over what other people say or do. She was the one who was rude."

"I'm still sorry." Especially that he hadn't considered by bringing her to his old stomping grounds, he'd be increasing the likelihood they'd run into people he knew.

More specifically, women he knew.

Dumbass move, Murphy.

"Then fine, apology accepted. You can make it up to me with chocolate."

"Done."

As they pushed through the crowd again, a sense of discontent settled deep in his gut as he thought about Nancy's words. The guys had hung the nickname Mighty Murphy on him years ago, because they were dickheads and that's what they did. He hadn't realized it had gone further than the firehouse, though.

Although maybe he should have.

A lot of badge bunnies and hose honeys were people already associated with the first responders' world. He'd enjoyed the company of more than a few nurses—and even a doctor or two—from the local area hospitals over the years. It only made sense some of them would know each other and share gossip. Being a tic mark on somebody's scoresheet hadn't bothered him before.

Now?

It kind of made him feel dirty, and not in the good way.

Thank God Miranda didn't seem too upset by the unpleasant encounter. In fact, the only thing that seemed to piss her off was how Nancy talked to him, like he was nothing but a living, breathing sex toy she wanted to jump on and ride. The way she'd leapt to his defense had taken him by surprise, but also warmed something inside him.

And made him wonder if maybe it was true.

Maybe it really wasn't the great sex that made her want to be with him.

Two customers were leaving the Creatively Cacao booth when they got there, allowing them to step right up to the table, which was lined with laminated pictures of the various artisanal chocolates being offered.

He greeted the man there with a clasp of hands over the display. "Raj, my man. I brought my lady over to try some of the good stuff."

"All my stuff is the good stuff." Raj paused and gave Miranda an appreciative closer look. "But for the beautiful lady, I'll be sure to show you only my very best."

"Miranda, this is Rajesh Agarwal, one half of CC Enterprises."

"The brilliant half."

"Don't let Prisha hear you say that," Ben replied with a snort. "Raj, this is my girlfriend, Miranda Hernandez." He enjoyed a small bite of satisfaction when disappointment flashed through Raj's dark eyes.

That's right, Casanova. She's taken.

"It's nice to meet you, Rajesh," Miranda said.

"Raj, please. And the pleasure's all mine." He shot her an appreciative smile, which only faltered slightly when his gaze swept down to take in the harnessed dog at her side. Not missing a beat, he explained to Miranda in detail about the proper way to get the full experience of the chocolate she'd be sampling.

"First, warm the chocolate, then cup it in your hand and inhale the aroma it releases. You'll be surprised how many undertones you can pick out once you pay attention."

"Like wine."

He grinned at her. "Exactly. Then you'll want to hold the piece you've chosen against the roof of your mouth and stroke it with your tongue, concentrating on how it feels as it melts. Is it firm?

Smooth? Silky? The experience should satisfy on multiple levels, and stimulate the senses."

Annoyance started to buzz in Ben's head like a pissed off hornet. What the hell did Raj think he was doing, using his chocolate pickup line on her in that flirty tone?

Wasn't *girlfriend* supposed to mean off-limits? Especially among friends?

He tried to tame the building buzz. Was he overreacting?

Maybe.

He wasn't used to these feelings of possessiveness. Women in his life had always been casual. Temporary. But Miranda was none of those things.

She was *his*, damn it.

"And then you want to concentrate on the taste. Not just the big one, but also the subtle ones as well. Does the flavor come on strong, or slowly build to a peak? How long does it last? That's called the—"

"I think she's got it."

Ignoring Raj's look of surprise that quickly turned to speculation, he picked out a half-dozen flavors for Miranda to try. Lucky for Raj and his perfect teeth, he took the hint and moved off to help a trio of new customers as his assistant bagged the purchase.

"Sorry if he made you uncomfortable with all the heavy flirting."

"Oh, I don't know. I kind of enjoyed it."

The annoyed buzzing turned into an angry swarm. "He didn't mean anything by it, you know. He flirts like that with everyone. It's good for business." Didn't she hear him using the exact same lines on the women at the other end of the booth?

"Wow. Good to know. Thanks."

Her flat tone was what broke through his jealous haze to realize he was acting like an ass. "God, I'm sorry. That wasn't what I meant."

"Then what did you mean?"

He ground his back teeth. "That I hated him flirting with you, especially after I told him you were my girlfriend."

The tight line of her mouth softened. "Yeah, you did tell him that, didn't you? I won't lie, it's not something I'll get tired of hearing anytime soon. And I'm sorry I enjoyed his flirting so much. It's just...that never happens anymore, and it felt kind of good. Which was wrong, and I'm sorry."

It was just...nice. Being talked to like a regular person for a change.

The memory of her wistful words had him wanting to kick his own ass. Again.

"It wasn't wrong. It was honest." And he'd gone and ruined it for her.

She relaxed against his side with a theatrical sigh. "So, do I ever get to try this supposedly amazing chocolate?"

"Only if I get a kiss."

"I think I can manage that."

"For each piece."

Her lips quirked. "Getting greedy."

"About you? Always." And it was the truth. She made him want more. Expect more. Of everything, including himself.

He knew exactly which one Miranda was going to love the most, but he took his time offering her the small bite-sized samples of each flavor in between claiming his kisses. By the time they got to the last one, he was so hot for her he was almost in pain.

"Oh." Her fingers flew to her mouth as she tasted the final piece. "Oh, my God. That's so freaking good."

"Yeah? Let me check." He kissed her, sweeping his tongue between her lips where he caught a hint of the jalapeno-laced candy. "Mmmm. Delicious."

"More, please," she groaned.

"More chocolate? Or more kisses?"

"Yes."

He obliged her by having Raj put together a box of her favorites to take home. The kisses would have to wait for home, too. It was already next to impossible to walk without having to adjust himself. Thank God his shorts were loose fit.

They continued checking out all the fair had to offer. But navigating with Sam was getting tougher as the streets got more crowded.

Most people were good about giving them a clear path once they saw the guide dog harness. But there were still several near-misses with people either in too much of a hurry or too inconsiderate to pay attention to what was going on around them. And the incidents of children running up wanting to pet Sam were increasing as well.

Miranda was patient and kind as she explained over and over that sorry, he was working and couldn't be distracted. But there was one mother who'd given her a hard time about it being "not a big deal" to just let her kid pet the stupid dog.

It had been damn near impossible for him to bite back a response to that bit of entitled bullshit. But somehow he had, letting Miranda handle it.

Which she did by calmly but firmly saying "Yes, ma'am, it's a very big deal, and I'd appreciate it if you'd educate yourself and your child about the proper etiquette when dealing with working dogs for the future." She'd given Sam his forward command and walked away before the sputtering woman could come up with a reply.

Talk about delivering a mike drop moment.

He leaned in and whispered, "That was so hot," making her laugh. That was when he noticed both she and the dog were starting to look a little stressed around the edges.

Damn, he should have picked up on that sooner.

"Do you want to call it a day?"

"Would you mind?" Miranda stroked Sam's head as he leaned into her leg. "It's getting a little too crowded for me."

"Not at all. I think we've had our fill of homemade soap and junk food. Unless you want to stop and get that funnel cake you were craving on the way out?"

She looked slightly nauseated. "Pass. I'm already going to be in a sugar coma on our way home."

On our way home.

He liked the sound of that.

Trying to stick to the edges of the crowd as much as possible, they slowly worked their way back toward the other end of the blocked off street where they'd parked. Before they got there, though, he heard an all-too familiar squeal right before a soft, warm body barreled into him like a heat-seeking missile.

He lost his hold on Miranda's hand as he staggered under the impact.

"Benny, Benny, Benny! It *is* you!"

"Jesus, Val." Disentangling himself from her, he grimaced as her perfume burned its way up his nose. "You have to stop doing that."

"Sorry. I was just so glad to see you, I couldn't help myself. It's been like *forever.*"

And yet, still not long enough.

"Yeah, well, we were just leaving, so..."

He started to reach for Miranda's hand again, but Val latched onto his arm with surprising strength, pressing her lush breasts against him as she did. "Oh, no, you can't go already! It's so early."

God, had he ever found that whiny pout attractive? Or had he just been so focused on the big boobs and talented mouth that he'd willingly overlooked the more annoying parts that came with them?

The more he was able to step back and take a good look at himself as he'd been the last few years, the less he liked what he was seeing.

Who he was seeing.

"Val, we talked about this, remember?" He tried to pry her fingers from his arm without hurting her, but damn, the woman was like a barnacle.

"You said we couldn't have sex anymore, but that doesn't mean we can't still hang out, right?"

Miranda made a small noise, drawing Val's attention. Her eyes narrowed, then widened in understanding as she noticed Sam standing stoically at Miranda's side, her hand firmly gripping the handle.

"Oh, hey, sorry, I didn't mean to ignore you." Val raised her voice slightly. "Can we help you get someplace? Sorry, sorry, that was rude, wasn't it? You don't even know who I am. I'm Valerie, and this is my really good friend Ben. He's a fireman, so he's, like, totally smart and reliable. Anyway, it's kind of crowded, so it's good you had him helping you. We can totally take you wherever you need to go so you don't get lost or confused or mugged or anything. We don't mind, do we, Benny? Then we can go see some more of the fair after. So, what do you think?"

If she hadn't sounded entirely sincere in her own ditzy way, it would have been horrifying.

No, scratch that. It was still horrifying, in a "watch your life crash and burn around you" kind of way.

"Yeah, Benny," Miranda said, eyebrow quirked. "What do you think?"

What did he think? That he was starting to regret ever suggesting they come down to the fair in the first place. Between Nancy, Raj, and now Val, he'd be shoveling shit off his head for at least a week before he could come up for air.

"Valerie, this is my girlfriend, Miranda."

"Oh, how silly of me." Val rolled her eyes and laughed. "Of course you're a friend of Benny's. He's always helping out people like you."

"Like me?" Miranda asked.

Uh-oh.

He recognized that silky tone. "Val—"

"Yeah, you know. Pretty women who need someone they can trust to help and take care of them." Val looked up at him with adoration in her eyes, making him feel like a heel. "Benny's really good that way."

"Ah…" Looking caught off guard by an answer she hadn't expected, Miranda had no comeback. "I see."

"Val, I don't think you understand. Miranda is my *girlfriend*." He put as much emphasis as he could on the word without having to spell it out.

He watched his meaning sink in as Val's expression shifted from confusion to disbelief. She slowly released his arm and took half a step back.

"But…you don't do relationships. That's what you said, right from the start. No relationships. Only sex."

He winced at the shrill words being thrown back at him. "Val—"

"Or was it just me?" Her raised voice garnered a few turned heads.

"No, Val, it wasn't just you."

"Then *why*? Why her, and not me? What did I do wrong?" The last word ended on a wail as tears started to fill her eyes.

Shit, shit, shit.

"You didn't do anything wrong. It just wasn't…there for us."

"But it is with her?"

He took Miranda's hand in his. Thank God, she let him. "Yeah. It is."

Tears dripped from Valerie's heavily mascaraed lashes. "It could have been there for us if we tried a little longer."

"No, Val. It either happens, or it doesn't." He hated hurting her feelings, but damn it, it was the truth. He hadn't planned to fall in love with Miranda. It had just happened.

Whoa.

Love? Where the hell had *that* come from?

He'd accepted they were in a relationship, sure, but *love*? Love meant long-term commitment. And hearts on the line. And a thousand and one chances for him to screw up and let his true stupid self show and chase her off, just like he always did.

He waited for the panic to set in, but all he got was a warm sense of contentment that soothed the emptiness he hadn't realized he'd been trying to fill with all that sex.

Son of a bitch. He loved her.

And he liked it.

With a sniffle, Val looked at Miranda, then away again, shoulders slumping. "I guess." She ran the back of her hand across her cheek, leaving behind a streak of black. "Is she why you wouldn't sleep with me the last time I saw you?"

He almost said no. He'd only known Miranda a few days when he'd run into Val in the lobby of his old building. But in a way, she'd started changing him from that very first time they met. "Yeah, I guess she was."

Val nodded. "Well, at least that makes sense, then. I mean, why else would you have said no?"

He winced at the implication. But honestly, she was right. He couldn't remember a single other time he'd turned down no-strings sex when it was offered. Even on the rare occasions he went out with absolutely no intention of looking for a hook-up, if a woman took it upon herself to come on to him, he was all in. No one but a fool would turn that down.

Certainly not someone who thought sex was all he had to offer.

Something he was only just starting to believe might not be true. Because of Miranda.

A quick glance at her told him absolutely nothing about what she might be thinking at this moment. Whatever it was, it couldn't be good. He needed to figure out a way to end this and get them out of there without Val going into a total meltdown.

"Val, look. I'm really sorry—"

"No, I'm sorry." Visibly gathering herself together, she wiped her face. "You never lied to me about how you felt. I just always hoped…" She gave an unhappy laugh. "I hoped this time, one of the good guys might actually want me for keeps."

"Jesus, Val." She was ripping his heart out.

"It was really nice to meet you, Miranda. I hope you guys are super happy together." She went up on her toes to kiss his cheek. "Bye, Benny." Before he could form a reply, she slipped away into the crowd.

"You should probably go after her."

He looked at Miranda in surprise before shaking his head.

"No. I definitely shouldn't." He slid his arm across her shoulders and pulled her tight against his body, relieved when she didn't try to stiff-arm him away even though she had every right.

He kissed her temple. "I'm so sorry about that. About everything that happened today."

"It's fine. Let's just go, okay?"

The ride home was made in silence. He knew every minute it continued was one more minute for Miranda to pick apart the conversations with Val and Nancy and find every little nuance she could use to string him up by his balls. He hadn't done anything wrong, but he wasn't sure how he could convince her of that.

By the time they finally pulled into his driveway, his guts felt like they'd been used for knot-tying practice by a troop of cub scouts. After they got out of the SUV, he waited while Miranda got Sam's harness and leash in hand, unsure which direction she was going to head. His house, or hers.

A silent sigh of relief left him when she picked his.

Not that he wouldn't have followed her if she'd made the other choice. But at least his anxiety came down a few notches from Defcon 1.

After letting Sam do his business and filling his food and water bowls in the kitchen, a still quiet Miranda left him greedily devouring his kibble and headed to the living room. Ben took a deep breath, then grabbed them a couple of beers and followed.

"So," he said as he handed her a bottle where she was curled up in the corner of the couch, "are we going to talk about it, or do we keep letting the tension build and see who cracks first?" He took a long swallow of his beer, steeling himself.

Cradling the bottle between her hands, Miranda tipped her head thoughtfully. "This is really bothering you, isn't it?"

"And it's not bugging you?"

She shrugged. "Not really."

"Oh, come on." He thumped his beer onto the coffee table. "You spent the whole ride home stewing about it."

"No, actually I spent it in a sugar coma, just like I said I probably would."

She had. But that was before his man-whore past had caught up with him. And as much as he hated the term, he was starting to realize it fit.

"So, running into Nancy and Val didn't bother you at all?"

"I didn't say that."

"I knew it." Why it felt he'd scored a point, he had no clue.

"But I got over it before we ever left the fair. Well, over Nancy, anyway," she added after a second of thought.

"And Val?" He braced for the worst.

"Val was...interesting. I wanted to hate her, but I couldn't." Miranda scrunched her nose. "She was kind of like one of those high-maintenance yappy dogs, always looking for attention and being a pain in the butt, but not a mean bone in their little bodies. I think I kind of liked her, to tell you the truth."

"Even knowing I slept with her?"

Why couldn't he stop poking at this?

"Let me ask you something. That time she mentioned, when she wanted to sleep with you and you turned her down. When was that?"

"The night after our first pizza dinner." The smile that crossed her face confused him. "Why?"

"Because," she said as she set her beer down and scooted closer to him, "it means you were telling the truth when you said you hadn't looked at another woman since the day you met me. And *that*"—she slid her hand up his arm to cup his face—"is all I need to know."

He was too stunned by her words to participate in the kiss she laid on him. All she needed to know? So, all of that worry and angst was for nothing?

It couldn't be that simple. He had to be missing something.

Breaking off the one-sided kiss she asked, "What's wrong?"

"Are you sure?"

She gave him the kind of smile that made his dick sit up and take notice. "Slick, I am one hundred percent sure. Now, are you going to keep your promise or not?"

"My promise?"

"To help me burn off all those calories."

"Oh." He scooped her legs up and brought them across his lap to straddle him. "That promise." He stood in one strong motion, his hands under her ass to support her. She let out a small yelp of surprise, followed by a joyful laugh.

God, he loved that sound.

"Boy Scout, remember?" He headed for the stairs, her legs wrapping around his waist as he climbed them. "We always keep our word."

For this woman, he always would.

She made him want to be a better person.

Hell, she *made* him a better person.

And after today, he knew there was absolutely no one else for him. It was Miranda, or nobody at all.

Chapter 18

"You ran into *two* of his exes?"

Miranda grinned at the amount of outrage Trixie infused in those seven short words. "Well, to be fair, only one of them was an ex." Although Nurse Nancy sure would have liked to change her status.

The memory of the woman's ballsy flirtation soured some of her amusement.

"According to him."

"No, she was pretty clear about her interest in getting to give his penis a tryout to see if it lived up to the hype." That announcement was met by sputtering. Probably Trixie choking on her wine.

"She did not!"

"She did." Miranda picked up the die and shook it in her cupped hands before dropping it to the well-loved kitchen table in Trixie's apartment.

"Six. Okay, you can go to either Sports and Leisure, or Science and Nature for the wedge."

"Science and Nature." Which was not her best Trivial Pursuit category. That frustratingly elusive green wedge had cost her the game more than once.

There was the soft hiss of a card being pulled from the box. Trixie cleared her throat and read, "What is the maximum amount of exes a woman can tolerate meeting in one day before being forced to commit homicide?"

Miranda lobbed a handful of popcorn across the table at her friend. "Not funny."

"No, it isn't."

"Trix..." Regretting her impulse to divulge the whole uncomfortable mess, she sighed. "It's not like he didn't tell me he's been with a lot of women."

Something she thought she'd made peace with. They'd both had lives before they met each other. His previous sexual excess had no bearing on their current relationship, as long as he remained faithful to her now.

Funny how much harder it was to remember that when faced with the living, breathing, crying proof.

"But he never said you were going to have to beat them off him with a stick, either."

True.

"Is he really that good looking?" Because honestly, she had no idea.

She knew every detail of his body. Her fingers had explored each delicious inch. So had her mouth. It was an outstanding body, if she did say so herself. All hard and buff, with just the right amount of muscle to give him definition without edging into gym-rat territory like some of the guys in her old unit had done.

Personally, she found Ben's sleek, panther-like physique much more attractive than bulgy muscles-on-muscles.

But his face? Not a clue.

Yes, she'd touched it. Many times. That's something lovers did, sighted or not.

The only thing it told her was that all of his parts were right where they belonged: two eyes, one nose, two oh-so talented lips. How those parts all looked when put together remained a mystery.

"Girlfriend, he's the kind of good looking that could tempt a saint to drop her robes and do him right in front of the Pope."

"Wow, lovely sacrilegious image, Trix. Thanks."

Her friend hummed, her thinking noise.

"He doesn't look like any one celebrity, but...if Chris Evans and Jensen Ackles had a baby, that would be Ben. Only with black hair and green, green eyes."

Captain America and the sexy, broody brother from Supernatural?

Oh, damn. Talk about some superhero level hotness.

Not that she cared about his looks one way or the other. Obviously. But if he was so freaking gorgeous, it meant she didn't just have to worry about the women he'd already slept with who might be looking for a repeat performance like Val. She'd also have to contend with all the ones who *hadn't* slept with him yet but wanted to.

Like Nurse Skanky.

Although she'd made it sound like it was his reputation, not just his looks, that had made her proposition him.

"They call him Mighty Murphy," she blurted.

That brought another hum, this one more intrigued.

"Because of the size of his package, or what he can do with it?"

"Oh, for...I didn't ask," she said with a sour tone.

"Well, you'd be in a position to know firsthand about both," Trixie replied with a sly note. "Care to make a guess?"

"No." Her face heated. Neither Ben's measurements nor his skills in bed were something she cared to discuss, not even with her best friend.

Although the truth was, it could have been either.

Or maybe both together.

"Spoilsport."

"Perv. Now, will you read me the damn question?"

"Geez, I thought getting regular sex was supposed to make you less grouchy. Okay, what fraction of the day does the typical cow spend chewing?"

"You know, if it was anyone but you, I'd swear you went looking for the stupidest possible questions every single time I land on a wedge." Because seriously. Cows?

"Does that mean you don't know?"

"Of course, I don't know. Who would know that?"

"It's three-quarters."

"Stupid cows." With a scowl, she slumped back and sipped her wine as Trixie took her turn.

"Entertainment for the pink wedge," she announced before pulling a card. "Who replies "I know" to Princess Leia's confession "I love you" in *The Empire Strikes Back*?"

Miranda thumped her glass down.

"Oh, come on! That's not fair. I get cows and you get Star Wars? I made you watch those movies!"

"And now I can thank you for it. Let's see…I'm going to say it was the deliciously snarky Han Solo. And hey, look, I'm right." Plastic clicked on plastic as she added the wedge to her playing piece. "That's all six pieces of the pie, girl. All I need to do is land on that center spot and you're toast. Want to concede now and save yourself the pain and humiliation?"

"Don't start doing your victory dance just yet. Gimme." She rolled, missed her question, and passed the die back.

"Getting back to the original topic," Trixie said after she missed her next question as well. "What did Ben have to say about being mauled by his groupies in front of you?"

"They didn't maul him." Although come to think of it, it had been pretty obvious from the amount of perfume clinging to his shirt afterward that Val had come close. "And he apologized."

"As he damn well should have."

"It wasn't his fault. They both approached him, not the other way around." Something she reminded herself every time the memory itched under her skin like a chigger.

Both women had singled him out of the crowd like lionesses targeting a choice bit of prey. And both had totally discounted the fact Miranda was right there next to him, simply because she was blind.

And *that*, if she was honest with herself, was the part really bugging her.

What would have happened if she hadn't brought Sam with them? If her blindness wasn't as obvious? Would Nancy or Val have refrained from trying to make a move on Ben with her there if they'd thought she was sighted?

Annoyed with herself for letting the possibility bother her so much, she rolled the die. Play continued with increasingly tense competition until finally Trixie landed on the center hub and Miranda got to pick the category for her final question.

"Geography." She grinned at her friend's pained groan.

"Where's the first point of U.S. land visible from a ship sailing from Hamburg to New York City? Hmm." The card tapped against the table as she thought.

"Come on, tick tock, Trix."

"I'm thinking, I'm thinking." More tapping. "I guess…Long Island?" There was a brief pause as she flipped the card for the answer. "Yes!" Trixie crowed, startling Sam out of his sleep with a jolt as she drummed her fists on the table. "I am still the trivia queen!"

"Congratulations, your highness," Miranda said wryly as she bent down to give Sam a comforting pat to let him know everything was okay.

A gracious winner Trixie was not.

The woman was a hard-core competitor. Which was why Miranda loved when they did game night. Everyone else always went easy on her. Half the time she won, she was sure it was because they'd cheated in her favor.

Trixie, on the other hand, always gave her best effort, no matter what. Even if it meant grinding Miranda into the dust.

Just like she would anyone else.

As they packed away the game pieces, she said as nonchalantly as she could, "Speaking of Long Island...Ben asked if I wanted to go to dinner at his parents' house out on the east end." Saying the words out loud made her stomach do a dip and whirl.

"He did?" Trixie sounded surprised. "That's a pretty big step."

"I guess. But it kind of seemed like he only asked because he felt he had to. And besides, he's already met most of my family, even if it was by accident, so maybe it's not? Big, I mean."

"Trust me. Any guy asking a woman to meet his parents is big."

"So, you think I should go?"

"You mean you didn't already say yes?"

She cringed at her friend's shrill tone.

"I asked if I could let him know." He'd seemed okay with it, but now she had to wonder if she hadn't hurt him a little with her waffly answer. She sighed. "That was a crappy thing to do, wasn't it?"

"Well, it would depend on why you had to think about it, I guess."

She swirled her wine and took a swallow of the zinfandel, savoring the sweet berry undertones as she considered the question. Why *had* she stalled?

Maybe because she'd just made this huge, scary gesture, offering him full access to her home and her life, and he'd come back with *maybe you might want to come with me to my parents' for dinner?* Talk about waffly.

But he'd still asked. That should count for something. Right?

"I guess because I'm a wuss."

"You are," Trixie agreed.

"Bitch." She laughed, then groaned and covered her face with her hands. "I have to go, don't I?"

"If you want things to get to the next level between you two, then yeah, you kinda do."

Did she want that?

Did Ben?

That was the million-dollar question.

"Things have happened so fast between us. I mean, we've only known each other a month or so, but we spend almost all our free time together. And most nights he ends up staying over." She hesitated. "Which is kind of why I gave him a key."

Trixie hauled in a gasp. "To your house?"

"No, to my gym locker. Of course, to my house."

"Girl, that's huge! Why didn't you lead with that?" She gave Miranda's arm a little play slap. "Did he give you one to his place, too?"

"Yeah, he did." The next day. It had kind of felt like an afterthought, truth be told.

Sort of like the lukewarm dinner invitation.

"Then I'd say you've already moved things to the next level."

"Does that mean I don't have to go to dinner?" The hopeful question was only half in jest.

"It means you'd better get your booty ass down to Long Island and score some major brownie points. Guys may say they don't do what their mothers tell them to, but that's bullshit. All men are momma's boys to some extent. And if momma ain't happy with you, nobody will be."

Great. No pressure there.

"So, what do I do if she doesn't like me, then?"

"Don't worry. You're smart and cute. How could she not love you?"

"I'm also loud, Hispanic, blind, and sleeping with her son."

"And which one of those is what's really bothering you?"

"Sometimes I hate it that you know me so well." She sighed, her hand dropping down to rub Sam's head where he lay beside her chair. "Being blind, of course. What if I go to dinner and they're all weird about it? About me?"

"Then they're idiots and you have my permission to school them on the facts of life, Hernandez style."

She laughed, but it did little to stem the worry that had settled in the back of her brain ever since Ben first uttered the half-hearted invitation.

"Yeah, well, things didn't go so smoothly the last time I tried being a part of his life outside of Kenoway. What are the chances this will be any better?"

"As good as you make them. Look, you can go into it expecting the worst, or you can show up ready to kick ass and take names. Nicely," she added after a second's thought. "No need to go all Jarhead crazy on them. You need to save something for the second dinner."

She laughed, but Trixie was right. She was a Marine, damn it. She knew how to improvise, overcome, and adapt. Surely, she could get through one lousy family dinner if that's what it took to make Ben happy.

Ben shut the study book on a groan. "That's it. I'm done. My brain is totally fried."

Cody never looked up from his own book. "Ten more minutes."

"Code, I'm serious, man. I'm toast. I've been reading the same question for, like, the past five minutes, and the only part I understood was the question mark." He tossed the study guide to the other end of the couch, when what he really wanted was to pitch it out the window.

Or set it on fire.

Or set it on fire and *then* pitch it out the window.

With a sigh, Cody closed his book and stretched his arms over his head until his back gave an audible pop. "Are you sure all this isn't making things worse instead of better?"

"This" being the extra study sessions they'd been doing at Cody's apartment every week in addition to the official prep class they'd both enrolled in. There were a lot of people taking the lieutenant's test he needed to score better than if he had any hope of promotion. Not necessarily people who knew more than him, but certainly ones who were better at taking tests.

And at the end of the day, that's what would matter.

"No. It's definitely helping." Continuing their self-study nights in between the official prep classes every week meant his brain was less likely to jam up under pressure in a room full of his peers.

Most especially Cartwright.

Cody glanced at his watch as he brought his arms down from his stretch. Something he'd been doing a lot of all night.

Usually, Ben was the one impatient to be done, so he could get home to Miranda. "Am I keeping you up past your bed time, Goldilocks?"

"Ha, ha."

"No, seriously. I appreciate the extra help, but if you've got someplace to be..."

"It's nothing. It's just..." Cody shrugged, looking uncomfortable. "I might have made a date for after we're finished is all. It's not a big deal."

It might not be a big deal, but it was definitely something, judging by the way Cody suddenly wouldn't meet his eyes. Ben couldn't resist the opportunity to needle his friend a bit over it.

"A date, huh? Let's see...is it the French stewardess, what's her name? The one you said had lips like a Hoover?"

"Yvette, and no."

"How about the model from the underwear shoot?"

Cody shuddered. "God, no. That was like having sex with a praying mantis, all legs and arms and no meat in between. All that was missing was her biting my head off after we were done."

Ben winced at the probably unintended double entendre. "Then is it—"

"It's Val."

"Val?" It took a second to process. "As in *Val*? Crazy stalker from downstairs that I moved to get away from Val?"

"She's not crazy," Cody snapped. He popped out of his chair and started grabbing up the empty water bottles from the coffee table. "And she's not a stalker. She just gets easily attached to people who pay attention to her, is all."

"Like a stalker."

"Fuck you, Murph. She's a good kid, and you kind of broke her heart."

He watched in surprise as his friend strode to the kitchen. A good kid? Broke her heart?

What the actual fuck?

"Since when did you become all Team Val?"

The bottles thumped into the recycle bin under force. "Since I found her crying her eyes out after she saw you and your girlfriend at the street fair last weekend."

Damn it.

He pinched the bridge of his nose. "I didn't mean to hurt her feelings, but it's not like I lied to her or anything. I told her we were over months ago, long before I even met Miranda. It's not my fault she didn't want to listen."

Even though, on some level, he did kind of feel like it was his fault she'd been hurt. He couldn't forget the look on her face when she realized he'd broken his one hard and fast rule about long-term romantic entanglements.

Specifically, not having them.

Coming back to the living room, Cody dropped into his chair with a grunt. "I know. It's just, she was so broken up, I couldn't leave her sitting there in the coffee shop looking like her last friend in the world had died. So, I brought her home."

Ben tensed. "And?"

"And we talked. Jesus, I'm not that much of an asshole I'd take advantage of her condition to get her into bed. I'm not Cartwright, for fuck's sake." He looked pissed at the mere suggestion.

"And yet you made a date with her for tonight."

"Yeah, I know, I probably should have talked to you about it first, since it kind of bends the rules about not going after the same women. But I figured you wouldn't mind, since you were pretty clear it was over."

"Why would I mind you keeping Val off my ass?" He made a giving gesture. "Please. Go for it. But Jesus, you know how she can get, and you still want to go out with her? What the fuck, Code? Are you suddenly a glutton for punishment?"

His friend shrugged. "I didn't plan it. I ran into her in the elevator this afternoon, and she asked if she could come over tonight, maybe hang out, have a few drinks, so I figured, why the hell not? My new roommate is always out, and God knows you're never around to hang with anymore."

Well, shit.

"Sorry, man. I'm just—"

"All wrapped up in your lady," Cody finished with a smirk. "Don't worry, I get it. If I had all that waiting at home every night, I wouldn't want to hang out with me either."

Cody had finally met Miranda a few days before the fair. Ben had been more worried than he thought he'd be about how it would go. They were the two most important people in his life right now. He wanted them to get along.

And they had. Better than expected.

Maybe a little too well.

By the end of their day of barbeque, beer, and bonding, Cody had given Miranda a sloppy kiss on the cheek, drunkenly confessing to Ben, "I never should have let you have her, Murph," before he staggered off to crash on his old foldout bed for the night.

Of course, that had led to Miranda wanting to know what he'd meant. He'd had no choice but to explain—in the vaguest terms possible—about their voyeuristic first glimpse of her from his bedroom window while painting. And Cody's magnanimous "gift" of not pursuing her even though he had dibs because he'd seen her first.

Thank God she'd found it amusing rather than creepy.

"Have you told her yet?"

"Told her what?"

"About what you're really doing here every week." He made a sound of disgust at Ben's guilty expression. "You're an idiot."

"I know what I'm doing." Probably.

"I don't like lying to her. And you shouldn't, either."

He didn't. But what had started as a simple misdirection about why he was driving down to Queens twice a week had become an entire house of cards, poised to collapse and rain down all over him like burning timbers at the first wrong move.

"The test is in four weeks. I'll tell her after it's over."

As long as he didn't choke and fail. If he did...well, then he'd never have to mention it at all, would he?

Cody was shaking his head. "I'm telling ya, it's gonna come back and bite you in the ass, bro."

"It'll be fine. It's not like I'm doing anything wrong. We're just studying."

"Whatever. It's your funeral."

A knock at the door ended the discussion. The eagerness to Cody's expression as he jumped out of his seat made Ben wonder if he'd been telling the truth about nothing happening between him and their sexpot neighbor. Or maybe he was simply anticipating making up for lost time tonight.

Either way, it was time to go.

Shoving his things into his messenger bag, he slung the strap over his shoulder and headed for the door. Val was standing there giving Cody the kind of possessive, hungry look that used to send Ben running in the other direction. She was dressed in super-tight skinny jeans and a blouse so sheer he could almost count the freckles on her shoulders.

Oh, it was *so* time for him to go.

"I'm hitting the road."

"You're not leaving because of me, are you?" She batted her heavy lashes, making clear she knew he was. "Look, I made Cody brownies. Because I know they're your favorite," she added with a smile for Cody before redirecting her gaze back to Ben. "Why don't you stay and have some with us."

Not a chance in hell.

"Thanks, but I need to get home."

Disappointment flashed across her expression, so fast he wasn't sure if he'd imagined it or not. By the way she smiled at Cody again, he must have. He gave his head a mental shake. He really hoped Cody knew what he was getting himself into.

With a quick goodnight, he walked past the two of them toward the still open door. His nose twitched as he passed through the cloud of Val's perfume. Jesus. He'd been to chemical spills that weren't as strong. She must have given herself a fresh dousing right before leaving her apartment.

Rolling the windows down once he hit the bridge helped to clear his nose. Too bad it couldn't do the same for his mind. All he could think about on the drive home was Cody's warning that his lies were going to catch up to him.

Then again, it had been Cody who suggested he tell his parents he was taking the test and look at how that had turned out. His mother's words of discouragement still stung.

Shit!

He almost swerved off the road when realization hit him. His family all knew about his plans to take the test. And Miranda didn't. If he put them all together around the dinner table, it would only be a matter of time before someone said the wrong thing and his little white lie would be outed.

Shit, shit, shit!

As much as it had rankled at first, maybe it was a blessing in disguise she hadn't seemed enthused with the idea of meeting his family.

Okay, new plan.

He wouldn't bring up the dinner thing again until the test was over. His mother wouldn't be happy, since he'd already mentioned bringing her, but it couldn't be helped. Not if he was going to keep Miranda from knowing the truth until he was ready to tell her.

Then, after the test, he'd confess all, apologize, and make a full-court press to get her down to the Island to meet the rest of the Murphy clan.

Confident he'd caught all the possible pitfalls that might trip him up, he cranked up the radio and checked the time. If he didn't hit traffic on the Hutch, he'd be home in time to tuck Miranda into bed.

With him, where she belonged.

Chapter 19

Breathing hard, Miranda fell back against what seemed to be the lone pillow they hadn't knocked off her bed with their enthusiasm. "You know, it's a good thing we're both in shape, or one of us would probably be in traction by now."

As it was, she wasn't sure she could feel her toes.

Then again, the rest of her felt so damn good, she didn't really care.

"Sweetheart, if we weren't in shape, we'd both be dead by now." Ben stretched out beside her, covering her right breast with his large hand. Little aftershocks of sensation rushed through her body at the possessive touch. "Damn, I just can't get enough of you."

It wasn't exactly "I love you," but she'd take it. Especially since she hadn't yet decided where she fell on that subject herself.

"Right back at ya, Slick." She rolled her head until it was pillowed on his shoulder and slid her arm around him, holding him close. "Mmm, I could stay just like this the rest of the night. The hell with dinner."

"I wish I could, but I need to shower and head down to Dom's."

She groaned. She'd known that, but all the endorphins flooding her system had obliterated the knowledge for one brief, happy moment. "Do you have to?"

"You know I'd much rather stay here with you." He nibbled along her neck, making her squirm and laugh. "But yeah, I do. In fact"—he twisted away, probably checking the time—"thanks to this little unscheduled treat, I have to skip dinner, or I'm going to be late." He gave her a smacking kiss before leaving the bed.

Disappointed, she swung her legs over the edge of the mattress and began to methodically search for and collect the scattered pillows and clothes from the floor as the old water pipes in her hall bath started singing their song. A twist of embarrassment hit her with every clunk and groan.

In all the months she'd lived there before meeting Ben, the noisy plumbing and simple tub/shower combo never bothered her. Now, she resented every time she had to use it. Ben's spa-like bathroom had totally spoiled her.

Everything about Ben had spoiled her. He was the best thing to happen to her in a very long time.

And somehow, she was screwing it up.

Just like she'd worried she would.

Oh, it was subtle. So subtle that at first, she hadn't even realized it.

But over the last few weeks, he'd started to pull back. They still ran, and trained in the pool, and went out to eat or to the movies or just for long rambling walks. And they definitely still had sex.

Lots and lots of sex.

But it was like the small window into his personal life that had been inching open had suddenly been slammed shut. Right on her fingers.

No more get-togethers with his friends. No more trips down to his old neighborhood.

And when she'd finally told him she would love to accept the invitation to dinner at his parents' house, that she was excited to meet them, the response hadn't been what she expected. In fact, he'd seemed more frustrated than pleased by her enthusiasm.

Not that he'd said so. But it was there in his voice, and the way he suddenly started making excuses every week.

The summer traffic is going to be a bitch. Let's skip this week and just stay home.

Sorry, something came up for this Friday and Mom needs to reschedule.

Don't worry, we'll get there one of these weeks. What's the rush?

The rush was that with every week that passed, she felt a little less sure of what direction they were heading in.

All too often, it felt like it was apart.

Then they'd have a perfect day like today, where all of his attention and desire made it feel as though they were the only two people in the world. And she was left not knowing what the hell to think.

Dragging on the shorts and top he'd stripped from her eager body a little while ago, she waited on the edge of the bed until he came back and started to dress before bringing up the question she'd been mulling over for the past few days.

"When you see Cody at Dom's tonight, why don't you ask him to come up here tomorrow?"

"What for?" He sounded distracted.

"Well, you're doing him a favor by helping him study. Why should you be the one who always has to drive all the way down there and back every time?"

"And he drove all the way up here when he helped out with the renovations." There was an edge to his voice she chose to ignore.

"Okay, yeah, obviously he had to come here for that, just like you have to go there to help out Dom. I get that. But you guys can study anywhere. If he came up here sometimes, you wouldn't have to spend all that extra time on the road every week."

When you could be spending it with me.

She bit the words back, because they were selfish as hell.

God, when did she become such a needy little whiner?

"I don't know why this is suddenly a thing." The mattress dipped as he sat to pull on his sneakers.

"It's not a thing." But clearly it was, if the fact he'd sat on the end of the bed as far from her as he could was any clue. "It was a question."

"Well, it sure sounded like it was a thing."

"I thought maybe you'd want to change it up a little, that's all. Tomorrow's supposed to be a gorgeous day. Instead of being stuck cooped up in his apartment, you could sit outside by the pool and get some fresh air and sunshine while you worked." The silence that met her suggestion was chilling. A small knot formed in her belly. "You know what? Never mind. It was a stupid idea."

He got up and came over to stand in front of her, bringing his warm, spicy, just-from-the-shower scent she took into her lungs like a hit of drugs. When he put his hands on her shoulders, the small contact sent wave of relief through her, loosening the knot.

"It wasn't a stupid idea. It's just...the test is only two weeks away. Things are working fine the way they are, so there's no reason to start changing them up now. Sometimes routine is good. Besides, if we were here, I'd end up being distracted by you." He gave her nose a playful tap.

His argument made perfect sense.

And yet, there was that little thread of something in his voice that was just...off. It was there every time they talked about that stupid test, which admittedly wasn't all that often. The few times she'd brought it up, he'd gotten defensive and weird about it, until she finally stopped trying to poke at something he clearly didn't want to discuss.

But not knowing *why* he didn't want to was like a splinter under her skin, annoying and ever present.

Hoping to lighten the mood, she smiled. "With all this help you're giving Cody, it's too bad you aren't taking the test yourself. You'd probably ace it."

It was said jokingly, but Ben's hands fell away from her shoulders like he'd been burned. "I have to go. Cody will give me nothing but grief if I'm late."

"Cody? Don't you mean Dom?"

"What?"

A small chill she couldn't explain rippled through her.

"Aren't you working on Dom's bathroom tonight? Because his mother is at her book club on Wednesdays?"

Which was evidently the only time they could work on the renovations, when she was out of the house. And why they could only get in a few hours of progress a week, making the project drag on for over a month now.

Or so he'd told her.

"Right. I am. Slip of the tongue." He gave her a fast kiss on the cheek. "See you when I get back." He was gone before she could say anything else.

With a groan, she fell back on the bed as the front door closed behind him downstairs.

No. Slammed.

"Couldn't leave it alone, could you, Hernandez? You just had to keep pecking away about that damn test. Idiot!"

She lay there, listening to the familiar sound of his SUV as it started up and backed out of his driveway. She tracked his progress down the street, going a little faster than he should be. Because he was running late, or because he was running from her?

By the time he turned the corner and the engine faded away to nothing, she felt his absence like a hollow ache in her chest.

So much for that perfect day they were having.

Why? Why did it bother her so much he was spending all this time with his friends? It wasn't like he didn't spend the rest of his free time with her.

And he was right. Cody had spent months coming up to help him work on his house on his days off. It was only fair Ben do the traveling now. That he was helping out two of his friends at the same time didn't change that fact, even if it did double the number of miles—and time—he was putting in on the road.

So why couldn't she accept things the way they were and let it go?

Maybe because somewhere, deep down where she tried to ignore it, there was a tiny grain of doubt rubbing her raw inside. After running into those women at the fair, and the way he'd started to close her off from the other parts of his personal life outside of Kenoway, sometimes it was hard not to wonder.

And worry.

And think about what she actually had to offer a man like Ben Murphy. Handsome, virile, charismatic Ben Murphy, who could have any woman he wanted. And, by his own admission, pretty much had.

Ones who didn't cling like a baby sloth, or make demands on all his free time.

Or wallow in the occasional pit of despair for no good reason.

"Pity party, table of one," she muttered as she forced herself to her feet. "God, I'm pathetic." It had to be the hormones. The tell-tale discomfort in her lower abdomen said her period, usually short but intense thanks to the Pill she took to regulate it, was imminent.

Normally she just got bitchy, though, not weepy. The guys in her unit had known when to tread lightly around her, and when to run like hell. Bitchy kept her strong. Weepy just flat-out sucked.

Going downstairs, she skipped the chicken frittatas they'd planned to have for dinner before ending up getting naked and crazy instead, and went straight for the gallon of caramel swirl in the freezer.

Fuck it. If she was going to be a cliché, she should at least enjoy it.

Sam padded after her into the living room and joined her on the couch, his snout resting on her knee mere inches from the bowl of ice cream. She laughed. "Yeah, I know, Mr. Mooch. I'll save you a spoonful, I promise."

She rarely gave him people food. It wasn't good for him. But she decided they were both entitled to a cheat-day from their usual healthy menu. Of course, the last time she'd had one, she nearly barfed up deep-fried Twinkie all over Ben's front seat.

Although it hadn't only been the junk food that made her nauseous that day.

After dropping the promised treat into Sam's bowl, she grabbed a bottle of water to try and mitigate the sugar crash she'd set herself up for and wandered onto the back patio. With the sun low in the sky, the searing July heat was finally starting to dissipate.

Birds filled the air with chirps and tweets as they swooped around the feeder Gail always kept full of seed next door. A squirrel screeched from the tree in the corner of the yard, scolding her for invading his territory. Other than that, it was peaceful and still.

But instead of being lulled as she usually was when she sat and let the quiet wash over her, all she felt was edgy and restless.

When had being alone started to feel so damned lonely?

Annoyed with herself, she stalked back inside and traded her water for a beer before going into the living room. She turned on the television, flipped through the entire lineup of channels twice, then turned it off again.

This was ridiculous. She was ridiculous. He hadn't even been gone two hours yet. How could she miss him so freaking much?

Face facts, Hernandez, you've got it bad for the guy.

Yeah, she did.

The question was, what did she do about it?

Did she continue to go on as they had, enjoying their time together and having brain-melting sex whenever the mood struck—which was always—or did she accept that her feelings for Ben had grown into something much more substantial?

Maybe not love. Not yet, anyway. But if the hollow ache inside when he was gone was anything to gauge it by, she was coming close.

The thought both excited and terrified her.

Mostly terrified.

Because she wasn't sure she would ever be enough for him. Not when he was used to having his flavor-of-the-week to move onto whenever he got bored.

Was he getting bored?

Turning the television back on, she tried to distract herself with the Yankee game. But even then, it was like she could feel the minutes ticking off, one by one, bringing her closer to seeing Ben again.

Damn. She really did have it bad.

By the time the Yankees lost and programming changed over to the local news, Ben still wasn't home. She checked her watch. He rarely ran this late, and when he did, he usually called to let her know.

Another half hour went by. Still no Ben. Still no call. The minutes ticking by inside her head started to take on a different kind of urgency.

It was stupid to worry. She was not going to be the needy girlfriend who checked up on her guy every time he was a few minutes late, damn it. She should just go to bed. He had the key. He'd use it when he got there, whenever that was. It was why she'd given it to him.

But then midnight came and went, and with it her last shred of restraint.

"Hey Siri, call Ben."

As she waited for her call to go through, she paced around the living room, unable to sit still. With every ring, her stomach twisted tighter. He was fine. There was a perfectly good reason he wasn't answering his phone. There was no need to panic.

Then, just before it would have rolled over to voicemail, the call was answered by a sleepy voice saying, "Hello?"

A sleepy *female* voice.

Miranda froze in place.

What. The. Fuck.

"Where's Ben?"

"What?" There was the sound of the phone being handled. "Oh, that makes more sense. I couldn't figure out how my phone got stuck in the sofa cushions. Because it's not mine!" The girlish giggle scratched Miranda's already frayed nerves like barbed wire. "I forgot we have the same phone *and* the same ring tone. Isn't that too funny? Anyway, Benny must have left his here by mistake. He was in kind of a hurry when he left."

Benny?

There was only one woman she knew who called him that.

"Yeah, I'll bet he was."

"When you see him, can you tell him where his phone is?"

"Oh, I will. Count on it." Blood was pounding so loudly in her ears she barely heard Valerie say goodnight. She ended the call and stood there, anger building inside her like a wildfire sweeping through a tinder-dry forest.

She'd been waiting here, thinking about him, *worrying* about him, and he'd been...

God, she couldn't even think it.

It hurt too much.

"There has to be a reason," she muttered as she started stalking around the room again. "Some reasonable explanation that doesn't include him being a lying, cheating bastard." But try as she might, she couldn't come up with one.

The sound of Ben's SUV coming down the street brought a harsh laugh. Five minutes. If she'd been patient for five more minutes, she might never have known the truth. How much longer would he have been able to play her for a fool before she finally caught on?

She was such an idiot.

After he pulled into his driveway and the engine cut off, she practically held her breath, waiting to see what he'd do. He wouldn't come to her fresh from screwing another woman, would he? Was he that much of a prick?

A minute later, the key turned in the front door, and she had her answer.

"Bastard," she hissed under her breath as she turned to face him.

"Oh, hey." He sounded surprised. "I didn't think you'd still be up this late. I figured you just forgot to turn the light off before you went to bed."

Something she did do sometimes, since she had no light sense. Which was why the living room lamp had a timer to turn it off at one a.m., just in case.

"Nope, I'm wide awake." In more ways than one now.

"And I'm glad." He slipped his arms around her, hesitating when she held herself stiff rather than melt into him the way she usually did. "What's wrong?"

"I was worried." And that made her feel like even more of a fool.

His tone was immediately conciliatory.

"I'm sorry, baby. We lost track of time, and then there was an accident on the Clearview that screwed up traffic all the way to the bridge. I was going to call you from the car and let you know, but I must have left my phone at Dom's."

"You did leave it." She twisted her body and stepped out of the embrace, when what she really wanted to do was punch him in the throat. Hearing him say "we lost track of time" was almost too much. "Don't you want to know how I know?"

"O-kay." He stretched the word out, sounding confused. "How do you know?"

"Because I called it."

"You did?" At least he was smart enough to start sounding wary.

"Yeah, I did. And guess who answered."

"Well, probably Cody."

The patronizing tone ramped up her temper a few more degrees.

"Really? Wouldn't it make more sense if it was Dom, since that's whose house you were supposed to be at tonight? Working on the big bathroom reno project?"

"Umm...right. I was. And then I stopped over at Cody's for a beer. You know, after."

"Uh huh. Well, surprise, it wasn't Dom *or* Cody who answered. It was a woman." Her heart sank even further when Ben pulled in a sharp breath. "Any idea who that might be?"

As she thought he might, he took the rope she'd given him and ran like a thief in the night with it. "It must have been Cody's girlfriend."

"Really? That's what you're going with?"

"Well, who else could it be?" He gave a nervous little laugh and rubbed her shoulder. "Come on, it's late and we're both tired. Let's go to bed."

In the past, his touch had always sent flames of desire licking along her body. Now, it left her cold and frozen.

Deciding she'd had enough, she yanked the rope tight around his lying neck.

"You should tell Val she needs to tone down the perfume. It's kind of hard to miss. *Benny*." The stink all over him was unmistakable.

His hand fell away. "Shit. Look, it's not what you think."

"No? So, what? Val was helping Dom redo his bathroom, too, and that's how she got her hands on your phone? And you?"

"She never...damn it! Look, I can explain."

"Oh, please do." She dropped onto the couch and crossed her arms. "I'm all ears."

Long seconds passed. He sighed. "Okay, look, you're right. It was probably Val who answered—"

"Probably?"

He took a deep breath. "But it's not because I was doing anything with her, I swear. All I did was leave my phone at Cody's."

"Cody's? Not Dom's?" she pressed, wanting to see if he'd lie. Again.

"No. I wasn't at Dom's tonight. But I guess you already figured that out."

She pretty much had. But the confirmation still stung.

"Were you there *any* of the nights you told me you were?" The silence sliced through her, only just beginning to realize how deep the lies went.

Unable to stay still, she popped to her feet and started to pace again. "Okay, so what were you doing at Cody's that you felt you had to lie to me about it?"

"It doesn't matter."

"Seriously? You lie to me for weeks, come home reeking of another woman's perfume, and it *doesn't matter*?" A memory kicked in, nearly gutting her. "Oh, God. Valerie lives in the same building as Cody, doesn't she?"

"That's not—"

"Doesn't she?"

"Yes." The word sounded strangled, like he was gritting his teeth. "But that doesn't have anything to do with anything. Val isn't important."

"No? You still haven't explained how she got her hands on your phone."

"I told you, I left it at Cody's. Val must have decided to answer it. Although fuck if I know why she would," he added on an angry mutter.

"Evidently you have the same phone and ringtone." And wasn't that just gag-worthy adorable? "So, if your phone was at Cody's, how did Val get it?"

"Because she and Cody hooked up."

"Valerie and *Cody*?"

"Why are you saying that like you don't believe me?"

"Uh, because the both of you told me you have some stupid 'bro code' thing that keeps you from going after the same women."

At the time, she'd found it amusing when Cody had drunkenly admitted why he regretted letting Ben have first crack at meeting her. Now it just seemed like a convenient lie.

Or maybe not so convenient, since it blew Ben's lame excuse into as many pieces as a frag grenade.

"That's not the same thing. We don't go after the same woman when we're, ah…"

"Hitting on them in bars?"

"Yeah."

"But what? It's different after you're done with them? Sloppy seconds is okay?"

"That's… No, we don't. Usually. But I told him I was fine with it if he wanted to go after Val. More than fine. He'd be doing me a favor, actually."

Did he even hear himself right now?

"Wow, how generous of you."

"Why the hell are you making such a big deal out of this?" Now he was starting to sound angry, too.

Which only made her madder.

"Aside from you sounding like a misogynistic asshole? How about because you lied to me."

"And I said I was sorry!"

"But you still won't tell me the truth, will you?"

"God *damn* it!"

She flinched at the fury in his voice, but didn't back down. "If being with me wasn't enough, you should have said something, not lied and snuck around behind my back."

"Is that seriously what you think? That I've been cheating on you with Val?"

"Honestly? I don't know what to think."

Because the Ben she knew—that she *thought* she knew—would never do that to her. But this Ben, the one who lied right to her face, could be capable of anything.

"Miranda, I swear to you. I never cheated on you, with Val or anyone else. You have to believe me." He waited a few long heartbeats. "But you don't. Do you?"

She swallowed down a bitter lump of confusion and despair.

"I don't know what to believe. All I know is you lied, and you would have probably gone right on lying for God knows how long if you hadn't forgotten your phone." She silently begged him to deny it.

Instead, he went on the attack.

"I'm not the only one who lied, sweetheart. You said you could handle the fact I'd had a lot of women in my life. You told me my past, my reputation, didn't matter. But that wasn't true, was it? You're judging me based on the man I used to be, not the one I started becoming the day I met you."

"I am not!" Was she?

No, damn it. She wouldn't let him turn this around on her. *He* was the one who lied. *He* was in the wrong here, not her.

"Look, all you have to do is tell me the truth. Where have you actually been going all this time?"

"No. Either you trust me, or you don't."

The rigid finality to his words scattered the last shreds of hope she'd been clinging to. He wasn't going to tell her.

"Then I guess maybe I don't."

"Then I guess I know where I stand."

There was a moment of painful silence, followed by heavy footsteps and the slam of the front door for the second time that day.

It took a minute for her to break the icy paralysis holding her captive and stagger to the couch, banging her knee on the table as she went. A sob choked her. Fighting it down, she dropped to the corner cushion, feeling as though her strings had been cut.

With an anxious whine, Sam pushed his nose into her face and gave it a lick. Closing her arms around him, she let him crawl into her lap as she wrapped her arms around his neck and finally gave in to the tears.

Chapter 20

"I told you this was going to happen."

Ben shot his friend a tired scowl. "Fuck you, Code."

Undeterred, Cody pointed at him with his half-empty bottle of Coke. "You need to apologize, and soon."

Not what he wanted to hear.

He took a long swallow of his own soda, grimacing as the icy coldness shot straight to his already pounding head. Perfect. He put it down with a thump. "Why should I have to apologize? I didn't do anything wrong."

Cody's bottle stopped halfway to his mouth. "Dude, you *lied* to her."

"But I didn't cheat on her, and that's what she thinks I did."

Hearing Miranda admit she didn't trust him had hurt worse than he could have ever expected. It was like all the air had been sucked from his lungs, with a fist squeezing his heart until it was ready to pop.

Her fist.

"Can you blame her?"

"Fuck yeah, I can!" Despite the lingering brain freeze, he took another swallow. Hell, maybe he could freeze out the memory altogether.

From across the table in the firehouse kitchen, Cody sighed and shook his head. "Murph, you lied about where you were. A woman answered your phone. A woman she knows you slept with." He sounded a little disgruntled about reminding them both of that fact. "What else did you expect her to think?"

"That I wasn't some lying asshole scumbag." He waved an impatient hand at Cody's incredulous look. "Yeah, yeah, okay, I lied. I get it. But it wasn't for anything bad."

"How is she supposed to know that? Just tell her about the fucking test already!"

"It's none of her damn business!" His hand sliced out to emphasize the words, knocking the Coke bottle on its side. "Shit!"

Jumping up to avoid getting a lapful of sticky soda, his chair went over with a clatter. With another curse, he grabbed a handful of paper towels and mopped up the mess, then tossed the sodden pile in the trash.

A vague sense of déjà vu hit him as he righted his chair. Of his very first fight with Miranda, in another kitchen, with another chair and a spilled drink to mop up. That had been about a lie, too. Hers, even though it was only one of omission.

He'd been so angry at the thought of her laughing at him while he bumbled along, not smart enough to figure out the woman across the table from him was blind. She'd accused him of having a chip on his shoulder that night, and she'd been right.

He also had a healthy dose of cowardice. Why else would he hold onto the lie now, when telling the truth could fix everything? Well, almost everything.

There was still the little matter of Miranda's lack of faith burning a hole in his gut.

"Things okay in here?"

Ben started and turned at Odell Watson's soft baritone. "Sure, Cap. Everything's fine." He managed a nonchalant grin as he retook his seat. Watson was a nice guy and a good captain, but he didn't tolerate any crap in his house.

After giving a quick look around the kitchen, probably to make sure there weren't any signs of the brawl he must have thought he'd find after hearing Ben yell and a chair hit the ground, he headed for the coffeepot on the counter.

Ben couldn't blame his caution. Ever since Cody had started dating Val, Cartwright had become douchier than ever. There had been several almost-fights cooler heads had only barely prevented from boiling over into the real thing.

Full mug in hand, he gave them both a look filled with "I'm watching you two" and walked back out. Ben's tense shoulders slumped in relief. Good guy or not, no one wanted to get on the captain's bad side.

"Are you really going to let this thing with your family mess up what you've got with Miranda?"

Great. Evidently, they weren't letting this go yet.

"What the hell does my family have to do with anything?"

"You're kidding, right? Your mother has the magic touch when it comes to screwing with your confidence. You told me how she reacted when you said you were taking the test."

"Yeah, thanks for that bit of advice, by the way."

"Hey, don't blame me for you not being able to deal with your mom's passive-aggressive shit by now."

He bit back his angry response as he mulled that over. He'd never really considered it before, but Cody was right. His mother often phrased her discontent in ways that made it seem like she only had Ben's best interests at heart. Anything positive she had to say about something he wanted to do was always followed by a great big *but*.

I know you want to be a firefighter like your uncle, but don't be too disappointed if you don't get the job, it just means it wasn't meant to be.

It's lovely you're buying a house, but I'd hate to see you waste your savings fixing it up just to sell it at a loss when it gets to be too much for you.

All simply nicer ways of saying she thought he was going to fail, so why bother trying.

He shook his head. "It doesn't matter what my mother thinks. That has nothing to do with what's going on between me and Miranda."

"Dude, it has *everything* to do with it." Cody leaned forward over the table. "Your folks didn't support you when you told them about the test, and you thought Miranda would react the same way."

"No, I didn't."

Yes, he did.

He'd panicked. Self-preservation had kicked in, and the lies had come spilling out of his mouth. Little white lies, he'd thought at the time. Ones she'd never find out about, so what would they really matter?

How could he have known it would all blow up in his face like a damned Molotov cocktail?

Cody snorted. "Whatever. But ask yourself this: is lying to protect your feelings from what she might say more important than losing her?"

The finality in those words sliced into him, making the ache throbbing in his chest even worse. Had he lost her? After storming out of her house two nights ago, he hadn't let himself think about it too much. He'd been too busy ping-ponging between being furious at her and feeling sorry for himself.

"We just had a fight," he said, hating the uncertainty of his own words. "That doesn't mean it's over." It couldn't be. She'd promised not to push him away if he screwed up.

And it was looking like he'd done that in royal fashion.

"It does if you don't explain your ass, which you keep saying you won't do."

"I shouldn't have to."

"Then what do you expect to happen? After a few days, you'll go home and both magically be over it, and everything will go back to the way it was before like nothing happened?"

"How the fuck should I know? I've never had a fight with a woman before."

Ben shoved back from the table and stalked to the fridge where he grabbed a bottle of water. Giving the top a vicious twist, he guzzled part of it down to help wash away the tinny taste of fear from his mouth.

"Never?" Cody's brows shot up.

"Not with one I cared about seeing again." He leaned his hip against the counter. "And neither have you, so don't give me that look."

"Hey, unlike you, I've had actual long-term girlfriends before. And I can guarantee this isn't the kind of thing a woman just gets over. Forgetting you made a date, or leaving the toilet seat up in the middle of the night? Maybe. But a big, fat lie you won't explain, that happens to involve your ex?" He shook his head. "You're gonna need to fix that shit."

"Fuuuck." He groaned it out like it had a lot more than one syllable as he tilted his head back to study the dingy ceiling tiles.

The thought of telling Miranda about how he needed to do twice the studying as everyone else just to take a stupid test made him want to vomit. Maybe there was another way to fix things without her finding that out. One that didn't involve baring his guts to the vicious claws of ridicule.

"What if I told her I was helping *you* do extra studying?"

"And why would you have needed to lie to her about it in the first place?"

Cody and his fucking logic.

"Then what if..." He came up blank.

"Face it, Murph. You need to find your balls and tell her the truth."

"What truth? That she's dating a moron?"

"No, I'm pretty sure she already figured that out for herself," Cody shot back with a sour twist to his lips. "Because only a moron throws away what you have just to protect his own ego."

"So, what? I put it all out there for her and hope she doesn't boot-stomp my heart into the ground?"

"No, you put it out there and *trust* that she doesn't."

There was that word again.

"Just like she trusted me when I said I wasn't sleeping around on her with Val?" That sparked a thought. "What if I got Val to talk to her? Tell her she's sleeping with you, not me, and that's why your apartment reeks of that damn perfume whenever she's there? She'd have to believe me then, right?"

Cody stared at him with in wide-eyed disbelief. "Jesus, you really are a moron if you think that would make things better."

"But—"

"You need to fix this, Murph. *You*. And there's only one way to do it. Tell her the fucking truth."

"But—"

"Do you love her?"

He paused, not sure he wanted to admit it. "I thought maybe I might."

"And what about Miranda? Does she love you?"

The air suddenly felt like syrup trying to fill his lungs. "I don't...I'm not..." Feeling like he was drowning, he shook his head. "I'm not that guy."

"What guy?"

"The one women stick with long-term. That they love. I never have been."

Miranda had tried to excuse it away, saying the women he'd been with were the reason things never lasted. And though he'd let her convince him of the possibility, deep down he always knew the fault lay somewhere within himself.

He was likeable. And fuckable.

He just wasn't good enough, or smart enough, or maybe just *enough* to be loveable.

Not even to her, it seemed.

"How do you know she doesn't love you?" Cody asked, breaking into his depressing spiral of introspection.

"Because she never said so."

"And you did?" He nodded when Ben looked at him like he was nuts. "Right. So, if you love her and never told *her*, how do you know she doesn't love you, and just didn't tell *you*?" Looking pleased with his reasoning, Cody sat back and drank the last of his soda.

That tantalizing possibility made his heart double-thump before reality crashed back in. "Because if she loved me, she'd trust me."

"Shouldn't it go both ways? You love her. Shouldn't you trust her, too?"

There was that fucking logic again.

Wanting to wipe the smug look off his friend's face with his fists, he put the violent energy into pacing instead. "What if I tell her about taking the test, and why I lied, and she still kicks my ass to the curb? What then?"

"Then you're no worse off than you are right now."

Not true.

It would be easier to live with Miranda's distrust and anger than any lukewarm support or, worse, any backhanded encouragement she might offer the way his mother had.

He froze.

Jesus fucking Christ. This *was* about his mother.

And he really was a coward.

"I fucked up."

Cody gave him an exasperated look.

"Yeah, you did. Now fix it."

"Aw, did poor widdle Benny have a fight wid his girlfriend?" The expression on Cartwright's face as he sauntered into the kitchen was pure malice laced with anticipation.

"Eavesdropping, Hoss? What are you, a little girl?" Cody shot back.

"Fuck you, Moore."

"No thanks, I have a much better standing offer at home." Cody gave him a nasty grin.

Cartwright's face went a mottled red at the allusion to Val, who'd turned down his advances more than once in the past when she was hanging around the firehouse trolling for info on Ben. "You're welcome to her. I'd never get much satisfaction from something that's been plowed so many times already, anyhow."

It was Cody's turn to darken with rage. "Shut your fucking mouth about her."

There was no chance of that happening. Not when Cartwright had gotten the reaction he wanted. No, he went right on pressing that button. "Or maybe you get off on knowing your buddy here was there first. Is that it? Are you two such 'close friends' that screwing the same woman is the next best thing to screwing each other?"

Cody's chair went flying back, hitting the wall as he rounded the table. "I warned you, asswipe."

Ben caught his friend around the chest with both arms before he got close enough to do something stupid, no matter how much Cartwright deserved it. "Walk away, Hoss."

The bastard had the nerve to laugh. "You seriously think either of you could take me?" He smacked his broad chest and spread his arms. "Bring it."

Ben snorted. "Right, like I'd risk my job over you. You're so not worth it."

"Oh, that's right, I forgot. Benny's scared of facing things head on. You'd rather run away and hide like the little bitch you are."

Before Ben could react, Cody lunged, almost breaking free of his hold. "You motherfucker," Cody snarled as Cartwright laughed. His body was all but vibrating with fury. "Keep laughing. You won't think it's so damn funny when you have to take us both on. Then we'll see who's the bitch."

Instead of looking worried at the threat, Cartwright seemed almost intrigued by the possibility. Before anyone could say anything else, though, Captain Watson strode into the kitchen. Displeasure was written all over his dark ebony face as he took in the tableau before him.

"Just what in the hell do you three think—" His words ended as the speaker crackled to life overhead.

"Engine 237...Ladder 192...respond to a phone alarm...Box 124...the address 7816 Fourteenth Avenue. Both units respond second due for a reported structural fire in a private dwelling."

Watson pointed at the men as a whole. "We'll be talking about this when we get back." He spun on his heel and exited, followed by the rest of them.

After donning his gear and climbing into his seat in the aerial truck as Cody slid behind the wheel as chauffer, Ben did his best to shove everything except the job from his head. Cartwright was easy to let go of. The burning need to apologize to Miranda was harder, but he managed, because he didn't have a choice.

There wasn't room at a fire scene for anything less than a hundred percent focus.

He slipped his arms through the straps of the SCBA tanks recessed into his seat as they roared through the streets, lights and sirens accompanied by an occasional descriptive curse from Cody at people who didn't get out of the way fast enough.

In the irons position this shift, he grabbed the axe and Halligan bar from under his seat as they pulled to a shuddering halt to the accompaniment of hissing air brakes. After he jumped to the ground, he got his first good look at what they had.

A large part of the calls they received were either total bullshit, smoke from burned food on the stove, or a small puffback from a cranky oil burner.

This wasn't any of those.

Huge flames shot from a front window on the second story of the residence like festive red ribbons. The hot glow filling the other upstairs window hinted there was a good chance the entire upper floor was already involved. The first due hoses were being dragged through the gaping front door, apparatus and firefighters clogging the street in both directions as frightened and curious neighbors huddled together to watch or take cell phone video.

"Murphy, Salazar, let's go," Captain Watson barked.

Pulling his mask on cut out most of the acrid scent of smoke, and helped pull Ben's focus in tight. It narrowed his world down to what was in front of him, the fire-retardant hood underneath muffling the discordant sounds of sirens and radios and people until they were muddled background noise mixed with the sound of his own breathing.

Every sense was fixed on the here and now.

He'd gone scuba diving once, and the isolating sensation was similar. Only underwater you felt mostly weightless and free. Decked out in full fire gear and equipment, he was humping nearly ninety extra pounds and lumbered like an overpacked trail mule.

Tools slung over his shoulder, he followed Watson to the front door of the house to the left of the one that was burning. Homes in this area of Brooklyn were mostly row houses, meaning they shared a common wall with the home next door, and the one next to that, and the one next to that. It gave the fire an almost inexhaustible supply of ready fuel as it burned through from one dwelling to the next.

They needed to make sure they stopped it before it consumed the entire block.

"Neighbors told PD an elderly couple lives here, and no one knows if they're home or not," Watson said as Ben forced the locked door open with the Halligan. The suck and whoosh of the breathing apparatus made the captain's already deep voice even more Darth Vaderesque. "Said the son had been visiting, but they don't know if he's still here or not, either."

"Seems to me nobody knows a whole lot of nothin'." Hector Salazar hitched the strap of the water extinguisher into a more comfortable position on his shoulder as he moved past Ben into the smoke-filled living room, ready to knock down any fire they found while Ben and Watson searched for victims.

With luck, there wouldn't be either.

Visibility went from almost normal to a hazy half-past dusk within a few yards of the front door. It was impossible to tell yet if the smoke was only seeping through from next door, or if it meant the fire had already breached the common wall and encroached into this house as well.

With practiced ease, the three worked as a unit to clear the rooms on the ground floor. Coming up empty, they headed for the stairs. Sweat started trickling down Ben's neck along his spine under the heavy bunker gear.

The haze grew thicker and darker as they went up.

Not a good sign.

The doors to the two smaller bedrooms facing the street were open. A quick search showed them both empty. So was the bathroom. The door to the last bedroom that faced the rear of the house was shut.

Ben's pulse sped as he pushed it open. If they had any victims, this was the only place they could be.

Entering the room, it looked empty, too, but that didn't always mean it was.

His breath whooshed in his own ears as he checked the floor on the far side of the bed and then underneath it while Hector checked the closet, before shaking his head at the captain. "Nothing."

"Nothing," Hector echoed.

Ben put his hand against the wall to help lever himself to his feet. And immediately yanked it back from the unmistakable heat that bit at him despite his protective gloves. "Cap, I think we've got fire in the walls."

As Watson called for a line to the second floor, Ben retreated to the hallway with him to give Hector room to probe the plaster-and-lathe connecting wall with the six-foot hook he carried. Every test hole he made released a belch of smoke and hot gases, but no flames.

Yet.

The hose team pounded up the stairs, forcing Ben and Watson to shuffle further back down the narrow hallway to make room. Cartwright had the nozzle, his size making the identification easy as he brushed by them even without being able to read his name on the back of his jacket through the thick smoke.

Cartwright and his backup were one step away from the bedroom when a muffled *whoomph* blew out from above their heads.

The force of the explosion took them all off their feet. Like the swat of an invisible giant's hand, the fire bottled up in the cockloft space above them flashed outward from a sudden influx of oxygen from somewhere, igniting the superheated gases in the air.

For a few stunned moments, Ben had no idea how he'd come to be laying on his back. His ears rang, muffling what was going on around him even more than normal, his vision blurring to black at the edges.

With a groan, he pushed himself over onto his side. The sight of everyone knocked over like dominoes among the burning debris from the partially collapsed ceiling brought his brain back online with a click.

Backdraft.

Thank God it happened above them and blew mostly outward. Otherwise…

Yeah, better not to dwell on that.

The first piercing chirps of PASS alarms began to sound, snapping him into automatic crisis mode. Act now, think later.

A quick headcount in the hall came up one short.

"Hector!"

Ignoring the pain grinding up his back from landing on his air tank—again, damn it—he managed to drag himself forward on his hands and knees, staying below the banked black smoke rapidly filling the hallway. He paused next to Captain Watson, who was getting to his knees, shaking his head as though to clear it.

He waved a hand to let Ben know he was okay.

Cartwright's backup on the hose, Eva Boone, was starting to roll over, seeming like her bell had been rung even harder than Watson's. Cartwright was still down but moving enough to deactivate his personal alert safety system alarm, looking like a big black sea turtle beached on its back by a wave.

Which left one alarm sounding, screaming that the person wearing it hadn't moved in over thirty seconds.

And it was coming from the bedroom.

Ben shoved aside a huge chunk of plaster and lath blocking the doorway and crawled in, afraid what he might find. The sinister crackle of flames surrounded him, the only thing visible through the blinding smoke. Every flammable surface in the room seemed to be burning with greedy intensity.

How the fuck would he find Hector in this?

If he's even still alive.

The flash of despair lasted only a split second before training kicked in. Listening to the high-decibel alarm, it seemed to be coming from everywhere at once, damn it, thanks to the muffling effect of his hood. He kept one hand in contact with the wall to stay oriented as he crawled. The other he swept out in search of Hector.

The Halligan, which he'd somehow managed to hang onto, extended his reach. But the room, which had seemed so small before, now felt like an endless blind maze.

Every second ticking by was another second Hector might be breathing in toxic smoke if his mask had been dislodged. Or flames could be licking past his protective gear to sear the tender flesh underneath.

A man might survive second- and third-degree burns.

But if they were bad enough, he might not want to.

Come on, come on…

Tension nipped at him while he worked his way around the bed in the thickening smoke. Was the alarm louder to his left? Or was that merely wishful thinking?

The clock in his head was ticking down with increasing urgency. *Where the hell—*

His Halligan connected with something metal under a large piece of the ceiling that had come down in the explosion. Thankful that plaster and lath didn't burn as easily as sheetrock, he flipped the smoldering debris aside.

Heart pounding like a freight train, he put his facepiece as close as he could to Hector's, trying to see if he was breathing. "Hector! Hey, Salazar! Talk to me!"

The most beautiful sight in the world was Hector's eyes fluttering open.

Relief flooded through his churning gut, leaving him almost lightheaded. "Welcome back, brother."

They might be open, but Hector's eyes remained unfocused. "Wha…"

Watson joined Ben on his knees at the downed man's side. "How is he?"

"Coming around, but out of it."

It should have been impossible to tell with all the gear, but Watson's shoulders seemed to slump in relief. "Stairs are compromised by debris, and we've got no water in the line. We'll have to go out the front window."

Fucking wonderful.

Gathering a groggy Salazar between them, they dragged him from the burning room and across the hall to the nearest street-facing bedroom, where the explosion had partially shattered the window. Boone took the Halligan from Ben and started clearing the rest of the glass from the frame. Cartwright closed the door behind them as best he could in the blast-torqued jamb, blocking off the majority of the heat and smoke.

From that direction, anyway.

After sitting Hector against the wall, Ben looked up at the somewhat intact ceiling as the trapped smoke rushed out the now wide-open window, giving them better visibility and lessening the pressing heat a few degrees. With the cockloft space above now fully involved, it wasn't a matter of if it all came raining down on them, but when.

Even now, small pieces of debris were dropping like burning confetti as they fluttered through the openings to the floor, the fire eating its way through the decades-old wood framing above like a starving beast.

Somewhere along the line, Cartwright had grabbed the extinguisher Hector carried in and was putting out the small fires around the room, buying them time. It wouldn't be much.

The can only held so much water.

Ben looked up as the ceiling made an ominous cracking noise. No hand extinguisher was going to stop what was up there. They needed out of the building.

Now.

Boone was at the window, giving hand signals to direct the aerial ladder as it was extended toward the opening. When she clenched her fist to signal "stop," Ben and Watson got Hector to his feet.

There was more walking than dragging this time as they moved him, but there was no way he was making it down the ladder under his own power. Luckily, helping hands appeared in the window.

Cody. No one else could scale a ladder in full gear that fast.

The man was part mountain goat.

Cody helped guide Hector out onto the ladder and clipped him into the safety line. As Boone waited, giving them time to get partway down the ladder before exiting herself, another loud crack came from overhead.

Ben instinctively ducked, arms coming up over his head as a small section of ceiling slammed to the floor near the door.

Cartwright attacked the new fire with the extinguisher as Boone practically dove out the window onto the ladder, both knowing they were running out of time. Watson motioned to Ben to go next.

He didn't even try to argue. As officer, Watson would make sure he was last out, no matter the danger. Which was one of the reasons his men would literally run into a burning building with him.

They trusted him to have their backs.

As he turned to the window, there was another crack from above, this time so loud it sounded like a gunshot. Everything slowed as Ben looked up and saw the beam sagging through the hole in the ceiling, its entire length being greedily consumed by flames.

Right over Cartwright's head.

Who didn't see it, because he was concentrating on putting the last of the water on the fire near the door.

There was no time to think, only react.

Ben launched himself at the larger man, knocking him sideways, both of them hitting the ground hard just before everything went black.

"I'm going to kick his ass."

Miranda barely resisted the urge to slam the door in Tino's face. She so didn't have the energy for his shit tonight. "And hello to you, too."

"I mean it. What did the bastard do to you?"

"He didn't do anything."

Nothing she wanted to discuss with her brother, anyway. But from the tone of his voice, he wasn't going anywhere without getting some answers. Resigned, she backed away from the open door and let him in.

"Bull. You've been crying. You never cry."

Not entirely true. She just didn't cry where anyone could see her doing it.

She had an image to uphold.

But she had shed so many tears since Ben stormed out on her two nights ago, she'd begun to worry she might never stop. As it was, her eyes felt raw and swollen, and her nose was so stopped up she could barely breathe.

She could only imagine what she looked like that even Tino, with his less-than-keen powers of observation, had known with one look what a mess she was.

"Why are you even here?" she asked as she walked back to the living room.

"Julietta said you sounded funny when she talked to you on the phone earlier, and she couldn't come herself, so she asked me to stop in and check on you on my way home from work. Don't make that face," he added. "Your family is allowed to worry about you, no matter how self-sufficient you think you are."

Normally she would have attacked that "think you are" statement, but she just didn't have any fight left in her at the moment.

Retaking her spot in the corner of the couch, she curled her legs under her. Her hand fell on the mountain of used tissues. She shoved them down behind the cushion, hoping Tino wouldn't notice.

Sam jumped up and curled beside her again. He hadn't left her side once.

At least she had one faithful guy in her life.

Digging her fingers into the dog's soft ruff, she hugged him close and sighed. "Ben and I had a fight, that's all."

"About what?"

"None of your business."

"Of course it's my business. You're my sister. He hurt you. I need to know how bad to hurt him back." The sound of knuckles cracking put her hackles up.

"This isn't the school playground, Tino. You don't have to fight my fights for me anymore."

"I don't care if you were a big, badass Marine. To me, you're still *mi pequeña mariposa*, and any guy who makes you cry needs to bleed."

As much as she wanted to stay annoyed at him, hearing the childhood nickname of little butterfly made it impossible. Which was probably why he dragged it out whenever he wanted to soften her up.

"You still don't get to kick his ass."

Tino sighed. "Then what *can* I do?"

"Nothing. Everything's f-fine." To her horror, she burst into tears.

The next thing she knew, she was cradled against Tino's shoulder as great, gasping sobs wracked her body. She clung to him, the comfort of having arms to hold her as she cried out her pain and confusion far outweighing the humiliation of appearing weak.

He spoke softly to her in Spanish, rocking her, until finally the sobs faded and the tears dried to a trickle.

"Feel better?" When she sniffled and nodded, he pressed a kiss to the top of her head, then shoved some tissues into her hand. "Good. Now, blow. You're getting snot all over me."

With a wet laugh, she did as instructed.

After mopping her face, she sighed and laid her head back on his shoulder. "Thank you."

"*De nada*. Now, do you want to tell me what really happened? And try to do it quick. Your dog is giving me the stink-eye. I don't think he's happy about getting evicted from the couch."

"He's just confused. He knows something's wrong but can't figure out what."

"Well, that makes two of us."

She sighed. What the hell. She'd already embarrassed herself. How much worse could it get?

As succinctly as possible, she told Tino about the events leading up to her fight with Ben. There was a muttered threat to Ben's manhood when it became clear he and Miranda were having sex. But otherwise, he listened without interruption until she reached the end, with Ben slamming out of the house and going radio silence two nights ago.

Using another tissue to capture the tears that had sneaked out as she spoke, she said, "I want to trust him, Tino. I really do. But why wouldn't he just tell me the truth if it didn't have anything to do with him seeing other women on the sly?"

"Because that's exactly what it had to do with," he replied in a harsh tone.

"But I don't know that."

And the more she thought about it, the less she believed it.

"Are you kidding? What about the *puta* who had his phone? The one he f—um, slept with. You think that's just a coincidence?"

"It could be. She's seeing his friend Cody now, and Ben admitted he was at his apartment that night." But he hadn't said why he was there. Or if that was where he'd been all the other times he lied about being at Dom's. "And she's not a whore, so don't call her that."

"Seriously? You're defending her?"

"You weren't there when we ran into her at the fair. I'm telling you, that conversation didn't sound anything like they were still sleeping together. Valerie was upset when she saw us together. I mean, she cried."

"Maybe because he was keeping you a secret from her, too. Playing you both."

Pain from that possibility zinged through her chest like a battery jolt, but she shook her head. "Why wouldn't she have said something, then? He made it clear we were together, and they never would be. She even said straight up he refused to sleep with her the last time she saw him."

She'd played that entire cringeworthy encounter over and over in her head since the wee hours of the morning when she gave up trying to sleep. Picked apart every nuance of what was said, and what wasn't. For a little while she even wondered if maybe he'd started up with her again after that encounter.

Maybe because of it.

But despite her initial knee-jerk reaction, the more she went over it, the more she couldn't believe Ben would do that to her. He just wasn't that guy.

"Okay, fine. If he wasn't sleeping with this *pu*—person, then what was he doing?"

"I don't know."

"Where was he going?"

"I don't know!" She rubbed her throbbing temple.

"Face it. He's a fu—freaking idiot to treat you this way, and you need to forget him."

"He's not an idiot," she snapped. "Don't you ever call him that."

"Jesus, do you hear yourself? You just finished crying your broken heart out over the guy because he's a liar, and now you're defending him. *Hermanita*, he's not a good man."

"He is!"

"Then he's just not good for you."

"But I love him."

It was a hell of a time for that realization to finally arrive.

But there it was.

Ignoring her brother's curse, she grasped his hand tight in hers. "Tino, I really do. I love him. Why else would this hurt so bad?"

"Damn it." He pulled her close again. "I told you to be careful, and look what you went and did. You wasted your heart on an ass."

"He's not." She sniffled. "Okay, he's an ass. But he's my ass, and I still love him anyway." Tino let out an *oomph*, and Sam was suddenly there, pushing his nose into her face, lapping at her wet cheeks with a whine.

"Your dog is standing on my balls," Tino gasped in a strangled whisper.

Biting her lip to keep from laughing, she pushed Sam away long enough for Tino to get to his feet. With a satisfied grunt, the dog hopped up and retook his spot, paws draped over her legs, head pressed to her chest in his version of a doggy hug. "Sorry about that."

"That dog has boundary issues."

It was true.

From the day she met him at Another Step Forward for their two weeks of training after being paired, Sam had bonded with her as if he'd been waiting for her all his life. He might have the goofy good-natured personality all golden retrievers had, but when it came to Miranda, she was his one and only focus. Unless she told him to, he deferred to no one but her even when off-duty.

Except Ben, she realized as she stroked the stubborn mutt's silky ears. It had taken some time, but it was clear that Sam had accepted him into their little pack, bringing it from two to three.

If even the dog trusted him, shouldn't she be willing to do the same?

From the coffee table, her phone rang, and Siri announced it was Ben calling.

Panic—or was it vanity?—made her shake her head. "God, I can't talk to him now. I sound like a bullfrog."

"Good. Then I'll do it for you."

"What? No, Tino, don't you dare!" She tried to push Sam off her lap so she could reach her phone first, but it was too late.

"My sister doesn't want to talk to you right now, asshole, but I've got a few things you're going to listen to."

She cringed as he paused for Ben's response. "I'm going to kill you," she growled between clenched teeth. If he chased Ben off with his ridiculous protective streak, she'd never forgive him.

"Who? Why should I..." There was another long pause. "Shit. Okay. Yeah. Thanks. Bye."

"Did you just hang up on him?" She really would kill him.

Tino knelt on the floor in front of her and took both of her hands in his. "*Bebé*, listen to me. There's been an accident."

Chapter 21

Cody's call from Ben's phone only said he'd been hurt at a fire and taken to the hospital by ambulance. Just enough information to keep her calm, because at least he was alive. And not enough to keep her imagination from constructing all the worst-case possibilities during the interminable fifty-two-minute drive there.

And yes, she'd counted every one of them.

Adrenaline and fear got her out of the car Tino stopped at the curb outside the emergency room entrance. But when the automatic doors *whooshed* closed behind her and Sam, panic fueled by memories took over, pinning her feet to the ground.

Oh God, that smell.

Even if she didn't know where she was, she would have recognized it anywhere. Harsh disinfectant ineffectually disguised by overly-sweet air freshener, but neither quite enough to mask the underlying bouquet of sickness, blood, and death.

Every hospital was the same, no matter where it was.

That smell sometimes followed her out of her dreams. The ones about the days and weeks when she'd been a prisoner to her injuries. Trapped in a bed, in a room, in a world where she had no control. No autonomy. Not even a say in her own care.

And sometime the dreams—and the smells—were so much worse. Because they were of the one place she never wanted to visit again.

Of all the odors a hospital held, the burn ward's was uniquely its own. One that stayed with you forever.

Her stomach roiled.

Please, God, don't let Ben have been burned.

It took everything she had to push the thought down where it wouldn't choke her. She couldn't change what happened to her team. She couldn't change what happened to Ben. But she could be here for him now to help him deal with it, whatever it was.

If she could ever get her damn feet to move again.

Stupid hospital phobia.

Maybe she shouldn't have insisted Tino drop her and Sam off at the emergency room entrance before parking the car. She could have used a little brotherly shove to get her going right about now. But she'd been too impatient to wait even those extra few minutes it would take to find a parking spot and walk back.

And now she couldn't even get past the damn doors.

Suck it up, Hernandez. This isn't about you.

This was for Ben.

"Sam, forward."

Her stomach did another rollercoaster-worthy dip as they advanced into the ER waiting room, but at least she got her feet to move without puking.

Yay, her.

"Miranda. I wasn't sure if you'd come."

Unnerved by the raspy unsteadiness of Cody's deep voice, she gave Sam his stop command, ignoring the fact her voice was equally shaky when she did.

"Of course I came. How is he?"

"He's still being checked out. They'll know more after the CT."

She sucked in a breath at the mention of the brain scan, nearly gagging on the thick scent of smoke Cody wore. "What happened?"

"There was a backdraft explosion at a residential—a house fire—and while they were trying to get out, part of the ceiling came down on him and Cartwright."

Another wave of nausea engulfed her. "Were they burned?" she croaked out.

No, no, no, please no.

"No, nothing bad. Their gear did its job."

Relief left her almost dizzy. "Good. That's good."

He patted her hand where it gripped his arm, something she hadn't even realized she'd done. "Want to sit down? It could be a while."

"Yes, please. Just...someplace where Sam will be out of the way, okay?"

Sam was one hundred percent allowed to be there. But she'd found out of sight went a long way toward out of mind for those who hadn't gotten the memo about guide and service dog privileges. As in, they could go wherever their humans did.

And while she could usually defend the Americans with Disabilities Act with composure and patience, right now she was pretty sure she'd lose her shit on anyone who tried to kick her and Sam out of the hospital.

She wasn't going anywhere until she knew Ben would be okay.

There was a low buzz of conversation in the waiting room, so they clearly weren't alone. And from the heavy stench of smoke as they passed people on their way to their seats, there were at least a few other firefighters there besides Cody.

She tried to counter the involuntary nausea from the acrid odor by reminding herself it came from the same gear that kept Ben safe. Saved him from the horror of being burned. Scarred for life.

Killed.

But try as she might, it was impossible to reprogram her brain into believing it was a good smell, not a harbinger of pain and death.

Tino joined them as she was settling Sam at her feet under the bolted-down row of plastic seats. She introduced her brother to Cody before asking softly, "Who else is here? And what about Ben's parents?"

"They're on their way. I called them right before you." He didn't sound like that had gone particularly well. "The whole truck company is out of service, so we're here for the duration until we get word on everyone's condition. The engine is still mopping up at the scene, but they'll swing by as soon as they can. Dom and the Cap went off to find something to eat while Bryan and I waited for you and the Murphys. Bry, this is Ben's girl, Miranda, and her brother Tino."

She hadn't heard anyone walk up, so they must have taken seats near him. She tried for a smile, though she was pretty sure she failed. "Hi, Bryan."

"Hey, Miranda. Tino. Nice to meet you. Well, not nice, considering why, but, well…"

"It's okay, I know what you mean." Something about his voice sounded familiar. "You were one of the guys helping Ben with his house, weren't you?"

"Uh, yeah. How did you…"

"You guys got pretty loud sometimes. I recognize your voice."

"Shit. Uh, I mean, sorry."

This time she managed a real smile, even if it was fleeting. "It's fine. It was always entertaining when you bunch got a few beers in you at the end of the day."

Bryan groaned. "You could hear us?"

"Kind of hard to miss." When he groaned again, she took pity on him. "I didn't stay outside and listen." Usually. "Your beer-secrets are safe."

"They were having drunken keg parties next door?"

This time *she* wanted to groan. "No, Tino, just friends hanging out having a few beers. I'm sure you do it with your friends all the time, too."

"That's how Murph paid for our labor," Bryan offered helpfully. "Free beer and barbeque."

Tino snorted. "You get what you pay for."

She swatted his arm. "Stop being all superior, Mr. Contractor. His house came out very nice. You guys did a great job," she added to Bryan. "The place is gorgeous."

"How would you...uh, I mean, thanks."

"She 'sees' a lot more than most people think," Tino said in answer to Bryan's obvious confusion, causing Miranda to gape in his direction.

A compliment? From her overprotective, uncompromising big brother who always acted like she wasn't a day past her *quinceañera*?

The evening was just full of surprises.

She got another when there was a commotion on the other side of the waiting room, where a woman demanded in a strident tone, "Where is my son?"

"Oh, boy," Cody muttered. He patted Miranda's knee before getting up and heading toward the upset woman. "Mrs. Murphy."

"Cody, dear, what's happening? How's Benjamin?"

"They're still running tests."

"What kind of tests? How badly was he hurt?"

Miranda's skin prickled as she listened to him give another succinct account of the accident. It only got worse with each telling.

And that was without all the details.

She had no doubt what actually happened was so much worse than the watered-down version Cody was offering them.

"I knew it. I *knew* this job would be the death of him!" There was anger in her words, but the undertone was pure fear.

"Deborah, please," an unfamiliar male voice said. From the well-modulated tone, Miranda guessed it to be Ben's father, the college professor who corrected strangers whenever they misquoted Shakespeare.

"No. I told you this would happen. It was only a matter of time."

"Why don't we go see what the doctor has to say before you start worrying about anything." His voice was calm, steady, and charmingly persuasive.

He sounded so much like Ben, she wanted to cry.

Their voices started moving further away before disappearing altogether. Probably through another door deeper into the ER, judging by the way they cut off so abruptly.

Cody retook his seat next to her with a sigh. "Man, I don't envy that doctor. Mrs. Murphy is like a momma grizzly when it comes to her kids."

"Isn't she a doctor herself?" At least, she thought that's what Ben said.

"Yeah. A pediatrician, but still. She's going to question every decision the poor guy makes."

Much as she wanted to sympathize with the ER doctor, she couldn't feel anything but relief someone would be making sure nothing got overlooked. Ben's well-being trumped any egos that might be bruised.

She knew firsthand how crucial hours, sometimes minutes, could be to get the diagnosis right and keep an injury from becoming permanently debilitating.

"Couldn't find a vending machine that worked, but I got us some waters from the nurse's breakroom. Any news on Ben?"

From the tang of smoke and sweat clinging to him, it was another fireman who'd joined them. And another voice she recognized from next door. The row of seats rocked slightly as he dropped into one.

"Not yet. But his folks just got here. They went in to see the doc. Where's Cap?"

"Dealing with Cartwright. He was giving the nurses a hard time. Said if Hector was already getting released, he should be, too."

Miranda could practically hear him rolling his eyes.

The name rang a bell. "That's the other fireman who was hurt with Ben, right?"

"You mean the one Ben got hurt while saving his dumbass life, yeah." The tone of the water-bringer's thick Bronx accent slid from annoyed to intrigued. "And who might you be, gorgeous?"

"Dom..." Cody made the name a warning.

She patted his arm to let him know she had this.

"I'm Miranda. This is my brother, Tino." She dropped her hand to the dog's head and felt his tail thump against her legs. "And this is Sam." Nothing derailed a would-be Romeo faster than bringing attention to her fully tricked-out guide dog.

Though Dom was evidently made of sterner stuff than most.

"Oooh, so, you're the sexy, sunbathing bikini goddess from next door. No wonder Murph kept you all to him—ow! What the hell, Cody? What was that for?"

"Are you a total idiot? Watch how you talk to Murph's girl-friend, numbnuts."

"Benjamin's *girlfriend*?"

Oh good, Ben's parents were back.

The chill in Mrs. Murphy's exclamation was the last straw for Miranda's already frayed patience. It snapped with an almost audible *ping*.

Spine straight, chin tipped to the 'bring it' angle she'd used whenever she had to prove herself to her fellow Marines just because she didn't own a dick, she stuck her hand out in the general direction she gauged the other woman to be standing.

"That's right. I'm Ben's girlfriend. Miranda Hernandez."

A moment later her challenge was met with an ice-cold handshake. Which told her more than words how frightened Ben's mother was, and deflated her own annoyance at the perceived slight from her tone.

A horrible thought occurred.

"Did you find out anything new from the doctor?"

"No. They couldn't tell us anything other than he's stable and getting tests." Her frustration was evident.

"Sweetheart, why don't you sit down and try to relax."

"How can I relax when my baby is hurt and they won't let me see him?"

"You can see him when they bring him back from his scan." He sighed at the unhappy grunt he got in reply. "Deb, trust the doctors to do their job. Aren't you always telling me how much you hate when your patients' parents helicopter?"

"This is different. I'm a doctor."

"Right now, you just need to be a mother." From the creaking sound, he managed to coax his wife into one of the uncomfortable plastic seats across from them. "Miranda, I'm Ben's father, Liam. I'm sorry it's under these circumstances, but it's nice to finally meet you. Ben has talked a lot about you."

That shocked her into blurting, "He has?"

"Yes. We've been looking forward to you coming to dinner one night soon so the whole family can meet you."

"You have?" Realizing she sounded like an idiot, she asked, "Then why was your wife so surprised to find out Ben had a girlfriend?"

Mrs. Murphy answered for herself. "It wasn't the fact you exist that surprised me, dear. Simply that Benjamin never once mentioned you were blind."

Clearly, they'd caught her little intro of Sam.

"And why should that matter?"

It was Tino who growled the question, making her wince.

"Sorry. This is my brother, Santino. Who seems to have lost his manners," she added with a small glare in his direction.

"To answer your question, young man, it doesn't. Not to us, in any case."

But Miranda had to wonder if it might have mattered to Ben.

Was *that* why he kept put off bringing her to meet his parents? Because he was embarrassed by her, despite all his assurances to the contrary? All that talk of compromise and fitting into his world, his life?

She shook off the thought. Now wasn't the time to deal with her own insecurities. There were far more important things to worry about.

More firefighters showed up as word spread through the department grapevine that some of their own had been hurt. The arrival that intrigued her most was Ben's uncle, who had a booming voice and a gregarious personality that matched his nephew's and felt almost out of place in the otherwise subdued hum of waiting room conversation.

"Deborah. Liam. How's our boy?"

"They're still doing tests," Mr. Murphy said. If she hadn't known they were brothers, Miranda never would have been able to guess, their voices and demeanors so different. But there were clearly pieces of both men in Ben.

Mrs. Murphy remained silent while her husband filled his brother in on what details they had to this point. Ben mentioned once there was a little animosity between his mother and uncle ever since Ben had followed him into the fire service.

Under the circumstances, she was surprised Mrs. Murphy wasn't letting her brother-in-law have it with both barrels.

After being brought up to speed, he greeted each of Ben's friends by name, obviously well acquainted with them all. It was also clear they all liked and admired the man, and not because—or maybe despite the fact—he was their superior officer.

Which, based on her own experience with those, spoke volumes about him.

"And you must be Miranda." His gentle words caught her by surprise.

"Um, yes. It's nice to meet you, Mr. Murphy." She shook a beefy hand calloused and scarred in a way she hadn't felt since her time in the Marines. He might be a Battalion Chief now, but he'd clearly come up through the ranks doing the same hard, dangerous work as everyone else.

"Please, call me Sean. It's nice to finally meet you. Ben's description didn't do you justice."

A blaze of a blush heated her cheeks at the unexpected compliment. Was there anyone in his family Ben hadn't talked about her to? Or that didn't seem to approve of her?

It was a little unnerving.

And sad. Because whenever she mentioned Ben to *her* family, it usually ended in an argument about how he was taking advantage of her.

Speaking of her family. "Sean, this is my brother, Tino." She listened to them exchange greetings before Sean moved off to speak with some of the other people there.

After that, the minutes ticked by slowly. The longer they sat there, the more Tino began to fidget in his seat. Finally, she leaned into him and whispered, "What's wrong?"

After a brief hesitation, he answered. "I was just thinking. About the last time we had to do this."

It took a second for her to grasp that the 'we' wasn't the two of them, but Tino and the rest of her family.

And she was the one they'd been doing it for.

Guilt, an old and true friend, rippled through her. "I'm sorry."

The deep breath he took seemed to take forever for him to exhale again. He switched to Spanish when he continued, his low voice strained.

"When I heard about the crash…God! I *know* what happens to a chopper when it goes down. I honestly thought you were dead. And you were. You died on that damn operating table, they said, before they managed to bring you back."

She sucked in a sharp breath. "They shouldn't have told you that." It was excessively cruel.

"I about died myself when they did. I mean, *Dios*, you're my baby sister."

Since Tino rarely talked about feelings, she was as shocked as she was touched by the raw emotion in his voice. Swallowing a lump, determined not to cry, she rubbed his arm gently. "*Mano…*"

"I never saw *Mamí* cry like that before. Or pray so hard. The girls, too. They must have said the rosary a hundred times over. And *Papí*…" He shook his head. "I swear he aged ten years in that waiting room."

For the first time, she truly understood what her family must have gone through when she'd been injured. Because she was feeling all the same things now with Ben. Fear. Worry. Pain. Confusion. The terror of not knowing was second only to the agony of not being able to do anything except wait.

And pray.

"I'm so sorry," she said again. "And thank you."

"For what?"

"Being there for me then. And now."

Especially since he wasn't a particular fan of Ben. And he seemed to share her aversion to hospitals. But he was here anyway.

Because that's what family did.

After what felt like a thousand years, a nurse called the Murphys in to speak with the doctor. Miranda was the one to fidget in her seat this time, wanting desperately to follow them. Tino took her hand in his and squeezed, and she leaned her head on his shoulder where the familiar scent of sawdust clung to his shirt.

"I don't know what I'll do if the last thing he ever heard me say to him was that I didn't trust him."

"Positive thoughts, *hermanita*. It's going to be fine."

"Yeah," Cody added from her other side, "Murph's tough. He's bounced back from worse than this."

"Oh, man, you're not kidding." Bryan said. "Do you remember that warehouse fire last year?"

Dom answered with the enthusiasm of someone about to tell a great story. "The one where the whole façade collapsed and trapped him on the roof with no line and no way down? Yeah, Murph almost bought it that day for sure. Ow! Damn it, Cody, stop doing that!"

"Then stop being an asshole."

"I wasn't...oh. Sorry, Miranda."

She smiled weakly. "It's okay, Dom. I know he has a dangerous job." Although she hadn't really had to face the reality of that until now.

Talk about getting a dose of her own medicine.

She seriously owed her parents a huge apology.

"Well, if it makes you feel any better, after he makes lieutenant, he might get transferred to a less busy house," Dom offered in a conciliatory tone.

Wait, what?

"Ben's getting promoted?"

"Dom, shut the hell up," Cody growled at the same time Dom answered, "Well, not yet, but he's taking the test, so eventually, yeah."

Her confusion deepened.

"He's taking the test? The lieutenant's test?" The one he'd told her he wasn't?

Only...he'd never *actually* said that, had he?

"Yeah, that's how you become a lieutenant." The *duh* was clear in his voice.

"Dom, seriously, shut it."

"What for? I mean, you've both been taking that prep class for it. It's not like it's a secret or anything."

Prep class?

"Cody?"

There was a long pause before he let out a small *fuck* under his breath. "It's not a big deal, really. But it's not my place to tell you about it, either. Ask Ben."

One more lie to wait for an answer about?

Screw that.

But before she could demand an explanation, Tino squeezed her hand. "They're coming back out."

Immediately, her attention refocused. "How do they look? Relieved? Upset?"

"His *mamá* is crying," Tino answered with great reluctance.

"Good or bad tears?"

"How should I know? What the hell are *good* tears?"

"This is why you can't keep a girlfriend. Learn the difference, *hermano*."

"Ben's going to be fine," Sean announced to the room at large in his booming voice. There was a loud murmur of relief from everyone gathered. "And both Cartwright and Salazar are cleared to be discharged."

"Thank God." The weight making it hard to breathe eased for the first time since Cody's phone call. Ben wasn't going to die. It wasn't too late. There was still time to fix whatever the hell it was that had gone wrong between them.

"Ben has a concussion, a couple of hairline rib fractures, and his knee got a little banged up," Ben's father added, to which Cody muttered *again*. "So, they're admitting him overnight for observation."

"I know he'll appreciate the concern you've all shown by coming here to wait with us, just like his parents and I do. But they've already said no visitors once he's settled in his room, so at this point there's nothing else for you to do here. So, everybody can head on home. Or, if you're so inclined, over to Calhoun's for a celebratory drink."

"You buying, Chief?" someone called out.

"In your dreams, boyo," Sean replied, earning a spattering of laughter. "Although I might be persuaded to drag out my pipes for a song or two if someone were to ask me nicely."

There were a few hoots and a lot of groans at that. The previously somber mood gave way to laughter and boisterous voices as people filed out. The silence left in their wake made Miranda realize how many people had been packed into the waiting room. It was clear Ben and the other two men had a lot of friends among their peers.

"I guess we should be going, too, then," Cody said. "Unless there's anything you need, Mr. and Mrs. Murphy?"

"Thank you, Cody, dear, but you all go on and join your friends. We're fine."

"We'll stay until he gets settled in his room, then we'll be heading home ourselves," Mr. Murphy added. The disgruntled harrumph his wife made said that was an argument he hadn't won quite yet.

As Cody, Bryan, and Dom said their goodbyes, Cody quietly added for Miranda's ears only, "Call me if you need anything. I still have Ben's phone." Then it was just Miranda, Tino, and Ben's parents in the suddenly echoey waiting room.

"You should be going, too, Miss Hernandez," Mrs. Murphy said. "I believe you have a long drive home."

She bit her lip. "Do you think I could see him first? Just for a minute?"

"It would be better if you came back tomorrow. I'm sure Benjamin will be in a much better frame of mind to see you then."

"But...I just want to see him, to tell him..." What? She wasn't sure herself. That she didn't hate him? That she was glad he was okay? That she wished the past forty-eight hours had never happened and she wanted a do-over?

All of those things.

But mostly, she just needed to see for herself he was alive and in one piece. Even if it was slightly bruised and battered.

"What you want, Miss Hernandez, is of little interest to me. The only thing I care about is what's best for my son. And right now, what he needs is his *family*."

She flinched at the chilly reminder she didn't fall under that category. "I understand. But—""

"No, you clearly don't. You are not seeing him. That's final."

"Sweetheart, why don't you go wait with Ben until they're ready to bring him up to his room?" As his wife's angry footsteps marched away, Mr. Murphy said, "I'm sorry. She's just upset about Ben. We live with the constant dread of getting the kind of phone call we got tonight."

"That's no reason to take it out on my sister."

She squeezed Tino's arm. "It's okay."

"No, it's not." Mr. Murphy sighed. "And tomorrow my wife will realize it. But for now...I think it best if you do as she said and go on home."

Pain lanced through her at the finality of his words.

Best for who? Not her, certainly.

But arguing would be a waste of time. He was right. Mrs. Murphy was looking for someone to vent her fear and frustration on, and Miranda had given her a convenient target by overstepping and trying to intrude on a family-only moment.

Brilliant tactical move, Hernandez. Way to draw enemy fire.

After waking up Sam, who'd been dozing out of everyone's way, she and Tino headed out to the parking lot.

They hadn't gotten far when a voice called from behind them, "Miranda?"

She stopped and turned, heart pounding. Had Ben suddenly taken a turn for the worse?

"Yes?"

Quick, light footsteps approached, indicating the woman who had hailed her was walking fast, but not running, so maybe it wasn't too urgent. She hoped.

"I was afraid I wouldn't catch you in time." There was an awkward pause. "Um, I'm Nancy. We sort of met a few weeks ago. Do you remember? At the street fair?"

As if she could forget the nurse who wanted to get Ben's pants off.

Seriously? Was the universe *that* pissed at her right now?

"Yes, I remember." What she hadn't remembered until now was that she was an ER nurse at one of the local hospitals. This one, it seemed.

Nancy snorted. "Yeah, I bet you do. I'm sorry about...well, never mind that. I heard what happened in there just now. Don't let it bother you too much. People say all kinds of stupid things they don't mean when they're scared and upset."

"Thank you."

"And I thought you should know Ben's been asking for you."

Her heart skipped a double-beat. "He has?"

"Non-stop. Which might be another reason his moms went a little Cujo on you."

Over Tino's badly stifled laugh, Miranda said, "Thank you for telling me. It means a lot."

No, it meant everything. Ben didn't hate her.

"If you hang out a little bit, I can get you up to his room for a few minutes after his folks leave."

She cocked her head in surprise. "You'd do that for him?"

Nancy sighed. "For you, actually. I figure I owe you one." She hesitated. "And him, too. I thought about what you said, and...you were right. If a guy had talked to me the way I talked to him, I probably would have cracked his mouth. Or given him a nut-ectomy."

A snort escaped at the vivid picture her words painted.

"Thank you." She turned to her brother, who'd been silent throughout the exchange. "Tino? Do you mind?"

"Sure, sis, we can stay. Tomorrow's my day off."

She wondered why he felt the need to tell her what she already knew. Or call her *sis*, something he never did. But as he and Nancy introduced themselves and she heard the underlying interest in their voices, she got it.

They both continued to chat while she gave Sam a quick potty break. By the time they all went back inside and Nancy left them by the elevators with directions down to the cafeteria for some much-needed coffee, phone numbers had been exchanged and a lunch date arranged for the following day.

Miranda could only roll her eyes as the elevator made its short, creaky descent. "Really, *bro*?" she teased.

He chuckled. "What can I say? She's got sass. I like that in a woman."

When Nancy came to get them a little over an hour later, Miranda was jittery from more than the extra boost of caffeine hitting her system. Drying damp palms on her jeans when she got off the elevator, she gave Sam the follow command and let Nancy lead them down the quiet hallway, Tino right behind her.

"He's going to be a little groggy," Nancy said softly when they stopped. "And probably cranky. He only took the bare minimum on the pain meds."

Stubborn man,

"I promise I'll only stay a few minutes. I just need…" She didn't know how to finish, but Nancy seemed to understand from the way she put a hand on her shoulder and squeezed.

"Take whatever time you need. Come on."

"I'll stay out here with Sam," Tino offered.

Miranda nodded. After giving Sam his release command, she turned over the leash to her brother and took Nancy's elbow.

She thought she'd already conquered her ridiculous reaction to being in a hospital. But the second they crossed the threshold into the room, the sounds and smells closed in on her like a pillow pressed against her face. Bile scorched up her throat in a fiery line as memories lashed at her brain with every step.

Waking to darkness.

Unable to speak because of the tube in her throat.

Not knowing what was happening.

Lost and so alone, no matter how many people came to hold her hand.

Trapped. Fire. She could smell the fire.

Burning. Consuming. Destroying.

She froze, feet once more pinned to the ground, forcing Nancy to a halt. No. She couldn't do this. She had to leave. Had to breathe. Had to—

"Miranda?"

Ben's voice blew over her like a reviving breeze, clearing away the panic before it could make her turn tail and run. Nancy took the hand from her arm and placed it on the metal railing of the bed, giving her both an anchor and a reference point, then retreated from the room, rubber soles squeaking faintly on the tile floor.

The door thumped quietly closed behind her.

She swallowed hard as her throat threatened to close up again at the sound.

"Hey there, Slick." Moving carefully to avoid disturbing the wires and tubes that would likely be running from Ben to an IV and the monitors tracking his vitals, she found his hand among the covers and laced her fingers with his.

The heavy odor of smoke he gave off stirred memories in the dark parts of her brain. Of other beds. Other men. Other visits.

She punched them back down with all her might. "So, I hear you went and got yourself all banged up."

"Couldn't let Cartwright get squashed." He muttered something else that might have been "the asshole."

"Yeah, I heard about that. I also heard you're going to be okay."

"Hard head."

The smug pride in that comment made her smile. "I won't argue with that."

"I'm sorry."

Words clogged her throat, but now wasn't the time or place to hash out their problems. "We'll talk about it when you're feeling better. I should let you get some rest. I just wanted to see for myself you were okay."

His hand clutched hers tighter. "Stay."

"Ben..."

"Just a little longer."

It was easy to give in since it was what she wanted, too.

Stroking her thumb over the back of his hand, she held it until his grip went lax as sleep finally overtook him. She reluctantly let go, but he wasn't as deeply asleep as she'd thought.

"Love you."

The slurred whisper shot straight to her heart like a mortar round. Only rather than exploding, it bathed it in healing warmth. "I love you, too, Slick." She waited, but the only thing she heard over the incessant beeping was his even breathing as he lost his last battle with consciousness.

God, she hoped that wasn't the concussion talking. Because she meant what she said. She loved the big jerk. Sitting in the waiting room not knowing if he was going to live or die had left her with no more doubts about that.

And if Ben truly loved her back, then there wasn't anything they couldn't fix.

Chapter 22

"ARE YOU COMFORTABLE, DEAR?"

"Yes, thanks."

"Are you sure? I can get some more pillows, if you want."

"No, Mom, I'm good. Really. Four is more than enough." Ben watched his mother, usually one of the most brilliant, rational, unflappable women he knew, dither and fret over the pillows she'd stacked and rearranged behind him—twice—after he'd literally crawled under the covers of his old bed after a much-needed but probably ill-advised shower.

Damn. He knew that look on her face.

Three...two...one...

"You look cold. Let me find you another blanket."

He wasn't cold. It was July, for God's sake.

But he let her go without argument. If it got her out of the room for a few minutes, she could hunt for as many blankets as she wanted. An hour in, and he was already regretting his decision to accept his parents' offer to stay with them for the forty-eight hours the doctors said he shouldn't be alone after his release from the hospital.

Not that he'd had a lot of other options. And not like his mother would have meekly taken a "no thanks" from him even if he had. From the second she showed up in the emergency room last night, she'd been a bulldozer. No one was doing enough, or doing it right, or doing it fast enough to suit her.

And if there was one thing Doctor Deborah Friedman Murphy wasn't, it was shy about letting the people she thought were slacking know about it.

He'd put out more metaphoric fires in the ER in one night than real ones in his entire last week on the job. It had been embarrassing as hell, how his mom had bullied all the doctors and nurses around like that. But in a weird, screwed-up sort of way, it had also made him feel kind of good, too.

In her own irritating fashion, it showed how much she cared.

Hell, it might have been a real Hallmark moment if she hadn't kept snapping at Uncle Sean about how it was all his fault Ben had joined the fire department in the first place whenever she didn't have a doctor or nurse handy to chew on.

"Here we are," his mother all but sang as she strode back into the room. With a practiced snap of the wrists, she unfolded the fleece blanket and spread it over the bed.

Even his toenails started to sweat, but he managed a smile. "Thanks, Mom."

Fussing with the edges of the blanket, she said, "There's water on the nightstand if you're thirsty. Or I can make you some soup. Would you like soup?"

"I'm not hungry right now, but maybe later."

His head ached so bad from the car ride home he was slightly nauseated. The last thing he wanted was food. Just give him a little not-poked-by-a-nurse-every-two-hours sleep, and he'd be fan-fucking-tastic.

With any luck, when he woke up again, the concussion would have settled down to a dull roar and his ribs and knee would have stopped throbbing like they were on fire.

His mother acted the way she always did when she heard something she didn't like.

She ignored it.

"You should have some soup. I'm sure they didn't feed you anything decent this morning before you were discharged. You need to keep up your strength."

"Mom..."

"I have some minestrone in the freezer. Or I can make fresh. How about some nice chicken soup? Would you like that?"

"Mom, I said..." He sighed, giving in to the almost frantic gleam in her eyes. "Sure. That sounds great."

"Good. You rest." She stroked the hair from his forehead the way she'd done when he was five and hurried from the room, purpose in her quick steps.

As the door shut quietly behind her, he immediately flipped off the blanket and closed his eyes with a relieved sigh. Maybe it still wasn't too late to pick couch surfing at Cody's for the weekend instead.

When he opened his eyes again, it was difficult to tell how much time had passed. The drapes of his old bedroom were drawn against the sun, since the light-sensitivity that plagued him on the drive home had been like sticking icepicks into his eyeballs. The deep twilight they left the room in told him nothing.

But his head no longer felt like a birthday pinata a few whacks away from spilling its candy, which suggested he must have been out for more than just a few minutes. So did the urgent pressure from his bladder.

He was weighing the need to pee against the risk of jarring his ribs to get up and take care of it when the door opened and his mother tip-toed in. For a split-second he considered closing his eyes and pretending to still be asleep.

In the end, his bladder prevailed.

Pushing himself gingerly up on one elbow, he asked, "How long was I asleep?"

"Oh, good, you're up. You drifted off about two hours ago. I was just coming to wake you."

He grimaced. Damn concussion protocols.

She hurried to his side. "What's wrong? Does something hurt?"

"No. I, ah...need to use the bathroom. And no," he said before she could ask, "I don't need any help."

That was more pride than truth, but he managed.

Barely.

Crawling back into bed when he was done, everything hurt again. Plus, he was a little dizzy and a lot out of sorts. Just some of the super-fun symptoms the doctors had warned he might experience in the first forty-eight hours after the concussion.

Add in all the other aches and bruises gnawing at his body from both the explosion and the ceiling collapse, and he was an inch away from asking for one of the heavy-duty pain pills he hated to take just so he could go back to sleep.

Sheer stubbornness had him gritting his teeth instead as his mother rearranged the sea of pillows behind him to her satisfaction. The hint of apples and cinnamon said she'd spent at least some of his time asleep in the kitchen baking.

"There!" she said with one final tuck. "How's that?"

"It's fine, Mom. Thanks." But when she reached to drag the blanket back up over him, some part of his tenuous hold finally snapped. "Mom, stop, okay? Stop fussing. I'm fine. Everything's fine."

"Everything is not fine," she snapped back. "You nearly got yourself killed."

Well, she had him there.

"But I didn't."

"But for God's good grace! Do you have any idea the things that went through my mind on the drive to the hospital after we got that call? The one I've dreaded getting all these years? All of the horrible things as a doctor I knew could have happened to you?" Her breath hitched in a tell-tale prelude to tears. "The sheer terror I might lose my baby boy without getting to say goodbye?"

Fuck.

He hated when his mother cried. It meant he'd *really* screwed up.

He tried for a bit of levity, giving her his most charming grin. Or, at least, the best he could manage with a pile driver currently digging into his skull. "I keep telling you, Caleb's the baby, not me."

"And I keep telling you, you will always be my baby, too." She gave him a smacking kiss on the cheek, then wiped it with her thumb to remove any lipstick. The familiar gesture brought on a wave of nostalgia and lessened his own temper.

"I'm sorry you were scared, Mom."

And he was. But he also knew what the next chorus of this song was, and he just wasn't up for another debate about his career choices.

Especially since lying in bed with a concussion didn't exactly work in his favor.

Hoping to head her off, he took a page from his sister's courtroom tactics and abruptly altered the line of questioning. "You know who else was scared for me? Miranda. What I don't understand is why you wouldn't let her come and see me?"

"What?" He'd clearly caught her off-guard with the question. Or with the fact he knew about her keeping Miranda out.

Thank you, Nurse Nancy.

"Miranda. I know she was out in the waiting room. But you told her not to come in to see me, even though you knew I wanted her to. Why would you exclude her like that?"

"Because it was a moment for family, and she's not."

"She's my girlfriend, and I wanted her there. That should have been good enough."

It was quick, and the room was dim, lit only by the small bedside lamp his mother had turned on while he was in the bathroom, but he didn't mistake the sneer of disdain that crossed her face.

His stomach went a little queasy again.

"Tell me you don't have a problem with her because she's Mexican-American."

She looked honestly shocked by that. "Of course not! How could you even suggest such a thing?"

"Then is it because she's blind?"

"Don't be ridiculous. Although knowing that beforehand would have made things a bit less awkward last night when we met for the first time."

It was the way she emphasized those last words that clued him in. "So, you're pissed because you hadn't met her yet?"

"I'm *annoyed*"—she changed his word choice with a pointed look—"that we were all eager to welcome her with open arms weeks ago, but she never bothered to come to dinner once despite my practically begging you every time we talked to bring her. How many insults should I take before deciding that if she isn't interested in even meeting your family, then she has no place being with us at your bedside?"

Well, hell. There it was.

Yet one more strand in his sticky web of lies coming back to choke him.

He sighed. "That was my fault, actually."

"Don't make excuses for her, Benjamin."

"No, really. She wanted to come to dinner. Weeks ago. But...I kept putting her off." He winced at the shocked hurt that crossed her face.

"Why would you do that?"

"Because I kind of let her believe I wasn't taking the lieutenant's test, and you all knew I was, so I was afraid someone might bring it up and she'd catch me in the lie." Which had somehow sounded perfectly logical in his head but now sounded so much worse out loud.

"Why on earth would you lie about such a thing?" A hint of predator-scenting-blood colored her next words. "She doesn't like your job, either, does she?"

"Sorry to disappoint you, but she has no problem with me being a firefighter. She was a Marine. She understands all about jobs that come with risks. I..." He let out a weary breath. "I just didn't want her to think I was stupid for taking the test like you and Dad did."

Her mouth dropped open. "We thought no such thing!"

"Oh please, Mom. I was there. You totally thought it was a bad idea."

"Only because you've never taken tests well."

It shouldn't have hurt, but it did. "See. Stupid."

"That is *not* what I said."

"It's okay. I always knew I was the dud of the bunch." He gave the devil-may-care grin he'd hidden behind for most of his life. "We can't all be brilliant, right?"

"Your father and I have never judged any of our children against each other. You all have your individual strengths."

"Yeah, I know. Abby's a maestro at law, Caleb's a savant at math, and me? What am I good at, Mom? Sports?" The memory of the coaching job she'd so casually brought up last month, like it was the perfect answer to the problem of her imperfect son, caused a sharp twist in his chest. "I'm not exactly in the same league as the rest of you."

"Yes, you were good at sports. Excellent, in fact. Which, if I might add, no one else in this family is. But that's not the only thing you excel at."

"Yeah, like what?"

"Being a firefighter."

Her words were like a physical blow.

"God, Mom. Just stop. You don't have to lie to make me feel better." Because he didn't. Not even a little. His self-esteem actually felt pretty damn battered.

"I'm not lying."

"You hate me being a firefighter."

"Yes, I do. Very much so."

Another hit landed. "You know what? I don't think I'm up for you stomping on my life choices right now. Maybe we can come back to trashing my career when I'm not flat on my back in pain." He turned his head away, signaling he was done with the conversation.

If he thought playing the patient card would deter his mother, he was sadly mistaken. Rather than back off, she crossed her arms and gave him the full force of her maternal ire. "Benjamin Xavier Murphy, you will do me the courtesy of listening to what I have to say and stop acting like an ill-tempered brat. Do I make myself clear?"

With that tone and the triple-name, crystal. "Yes, ma'am."

"Good." She sat on the edge of the bed next to him, her face softening. "Benjamin, sweetheart. I know you're very good at what you do. Extraordinary, in fact. One of your friends is alive today because of your quick thinking and actions."

Warmth spread up his neck in an embarrassed flush. "It was just reflex." The friend part he left alone. It had been clear when Cartwright stopped into his room this morning that even a close call with death wasn't enough to stop him from being a prick.

But he was still around to be one, which made it a win in Ben's book.

"And that reflex is you being good at your job." When he shrugged, she put a hand on his arm, her expression distressed. "I'm so sorry. I never realized how much my hating your job and harping on wanting you to find another one would make you think it had anything to do with you."

"Kind of hard not to."

"I see that now. But Benjamin, try to understand. Most people don't truly appreciate the dangers of being a firefighter. Even your father and I didn't really grasp it, not even with his brother on the job. Not until after 9/11 happened."

A lump of tangled emotion formed in his throat. "That was...unimaginable."

"It was. But it was everything afterward that brought home to me the sacrifice of not just the men and women who have the job, but their families. All those funerals. All those wives without husbands, children without fathers, parents without children. It was..." She shook her head, tears shining in her eyes. "All I kept thinking was, what if that was us? What if Sean had died? How could we have handled that?"

They'd lived through the same hellacious hours of fear and uncertainty as thousands of other families who had loved ones in the city that horrific Tuesday morning, first responder and civilian both. He'd thought it would be the worst day of his life.

Until the days and weeks that followed.

"But he didn't die."

"No, thank God. But he was different after that. We all were. How could we not be?" She took a deep breath and brought her composure back under control. "Did you ever wonder why Sean never got married?"

"Not really. I mean, I guess I just figured he was happy as a bachelor." His uncle had always seemed to revel in his unmarried state. Something Ben had planned to emulate until a certain dark-haired selkie came into his life.

"Not happy. Safe. He was engaged once, for all of about two seconds. His fiancé gave him back the ring a few months after the attack, saying she couldn't live the rest of her life with that kind of fear hanging over her head every day. Sean didn't even try to argue with her. And he never got serious with another woman again."

It was hazy, but he kind of remembered the short, blonde-haired woman his uncle had brought around to family dinners and holidays for a while before he'd just...stopped. And Ben had been too much a self-absorbed teen at the time to bother wondering why.

"Like I said," his mother continued, "that day changed us all. Sean gave up on marriage, and I suppose I got a little more over-protective of you three—"

"A little?"

She tapped his arm in admonishment for interrupting, but her flicker of a smile acknowledged he was right. "And I guess I reacted badly when you announced you were going to be taking the test for the fire department because of it."

"You told me it was a waste of my time, and I should find a nice, easy job instead." It was still one of his most painful memories.

And the one that had made him study his ass off to prove her wrong.

She raised a hand to her heart as she made soft, anguished sound. "I'm so sorry. I never, ever meant it the way you clearly thought I did. I didn't want you to be a firefighter. But I never thought you weren't intelligent enough to get the job. I knew you could. *That's* why I tried to discourage you."

"Oh, come on, Mom. We both know that's not true. I've never been anywhere near as smart as Abby or Cay. Or you and Dad. Face facts. I'm the dumb one."

"You are not dumb. You never were. Yes, you had some problems in school early on, but that was because you had a short attention span and kept losing focus. It got better as you became older."

"I still can't take a test worth a damn."

"Obviously you can, or you wouldn't have a job."

"Yeah, well, I have to study twice as hard as everyone else." He was starting to sound childish even to himself.

"Performance anxiety."

He nearly choked. "Excuse me?"

"Well, more specifically, test anxiety. It's a legitimate psychological condition where people experience extreme distress while taking tests."

"Great, so I can't take tests because I'm afraid of taking them?"

"Of not doing well on them." She paused before continuing with a pained look of apology, "Or maybe of being compared to a brother and sister who got A's without all the extra work you put in." She put her hand on his and squeezed. "I'm so sorry I didn't realize that at the time. That I didn't know this was even something that existed. I'd go back and change it if I could."

It felt like everything he believed about himself was suddenly being knocked out from under him. "Why do you seem so sure I have this anxiety thing?"

"You tell me. When you're taking a test, do you find yourself blanking on answers you know that you know? Does your mind start to race and make it even harder to concentrate on the test as you go? Afterward, do you get angry at yourself for it?" She gave him a pointed look. "Think of yourself as stupid?"

Every word was like she'd peeled back a piece of his skull and was peeking inside.

With a hard swallow, he nodded. "Yes. All of that."

"There are other symptoms, but that's test anxiety in a nutshell."

Could it be true? Could most of his problems have come from his own feelings of inadequacy next to his brilliant siblings? He'd worried about doing badly so he did, like some kind of horrible self-fulfilling prophecy?

"But I'm really not as smart as Abby and Cay."

"And Caleb can't throw a football like you can. Abigail can't make friends as easily as you do. Hell's bells, you've got us all beat on that particular skill. People *like* you."

The unexpected curse surprised a laugh out of him. "It's not exactly the same thing."

"I know. But we all have our strengths, sweetheart. So, yours may not be in the classroom. That doesn't make you stupid. Something you proved by doing so well on the fire department exam and getting hired."

Maybe because that had been his own thing, and he didn't have to worry about competing with his siblings.

Huh. Maybe there was something to his mother's theory after all.

She sighed. "And...as much as I hate it, I know you're going to do well on your lieutenant's test, too. Which is good, because they need talented men like you doing that job."

He squeezed her hand, feeling an odd lightness inside that hadn't been there before. "Thanks, Mom. Knowing how you feel about the job, and why, I know that had to be hard for you to say. It means a lot to me."

"Hmph." She got up. "Let me go get that soup now. You must be famished." Reaching down, she yanked the blanket up over his legs before leaving.

With a grin, he left it. His mother was going to coddle no matter what he did or said to dissuade her. He might as well lay back and enjoy it. Maybe with this newfound understanding between them about his job, spending a few days here wouldn't be as difficult as he'd feared.

Thank God I'm home.

As his brother's Camry pulled into his driveway, Ben couldn't hold back a sigh of utter relief. After two endless days of his mother's tender loving care, he'd been ready to crawl back to Kenoway on his hands and knees if necessary to escape.

Thankfully, Caleb had taken pity on him. It wasn't until they were on the Hutch, more than halfway home, that he thought to ask why his brother had a Monday off to drive him around when he was supposed to be teaching the summer math course at Whitman.

"I told them I wouldn't do it."

That his dutiful, don't-rock-the-boat brother had refused what was essentially a command from the school board wasn't nearly as surprising as what he'd said next.

"I'm also thinking of turning in my resignation."

"Wow. That's kinda out of left field, isn't it?"

"Not really. I've been thinking about it for a while now. I was going to talk to you about it at dinner last month. To ask your opinion."

And he'd cut and run before he had the chance, then never followed up when Cay hadn't replied to his text to call him.

I'm a sucky brother.

"Why do you want to quit?"

Caleb had chewed his lip for a moment before sighing. "Because I hate my job. Well, not teaching. I love that. But I hate doing it at the university."

"You mean, at the same university where Dad works?"

Caleb's expression was answer enough. "Don't get me wrong, I love him and all, and I appreciate that he went to bat for me to get the job there even though I didn't ask him to." His tone said he hadn't wanted him to, either. "But the truth is, I already knew what I wanted to do when I got my degree, and this wasn't it."

"So, what was it, then?"

"Teaching high school remedial math."

"Really? Isn't that a pretty big come-down from becoming 'the youngest department head Whitman has ever seen?'" The verbal mimicking of their father had been subconscious, but spot-on.

An honest-to-God growl had left his brother's throat in response.

"That's Dad's wet-dream. I just want to help kids learn. And the ones who need it the most aren't at the university taking advanced trig. They're the ones who can't grasp simple high school math well enough to get the test scores they need to get *into* college."

The words had been like a jab to Ben's solar plexus. "Like me, you mean."

"And hundreds of other kids who just need someone to show them how."

Either the exhaustion of the past few days or the talk he'd had with his mother kept Ben from working up the usual irritation at being reminded how stupid he'd felt being tutored by his little brother.

And because of that, he was able to see past his habitual knee-jerk self-defenses and realize this wasn't about him. It was about Caleb.

"You really were good at it." The admission had been gruff but honest. Caleb absolutely *rocked* as a teacher to the thick-headed.

He should know. He had one of the thickest.

"Thanks. And I enjoyed doing it. I felt like I was accomplishing something important, not just going through the same academic motions every semester the way I am now. I want to feel that way again." He'd flicked a nervous glance at Ben before hunching back over the wheel. "So? What do you think?"

"Does it really matter what I think?"

"Yeah, it does. Mom and Dad are already freaking out about me turning down the summer session, so I can't talk to them about it rationally. I need someone to give me an honest opinion about whether I'm crazy to even be thinking about this. Someone I trust to tell me the truth."

It might have been the concussion, but that had made him feel all warm and fuzzy toward his brother. Feelings that normally didn't apply in the Murphy household.

It had been the weekend for strange miracles.

"Then, for what it's worth, I think you should do what's going to make you happy." God knew life was too short to do anything else.

A truth he'd just had hammered home with blinding clarity.

Literally.

Caleb's shoulders had relaxed for the first time since he'd started driving. "Yeah. So do I."

"Mom and Dad will try to change your mind, you know."

"I know." Then the hard press of Caleb's mouth had tipped up into a quirky half-smile Ben was more used to seeing in his mirror than on his little brother. "Which is why I plan to wait until after Abby tells them about her promotion before I bring it up. Hopefully, they'll be too proud of the new junior partner in the family to get too worked up over it."

Ben had grinned back. Using a sibling as a distraction tactic. Now *that* was how they rolled in the Murphy clan.

Getting out of the car after suffering through over two hours of stop-and-go traffic brought on an involuntary groan. Damn, everything ached. All he wanted was an hour under the massaging shower jets in his bathroom, a handful of Tylenol, and Miranda.

Not necessarily in that order.

They'd detoured into Brooklyn to the firehouse to pick up Ben's keys and wallet from his locker. His SUV stayed in the lot, though, since he still wasn't allowed to drive. Digging into the pocket of the sweats his brother had lent him, Ben pulled the key out and let them in. Never had coming home felt both so good and so damn lonely.

Caleb let out a low whistle of appreciation. "You did a nice job with the place. I don't even recognize it."

"Thanks. Give yourself the nickel tour while I go get some aspirin."

"That's okay, I can wait."

Ben scowled. "You don't have to babysit my every step. I'm fine."

"And if you fall and crack your head open, *I'm* the one Mom's going to kill, so deal with it."

He wanted to argue, but there was no point. When she went into badger mode, their mom could be terrifying. Resigned to his shadow, he shuffled to the kitchen and grabbed the bottle of Tylenol he kept in one of the cupboards.

As he knocked two into his hand, his fingers touched the raised bumps of the Braille label stuck to the bottle, bringing a lump to his throat.

Two days he'd been out of the hospital, and all he'd gotten from Miranda after Cody returned his phone were a few short texts asking how he was. No calls. No questioning when he was coming home. Not exactly encouraging.

Especially after what he'd told her in the hospital.

And what she'd said back.

At least, he thought she had. The memory was still hazy, but he could have sworn...

Opening the fridge to grab a water to wash the pills down with, he stared. Shelves that had been mostly bare were crammed with covered casserole dishes and plastic containers, all neatly labeled with what was in them and proper heating instructions.

He would have suspected his mother if she hadn't spent the past two days barely letting him breathe without being there to make sure he wasn't exerting too much effort doing it. Then he recognized the names of some of his favorite dishes from Mrs. Hernandez's repertoire that Miranda had shared with him.

Miranda.

A tiny slice of the pain her silence caused slid away at the proof of her presence in his home. It wasn't a phone call, but it was something. At least she'd been thinking about him. He could work with that.

After heating up a couple of the massive, mouthwatering burritos for lunch, he showed his brother the rest of the renovations he'd done to their grandmother's old house. When they reached the master bedroom, Caleb shook his head. "I had no idea."

"About what?"

"That you were doing all *this*." He gestured around the room.

"What did you think I was doing all these months when I said I was busy fixing the place up?"

"Hiding from Mom's Friday dinners." They grinned at each other. "I don't know. I guess I thought you'd just slap up some paint and maybe put down new carpeting or something. I'm sorry. I should have given you more credit than that. This place is incredible."

"Thanks."

The warmth in his chest from his brother's words was unsettling. He was used to having his family underestimate him.

Praise and admiration would take some getting used to.

"I'm going to take a long soak in the shower, so why don't you head home?" He wasn't surprised when his brother gave him a "get real" snort and plopped himself on the bed, picking the remote up from the nightstand. "Suit yourself."

While Caleb explored the sports package on his tv, he grabbed a pair of gym shorts and went into the bathroom. As he waited for the LEDs in the shower to turn red and steam to start curling along the ceiling, he flicked on the towel warmer, then stripped off the borrowed clothes with careful movements.

The hiss as hot water hit his skin turned to a groan of pleasure as the heat seeped deep into tight, aching muscles, easing them a fraction at a time. A hot tub. He was definitely adding a hot tub when he got around to fixing up the backyard.

Bracing his hands against the wall, he let his head hang between them as the multiple massaging jets worked their magic. He was in such a state of bliss that he didn't bother to move when the bathroom door opened.

"I'm fine, Caleb. Go away." The door closed again, but he caught movement out of the corner of his eye and sighed. "Damn it, Cay, I said I was—" He looked over and immediately forgot what he was saying.

That wasn't his brother on the other side of the fogged glass.

He stared wordlessly as Miranda shed her clothes and carefully stepped into the enormous shower with him, one hand on the wall. Maybe he was hallucinating. Or asleep. Or dead and gone to heaven.

But when she reached out to touch him, everything snapped into place with blinding clarity.

Sweet holy fuck.

She was here.

Really here.

With him.

He rasped out her name and kissed her, wanting to punish her for leaving him alone, for not trusting him, for all of it. Instead, he ended up worshipping at her mouth, taking it in small nips and sips, which she met with equal desperation.

Finally, he managed to regain some tiny bit of sanity. "Caleb." The bathroom door was closed, but his brother was right on the other side of it.

"Gone." Her voice was just as hoarse with arousal as his. "You're all mine now."

The possessiveness of her words caused a painful rush of blood to the erection caught between their bodies. He took her mouth again, dragging a groan from her as his tongue dueled with hers while his hands roamed and reclaimed her body.

A rumble of frustration left him when she pulled back, breaking the kiss and stilling his questing fingers.

She laid a single finger over his lips.

Silently, she took his hand and led him out of the shower, pausing only long enough for him to turn the water off. He stood passively as she used one of the warm oversized towels to gently dry him, one body part at a time, until every inch of his skin was alive and humming with anticipation. Then she used the other towel to do the same to herself.

He didn't think it was possible, but watching her caress the plush terry over her own body was even more arousing than having it used on him.

After placing the damp towels on the vanity, she took his hand again and led him into the bedroom. Touching the doorframe, she walked to the dresser, touched for orientation, then led him to the bed, all still without a word.

Using gentle pressure, she urged him onto his back. He went willingly.

Whatever she wanted to do to him, he was all hers.

Miranda followed him onto the bed, straddling him. His erection bobbed up to say hello. To his immense disappointment she ignored it, instead leaning forward and kissing him softly on the mouth. The cheek. The jaw. Her lips touched all of him, working her way down his body slowly, gently, just as she had with the towel.

Nerve endings already aroused became even more inflamed, leaving him quivering and on the brink by the time she came to the part of him she'd previously overlooked.

Eyes closing on a groan of pure sensual torture, he lost himself to the warm caress of her mouth. She knew what he liked, and she gave it to him, bringing him close to the point of no return before she backed off and released his erection with a small pop.

Before he could form the words to protest, she adjusted her body and slowly lowered herself onto him, taking him inside of her in one long, easy glide that made them both groan this time.

With agonizingly slow movements, she rose and fell, not letting him do any of the work as she gave them both pleasure. That didn't keep him from reaching down to stroke her with his thumb in time with her unhurried riding motion.

Two could play the teasing game.

Too soon, the tell-tale tingle that the end was near crawled up his spine. He squeezed her hand to let her know, but she kept up the same, steady pace, and he went over the edge, her body gently milking his, stroke after lazy stroke.

Even through his own orgasm, he knew the instant she went over, too. Her body arched and tensed and quivered, her inner muscles squeezing him as she found her own leisurely release right after his.

All without a word.

Rather than collapse onto his chest like a warm, living blanket the way she usually did, Miranda slid over to lay beside him instead. He rolled to his side to face her and winced at the quick stab of pain. Good thing one of them had remembered his injured ribs.

"I'm sorry I lied to you."

"I'm sorry I didn't trust you."

He snorted. "Like I gave you any reason to. No," he said, cutting off her protest. "I was wrong to lie about where I was going all those nights. It was…" Embarrassing. Humiliating. "…stupid, really." Not a word he liked to use about himself, but when the shoe fit…

"You weren't cheating on me."

The fact it was a statement and not a question erased another layer of the pain he'd been carrying the last few days. "No, I wasn't. I'd never. Why would I, when I have you?"

She swallowed. "Because maybe I'm not the right woman for you. Why else would you have lied to me?"

Her words sent a bullet of panic through him.

"You are everything I need. Everything I want. Christ, if you were any more, you'd have killed me by now."

"I'm not talking about sex."

"Neither am I."

Uncertainty still clouded her expression despite his words.

Damn. He'd been so blinded by his own insecurities he hadn't even thought about how they might end up feeding into hers.

Time to set that shit straight right now.

He gently cupped her face in his hand. "Sweetheart, you're one of the bravest, most determined people I've ever known. You set your mind on something, and you do it. You're *exactly* the right woman for me. You're already a part of my life, and I'm not letting you go without a fight."

Miranda's lips trembled before she pressed them tight, blinking away the sheen in her eyes. "You and your sweet talk."

"Just the truth. Speaking of which..." He hesitated only a second, then dropped his hand and tore the proverbial bandage off in a rush of words. "The real reason I was driving down to Queens twice a week was because I was studying for the lieutenant's test that's coming up soon, and I didn't want you to know."

Confusion brought her brows together. "But...why not?"

"Because chances are good I'll totally fuck it up and fail."

"So what?"

He blinked. "What?"

"So what? What if you take the test and don't do well. What happens?"

"Um, I don't get promoted."

"And?"

A trickle of frustration slid into his tone. "And what?"

She countered his frustration with a little exasperation of her own. "And will anything bad happen to you at work if you do poorly, besides not getting the promotion and whatever raise and perks go with it?"

"Well, I'll get my balls broken by everyone." Especially Cartwright.

She snorted. "If the fire department is anything like the Marine Corps, that'll happen no matter how you do."

"Yeah, true."

"So, what's the real reason this test has you all twisted up in knots?"

Trapped, he had no choice but to tell her the truth. "I don't want you to be disappointed in me."

Like everyone else.

Although...that wasn't as true as he'd once thought it to be.

"Why would I be disappointed in you? You're doing what you can to give yourself the best possible chance. You can't do more than that."

"I'm doing twice the studying, and I probably still won't do as well as half the guys who take it." People who were his peers. His friends, his *uncle*, all of them would see his score when the results came out and know the truth.

Ben Murphy was an idiot.

Being able to put a name to his problem thanks to his mom didn't change anything. In a way, it kind of made it worse. It meant that no matter how hard he worked, how much he studied, he'd still always come up short.

Miranda was quiet for a long minute before she raised herself up on one elbow, giving the illusion she was looking right at him. Seeing him.

"Let me ask you this. I've been training for the Marine Corps Marathon for months now. It's important to me I give the best showing I can. For my guys. I've been doing okay running tandem with you out on the high school track, where it's just us and a perfectly surfaced oval, but honestly? I have no idea how I'll perform once I get to the real thing, out on open roads with a bunch of other runners and a different guide."

"You'll be fine." He had zero doubt of that.

"You don't know that. Maybe I'll trip. Or get freaked out and have a panic attack when I'm in the middle of a crowd of thousands. It almost happened at the fair, and I had both you and Sam with me. I won't have either of you when I'm running. What then?"

His stomach dipped at the thought.

"Then you know you tried hard and did your best."

"And if I decide halfway through the race I've had enough and quit? Would you be disappointed in me for giving up?"

"Of course not."

She leaned closer until their noses nearly touched. "Then why the hell would you think I'd be disappointed in you for doing the best you can, no matter what your stupid score ends up being?"

"Because..." Because it was what he'd come to expect from the people who were supposed to be behind him when it mattered most.

Worse, it was what he'd come to expect of himself.

"Because I'm an idiot?"

Her lips twitched at his self-deprecating reply. "I think we can agree on that." She pressed a kiss to his nose. "Take the test. Do the best you can. But for God's sake, stop worrying about what everyone else is going to think. Especially me. Do this for *you*."

Damn, had he just thought it seemed she could see him?

More like see *into* him.

His mood lightened, only to plummet again in the following heartbeat.

"It's probably a moot point, anyway. The test is next week. I already missed the second-to-last prep class, and with this concussion who knows if I'll even be able to concentrate well enough for the final one. Or to take the test."

Damn it. All that hard work for nothing.

"Then we figure out how to make up for what you missed. I'm sure Cody will help. So will all your other friends. And if it turns out you can't take the test, then you see if they have some kind of make-up exam. You did get hurt in the line of duty. Or you take it next time. You have options, Slick, and people who are willing to be there to help you out."

Yeah, he did. He was only just starting to realize that.

He hesitated. "It's not just that. My mother thinks I have a mental problem with taking tests. That I worry too much about doing poorly, and then I end up doing exactly that."

She gave him a saucy smile. "Then I guess I'll have to come up with some way to keep you distracted from thinking about it, won't I?"

How did he get so freaking lucky to find this woman?

"God, I love you." He grinned when she sucked in a shocked breath. "Didn't think I'd say it again, did you?"

"I wasn't sure you remembered saying it the first time."

"I remember. I also remember what you said."

"Me? I don't remember saying anything." She squirmed and laughed when he tickled her as punishment for teasing. "Okay, okay, I might have said something like…I love you, too." All the laughter was gone from her voice when she gave him the words. "I do. I wasn't sure yet, but after you were hurt, and I didn't know…" She cleared her throat. "Don't ever scare me like that again, Slick."

"You know I can't promise you that."

She sighed. "I know."

His mother's words itched at his brain. About her worrying about him every day. About his uncle losing his fiancé and choosing the bachelor life rather than trying to find someone who could deal with the strain of his profession.

Something he now knew he *didn't* want to emulate.

"I could find another job." The words tasted vile, but he meant them. If the alternative was losing her because she couldn't stand the constant state of fear, he'd leave the department in a heartbeat.

"Only if you want to find another girlfriend, too."

Confused by her angry tone, he asked, "Because I don't want you to worry all the time?"

"Because I don't want you to change who you are to try and make me happy. I love you just the way I found you. That means loving everything about you, even your dangerous job. Will I worry every time you go to work? Absolutely. But I'll also worry whenever you drive down to see your parents, just like you'll be thinking about what could happen every time Sam and I cross Main Street."

Something that still made him break into a cold sweat.

"I still can't believe you came to the hospital, after saying it would take a miracle to get you to walk into one again."

"That should tell you something, Slick."

It did. Hearing she was in the waiting room had done wonders for his aching head.

And heart.

"But then you didn't call after I got out, and I wasn't sure what to think."

"You were with your family. I didn't want to intrude. Cody kept me updated on how you were doing."

"You wouldn't have been intruding."

Her nose wrinkled. "Your mom might have had a different opinion. We, ah, had a small thing in the waiting room."

"Yeah, she mentioned that."

"She did?" Miranda sounded surprised. And a little bit guilty.

He kissed the tip of her nose. So freaking adorable.

"She had a feeling that might be the reason you didn't call, so she told me what she said. She also said she owes you an apology."

"She really doesn't. Everyone was kind of on edge that night. Besides, I made good use of the time you were gone."

"I saw the results in my fridge."

She lifted one shoulder. "Hernandez women cook when they're upset."

"And they do it very well. In fact, Caleb might try to steal you away for your burritos."

Her laughter was a beautiful sound. One he'd missed hearing.

"He's too late. I've already got the guy I want, and I'm keeping him." She hesitated. "I hope you don't mind that my mother and I invaded your kitchen to cook. It was easier to do it all here rather than drag it all over from my place."

"Yeah, yeah, you just love me for my appliances," he said with a grin, which she matched with her own.

"Well, you do have all the best toys. I think my mother's going to be bugging *Papí* for a new stove now after using yours." She sobered. "I'm so glad you're home. I don't think I could have gone another day without seeing you. I love you, Ben Murphy." She spread her hand over his heart. "All of you."

Emotions threatened to swamp him as he looked into her eyes. Beautiful eyes. Eyes that saw straight to his soul, even if they would never see his face.

Or maybe that was the reason she was the one person who could see him so clearly.

He put his hand over hers, sealing it to his body. "And I love you, Miranda Hernandez. All of you. Just the way you are."

Epilogue

3 MONTHS LATER

The air Miranda sucked in couldn't seem to fill her burning lungs with enough of the oxygen her tortured body needed. Fatigue pulled at her from all directions, urging her to stop the abuse and give up. The pain radiating from her feet and legs agreed.

It didn't matter what her good intentions had been at the start of the race. Nothing was worth this kind of punishment.

Quit. Quit. Quit.

The words whispered in her brain in time with the slap of her sneakers as she picked them up and put them down, the action more mindless muscle memory than real thought at this point. It was tempting to give in. So, so tempting.

"Last mile marker coming up!"

Like a switch had been thrown, her body found its kick, that final bit of energy when the end of the race was near. The pain and fatigue melted away. They'd be back, but not before she crossed under the red and gold arch at the finish line with the rest of her unit.

The exhilaration of that thought thrust an extra burst of adrenaline through her weary muscles and smoothed out her pace even more.

Cash's shout might have been mostly for her benefit since she couldn't see the sign, but it seemed to have the same energizing effect on everyone else.

It was as if she could tell exactly which of the feet pounding the street around her belonged to her guys. Like their old training days, they ran as a tight group in perfect step with one another. The well-oiled machine the Marine Corps had forged them into.

Unlike those days, though, this machine was a little less oiled and now included a wheelchair, the blade Cash wore for a leg to run, and her. Damaged pieces, running to honor the missing ones.

But damaged or not, they were going to finish this damn race.

All of them.

"You doing okay, Hernandez?"

As her guide for the last leg of the marathon, Sergeant Kevin Vonderman had done a great job of keeping her on course and motivated through the physical slumps that came with a race this long.

"Pain is weakness leaving the body, Sarge," she panted out.

"Oorah, Marine!"

There was an echo of "oorahs" from all around that she joined in.

For days before flying to Virginia, she'd worried about seeing them again after all this time. It would be the first time they'd all be together, face-to-face, since their chopper went down.

Neither she nor Gator had been able to attend any of the funerals, and by the time she'd been released from the rehab facility, Stubbins and Vonderman had been cleared back to duty, and Cash had been discharged and sent home.

A decision he'd fought tooth and nail. And had won the right to return to active duty, prosthetic leg and all.

She'd expected things to be awkward when they all met for lunch yesterday. And it had been. For all of about two minutes. Then Gator had let loose with one of his usual raunchy comments, and suddenly it was like no time had passed at all.

A change in pressure on the short tether pulled her a little to the left as Vonderman adjusted them with the curving course as it wound toward the Iwo Jima memorial. The sound of the crowd began to build, signaling they were getting close to the finish line.

You fucking did it, Hernandez. You actually fucking did it.

Though not alone.

Von and Stubs had both done incredible jobs being her guides. Since Ben had missed the application window to join the race, they'd stepped up in his place, training on their own for weeks to learn how. And despite a few hiccups early on, it had been smooth going almost the whole way.

But a part of her still missed having Ben at her side.

A tingle of happiness filled her just thinking about him. He hadn't been able to keep training with her after his injuries a few months back, but he never stopped being her biggest champion. He'd even rounded up people to run with her while he couldn't, so she wouldn't lose momentum.

But the biggest, most wonderful thing he'd done for her was to take time off to come with her and cheer her on. She'd heard him yelling his fool head off at three different spots along the route, which meant he'd been using the Track-a-Runner feature on the marathon app to keep up with their progress.

If it wouldn't have screwed up everyone else's pace, she'd have gone to the sidelines and kissed the big goof to show him how much his support meant to her.

"Home stretch, boys and girls!" Cash called out.

The roar of the crowd was disorienting, but Von led her with unerring confidence across the finish line, where they were each given their finisher's medal.

She didn't need anyone to tell her what it was. Her fingers curled over the familiar shape of the Eagle, Globe, and Anchor at the end of the ribbon around her neck, a sense of satisfaction and pride countering the draining loss of endorphins.

She didn't even bother asking what their time had been. It didn't matter.

It only mattered that they'd done it together.

"We did it, *cher*." Gator's hand closed around hers and gave a good squeeze as he echoed her thoughts out loud. "We done beat dat bitch."

"We beat dat bitch to death," she agreed with a laugh. Gator always pressed hard on his unique Cajun syntax when he was feeling particularly feisty. After what they'd just accomplished, she had a feeling he'd be laying the accent on like thick bayou mud for the rest of the day.

Water, a banana, and a handful of nuts were all the recharge she had patience for before they all headed for the area set aside for runners to meet back up with friends and family. The excitement of it all kept her from crashing just yet, but there was definitely a nap somewhere in her near future.

"Miranda!"

"Ben!" She gave a joyous laugh as his arms came around her, lifting her feet from the ground with the exuberance of his hug. She pushed at him half-heartedly when he set her back down. "Stop, I'm all sweaty."

He leaned closer to her ear. "Just the way I like you."

Before she could decide between telling him to behave or asking if he wanted to go to their room and work up a matching sweat of his own, he moved away to make way for someone else.

"You were awesome!" Julietta gave her a quick hug. "I'm so proud of you."

"Thanks, Jules." When her sister stepped back, Miranda expected her mother to step into the void. To her shock, it was Isobel.

"Sorry, but I'm not hugging you while you smell like a locker room." Although she did brush a kiss on Miranda's cheek in greeting.

"Izzy? I didn't think you were coming."

"Are you kidding? With this many hot guys, how could I not?"

And there it was. The one reason her sister would waste her time and money coming down to Virginia for the day. Herself.

Isobel let out a small grunt. Probably from Julietta's elbow. "And, I guess maybe I wanted to see my big sister do something pretty incredible." The words seemed sincere despite having been coerced.

"Wow. That's...wow. Thank you." She threw her arms around her sister's neck and hugged her tight. In spite of Izzy's heartfelt "eww!" she hugged her back. Maybe she was finally growing up and figuring out who she was supposed to be.

Maybe they both were.

Tino hugged her next, whispering how proud he was in Spanish like he had when she was a little girl. Then her mother enveloped her in a citrusy cloud as she wrapped her arms around Miranda and held on, slowly rocking her.

It wasn't until she felt something wet on her neck that she realized her mother was crying. "Mom?"

Her mother loosened her hold but didn't let go. "I am so proud of you, *mija*. And so ashamed."

Shock would have made her step out of her mother's embrace if she hadn't been holding on. "Ashamed? Why? What did I do?"

"No, no, not you. Me. I did this. In all these months you've been telling me you were ready to start living your own life again, I couldn't see the truth. That it was *me* who wasn't ready. I was afraid to let you go and watch you fail. But you're not going to. I believe that now. You...you're a strong, amazing woman, and I can see now you're capable of handling anything you set your mind to."

Emotion clogged her throat at the words she'd never expected to hear.

"Thank you, *Mamí*. You don't know how much that means to me." She hugged her mother again. When they both finally let go, she thought they were done and started to turn back to Ben.

"*Mijita.*"

Just one word, but it was enough to make her knees almost buckle.

"*Papi?*" She gasped as her father's strong arms came around her, her suddenly damp face pressed against his shoulder as she breathed in the familiar scent of Old Spice and new wood that always clung to his skin. "You came. I can't believe you came."

"I'm so sorry, *mija*. I let my pride stand in the way too long."

"No, it's my fault, too. I know how much trouble I've been to you since I lost my sight."

"Trouble?" He held her tighter and rocked like her mother had done. "You're my daughter. You aren't *trouble*." His breathing hitched, the closest he'd ever allow himself to crying in public. "And your mother is right. You're a strong, amazing, *incredible* young woman, and I've never been prouder of you in my life."

His husky words helped take the sting from all of the angry ones they'd tossed at each other over the years since her defiant enlistment in the Marines. They'd never erase them, but maybe it was the balm they both needed to be able to put the past where it belonged and heal the rift in their family's core.

While she was still hugging her father, her mother came and wrapped her arms around them both. Julietta did the same, and Tino, and even Isobel after she heaved a loud sigh about more sweatiness. Tears and laughter filled the circle, but something was still missing.

Something important.

Miranda picked her head up and held out her hand. A moment later, Ben took it. Jules shifted from her side, making a place for him to move in and become a part of the group hug. His breath touched her cheek in a warm puff as he pressed his head to hers.

She smiled at the familiar feel of him. Perfect.

Now her circle was complete.

"I think your friend Gator wants to rip my nuts off."

Still riding the emotional high of the day, Miranda laughed and ignored the fresh beers Ben had spent far too long retrieving from the bar, wrapping her arms around his trim waist instead. "Why would you think something like that?"

"Maybe because he said, and I quote, 'If you hurt my Boo, I'ma hafta pull your nuts off like grapes from da vine, you got dat, you?'"

She laughed again. That sounded exactly like something Gator would say, crazy accent and all. "Well, you're safe from any nut ripping, aren't you, since I've never been happier in my life."

And she was. Gloriously, deliciously happy.

Something that surprised her each and every morning when she woke up in the arms of the man who had turned the light on inside her again.

"Same goes, Legs." He nuzzled her neck, both of them ignoring the hoots and whistles of the Marines packed in tight around them.

"Best get a room, you."

"Already got one, thanks." Miranda reached down to the electric wheelchair Gator had somehow managed to maneuver through the dense crowd and patted his arm. The uneven, waxy texture of the old burn scars that covered most of his body still evoked the same deep guilt and sadness in her chest they always had, but she kept her smile in place.

The time of grieving for lost things was over.

Today was all about new beginnings. For all of them.

"You really shouldn't be threatening my guy's junk, Gate. I'm kind of partial to it."

Gator snorted. "No doubt, when he look like dat." He tugged her arm, pulling her down closer so he could lower his voice. "You happy, *cher*? I mean, for real happy?"

"I'm more than that. I'm for real in love."

"Dat's all I need to know, then." He pressed a smacking kiss to her mouth, no doubt to irritate Ben, before releasing her.

Predictably, Ben slid his arm back around her and pulled her tight to his side. In the tense silence that followed, she could only imagine the staring contest being held to prove who was the bigger alpha dog in her life.

Idiots.

Finally, Gator chuckled. "You'll do, Slick. You'll do."

"I hate when he calls me that," Ben muttered after Gator had wheeled off to answer someone's hail from somewhere across the bar.

"Which is why he does it." Though she had to admit it annoyed her a little, too. Again, probably why he did it. Gator was a master button pusher.

"Well, at least he hasn't started calling you Legs yet."

If Gator knew just how much it would piss Ben off, he'd never call her anything else. "Let's make sure he never hears you call me that, okay?" It would be a shame if she had to kill one of her best friends for being an ass.

When she covered a yawn with her hand, Ben asked, "Tired?"

"Exhausted," she admitted.

The combat nap she'd taken after the race had gotten her through dinner with her family and the round of congratulatory phone calls from Trixie, Robin, Cody, and the rest of Ben's friends she was coming to consider hers as well.

But after meeting back up with the guys for a few beers, plus a couple of shots in honor of those missing, her ass was starting to drag low to the ground.

"Hopefully not too exhausted," Ben murmured against her ear. His hand slid down to caress her hip. "I promised to pamper and take care of you tonight, to make you feel *outstanding*, remember?"

An incandescent spark spread throughout her body.

Oh, she remembered. Vividly.

Some words were hard to forget, especially when the man uttering them was buried deep inside your still throbbing body.

"I'm never too exhausted," she murmured back, flicking her tongue out to catch the edge of his ear, "for a nice, satisfying...foot rub." She grinned against his neck as he groaned. "Seriously, my feet are killing me."

"Give me half an hour, and you won't even remember you have feet."

"Promises, promises."

"Not a promise, *cher*," he replied, leaning on a bad Cajun accent tinged with Long Island, "it's a guaran-damn-tee."

They worked their way out of the bar, leaving Gator and the rest of the guys still drinking and talking old times. A bout of laughter that rang out made her smile. Seeing her friends celebrate life despite their losses eased the weight of guilt and sorrow she'd been carrying for so long.

It was finally time to leave the past behind and move on.

Sam greeted them at Julietta's motel room door with his usual exuberance. He hadn't been happy about being left behind tonight, but she hadn't wanted him in the crowded bar. He was trained to handle situations like that; it didn't mean she had to take him there. Not when she had Ben to be her guide.

To be her everything.

She'd told Gator the God's honest truth. She was for real in love with the guy.

As she listened to him wrestle with Sam over his favorite tug-toy, she tried to imagine her life without him and couldn't. In just a few short months, he'd turned her whole structured, solitary world upside down and inside out.

He kept saying she was the best thing that ever happened to him, but she knew it was the reverse that was true.

His constant encouragement and belief in her ability to do whatever she put her mind to had lit a fire under her butt about her future. She'd gone and talked to a counselor at the local college about maybe enrolling in a few classes for the spring semester. And while she didn't know how it would go, she'd at least put herself out there to try.

Like she'd asked him about the lieutenant's test, so what if you fail?

Which, in fact, he hadn't.

When the scores came out a few weeks ago, Ben hadn't just passed, he'd done exceedingly well. He'd even scored half a point higher than Cody did. Something he wasn't likely to let his friend forget anytime soon.

Then again, Cody was so busy being happy with Val—the woman was actually starting to grow on her—he probably wouldn't care.

As Ben took Sam out for one last potty break, she stripped down and crawled under the covers with a sigh to wait for him. The past three days had taken their toll, both emotionally and physically. She wasn't sure how well she would have handled it all if Ben hadn't offered to come along.

He didn't try to fix her problems for her. His rock-steady presence at her back just made it easier to face her fears and doubts on her own terms.

Just one more thing to love about the man.

When Ben joined her, she snuggled against him, breathing in his familiar mix of smoky musk and sexy man. The scent of home. "Thank you."

"For what?"

"For being here. For being you." She kissed him, long and lingering. "For being mine."

With a low chuckle that sent tingles of excitement to wake up the tired parts of her body, he rolled her underneath him. "I'll be yours for as long as you want me, Legs."

She wrapped those legs he was so fond of around his hips and smiled. "I will always want you, Slick. Always. That's a guaran-damn-tee." With a shift of her hips, she opened herself to him and drew him deep inside, body and soul.

Right where he belonged.

A Note From the Author

I hope you enjoyed Ben and Miranda's (and Sam's) story!

This series holds a special place in my heart, as my husband is a retired Marine, and one of my brothers is a retired Battalion Chief with the FDNY. But I think the real inspiration for these books sprang from seeing guide dogs being trained all around my home town when I was growing up and, later, meeting a family who fostered guide dogs-in-training during their first year, teaching them basic social skills and commands. With all of that marinating in my brain, it was only a matter of time before the Wounded Warrior Legacy books were born.

I'd like to thank everyone who helped me with this book (and there were many!). First, my husband, whose understanding when I lock myself in the office to hit my deadlines is boundless. Thanks to the folks at America's Vet Dogs, who graciously answered my one million questions when I was still fleshing out the idea for this series. A huge shout-out to my sensitivity readers, Bee, ER, and Amanda, who helped make sure I didn't muck things up about Miranda and Sam too badly. Big thanks also go to my brother, BC Brian M. White, FDNY-Ret, who let me pick his brain whenever I had a question about anything fire related. And finally, many thanks to my late sister-in-law, Liz, who helped me with some of the Spanish before she was taken from us far too soon. *Te echamos de menos.*

Any inaccuracies that remain are mine alone, and were sometimes necessary for the story.

We still have two more service dogs with veterans to help, so keep an eye out for the next Legacy book, A Light in the Darkness, coming out later this year. Not all wounds are physical, and Neil Crawford is in a fight for his future against the PTSD that's followed him home from the battlefield. This was a tough book to write, but I think the results are worth it, because everyone deserves their HEA, in both love and life.

If you want to know more about my other books, scan the QR code below to visit my website (nikarhone.com). While you're there, claim your FREE book just by signing up for my newsletter. You can also stay up-to-date on all future releases by following my author page on any of the major book retailer websites.

And finally, if you enjoyed this book, please take a moment to leave a review with your favorite book retailer. They're what feeds an author's creative soul. Thank you!

Claim your FREE book now

Resources

If you or someone you know are in crisis, please reach out:

Suicide & Crisis Hotline: (toll-free 24/7) call 988 and press 1
Suicide & Crisis Website: 988lifeline.org
National Call Center for Homeless Veterans: 1-877-424-3838
Americans With Disabilities Act information: ada.gov

Please consider volunteering or donating to your local guide/service dog organization. If you don't have one, here are a few that I know of:

America's Vet Dog: vetdogs.org
Guide Dog Foundation for the Blind: guidedog.org
Guiding Eyes for the Blind: guidingeyes.org
Guide Dogs of America: guidedogsofamerica.org
International Guide Dog Federation: igdf.org.uk
National Federation of the Blind: nfb.org
Paws of War: pawsofwar.org

Also By Nika Rhone

<u>Boulder Bodyguards series</u>
What the Lady Wants
Finding Forever
Can't Help Loving You

<u>Boulder Beaumonts series</u>
Worth Any Price
Never Let Me Go
All I Need Is You

<u>Wounded Warrior Legacy series</u>
Just the Way You Are
A Light in the Darkness (coming 2025)

About the Author

Nika Rhone spent her childhood wearing out library cards as she read her way through the extraordinary worlds far beyond her small hometown on Long Island, NY. By her teens, her imagination was taking her places all on its own, forcing her to learn how to type (badly) so she could get all the stories down on paper. After a long love affair with science fiction and fantasy, she finally discovered romance, fell head-over-heels, and now spends her days crafting happily-ever-afters for the characters who still tell their stories faster (and better) than she can type them.

You can keep up with all the latest book news, events, and give-aways by visiting her website www.nikarhone.com and joining her newsletter.

My experience with cancer before my own diagnosis had been limited to family. My dad's oldest sister had passed from breast cancer. She found the lump one month after a full physical, underwent surgery, chemo, and radiation and died within six months almost to the day of finding the lump. My oncologist told me that her cancer was likely triple negative due to the quick progression of the cancer.

My father had fought multiple myeloma for eight years. I had seen the effects of chemo and radiation on his body and naturally assumed that I would experience the same types of effects. However, cancer treatments have come so far in the last few years that nausea is almost a thing of the past. My mom was diagnosed with ovarian cancer in December of2009 and passed away in January of 2010. I have had other aunts, uncles, and cousins with cancer, so it was amazing that all my genetic testing came back negative.

I continued to work through my chemo months. As a teacher, I felt I owed it to my students and parents to give them my best effort. I had planned in August of the school year to retire the following May. My diagnosis seemed to confirm this decision. Throughout my treatment, my students were my rock. They were amazing from the notes they would leave on my desk to the sanitizing they would do each day to make sure I stayed healthy.

That's how my journey began. The next few chapters are going to address specific things such as: chemotherapy, fear, depression, surgery, radiation, oral chemo and suggestions for you in your journey. Again, let me say, everyone's cancer journey is different. I'm not trying to tell anyone how to walk their journey, but I simply want to share the knowledge I've gained to help you know that you are not alone.

Chemotherapy

My diagnosis was Triple Negative Breast Cancer (TNBC). TNBC is negative for estrogen receptors, progesterone receptors and excess HER2 protein. This means the cancer is not fueled by estrogen, progesterone, or by the HER2 protein. Those at risk for TNBC are women younger than 40, African Americans, Hispanics, and those with a BRCA1 gene mutation. TNBC accounts for 10-15% of all breast cancers. I was diagnosed as a 59-year-old Caucasian who did not have the genetic component. Triple-negative breast cancer (TNBC) is considered an aggressive cancer because it grows quickly, is more likely to have spread at the time it's found and is more likely to come back after treatment than other types of breast cancer. The outlook is generally not as good as it is for other types of breast cancer. According to the American Cancer Society, the five-year survival rate for TNBC is 77%.

The best chance for survival with Triple Negative Breast Cancer (TNBC) is to begin with chemotherapy. Having surgery first could allow cancer cells to migrate to other areas of the body. After surgery, a minimum of six weeks is necessary for healing which would postpone chemotherapy. Since TNBC is aggressive, treatment must be aggressive.

I have always taught my students that chemotherapy doesn't just target the cancer cells but all cells. The ability of chemotherapy to kill cancer cells depends on its ability to halt cell division. Usually, the drugs work by damaging the RNA or DNA that tells the cell how to copy itself in division. If the cells are unable to divide, they die. The faster the cells are dividing, the more likely it is that chemotherapy will kill the cells, causing the tumor to shrink. They also induce cell suicide. Chemotherapy is most effective at killing cells that are rapidly dividing.

Unfortunately, chemotherapy does not know the difference between the cancerous cells and the normal cells. The "normal" cells will grow back and be healthy but, in the meantime, side effects occur. The "normal" cells most affected by chemotherapy are the blood cells, the cells in the mouth, stomach and bowel, and the hair follicles. This is because these cells are the fast-growing cells in the body. Because normal cells are affected, side effects occur. Not everyone has the same side effects but the ones most related to the Taxol/Carboplatin regime are nausea, vomiting, low blood counts, hair loss, joint and muscle pain, neuropathy, diarrhea, mouth sores, thrush, and fatigue. I experienced all of these except for vomiting.

Initially, I was told I would have sixteen rounds of chemo. The first twelve treatments would consist of Taxol with Carboplatin added each third treatment. This is the standard for treatment of TNBC. Treatments would be every week unless my blood counts were too low for chemo. This would be followed by four treatments of Adriamycin, every two weeks. Adriamycin is nicknamed "Red Devil" because of its bright red appearance. Medical professionals do not like to use that term, but in my mind that is what it should be called. Not only is it red in color but it is a one of the most powerful chemotherapy drugs ever invented. It can kill cancer cells at every point in their life cycle and the side effects can be devastating.

My first day of chemo arrived and I kept stalling. I knew I had to go, but I kept thinking back to my dad and how his chemo journey had progressed, and I ended up feeling nauseated BEFORE chemo. I carried a bag in the car with me because I felt so sick. Fortunately, it was not needed.

My nurses were awesome in getting me ready and explaining each step of the process. My first chemo lasted six hours. It was a slow drip to make sure I didn't experience any adverse reactions. I had received IV steroids to postpone nausea for at least forty-eight hours and IV Benadryl to negate any allergic reactions. Unfortunately, the Benadryl caused restless leg syndrome and I was unable to sleep through any of my chemo treatments.

The first treatment wiped me out for the entire weekend. I had my treatments on Thursday and my plan was to go to work each following Friday. With my first treatment I went ahead and took Friday off from teaching because I wasn't sure how my body would react to the drugs. I slept most of Friday, Saturday, and Sunday.   I woke up Saturday night with dry heaves and immediately started my anti-nausea meds. They kept me from throwing up, but between the chemo and anti-nausea meds my appetite was gone.

I opted not to do a cooling cap during my infusions. I might have been able to keep my hair during Taxol/Carboplatin but was assured that I would lose my hair on Adriamycin. I could not justify spending an extra fifteen hundred dollars on something that might help me keep my hair. I opted to wear baseball caps and looked for fun caps that I could wear to school.

Emotionally, I thought I could handle losing my hair. After all, it would grow back, but the actual hair loss was gut-wrenching. For me, my hair loss was so personal, I did not allow or take any pictures of my bald head.

Infusion days always began with blood work to make sure my counts were high enough to have a treatment. One of the first things I noticed was my hair hurt.   It's hard to explain. It wasn't my actual scalp, but it felt as though the actual hair on my head was hurting. I had been told by a friend that when she started chemo her hair hurt and the only thing that helped was shaving her head. I took the initiative and shaved my head leaving a mohawk.

Jason Bowen, my worship pastor at church had a mohawk and he was coming to my infusion that day. Imagine his surprise when he walked in and saw me sporting the "hawk"! We had a great laugh about it, and he kept me company as my body was pumped with the toxic chemicals once again.

I had missed church the Sunday before, so Jason brought communion to share with me once my infusion was over. We gathered, Jason prayed, and then we took communion together. A solemn moment turned into a hilarious moment when a voice from the nurse's station said, "Are you all doing shots up there?" Jason and I looked at each other and burst into laughter. I think we laughed until we cried.

After my second infusion, my hair had to go. I took out the clippers and buzzed the rest of my hair. I chose when to cut my hair. I didn't wait until it began to come out in clumps. There was so much out of my control at this point that I felt the only thing I could control was to shave my head. Remember, how I said that I thought I could handle losing my hair? Well, it wasn't true. It hurt to cut my hair. Not because I'm vain, but now everyone would know that I was sick. I didn't want to be sick, and I didn't want to have cancer, but I had no control. I didn't shed tears until it was all off and then I fell apart.

I tried to maintain some sense of normalcy during chemotherapy. I continued to teach my students and they were awesome. Each afternoon my last period would sanitize my room to make sure I stayed healthy. I wore masks to school and tried to have fun finding the most ridiculous and outrageous masks. My students were particularly excited when I showed up wearing shark masks during our shark unit. Focusing on things other than my illness helped keep my spirits up and my mind off what I was experiencing.

My chemo continued and I was hoping to be completely done by April, but then low blood counts hit. I couldn't have a treatment and it was frustrating. I was given shots of Neupogen to bring up my white blood cell count. My bone marrow was taking a hit from chemo and these cells had plummeted. As with any drug, I had to watch for side effects, with the main side effect being bone pain and the most serious being a ruptured spleen. As if cancer isn't bad enough, now you must contend with all the vicious side effects from the treatment.

Due to low blood counts, I had to have two blood transfusions which last almost as long as a chemo infusion. My counts never recovered, and my oncologist decided at the end of April to cancel the last two Taxol treatments (I had all the Carboplatin treatments) and move forward with Adriamycin (AC). I was concerned though and voiced my fears to my oncologist I was afraid, that since I hadn't had all the treatments and there had been weeks between some treatments, my tumors were growing.

My oncologist, Dr. Minesh Patel, with the Piedmont Cancer Institute, was an absolute Godsend. Not only did he listen to my fears, but he sent me immediately down to the Breast Clinic for an ultrasound to check the size of my tumors. My report this time read as follows:

At the 6:30 position 5 cm from the nipple the largest mass which has undergone prior biopsy has decreased in size currently measuring 2.0 x 0.9 x 2.0 cm. Previously this measured 2.3 x 3.2 x 3.4 cm. Pretherapy ultrasound demonstrated masses at the 6:00 and 7:00 positions in the right breast. Neither of those masses could be visualized at this time. At the 9:00 position 3 cm from the nipple there is a 0.6 x 0.5 x 0.4 cm mass. Previously this measured 1.2 x 0.4 x 0.8 cm. At the 9:00 position 8 cm from the nipple again visualized is a cyst not significantly changed currently measuring 1.0 x 0.8 x 0.9 cm. At the 10:00 position 10 cm from the nipple the second lesion which underwent biopsy is visualized. Currently this measures 1.3 x 0.7 x 0.9 cm. Previously this mass measure 1.6 x 0.9 x 1.2 cm.

Not only were my masses reducing in size, but some had completely disappeared! Chemo was working! I must be honest and say that if positive results hadn't been found, I'm not sure I would have continued chemotherapy. It had been so hard for an active person to now struggle walking from the front door to the mailbox. Chemotherapy zaps your energy. The fatigue that comes with the treatment is like nothing I have ever experienced! Rest and more rest didn't help. It is a constant fatigue that is not alleviated by anything! I went from my 5K's, 10K's, and maintaining my lawn to just trying to get out of bed daily to go to work.

Some days I just felt like giving up and giving in to the feelings of despair. Physically I was exhausted from the stress on my body. Mentally I was exhausted from trying to stay the course and be upbeat. Emotionally I was exhausted and just felt like crying, all the time. Though I pushed through all the feelings, some days were simply hard. Nothing seemed to help. I knew that with AC things were going to be much harder.

After first round of AC, I lost all my body hair. I cried when I lost my eyebrows and eyelashes. I looked in the mirror and did not recognize the person looking back. I hated the way I felt. I was tired of being tired. My chemo journey that was supposed to be over by April was now heading toward June before being finished. A result of AC is chemo brain or chemo fog, and it began to affect me. I couldn't remember things. I struggled to put sentences together. I cried myself to sleep frustrated because I felt stupid. I stumbled over words and I was worried about my hearing.

I already had a hearing loss and suffer from auditory processing disorder. Another possible side effect of my chemo treatment was losing even more hearing. I was devastated to think I could possibly lose even more. I cried more. I felt helpless and, at times, alone. Knowing my concerns, my audiologist kept a constant check on my hearing, and we were both pleased that I made it through chemo without additional hearing loss.

After two treatments with AC, Dr. Patel ordered another ultrasound to alleviate my fears. This time my results read: *Favorable response to treatment. The biopsied masses at 6:30 position 5 cm from the nipple and 10:00 position 10 cm from the nipple, have both decreased in size. Mass at 9:00 8 cm from the nipple has decreased slightly in size. Mass at 10:00 11 cm from the nipple has decreased in size. Mass at 9:00 3 cm from the nipple is unchanged.*

Dr. Patel assured me that even with two treatments left, tumor sizes would continue to decrease and after treatment was finished, the chemo would continue to work in my system for some time. He was thrilled with my body's response to chemo. It was obviously working, and I realized that what my body was going through would be worth it in the long run. My last chemo treatment was June 13, 2019. With my last two Taxol treatments cancelled I had completed 14 out of the 16 treatments. Now it was time to rest and prepare for surgery.

Surgery/Drains/Complications

The last chemo was finished and now my body had a month to recover as best as possible before I would be scheduled for surgery. I met with my surgeon and he ordered a new PET scan to identify any areas of active cancer. My PET scan came back showing no active cancer cells. The tumors had shrunk, no lymph nodes showed activity and the intramammary gland was inactive. I was thrilled and my oncologist was excited and told me how I had a tremendous response to chemotherapy. Next step, surgery.

July 16th arrived quickly. I reported to the hospital early to have lymphatic mapping for the sentinel lymph node biopsy prior to my surgery. Lymphatic mapping requires injections around the areola of the affected breast. Then, for ten minutes after the injection, you are required to massage the breast to help the radioactive material flow to the sentinel nodes. I won't lie, the injections were painful, even with the numbing cream that was used.

Lying on a gurney, rubbing your own breast is also weird, but the massaging is necessary so they can map the lymph nodes for the surgeon to know where the nodes are located, and which ones must be removed. After the "massage", the imaging scan was completed (five minutes of no movement for each picture). The entire scan took about fifteen minutes to complete. Once the scans were completed, I was sent upstairs to the surgical suite.

After checking in I was taken back and prepped for surgery. Since my head was bald, I was given a special surgical cap to keep my head warm during surgery. My IV was started and my "5K crew" could come in two at a time to visit me. My surgeon, Dr. Frank Powell, arrived and discussed my surgery. His first surgery was over, and my surgery would begin earlier than scheduled.

The anesthesiologist arrived and began my pre-meds. I remember being rolled out of my cubicle bidding everyone farewell and that is the last thing I remember. I had opted for a bilateral mastectomy and I knew when surgery was over, I wouldn't look the same. I was undergoing an amputation and I had opted for no reconstruction.

I was offered the opportunity for a "tummy tuck" and immediate reconstruction. After doing several hours of research and talking to women who had reconstruction, I decided this was not for me. I did not want to undergo more surgeries (except for revision to clean up any scar tissue and skin flaps) and I heard nightmares about infection, and the body rejecting tissue, so I decided to remain flat. I do not need breasts for my identity. I was comfortable with the decision and my surgeon was respectful of my wishes.

Surgery lasted over three hours.   At different stages throughout my surgery, tissue samples were sent to the lab to check for cancer cells. Lymph nodes shown on the mapping were removed and sent to the lab. Tissue from the left breast would also be sent to identify any possible cancer cells. PET scans are great for detecting cancer cells but will not identify any cells less than one centimeter. Pathology would be the only way to determine if any cancer remained in the breast tissue.

I vaguely remember coming out of anesthesia in recovery and being asked if I was in any pain to which I responded "Yes, just a little". I must have received a dose of pain medicine because my next memory is being wheeled into my room where my crew awaited my arrival. I also vaguely remember a semi-wave (and I'm sure a goofy grin) as they left the room for my team to get me positioned in the bed.

A blood pressure cuff was on my left ankle along with the cuffs on my legs to prevent blood clots. I had one drain on the left side and two drains on the right. I was in a surgical binder and unable to see the incision. Drains are important after a mastectomy because of the danger of seromas (This is a collection of fluid that builds up under the surface of your skin after tissue has been removed). With the removal of breast tissue there is a natural "gap" left where the tissue was and this area can fill up with fluid. To prevent this, a drain is inserted into the area and the fluid is collected.

The surgical drains consist of long tubes inserted into the breast area or armpit and have plastic bulbs at the end to collect the fluid. Since I had lymph nodes removed on the right side, I needed two drains. One for the area where breast tissue had been removed and the other in the armpit.

I had never spent a night in the hospital as a patient. I now understood why people talk about how you can't get any rest. My stay was going to be one night, and I think they purposely tried to keep me up! Vitals every two hours, blood draws, checking to see if I needed anything. I was exhausted the next morning!

I had endured a liquid diet for dinner the previous night. My surgeon was being cautious knowing I had been under anesthesia for several hours. He wanted to make sure I didn't have a stomach problem on top of everything else. Imagine waking up (from maybe an hour nap), preparing for what I knew would be an eggs and toast kind of morning and having another liquid diet delivered for breakfast. WHAT? At least there was coffee, but have you ever tried to drink chicken broth for breakfast? If not, trust me. Do not try it.

This situation was quickly addressed when I saw my surgeon that morning and begged for a normal lunch. Dr. Powell caught me doing laps around the floor because my nurse encouraged me to get up and move. They were all amazed because I was moving, and I hadn't had any pain medicine since the shot right after surgery. I didn't need it. I felt a little sore but nothing to warrant pain meds. Dr. Powell wanted to check my incisions and I got the first look at my chest. No bruising but lots of staples and drains coming out of my body. It was a little overwhelming.

I had been watching the nurses empty my drains. The fluid is measured in cc's and had to be documented each time. My drains were numbered, and I had a form to document how much fluid was being produced by each drain. I would have to show the nurses that I could handle my drains before I would be released. Being the good student and overachiever that I am I, passed without a problem.

I had ordered a couple of shirts from a breast cancer patient who realized that when women have a mastectomy, they need some way to hold the drains. You cannot just let them dangle because they are stitched into your body and the weight of the fluid could cause them to tear from the stitch. The drains fit perfectly inside the shirt pockets and I was able to go home with my new hardware.

Sleeping with staples and drains was difficult because I'm a stomach sleeper and don't sleep well on my back. Fortunately, I was able to sleep on the chaise on one end of the sectional with pillows on my chest to protect my incision. Every day I stripped and emptied my drains in the morning and in the evening and recorded my numbers. My numbers would have to be lower than twenty cc's for drain removal.

At my first surgeon's visit, I was told no drains could be removed. I was disappointed but if drains are removed too quickly fluid can build up and require more surgery. My next appointment a week later, I was able to lose two of my drains. At the two-week point, I was able to finally have the last drain pulled. Marlo, my nurse practitioner, also removed half of my staples. I was ecstatic because this meant I could finally shower!

Dr. Powell had recommended no shower until after all the drains were removed. The chance of infection was too high, and I did not want an infection. Imagine how long my shower was that first time. It was awesome! Baby wipes just didn't give the same sense of cleanliness.

A week later, I took another trip to the surgeon to have the rest of my staples removed.   I felt relieved this part of the journey was over. I was ready to get on with radiation and finish this journey. But my journey was going to take a detour.

My pathology results came back, and the great news was only four millimeters of cancer had been found in the breast tissue. This was great and Dr. Patel said I had a "phenomenal response to chemo". This didn't show up on the PET scan since it was under a centimeter. The lymph nodes that had been removed showed no cancer activity. Everything looked great. But remember that detour…

Five weeks out from surgery, I was scheduled to have another post-op with Dr. Powell's office. The night before, I couldn't catch my breath. Every time I tried to get a deep breath; I was having chest pains. I thought I had probably pulled a muscle doing some arm stretches to be able to reach up. It was bad enough that I reached for a pain pill and went to sleep.

The next day, I happened to mention to Marlo, the nurse practitioner, that I couldn't draw a deep breath. She was immediately concerned and ordered a CT scan immediately. I was five weeks out from surgery, and it was probably a pulled muscle, but she had a "gut feeling" and she wanted to check.

Imagine my surprise when the results came back that I had bilateral, multiple blood clots in my lungs. No sooner had I left the CT scan than I was receiving a call from Dr. Powell's office. He was in surgery but had been called and told of my diagnosis. I was told to immediately go to the emergency room where I would be admitted to the hospital.

Upon arrival I was taken back (shortest emergency room wait EVER) and placed on a heparin drip. I was admitted to the hospital and told my stay would be at least two days while I received heparin. I would also have to learn to give myself shots in the stomach of Lovenox for six weeks, followed by six months of Equilis.

Through all of this, I must admit that I really didn't look in the mirror. I was afraid that I would break down. Not because of the loss of my breasts, but now I felt like Frankenstein with scars. I've always struggled with my self-image. As a child, I was extremely shy (I'm sure this comes as a shock to people who know me now) and it was always hard to make friends.

Looking in the mirror was huge, and when I finally looked, I cried. I cried because I felt I looked funny with my scars. I cried because I was no longer whole. I cried because cancer sucks. Then I picked myself up and moved forward. There was still a war to wage.

Radiation and Oral Chemo

I find it interesting that one of the ways we fight cancer is to use radiation, which in large doses can cause cancer. I met with my radiation oncologist before chemotherapy. My oncology nurse navigator scheduled all my appointments and had me meet with my oncologist, surgeon, and radiation oncologist prior to beginning any treatment. Looking back, I believe this helped me be more at ease about everything.

At my first radiology appointment, I had to watch a video about what to expect with radiation. Imagine my surprise during the video when it was mentioned that you would not "glow in the dark" nor would you be "radioactive" during your treatment. Okay, being a science teacher, I just snickered my way through. Knowledge is power and I was shocked to hear that people think those things. I wish people would educate themselves on treatments and how they impact the body.

After chemo and surgery, it was time to begin radiation. My first appointment was the most interesting. A sharpie was involved and when I came home, I looked like a first grader had been drawing on my chest! There were all kinds of marks. Some marks were covered with plastic stickers. These were the markers that would be used to "line me up" for radiation. I was told to be careful showering because I did not want to "erase" my marks. The next day, it was time to start.

I arrived with my key card and signed in. About five minutes later, I was told to come back and change. I entered the room where the huge radiation machine is located and of course, the first thing I noticed was the thickness of the door to "lock" me inside while everyone else is outside. The techs positioned me on the table and then laid a brass piece of mesh on the right side. This is to be sure the radiation is being absorbed by the skin. To be honest, I kind of felt like Cleopatra, with a fancy breast plate, but wait, I have no breasts!

Everyone left and I was left alone with the machine that would move, take pictures, and shoot targeted radiation into my body.   The longest part of radiation treatment is the positioning. The actual radiation times are a few seconds.

There were several areas they were targeting an intermammary lymph node (which received five extra radiation rounds), lymph nodes under the arm and the breast area. Actual radiation was probably about five minutes. This would continue five days a week, until thirty treatments were complete.

Since even Sharpies do not last forever, I eventually received four tattoo marks that would help line me up for radiation. These are permanent and are a reminder of what my body has been through. One of my doctors suggested getting a tattoo to connect the dots in some fashion. I think I'll pass.

Radiation causes fatigue. Great, just what I needed more of in my life. It also causes browning and burning of the skin. That is how they know the treatment is working. My burns blistered and oozed at time. Dr. Santiago made sure I had creams and lotions to help with the burning. When my skin reached a point that she was uncomfortable with continuing, she switched to "zapping" the intermammary lymph node for five treatments. Then we went back to the right chest.

The radiation center also provided me with a pillow, made by volunteers, to wear in the car between my chest and the seatbelt. I would love to meet those ladies and hug every one of them because their thoughtfulness makes radiation life much easier. It also came in handy for just putting under my arm to ease the discomfort after treatment. Radiation is basically a second-degree burn, and it hurts just like a burn from cooking or an iron. Having something to place under the arm was wonderful.

One funny thing that happened during radiation was the day I was lying on the table and I thought something is just not right. Then I realized that the brass material was sliding ever so slowly toward the right. When you are in radiation, you must maintain your position. You do not want them shooting radiation in some random part of your body. I laid perfectly still hoping it would not continue the slow, gradual slide. Before I knew it, yep, it hit the floor. I did not move. The door opened and here came the tech saying, "Don't move". I replied, "I haven't, and I won't."

Moving would have caused us to have to start all over. She picked up the mesh and went to the sink to wash it off. Normally, the mesh is in a warmer prior to placement. She rinsed it and came to put it back on. Needless to say, it was cold, and it took my breath away. She apologized and I told her it was okay; it didn't make my nipples hard. She paused, looked at me, saw the twinkle in my eye, and burst out laughing. After all, no nipples to make hard!

Radiation ended and I cannot even begin to tell you how great it felt to ring the bell in the radiation center. The techs in the back could hear my bell ringing! I was presented with a picture of my bell ringing and a bag of goodies to celebrate. Another milestone reached and I was ready for the next step.

Oral chemo began two weeks after radiation. I would be taking Xeloda for the next six months. Xeloda has primarily been used in the treatment of colon cancer but has been found to be useful in treating breast cancer after IV chemo, surgery, and radiation. The purpose was to wipe out any remaining cancer cells that might remain in my body.

I had to go to chemo education again and learn all about my new medication. The side effects would not be as drastic as IV chemo but there would be side effects such as neuropathy, nausea, hand and foot syndrome, mouth sores, diarrhea, and constipation to name a few.

I learned quickly how to prevent the mouth sores. I took my pills (that look like horse pills) after I had filled my mouth with water. This prevented the pills from touching the lining of my mouth. Some women experience darkening of their nails during Xeloda. Others experience hand and foot syndrome which can lead to problems with walking and doing everyday tasks. I had some redness in my hands which at times made them feel like they were on fire, but none of the excess peeling that happens to some.

Originally, my doctor wanted to place me on 3,000 mg of Xeloda a day. However, my blood counts were still so low that he reduced it to 2,000 mg a day. Two pills in the morning and two at night. I always took my meds about thirty minutes after eating. Every month I had to go in for blood work to check my counts. At times through this journey, I have felt like a human pin cushion.

Xeloda is taken for fourteen days and then seven days off. The main effect of Xeloda was on my digestive system (diarrhea, nausea, loss of appetite, constipation, changes in taste).

There were days I had to make myself eat but I never experienced nausea like I did while receiving Taxol and Carboplatin. My oncologist was sweet enough to give me two weeks off at Thanksgiving so I could enjoy the holiday.

Thanksgiving and Christmas 2019 were extra special. Even though I was still in active treatment, I was so close to the finish line. The year before my Christmas present was my diagnosis and I was not sure how I would respond to treatment. I was grateful to have another year.

In April of 2020, one month after the pandemic started, I finished Xeloda. I went to see my oncologist and had blood work again. This time, I took my extra Xeloda with me. I was finished and it felt great. My oncologist office takes any extra meds and uses them for women who cannot afford their medication. Not only was I happy to be finished, but I hoped in some small way I was helping someone else in their journey.

Loneliness, Depression, Anxiety and Fear

Many of my friends may find this shocking, but I was shy as a child. I would hide behind my mother whenever someone spoke to me. I lost myself in literature and between first and second grade I read over 120 books during the summer, chapter books, and I still have the certificates to prove it! If I ever felt lonely, I would lose myself in a book. However, throughout my cancer journey, books no longer were a solace to me.

I was never completely alone during my journey, but I felt alone. Even though I spoke with other patients there were always differences in treatments, emotions, and physical side effects. This is a journey that is different for every person. When my aunt passed from cancer it was simply referred to as breast cancer. Now, with further research, breast cancer can be ductal carcinoma in situ, invasive ductal carcinoma, lobular carcinoma, estrogen positive, progesterone positive, HER2 positive, triple positive, inflammatory breast cancer, triple negative, Paget's disease of the breast, papillary carcinoma, or metastatic breast cancer.

There were times at school among a group of middle school students, at church, with friends, I felt totally alone. I wanted to be the best teacher I could for my students. It was my last year in the profession and I wanted to give my students the best. I was not sure how to navigate the role of being upbeat and dealing with the loneliness I was feeling, not just some of the time, but all time.

For me, there is a fine line. How much do I share and how much do people really want to hear? You know the feeling when you are talking to someone and you see them zone out? They may be looking at you, but you can see they really are not into the conversation and wishing they were somewhere else. When people asked how I was doing, my pat answer became "I'm fine." I did not want them to know the feelings, that at times, scared me.

The World Health Organization reports that more than 264 million people of all ages suffer from depression and more women suffer from depression than men. Breast cancer treatments can contribute to depression. The American Cancer Society reports that one in four people with cancer suffer with depression. A cancer patient can appear to be fine on the outside but inside depression is real. Often if they focus on others, they can pretend to be okay. But it is easy to slip down the rabbit hole and then difficult to fight your way back to the surface. Cancer forces you to face changes that you are not prepared for, and let us be honest, never wanted, and life has become painful.

With my cancer diagnosis I found myself feeling so depressed that I did not want to get out of bed. I no longer enjoyed reading. At times, I could not sleep and then other times all I wanted to do was sleep. I felt helpless in my situation and would have difficulty focusing on tasks. My blog became a place that I could share my feelings and talk about the hard times. Many of my friends commented and told me they appreciated my candor. However, at times I felt that I might be sharing too much.

Writing became important, whether in my blog, or in my journal. I also spoke with my doctor and together we developed a plan. Talking to my friends was a tremendous help and they encouraged me to be open with my feelings and call them at any time of the day and night. My support group played a vital role in my overcoming depression.

Anxiety is considered a normal emotion. However, when levels of anxiety rise, it can become a medical disorder. With a cancer diagnosis, anxiety can become a way of life. Not only does one become anxious about their future, but every test, every scan creates more anxiety. Even though I am through with my treatments, I still suffer from what I call "scan-xiety".

I have CT scans every six months to check on the right lung nodule. My oncologist believes it to be scar tissue from bronchitis or from surgery. Recently, I had a scan at a different location and they recommended a scan in three months, instead of the usual six.

Of course, my scan-xiety went off the charts. It was not until my oncologist explained that they had no baseline data to compare it to, that I felt any less anxious but let me be honest, until the actual results are posted I will not rest easy.

Every ache and pain can cause the anxiety level to rise. Thankfully, I have a doctor who immediately orders an ultrasound or other test to make sure the cancer is not reoccurring and to alleviate my fears. Triple Negative Breast Cancer commonly returns in the liver, brain or lungs and I had an intramammary lymph node that could not be removed, so all these areas are checked on a regular basis.

Will the anxiety ever go away? I doubt it. It is a part of being a cancer patient.

Along with the anxiety comes fear. The *Neuropsychiatric Disease and Treatment* journal (2019) suggests that 31% to 52% of cancer patients fear that cancer will return. I refuse to let fear rule my life, and I do not hide under the covers in a constant state of fear. I will be the first to admit that with every scan and every twinge the fear comes with the anxiety.

Let me be completely honest (although I have been through all this book, but let me underscore this particularly), I am a cancer patient and I realize that my chances of dying from cancer are greater than someone who has never been diagnosed. It may ultimately claim my life, with either a reoccurrence or a new diagnosis of a different cancer.

My fear is real but not crippling. Most days I can put it far from my mind, while other days it hits me smack in the face. First, I think one needs to realize it is natural to be afraid. It is what we do with the fear that makes the difference. If it becomes excessive, it becomes crippling. There are things I do when I feel the fear "creeping up" and perhaps some of these suggestions will help others.

I have noticed that I have "fear triggers". When I hear of others being diagnosed or even of those passing with cancer, my fear becomes more prominent. That is when I turn to my support group and talk it out or I write in my journal. Acknowledging the feelings helps me to "get it out" of my system and I feel calmer.

I try to do something constructive. Either I take a walk, read a book, or immerse myself in a project that I have being putting off and trying to find the time to complete. I do not have time then to sit around and focus on the fear that can become overwhelming. I also try to be proactive. If I have a medical issue that I think needs to be checked, I do not hesitate to have it checked out. I stay in touch with my medical team and as I have mentioned before I have a great oncologist who listens and will not hesitate to send me for a scan or a test. He has even told me not to worry, while I know he worries until the result comes back. He has told me that at times he has been accused of being OCD about things, to which I tell him I am paying him to be OCD in my place!

I focus on enjoying life and trying to spend time being mindful of the blessings I have and how grateful I am for my life. I am constantly looking for ways to help others because I find that focusing on what others need takes my mind away from my struggles. It would be easy to fall into a pity party, but life is too short. I would rather spend my remaining days being a help to someone rather than a hindrance.

Booker T. Washington stated: "If you want to lift yourself up, lift up someone else". That is my purpose now, speaking to other women who may find themselves on this journey. Lifting other cancer patients by simply saying: "I understand. I have been there. I hear you."

Survivor's Guilt and Anger

According to the CDC, breast cancer is the second leading cause of death in women. Black women die at a higher rate than white women. **Breastcancer.org** reports: *1 in every 8 women will develop invasive cancer over the course of her lifetime. In 2021, it is estimated that about 30% of newly diagnosed cancers in women will be breast cancer. About 2,650 new cases of invasive breast cancer are expected to be diagnosed in men in 2021. A man's risk is about 1 in 833.*

The American Cancer Society states that the estimates for breast cancer in 2021 will be: *281,550 new cases of invasive breast cancer along with 49,290 cases of ductal carcinoma, and 43,600 women in the U.S. will die from breast cancer. As of January 2021 more, than 3.8 million Women will have a history of breast cancer. Breast cancer is the second leading cause of death Among women and there is a 1 in 39 chance that a woman will die from breast cancer. In women under 45, breast cancer is more common in Black women than white women. Black women are more likely to die of breast cancer. About 85% of breast cancers occur in women who have no family history of breast cancer.*

I was not sure I would include this chapter in the book, but with these statistics and my recent emotions, I felt it was necessary. For months, I have not been able to pinpoint exactly what I was feeling. I could not put it into words. It was different from all the other emotions that I felt and finally the other day while walking, it hit me. I have survivor's guilt and I am angry.

Recently an event occurred in my life that made these emotions bubble to the surface. They have been there all along under the surface and have now risen to the top.

I had a friend who had been diagnosed with leukemia and recently learned that he had colon cancer. The colon cancer could not be dealt with until his counts came up from the chemo for his leukemia. His counts had come up and they were looking at surgery when he found nodules while showering. Previously when he had found the nodules, they were leukemia that had risen to the skin. His chances of survival from the colon cancer was 30% and now, with the rise of more nodules, it would mean postponing surgery yet again. My friend decided to take matters into his own hands. I believe he did not want to put his wife through a prolonged sickness, and he was in pain. Our theatre community is still reeling from our loss.

I feel guilty. I have felt guilty for some time. There was a young female undergoing treatment at the same time I was in treatment. Her tumors did not respond to treatment. There are women losing their lives every day to TNBC and what breaks my heart daily are the children that have cancer and do not survive. I feel guilty that my cancer responded and others have no response. I look at the stats I mentioned, and I am blown away by how many have survived but I am broken-hearted by how many have not.

I have been told that my faith played a huge part in my recovery. While I believe it did, It does not answer the question of why I lost both parents to this disease. My dad was a minister, and my mom was one of the strongest Christians I have ever known. An acquaintance recently lost her battle to breast cancer and left behind a husband and two children (one whom is six years old). I have no children, yet I survived. Do not get me wrong. I am thankful for my survival, and I thank God every day for a new day, but the guilt is real. It is real for cancer survivors just as it is real for our military who experience similar feelings.

I am also angry. Angry that we have not been able to find a cause or a cure. Yes, we can point to some things that put you at higher risk but in many cases oncologists have no clue as to why some develop certain cancers, and some do not. Cancer is now considered a genetic disease (National Cancer Institute) and it is known that if a parent has cancer, the risk to the children is higher.

I am angry when I see young children who receive a cancer diagnosis. It was hard enough as an adult to tolerate chemotherapy, surgery, and radiation. I cannot imagine having a child that must go through this horrible treatment, and I cannot imagine having to bury a child. As a teacher, I have lost students to this beast, and it breaks my heart to see someone with Such a bright future have their life cut short.

I am angry that some cancers are being ignored and do not have the research that is needed, such as pancreatic cancer. I am angry that some cancers have become more dollar oriented and everyone jumps on the bandwagon to make a profit off this disease.

I am angry that some people treat others as a pariah when they are diagnosed, as if they are afraid that if they encounter the patient that somehow it will magically transfer. I am angry that it cheats people out of their future, their dreams, their ambitions. It leaves one feeling tired and like you must make excuses for why you just do not seem up to par. I am angry that it robs us of friends, parents, children, spouses, relatives and never seems to stop.

Yes, I feel guilty, and yes, I am angry. However, I use that guilt and anger to try to educate and share with people what someone goes through during cancer treatment. I have had several women call me to talk to me about their journey they are just starting. I am brutally honest with them. That is what I wanted, and I refuse to sugar coat the truth. I have even been known to raise my shirt and show my scars because that is what cancer is, scars.

It is not a pretty color, it is not an unaffected body, it is not attractive. It leaves you with scars, feelings of guilt, and feelings of anger. It leaves you forever a cancer patient with a message that you can share with others.

What I Have Learned

The following are things that I have learned during my cancer journey. Some of these you may know. I did not, and my purpose here is to give you some insight about things you may experience and how I handled it.

Be an advocate for yourself. I wanted the best treatment, so I sought out the best team. During the weeks as treatment progressed, I would think of questions I wanted to ask. I simply opened my phone and, in my notes, wrote down all the questions that came to mind during the week because I knew by the time, I reached my appointment I would not remember.

All my appointments ended with my question-and-answer session. Since I have a hearing disability, I asked my doctors if they were comfortable with me recording our conversations to go back and listen to the information at home. Everyone agreed. I downloaded a recording app on my phone. Having these recordings was extremely helpful in the beginning of my treatment due to all the appointments and overload of information I was receiving. If you do not understand, ask questions. If you feel you need a second opinion, get one. This is about your health, your body, and your journey.

Treatment. Find the best place for your treatment. Choose the place that specializes in your cancer. Make sure your doctor is up to speed on the newest treatments and current trends in your type of cancer. Breast cancer has more than one type of cancer and many kinds of treatment. Treatment also depends on how aggressive the cancer is and the stage of cancer. I was fortunate that my cancer institute was a member of M.D. Anderson in Texas. They are number one in fighting cancer. I wanted the treatment that would give me the best outcome. Choose the place that is doing research in your cancer and is up to date on the latest treatment and trials.

Choose what is best for you. I chose a bilateral mastectomy. Several years prior, I had been diagnosed with atypical hyperplasia in my left breast, and under my doctor's advice had taken Tamoxifen for five years. Imagine my surprise when the cancer showed up in my right breast! I made the decision to remain flat and not have reconstruction. There were some who questioned my decision. It was MY decision. I did not want to have more surgery. I did not want to deal with possible infections from expanders. I did not want to deal with implants. I made the best decision for me. I researched; I asked a lot of questions of those who had tummy tucks, reconstruction, or expanders, and I made my decision. You must choose what is best for you and your body.

Google is NOT your friend. I knew this before I had cancer, and I was told by my oncologist and my oncology nurse navigator NOT to Google things. What did I do? I used Google and looked up all sorts of things. BIG MISTAKE! You can find all sorts of information about cancer and some of it is quite frightening. There are myths about sugar, drinking milk, using all-natural remedies, and so much more. The best information you will receive is through the American Cancer Society and your doctor. Your doctor and nurses will tell you not to Google things, but I know you want to know more, and you will resort to Google regardless of what anyone says. Talk to your doctor about what you find. I did and it led to great conversations, and I was able to understand more about cancer and the misinformation that is on the internet.

Google was useful for the latest information about ongoing research in the world of Triple Negative Breast Cancer. I would always take notes and discuss them with my oncologist. Fortunately, I had an oncologist who was keeping up with the current research and could share even more about possible treatments and new treatments.

Listen to your doctor. You would think this would go without saying, but then you would be wrong. I cannot tell you how many times I went for my infusions or doctor's visits and had the nurses and doctors thank me for following their advice. They told me to use the numbing cream on my port and I did. Many people do not, then complain when the needle stick hurts. They gave me advice, and they are the professionals. My team had treated numerous cancer patients. I was new to the game, and I figured they knew what they were talking about, so I followed their advice.

Prepare for people to be uncomfortable. I saw this happen with my dad. People who had been close friends quietly faded away into the background. It happened with me. Cancer

makes people uncomfortable, and they have no idea what to say. It can hurt because at this point you need people in your life. I had to quickly understand that I looked different and now I was faced with a possibly terminal disease and people just do not know what to say or do. Maybe they have the irrational fear that cancer is contagious (you would be surprised how many people believe that myth), or perhaps they are preparing themselves for losing you to the disease. Cancer makes people uncomfortable. Often, they cannot relate to what is happening and want to be understanding. Many conversations people had with me would begin with, "I had a friend/relative with breast cancer; she died." As awful as that sounds, they are trying to understand and sympathize. Unfortunately for me, I have no recollection of the rest of the conversation because I was hearing "she died "over and over in my mind. Nothing else registered.

Attitude determines altitude. Understand that your attitude throughout this whole process is, I believe, the thing you can control in an uncontrollable situation. Were there days I was down? Hello, did you read *Loneliness, Depression, Anxiety and Fear?* There will be days that you feel lonely, you are depressed, and you fear that your cancer will return. However, I have had more positive days than negative. I struggled at times, but I pulled up my big girl panties and went on. I could not dwell on the negative emotions because I believed that staying in the negative would impact my treatment.

Start a blog or a journal. I decided early in my journey to write a blog using Caring Bridge. I did not want to post all my information and feelings on social media like Facebook. If friends wanted to follow my journey they could read my blog. I shared all my feelings, fears, and frustrations, and it was cathartic for me to write. Many of my friends would post comments, hearts, and tell me I was in their continued prayers. Their words were comforting to me, assuring me that I was not alone, and they were rooting for me. I know they will never understand how much it meant to me to have that support system. They laughed with me and cried with me through my blog. Caring Bridge offers free blogs for people undergoing things such as cancer or long-term illnesses. If you are not comfortable with blogging, start a journal. You will be amazed at how your thoughts and feelings change throughout your journey and when it is over you can look back and be amazed at how far you have traveled.

Supplements. You are going to be inundated with people recommending supplements for you to use during your cancer treatment. The problem with supplements is some of them interfere with chemotherapy. For example, a multi-vitamin can work against chemotherapy. If I was putting these chemicals in my system to kill cancer cells, I certainly did not want to take something that was going to negate the effect of the chemo. I did not take anything my oncologist did not recommend and he only recommended B6 to counteract the neuropathy that I experienced in my hands. I was amazed at how many people became cancer experts with no medical degree. I know they meant well but always run supplements by your oncologist.

Chemo brain. Chemo brain or chemo fog happens and involves thinking and memory problems. At times, I struggle to find the words I want to use. I forget names of people I have known for years. You will come across people who will tell you that is a part of getting older, and it can be, but this is brought on by the treatment for cancer. It is a real side effect of chemotherapy, and sometimes radiation therapy. For me, chemo brain was one of the most frustrating side effects. There are times I feel stupid, and I must remind myself that it is an effect of the chemo. It may never pass for me and as time goes on it may improve but do not let anyone tell you it is not a side effect. For most people. Chemo brain can continue from nine months to a year after completing treatment. I am surrounded by a great group of people who often will either wait patiently for me to figure out the word or try to help me with the word.

Fatigue. I have always been an active person. In high school, I played tennis, and in college I played basketball and tennis. I used to run but as I began aging, I began walking. I loved doing 5K's and even did the Peachtree Road Race, a 10K. I had heard about the fatigue aspect of cancer treatment but did.not realize the extent of exhaustion. There were days I struggled to walk to the mailbox or get dressed. More sleep does not help. Resting does not help. It is a side effect of the treatment and one for which there is no fix. Just know that it is temporary. It does get better. Sometimes it will be hard to have any energy but understand that this will pass and there will be a day that you feel stronger. I am back to walking and that has helped me cope more than anything.

You are different. I am no longer the person I was before cancer. I have been changed physically, mentally, emotionally, and spiritually. I cannot go back to the person I was before cancer. My body bears the scars of the battle. I look at things with a different perspective. Your mindset becomes different. I appreciate the small things now more than ever: hugs, laughter, good jokes, time with friends, being able to sit and watch the birds at my feeders. I had a good appreciation of nature but now have a greater perspective on nature. You find you do not sweat the small stuff because you have been through the tough stuff and are still standing.

People will tell you how great you look. Many will think that because you are through treatment that all is well. It's hard to understand that just because treatment is over it does not mean that everything is the same. It's not, you are different. You have faced a beast and that beast will always be in the back of your mind. Control it; do not let it control you.

Support. Find a support group. Most of my friends would NOT agree with this, but I tend to be shy. I grew up painfully shy and with my father being a minister, we moved a lot. It was hard for me to move and make new friends. Even today, I must force myself to introduce myself to people and overcome my initial shyness. Face to face support groups are not my thing.

I joined several private groups on Facebook: Flat and Fabulous, Triple Negative Breast Cancer Survivors, Triple Negative Breast Cancer Foundation, Breast Cancer Survivors and Warriors, and others. These groups are closed and usually ask you to share your diagnosis prior to being admitted. They are safe groups where you can post pictures, ask questions, and share concerns.

I had (and still do) a group of close friends, known as my 5K Tribe, who supported me though my journey. We originally met through WW (formerly Weight Watchers) and when they found out about my cancer, they were there for me. I am a retired teacher now, but during my chemo I was teaching, and the administrators and fellow teachers helped me in any and every way. I had an on-call sub, Denyel Davis. If I got to school and started feeling the effects of chemo and just could not make it, she was a phone call away. Dr. Sarah Klein (my editor), Dr. Mitch Bailey, and Diana Harper went above and beyond and checked on me to make sure I did not over do things. My church was hugely supportive of me. I had calls, texts and pastors who sat with me during chemo and visits during my hospital stays. When I finished my last treatment, my church did a drive by parade in my neighborhood (due to COVID-19) with signs and cheered from their cars. They provided lunch for me that day and chocolate!

Ask for help. This is a hard one especially for me because I like to believe I can do things on my own. During cancer treatment that is not the case. There were times I needed help with simple tasks, times I needed help understanding treatment, times I just needed to talk. As I have mentioned before, not everyone will be there, but someone will. If it was a medical issue, I always asked my medical team. One of the greatest comforts to me was my Oncology Nurse Navigator, Stephanie Martin-Rohling. She met with me when I was diagnosed and scheduled all my first appointments. She was with me when I met with my surgeon, dropped in on infusion days and even gave me her cell phone number to call with any questions I might need to ask.

When I felt my nausea meds were not working, I called my oncologist, and they prescribed a different med. When my hands felt like they were burning (hand and foot syndrome) I asked my oncologist what I could do. If I had an unusual symptom or concern, I asked for help. Your team is there to help you get through this journey. Ask for their help. Your friends are there; ask for their help. I had several friends that cooked for me during chemo, and I had several others that offered. If I had wanted a full course meal, I had those willing to provide if I asked. Do not be afraid to ask. You will be amazed how people will reach out to help if you just ask.

Cry if you want. I am not much of a crier, but I have shed more tears during my cancer journey than ever before in my life. There are going to be days you feel lost, you feel confused, tired, lonely and all those emotions bubble to the surface and you cannot hold them any longer. Allow yourself tears for relief during this struggle. I have found that tears can be cathartic, not a sign of weakness. In your journey, allow yourself to express the emotions that well up from deep inside. No, they will not change the journey, but they will relieve the tension and frustration.

Pick a playlist. I am serious. Pick some music that speaks to you to play during your chemo, on the way to your appointments, when you are feeling down. My chemo playlist has become my go to when I am walking or driving to another appointment. Some are songs about cancer (Melissa Etheridge *I Run for Life)*, others are just upbeat songs that make me smile (Bob Marley *Three Little Birds)* or songs with a personal message that I hear (Michael Jackson *Beat It).* Any music that speaks to you, use it, embrace it, sing along, who cares if you cannot carry a tune. I promise you it will make you feel better. I have included my playlist at the end of this book. These are songs that spoke to me during my journey. Some may speak to you.

Surround yourself with positivity. For me, this took a variety of different forms. I had a t-shirt that referenced my superpower as fighting cancer and, on the back, I used the hashtag #hyderstrong. My hashtag was important to me and spoke of how I wanted to feel through my journey. I embraced it and used it on shirts, posts, and a dear student even used her Cricut machine to print it for my car. Several of my friends purchased shirts (I received no money from the sale) and took pictures of themselves in the shirt. I printed out every picture and put it in a journal.

My students designed a shirt (Hyder's Fighters) and I took pictures of them and posted in my journal. I had quotes around my home office and classroom that helped me focus on the positive. Were there times I wanted to give up? Yes, but by surrounding myself with these things, I continued the fight. Focusing on positive things helped combat the feelings of fear and anxiety. A simple sign I purchased from a friend that says "Grateful" reminds me every day that I should be grateful. It is the small things. Never again will I take my health for granted.

Things to Not Say to Cancer Patients

I don't know who will read this book, but I wanted to include some things that have been said to me and why it might be best not to say them to a cancer patient. No one intentionally tries to hurt your feelings, but I think people are extremely uncomfortable when it comes to cancer. They want to say something but are at a loss of what to say. My advice: do not say the following. Yes, these were said at one time or another during my journey, and I follow up with what I thought.

I had a friend who had breast cancer, she died, but. All I hear is that someone died from breast cancer. I do not remember what was said after because in my brain the "she died" is still echoing.

You are so lucky; you don't have to wash your hair. No, I am not. And, I have lost my hair, everywhere. It is a very traumatic experience and I wanted to say, "If you think it's so great, shave yours." Of course, I did not say it, but I did think it.

If you need anything, call me. Honestly, I am not going to call. I do not want to be a bother to anyone, so I just never called anyone. The best thing to do, drop by with a meal, ask when the next chemo is and drop by, send a card that says I am thinking of you,
or call.

You just need to rest. Wait? What? That is all I feel like I am doing, and I am still tired. Cancer fatigue does not get better with extra sleep. They can control the nausea but there is nothing that can help with the fatigue. Understand that just walking from the bed to the sofa is a chore. It is unlike anything I have ever experienced.

You are so strong. No, I am not. I am just trying to survive. Think about it, what choice do I have but to fight and that does not make me strong. How did having breast cancer make me strong? It is one day at a time survival.

Have you tried (fill in the blank). No, and I am not going to try anything that my oncologist does not recommend. I followed his plan. Vitamins and other remedies were not a part of my treatment. In fact, I was told specifically not to take vitamins because they interfere and work against the chemotherapy.

Hang in there and fight. What do you think I am doing? I am allowing toxins to buildup in my system to do just that.

You aren't doing reconstruction? Okay, so I had a pat answer for this one and I would respond with: *Why do I want to put something back on my body that was trying to kill me?*

Wow! You are getting new breasts? No, I'm not! Nothing, let me say again, nothing replaces the real thing. Cancer patients call fake breasts "foobs". Foobs are either silicone or saline filled. They usually have no nipples unless they are tattooed, or nipple-sparing surgery is accomplished. They are cold to the touch and they have no sensation. Prosthetics are the same. This is not a free "boob" job; it is a matter of survival.

Don't worry, you'll be fine. First, you do not know this, and second this makes all the fear and anxiety worse. You begin to think maybe you don't have enough faith because you are worried. The funny thing I see in this statement is that most people that say it worry themselves. It downplays everything a cancer patient is feeling.

Everything will be okay. This is usually said right after don't worry. This is easy to say for someone not facing cancer, not feeling ill all day and most days, and not facing the mounting bills that come with cancer. Not every cancer patient's journey is smooth and carefree.

You don't look sick. I tried hard not to "look sick." The hardest part of my hair loss was when I lost my eyebrows and eyelashes because then I thought I looked sick. Just because a cancer patient might not look sick doesn't mean they are okay. Side effects from chemo, fatigue and even weight gain are daily battles.

You must be happy you are cured. Once a cancer patient, always a cancer patient. There is always a blood test or another scan. There is always the fear of cancer returning. Cancer patients are not cured; they are in remission and they pray it will not return. Life Is never going to be the same for cancer survivors.

You don't really need your breasts anymore. Really? When did breasts start coming with an expiration date? Women struggle with self-image after a single mastectomy, imagine a bilateral mastectomy. Now your body looks different, and scars take the place of breasts. You begin noticing your stomach looking bigger. It's hard to lift your arms and the area itches and because of damaged nerve endings, scratching doesn't help. I have learned that gently patting the area that is itching eventually eliminates the itching.

And then the last thing that was said was *nothing*. Not a word. This was the one that probably hurt the most. People who I thought were good friends said nothing, and the silence was deafening.

What can you do...

I mentioned things not to say, but there are things you can say. *I love you, you are in my thoughts and prayers, I hate cancer and I'm coming over with chocolate, What day works for a visit, I'm coming by to (mow, clean, do laundry), I'm heading to the grocery store, what do you need, I'm so sorry or I really don't know what to say.*

Asking a friend if they want to talk about it. Some may and some may not. If you ask be prepared to listen. Just listen without judgment, without platitudes, simply listen. Lending an ear and allowing a cancer patient to purge their feelings can be powerful.

Just visit. Sit and hold their hand. Let them cry on your shoulder. Just be there.

For a cancer patient, being there speaks more than actual words.

Final Thoughts

I have some final thoughts, and not sure where else to put them, so I am adding an additional chapter about my journey. These are the things that have bothered me throughout my fifteen-month journey and I continue to mull over in my mind. One thing I learned in writing my blog is that people appreciate honesty. The thoughts in this chapter may come across as bitter or angry but I am neither. My journey has shown me that I had a strength that I did not know I possessed, and I believe as a cancer patient I have the right to express the following.

I hate pink. I have always disliked the color on me. My sister had pink bridesmaids dresses, so yes, a picture of me in pink exists. It is a beautiful color when associated with the setting sun or flowers. My question is why we have taken a color and made it the symbol of something that is awful? I think I understand the intent but pink? Men get breast cancer not just women.

Breast cancer is not pretty. Breast cancer is the scars of the mastectomy or lumpectomy. Breast cancer is the dry heaving or vomiting from the chemotherapy. It is the toxic treatment that has numerous side effects. It is losing friends and families and in some cases spouses because they cannot deal with the disease. It is sleepless nights because of steroids and anger because of those medicines. It is losing your hair from all parts of your body and having people look at you with sympathy when you go out. It is suffering from PTSD when seeing, smelling, or tasting something that reminds you of chemo. It is the fear that happens every time you get a twinge or a pain and you think the cancer is coming back. It is a monster seeking to destroy your life.

Some say that breast cancer gets too much attention when there are many other cancers. Breast cancer is the most common cancer among women. One in every eight women will be diagnosed with breast cancer. What upsets me is breast cancer has become commercialized. Businesses have jumped on the breast cancer wagon and sell everything pink during Breast Cancer Awareness Month.

How much of that money is funding breast cancer research? How much of that money is pure profit? Would you buy pink if you realized only 5% - 10% of the cost is going to research. People with great intentions of supporting breast cancer research are falling into marketing traps and schemes. Do not misunderstand me. Any money donated to research is great, but there are organizations that donate 100% of their proceeds to research without the cute gimmicks.

I am tired of seeing the catch phrases: *"Save the Tatas" or "Save the Boobies"*. What about save the woman or save the women? Saving the lives of the women is more important than saving the part of their anatomy that is trying to kill them. That is why I chose to remain flat. When my surgeon offered me reconstruction, I simply looked him in the eye and asked: "Why would I want to have something to remind me of what was trying to kill me?" He smiled and said: "I understand".

I do not consider myself a warrior or survivor. I am a cancer patient. I will always be a cancer patient. There will always be another test or another scan. There will always be doctor's appointments and another specialist to see. It is never ending. First, every three months I will see my oncologist, radiologist, or surgeon and then it will progress to every six months. If the cancer does not return; I will graduate to yearly exams. Life is forever changed.

I will always have scan-xiety. This is a cancer patient word that every cancer patient understands. Every time the doctor wants you to have another scan, the fear comes back, and for me, it's a sleepless night. The "what if's" always rear their ugly head at this time, and I am on pins and needles until the results are released. I have scans every six months. With my type of breast cancer there isn't a blood test to check markers. If I have a pain that lasts for some time, it will be another scan to see if the cancer has returned. For breast cancer, the cancers can return in the lungs, brain, liver, or bones.

Chemo was hard on my teeth. My dentist provided me with a prescription fluoride toothpaste to hopefully prevent tooth decay. Unfortunately, at my last visit, he found decay under one of my anchor teeth that holds in a bridge. At the appointment with the oral surgeon, I was told that the possibility of implants was improbable. This is because of the Prolia I am currently taking for osteoporosis. After treatment, I had a bone density and was told I have osteoporosis and osteopenia due to chemo. Prolia strengthens the bones except for the mandible. Implants will probably not take because the Prolia prevents healing in the jaw. I also found out that due to this I should be using a prescription mouthwash prior to any dental treatment and it is advised that I take antibiotics before and after treatment. Even having my teeth cleaned can cause osteonecrosis.

Even though I am out of treatment, cancer and its treatments continue to give. Some days are easier, and some days are harder. It is my new normal. I have a choice and you have a choice. You can either embrace it or give in. I refuse to give in. Even if the cancer were to come back tomorrow I believe I still win. I will not let it control me. I will not give into the fear. I will make my life meaningful and continue to live life to its fullest. I encourage you to do the same. Stay the course.

I am a Cancer Patient

I am a cancer patient
I understand fear…
>Fear that comes with a diagnosis
>Fear that chemo is not working
>Fear of losing family and friends
>Fear of rejection
>Fear of never being the same
>Fear of looking different
>Fear of the future
>Fear of not having a future.

I am a cancer patient
I understand loneliness…
>Loneliness from cancer
>Loneliness and losing one's self
>Loneliness through treatment
>Loneliness in a crowded room
>Loneliness when losing friends
>Loneliness through isolation
>Loneliness and depression
>Loneliness of saying goodbye.

I am a cancer patient
I understand changes…
>Changes in mind
>Changes in body image
>Changes in soul
>Changes in mental fortitude
>Changes in daily living
>Changes in the future
>Changes in thoughts
>Changes in attitude.

I am a cancer patient
I understand being resilient…
 Resilient through treatment
 Resilient through surgery
 Resilient through radiation
 Resilient through fear
 Resilient through loneliness
 Resilient through changes
 Resilient through cancer
 Resilient and still here.

Tammy D. Hyder

Resources and Song Lists

When I started my cancer journey, I had no idea what I would need and where I might find help. In this chapter, I have included two things that I hope will help you. First, a list of resource sites that I found items I needed for surgery and other things. Many of these resources were started by women who experienced breast cancer.

Second, I have included two song lists. One is my chemo playlist that I listened to during chemo and still listen to when I walk. Most of the songs have nothing to do with a cancer journey, but they spoke volumes to me. The second song list is Christian music that also helped during my journey. I hope you find these resources and songs helpful.

Resources:
https://www.knittedknockers.org/
A group that provides knit prosthetics to women with breast cancer. You can either knit
Knockers or request a pair. They are more comfortable than the traditional prosthetics.

https://www.etsy.com/shop/ConquerRecovery?ref=simple-shop-header-name&listing_id=267660187
ConquerRecovery is a group, on Etsy, that specializes in mastectomy shirts that help manage
drains after surgery. Made from comfortable fabric, they have pockets to hold the drains. The
shirts have snaps for easy on and off and there are four drain pockets.

https://www.etsy.com/listing/635902369/mastectomy-pillow-for-breast-cancer-post
Pinkpepperco is another company on Etsy that specializes in products for breast cancer patients. They have mastectomy shirts and mastectomy pillows. I ordered my shirts and pillow from PinkPepper. When I was finished with both, I donated them to my cancer center for other women to use.

HOPE Kit - National Breast Cancer Foundation
The National Breast Cancer Foundation provides these free of charge to women with Breast cancer. They are filled with fuzzy socks, tumbler, tea, a Hope Journal, Lip balm, and many other items.

Free Cancer Hats, Scarves & Jewelry Gifts | Chemocessories
Started by Iris who wanted to continue to look good during chemo, so she wore turbans, scarves, and jewelry that matched her outfits. Today sets of scarves, turbans, and jewelry are donated to women going through treatment to boost confidence.

awesomebreastforms.org | Home of Awesome Breast Forms!
Another group that provides knitted prosthetics for women. They also have Awesome
Swimforms.

Cleaning for a Reason – Free house cleaning for cancer patients
A non-profit organization that provides three free home cleaning services to cancer patients.

Sisters Network Inc. : A National African American Breast Cancer Survivorship Organization
Committed to increasing local and national attention to the impact that breast cancer has

on the African American community. Lots of resources including ongoing trials, support groups, and financials.

Home - Little Pink Houses of Hope
Free weeklong retreats for patients and families to celebrate life in a new way. Little Pink
Houses of Hope was started by breast cancer survivor Jeanine Patten-Coble.

https://wwwdivaforaday.org
A day escape for women dealing with cancer to enjoy a complete day of pampering at a
Salon/Spa. A day to relax and restore.

Home | Triple Negative Breast Cancer Foundation (tnbcfoundation.org)
TNBC foundation partners with CancerCare to offer free and professional support services
to patients and families.

<u>Chemo Playlist</u>

Stronger (What Doesn't Kill You)
    Kelly Clarkson

Fight Song
    Rachel Platten
I Got This
    Jennifer Hudson

Three Little Birds
    Bob Marley

Roar
    Katy Perry

Girl on Fire
    Alicia Keys

I Run for Life
    Melissa Etheridge

Fight Like a Girl
    Anita Cochran

Survivor
    Destiny's Child

Invincible
    Kelly Clarkson

Pink
    Dolly Parton, Monica,
    Jordin Sparks, Rita Wilson,
    and Sara Evans

Beat It
 Michael Jackson

Eye of the Tiger
 Survivor

Don't Stop
 Fleetwood Mac

I Will Survive
 Gloria Gaynor

Happy
 Pharrell Williams

Don't Stop Believin'
 Journey

Gonna Fly Now (Theme from Rocky)
 Bill Conti

Another One Bites the Dust
 Queen

Warrior
 Demi Lovato

I am Not My Hair
 Indie.Arie

Rise
 Katy Perry

I Won't Back Down
 Tom Perry

Break My Stride
> Matthew Wilder

Scar
> Carly Simon

Make It Go Away (Radiation Song)
> Sheryl Crow

One Day You Will
> Lady A

I'm Gonna Love You Through It
> Martina McBride

Christian Music

You Say
> Lauren Daigle

God's Not Done with You
> Tauren Wells

I Will Fear No More
> The Afters

Good Good Father
> Chris Tomlin

Never Gonna Steal My Joy
> Mandisa

Shoulders
> For King and Country

Even When it Hurts
Hillsong United

Waking Miracles
Matthew West

Light of the World
Lauren Daigle

Turn My Eyes
Bonray

Whom Shall I Fear
Chris Tomlin

Oh, My Soul
Casting Crowns

Look Up Child
Lauren Diagle

It Is Well with My Soul
Matt Redman

Praise You in This Storm
Casting Crowns

Healer
Hillsong

It's Not Over Yet
For King and Country

Faith
Jordan Feliz

Warrior
Hannah Kerr

You Never Let Go
Matt Redman

God Who Listens
Chris Tomlin

Unstoppable God
Elevation Worship

Blessed Be Your Name
Matt Redman

I Will Rise
Chris Tomlin

Everyone Hurts
Kirk Franklin

Trust in You
Lauren Daigle

Out of My Hands
Jeremy Camp

Surrounded (Fight My Battles)
Michael W. Smith

Cancer Blog

The following is my blog that I kept on Caringbridge.org during my cancer journey. It is in an unedited form, but I wanted to include it. Writing this book was cathartic and including the blog gives one insight to how I felt during the journey. Many of my friends made such positive comments on my blog. I have not included the comments, just my writing. I hope this helps you understand a cancer journey that you or a loved one may be going through.

The Start
December 18, 2018

I have decided that this is a great way to keep everyone up to date that is interested in my journey. I will be keeping a daily journal and will add things from it to this site at different times. I never expected to hear the words I have cancer, but now that I have, I am trying to wrap my mind around all of this. Friday, I met with my oncologist and he is a cutie and I believe a great doctor. I have heard nothing but positive about Dr. Patel. I meet the other doctors this coming Thursday and Friday. Today, I got called to Piedmont Fayette to complete my genetic testing. My doctors wanted this done before I go for my surgical consult on December 31st. Am I scared...well, duh. Of course, when you hear the word "cancer", it raises an alarm. In all my 59 years I have never spent the night in a hospital, at least not as a patient. So that thought is petrifying... Losing my hair, well I am a tad bit vain, but I'll just have to find some cute ball caps to wear to keep my head warm. I'm not on this journey alone...and for that I am thankful.

It Is What It Is!

December 20, 2018

A lot of people have told me they are amazed by my attitude about this whole cancer thing...to which my response is simple. It is what it is. I can't change it. If I could, of course I would but I can't. What I am going to do is NOT let cancer define me. It is NOT who I am it is something that is happening in my life at this moment in time for whatever reason. Attitude is half the battle. Am I scared, right now no, but ask me that when they get ready to wheel me in for surgery and that answer will probably change. I just left the radiation oncology doctor. My blood pressure was 120/78 and they were surprised since we were going to be talking about the radiation procedure, etc. But it is what it is and I can't change it. My attitude toward this is a big part of the picture and I intend to face this head on. Does this mean I won't sit down something and have a pity party? I probably will but I promise not to dwell there. I have great team of doctors that are going to work to get me ready by July 4th for the 50th Peachtree Road Race! Enough about that stuff...so let me share what I learned today. I have various lumps and bumps. This I knew already, but let me share exactly how unique and special I am. First, I have not one type of breast cancer, but TWO! Yes, you heard it here first, I am just that special! I like to do things big, so I go and have two types. I am estrogen positive in one area and the other area, negative. Hmmm..go figure. Second, due to the variety of lumps and bumps, I will have to have a mastectomy. We don't know yet if I will have chemo followed by radiation, just radiation or just chemo. That won't be decided probably until the pathology comes back after surgery. Third, it is NOT in my lymph nodes, which we probably already knew, but that was good to hear it again. Fourth, Tammy has some decisions to make. Not easy ones and once they are made, they cannot be changed. But you know something...It is what it is...

Treatment Plan

December 26, 2018

I have known now for several days what my treatment will be but didn't want to post before Christmas. I hope everyone has had a wonderful Christmas. I enjoyed a quiet day on the lake and took some time to reflect and to try to come to terms with all that is going through my head. I met with my surgeon last Friday and now I have an idea of what is going to happen over the next few days. Tomorrow I am scheduled to have a port installed. This will make it easier to have chemo since it is so hard on the veins. Dr. Powell will be placing this and my plan is to start chemo on January 4th. I will have chemo prior to surgery. This is for several reasons. One it will help reduce the tumor size and it is looking more and more like I have triple negative breast cancer, which is classified as aggressive. It is not in my lymph nodes so that is a huge positive. I don't know yet how many chemo treatments, but I do know that surgery will be after the chemo. I love my surgeon, Dr. Frank Powell, and have heard nothing but positive about him. I do believe I have the best team of doctors for my care and that makes me feel comfortable with everything. He and I spoke about surgery and I have decided that my best course of action is a bilateral mastectomy. I made the decision and after I told him, he agreed that this is the best course of action. I feel confident in my decision. The only thing that is freaking me out a little is the prospect of losing my hair. I know, hair will grow back. I think the thing that freaks me out the most...the sympathetic looks I will get when that happens. That I don't want. I don't want to be treated any differently. Cancer does NOT define me. This is a mere bump in the road. Let's treat it as such.

Finalized Treatment Plan - Plans blown...

December 28, 2018

My port was placed yesterday. I am one step closer to beginning chemo. Everything went well with no complications except being extremely hungry! I couldn't have anything after midnight and the port didn't get placed until around 4. But it was a great sleep!

I met with Dr. Patel today and we discussed my treatment plan and put some things in place. The first thing I asked him was about my prognosis. I have triple negative breast cancer which is the most aggressive form of breast cancer. There are several things in my favor: my genetics test all came back negative; the lymph nodes are not involved, and it is stage 2. Next Friday I am having a PET scan to look at the nodes once more. Then I will have an electrocardiogram to check out the heart. This is being done because some of the chemo's I will have can make the heartbeat differently.

Now, about chemo. I will be involved in chemo treatment for 5 months. A total of 16 chemo treatments, prior to surgery. He gave me two choices of chemo and I chose the one that is the most aggressive and has only been used for about 14 months but the rates of remission before surgery are high. I'm going to be as aggressive toward this cancer as it is toward me.

I will lose my hair probably after the second treatment. He gave me the option of a cooling cap to use during the first few treatments that might help save my hair, but by the second round of chemo, it won't work, and my hair will fall out anyway. I can't justify that expense for something that will not work the whole time and isn't a full proof guarantee. This means that surgery will probably not be until I retire. If things go as planned with the chemo then we are looking at June/July for surgery.

The thought of losing my hair is freaking me out a bit, so tomorrow when I have my appointment, I'm going to have my hair cut shorter than it has ever been.

I can work during chemo and will work as many days as I can because my students deserve a teacher who is teaching and not someone who is just filling in for me.

However, my teaching will be a little different. I will probably wear a mask most days to prevent catching anything from my students. All of these things are necessary, but I must admit, my heart is broken as to the things I will NOT get to do.

I can't go with the band to Universal during winter break. Craig Owens has asked me to chaperone since it is my last year teaching....now, I can't go. I was planning on going to Guatemala this summer to help build houses. Now I won't be able to participate in this trip. I had hoped to walk the 50th Peachtree Road Race and now it looks as though I will be recovering from surgery. I was scheduled to direct a show that I put up last year to the script committee and now I won't be able to see that dream realized.

Plans blown...but I have to focus on my health...I want to be a survivor, not a statistic.

Shorter hair...Hair today...gone tomorrow...
December 29, 2018

When I met with Dr. Patel yesterday, he told me that I will lose my hair. I took matters into my own hands today and had the fabulous Candi cut it shorter and shave the sides. I like it and everyone who has seen it likes it. Then I headed to Renew in Fayetteville. My other fabulous friend, Jill Lucas, suggested going by. The lady there was extremely helpful, and I walked out with a couple of options to wear on my head when the hair goes. Dr. Patel gave me the option of a cooling cap during the first part of treatment, but I cannot justify that expense when he told me that during the second phase of chemo, nothing will stop the hair loss. I know that I'm going to be facing some big bills in the near future and could not in any way justify one that won't work.

I'm not looking forward to chemo. It is going to be a long road. But on the other hand, I want to get this started so I can get to the other side. So many people are angry on my behalf, knowing that at the end of this school year I am retiring, and they don't think this is fair. I've got friends that want to call but don't know what to say. Just remember...hair today...gone tomorrow...but I'm still the same person...with or without hair...I want to laugh and have fun...not dwell on what is going on...I want to remain positive, and I need those positive vibes...

If you are scared for me, worried for me, or angry for me...thanks. But let's focus on fighting this together...I need your support. I may need your shoulder to cry on...I may need you to pick me up when I'm lost...I may need to borrow your hair!

I would...
December 30, 2018

It's 3:25 AM and I'm awake having a bit of a pity party. I don't know what triggered it but I have an overwhelming sense of sadness. I don't know if anyone is reading what I am writing but I'm finding it cathartic to write, so I will continue. It's easy when you don't have a diagnosis to say the words "I would..." I'm guilty myself of saying what I would do if certain things happened to me. It's different when it does happen. When you are faced with the reality of things that are coming, it's different.

I've had to make some hard choices the past few days. Choices that will change the way I look, choices that will be hard for my body to handle, choices that will make looking in a

mirror painful. It's easy to say what one would do in a situation, it's hard to actually have to make the choices.
I don't know why I have cancer. It's not a genetic mutation and currently, I'm the healthiest I've ever been. I'm not sure how strong I am for this journey and this isn't a
journey I would wish on anyone. There are so many things I had hoped to accomplish with the end of my teaching career, but this was not one of them.
I saw my father struggle through chemo, and I remember boldly saying I would not put myself through it. Now, I have no other choice. I've seen women have a mastectomy and boldly said, "take them, they don't define who I am" and now I have no other choice. I've seen cancer patients lose their hair and boldly said, "it's hair, it will grow back" and now I'm going to lose mine.
I've made a lot of "I would" statements and now they are reality. Reality hurts....cancer sucks.

Getting Real
December 31, 2018

I met with Dr. Powell today and he is pleased with the port installation. Everything is healing great. The bruise has already turned a lovely yellow. Dr. Patel's office called while I was in the waiting room and requested me to drop by (just a few doors down) and pick up my schedule. I thought I would take this time to let you know what's happening.
On Thursday of this week, I will go for a PET scan. This will determine the areas of cancer. It will also be a chance to verify the lymph nodes although an ultrasound and
MRI usually are best for looking at the nodes. Basically, I will have radioactive sugar...and then they will scan to look for where the sugar is being sucked up. Pray that it is only in the breast tissue.

Next Tuesday morning, the 8th, I will visit the infusion center where I will meet with the nurses and they will go over all the information I need to know prior to beginning chemo. Thursday, January 10th is C-Day. First chemo infusion and they have me on the schedule for 4 1/2 hours. It's getting real...I'm getting nervous...like don't want to eat nervous...like chewing nails nervous. I want this to get started, but I am nervous. Did I mention I was nervous? Oh, and in case you forgot...I'm nervous. I've also purchased my anti-flu masks to wear at school. This should be interesting both for me and my students. This will be a new experience...wearing hats to school and a mask...It's my new normal and I really want to work as much as possible through this; I want my students to enjoy my final year with them.
So everything is getting real...real scary...I know you are supporting me...I feel your words as I read your comments. I know God has got this...but you know....it's getting real....

It's 1:40 AM...Are you sleeping? I'm not! The New Normal...
January 3, 2019

I find myself waking at odd hours and not being able to go back to sleep for some time. This is when writing becomes so important to me. It is the time when my feelings are raw and writing helps. PET scan is today at 4:15 and I would appreciate prayers and thoughts during this time. No cancer other than breast cancer is what I want to hear. Not that they think it has spread anywhere, but this is just to make sure of that fact. Sigh...another 6 hours of fasting...I don't know what Dr. Patel is thinking...he wants me to gain weight and then has me fasting again...LOL! I have so many people who have volunteered to go with me to chemo that I am having to turn people away! Which is a great problem to have but I don't think the infusion center would look to kindly at me if I had 30 people all sitting with me. Of course, it would be a great time, full of laughter and talking but I don't think it would be appreciated. For those who have volunteered to go, thank you so much. I'm sure that over the next five months, you will get your turn! So, keep those cell phones handy! Nerves are still raw. This weekend I am going to enjoy some time with some special friends as we head to Ponce City Market for the best noodles anywhere! I am going to savor every mouthful! And I am going to enjoy every moment of being surrounded by some of the best friends anyone could have in this life. Friends who also plan to take off work to be there on the day of my surgery...whenever that is. I have some of the greatest friends! I'm still scared and anxious. Most days I am forcing myself to eat and today of course since I can't eat until after the PET scan...I will probably want to eat the entire 6 hours leading up to the scan! Isn't if funny how that works. Kind of like you have a car problem, and it goes away the minute you drive it to the mechanic. Changes are coming and I think I'm ready. Yet, I'm not. No, that doesn't make sense, I know. It's just the new normal.

Devastated...
January 7, 2019

There is no other word to describe how I feel now. Dr. Patel called me with my PET results. There is lymph node involvement in a lymph node behind my chest wall. The good news is they believe it is contained to that node and there is no sign of cancer anywhere else...lungs, bones or any other organs.

This isn't what I wanted. This lymph node cannot be removed because of its location. This means radiation after surgery...this reduces my survival rate. Triple negative often comes back somewhere else within 5 years. I can't explain how I feel. I don't understand it...I had my checkups, my mammograms. I want to scream, punch something...I feel so defeated and I haven't even started chemo. The only word that fits is devastated. Please don't tell me to get over it...I need some time to process, to cry, to mourn. I will fit, but today I just want to have a good cry...I'll be better tomorrow, but today I just have to come to grip with something else...I'm devastated...

The Rainbow
January 8, 2019

I went for my chemo education this morning and as I left, I saw a beautiful rainbow. I'm claiming that rainbow as a promise, that everything will be okay. I now know my treatment plan, so for those of you following, here goes. I will be starting chemo Thursday. Yep, day after tomorrow.
My treatment is going to be once a week for 12 weeks. Infusions will be about 2 ½ hours per infusion, except for the first one which will be 4 ½ hours. This is aggressive

because my cancer is aggressive, and Dr. Patel is going to everything he can to knock this out.

After 12 weeks, part B will be every other week. This will be the chemo lovingly referred to as "Red Devil". This is the chemo that is the hardest on my other body systems and has the harshest side effects. It can affect my heart, my bone marrow, etc. I will have 4 treatments of this chemo cocktail.

I feel better than yesterday. Dr. Powell's office (my surgeon) called to reassure me that he plans to get rid of all the cancer cells, including the lymph node that is showing activity. I love my team of doctors. They have responded to all my requests and answer all my questions.

I believe I am in good hands. Both my doctors and the Great Physician. I covet your prayers, your love, and your positive thoughts. I believe that 99% of my battle is mental. I know I will have days I want to scream, shout and cry. I have a wonderful cousin who has promised to replace any drywall that I might abuse in my fit of rage! (LOL)

I have a wonderful support team. I cannot do this alone and you all are a vital part of my journey and my recovery. Thank you for listening, thank you for caring, thank you for your prayers, your love, your positive attitudes, your willingness to listen. I am going to kick cancer's ass. I am claiming that rainbow!

And so it begins...
January 10, 2019

Yesterday I was totally fed up waiting for my infusion to be certified. I decided to take matters into my own hands and go ahead and come, which means I had to pay out of pocket for my medications. Hopefully, insurance will come around before next Thursday. I am almost through my first bag of chemo as I write this entry. This morning was nerve-wracking.
I got up at my normal breakfast and promptly begin to feel nauseous. Felt nauseous all the way to Dr. Patel's office. Simply nerves...when I get nervous, that's what happens.
I've been giving all sorts of medications through my IV before the actual chemo even started. Jeani and Patti are keeping me company. All is good in chemo land...1 down, 15 to go. It has begun.

The Normal: Laughing and Liberating!
January 18, 2019

I haven't updated in a week because I really haven't felt good. The first infusion hit me about 1:00 AM on Sunday morning. Saturday, I had spent mostly sleeping. Sunday and Monday were spent taking nausea meds and trying to hydrate and sleeping. Monday, I called the office and they prescribed me a new nausea med which seemed to help. I was able to work Tuesday and Wednesday and begin eating again, so that helped with my energy level. Yesterday it was my second infusion. My friend, Jason Bowen sat with me during the infusion and asked all kinds of questions which was cool to help educate someone else about the process. And he made me laugh and laugh hard. We had a blast! I'm sure there were some there who wondered what I was laughing about with these toxic chemicals being pumped into my body, but you must laugh people!

Knowing that Jason was coming yesterday, I took out the trimmers on Wednesday night and proceeded to trim the hair. I am now sporting a Mohawk! Jason has a Mohawk and I knew he would be stoked to see my hair...he was. I've now officially been called a "Badass Cancer Warrior"! The ladies in Dr. Patel's office loved it and so did Stephanie my Oncology Nurse Navigator. With this second treatment of Taxol my hair will start coming out.

I thought it would be a traumatic event, cutting my hair. But you know what it was really liberating. It is like hey this is the new normal. I'm going to enjoy it and I've had so many laughs. I was even laughing the whole time I was cutting! No, it was not hysterical laughter. It was later though when the tears came. Now, I look sick. This can't be happening.

I'm feeling pretty good right now. All the meds they gave me yesterday to make the chemo easier to tolerate are still in my system. Saturday and Sunday are the worst days. My nurse practitioner told me when to start my nausea meds and how to keep them in my system over the weekend, so we have a new plan this weekend and we will see how it goes. If this doesn't work, then we will try other meds on the market. My team is working hard to keep me comfortable, and I believe in them.

I will be getting the carboplatin every 4 weeks in addition to the Taxol. The latest research, only about a year old, has shown that when carboplatin is added to the chemo the treatment is more effective. They attack the cancer cells in different ways.

With standard chemotherapy, there is a 76.1% disease-free after three years and with adding carboplatin there is an 85.5% overall disease-free after three years. Right now it is only three years because this is a new study that was only started three years ago.

Use of the carboplatin in TNBC patients only started about 14 months ago. When I get the Carboplatin with the Taxol, I'm getting double dosed so that is harder on my system.
Keeping my fingers crossed that this weekend will be a little easier.
Still laughing. Still feeling liberated.
I have my down moments. Mostly, I feel guilty. Guilty that I can't give my students the best "me" my last semester of school. Guilty that I can't be the normal energetic teacher that I try to be. Guilty that I can't pull my weight with duties and such at school.
I'm working through it. Wow! I think I've written a chapter in a book! Thanks for reading! And thank you for following me on my journey! Your notes, your cards, your gifts, your positive thoughts in your texts and comments mean so much and always arrive at the right time for a pick me up! God's timing and your timing is perfect!

I'm Not Contagious!
January 21, 2019

When I met with my radiation oncologist, they had me watch a video explaining how they do radiation treatment. I still don't know if I will have to have radiation, but they wanted me to see it so I would know what to expect. At least 3 times during the video, the guy said, "You won't be radioactive" and "You won't glow in the dark." Okay, being a science teacher, I laughed...because...DUH...really? I even asked do people really believe that? The answer was a resounding yes. Unbelievable.
I have noticed some things though since my diagnosis. I really think people think I'm contagious. I mean I get the not wanting to hug...because frankly, I don't want or need

your germs. Nothing personal. That's why I wear a mask in public. I'm not contagious to you but you are to me! I've seen people completely drop off the radar. Haven't heard from them in any form or fashion. Not even to see how life is during this journey. Interesting...

I know when Dad fought his battle against cancer, some of his closest friends went AWOL. I'm not sure why. But cancer isn't contagious. Maybe it's because people don't know what to say. Maybe they are uncomfortable because you look different. I'm not sure but it is interesting studying human behavior, which is currently what I'm doing. Take last Thursday. My dear friend Jason came to sit with me and asked me all kinds of questions about my treatment. I LOVED the conversation. It gave me a chance to share what I've learned and to educate someone about what's happening. (On a side note, the doctor wasn't really happy that I had lost 9 pounds my first week of chemo...but that's another story).

I'm still the same...yet I'm not. I still love to read, love to laugh, have the weird laugh that everyone can pick out, love to sing, love to think, love life. I'm different because I have a disease that has to be treated harshly and the treatment wipes out my immune system causes my hair to drop and makes me ill at times. Same, just different. You don't have to know what to say and if it makes you uncomfortable, don't talk about the cancer. It's going to go away and I'm fighting this beast with every ounce of strength I have in my body. It can be beaten, and it will be beaten. But the next time you see someone, even me, that might have cancer, don't forget we aren't contagious and we love saying hello. No need to be scared...BOO!

GREAT NEWS! Attitude determines Altitude!
January 24, 2019

Okay, so today was to be a chemo day. Arrived at the office and my dear friend, Ana met me. When I met with Dr. Patel, we went over my recent tests. Genetic tests show NO mutations for cancer on any gene.... awesome!
Echocardiogram shows I do have a heart and it is a great functioning heart...Great news. Had gained 2 pounds...Great news.
BUT THE BIG NEWS...Dr. Patel wanted to check the tumor...Remember my tumor was 3.3 centimeters when we started. The tumor is now 1 centimeter! The chemo is working! The idea behind the Carboplatin is to reduce the tumor size and have me cancer free BEFORE surgery! This is awesome!
I did not do a treatment today because the blood work showed that my white blood cell count has dropped and more importantly the cells that help fight off infection (other than white blood cells) are low. With a treatment today that would put me at great risk of infection. Tomorrow and Monday after work I go to the office for a booster shot for my cells.
Even though I didn't get a refill...as I lovingly call it, I did say hi to all my infusion nurses in the back. Dr. Patel told me I have to be his happiest cancer patient of the week and so did they. But you know, it's all about attitude. I've always told my students that your attitude determines your altitude. Yeah, I have bad days but don't we all? I want to beat this beast and beat it badly. One of my all-time favs, Pat Summitt said: "You can't always control what happens, you CAN control how you handle it." This is so true. We can't control some of the situations we find ourselves in. I can't control having cancer. Would I if I could...Oh yeah. Did I choose this journey? Oh, no...but you know what? I'm not going to curl up in a fetal position (unless it's really bad chemo reaction...lol) and let cancer win. My attitude is I'm

kicking this stuff to the curb. I'm in this fight to win it. AND we have got to do more to find out why 1 out of 8 women will be diagnosed. CANCER is a scary word. But I chose words like ATTITUDE, COURAGE, HOPE, FAITH, LOVE. I choose the positive. Maybe I'm meant to have this journey to show my students how to overcome adversity. Maybe I'm meant to have this journey to help someone else. Whatever the reason, I'm going to fly high and control how I handle it! Let's soar together and beat this beast!

Alone, but not alone. Ramblings....
February 3, 2019

Everyone's cancer journey is different. What works for some, may not work for others. You have to figure it out as you go along. I decided that this past Thursday, I would go to my chemo alone, for several reasons. I just wanted to have a little quiet time to reflect on all that is happening. I am alone in this journey, yet I'm not alone. It's my body that the chemo is attacking and fighting with the cancer cells. Unless you've been through chemo, you don't know how hard some days can be. Yet, even if you have been through chemo, it's different for each individual. So, you are alone. But with so many friends surrounding you, you aren't alone.
I don't ever feel alone in my journey. I've had so many calls, texts and cards from my friends letting me know they are thinking about me. So may offers of food, rides, etc.
have come my way that I might not need to cook for the next year...and we all know how I just love to cook (NOT)!
Being alone at chemo Thursday gave me a chance to just relax and go with the flow. I people watched and that was interesting. People react to things in so many ways.

I don't consider myself a strong person. I suppose it is all in perspective. I hope that I am teaching my students that even though life is tough...you suck it up buttercup and go on about your merry way. There are days I wonder what caused my cancer, why I have cancer and will I beat it? Those, from everything I have read, are normal thoughts.
Chemo is tough. This coming Thursday will be some of the roughest chemo with the Carboplatin, but nothing like Red Devil (named for its color and stress on the body) that is coming in April. I just want to get through this part of the journey so I can move on to the next phase.
I try to stay off the internet looking for information about TNBC...so much is out there, and it can be scary...don't drink milk...don't eat sugar...you can drink milk...you can eat sugar...do this, do that. It can be overwhelming at times. Me, I'm listening to my doctor and taking his advice. He is the expert, not me and certainly not the internet!
As you can see my mind is all over the place today. My thoughts come all at a mad rush...so I am just typing to share my ramblings with you. I know I am alone through this, but I know I'm not alone with you my friends supporting me. You DO NOT KNOW how much it means to have you call, text, etc. I'm savoring every moment of your support and love. Your encouragement is what keeps me going on the days when it's hard to get out of bed. Thank you from the bottom of my heart. If you have sent a text, called, or mailed me a card know that I do not take our friendship lightly. I treasure you and your friendship.

Ramblings of a Steroid Induced No Sleepy Time!
February 7, 2019

Okay, so what do you do when you have received steroids in your IV and have slept for three hours (don't be jealous that I went to bed at 8:30) and now you can't sleep because you are wide awake? You write on your Caring Bridge site and have really long sentences that drive your friends who are ELA teachers crazy!

Seriously though, this is when I feel the most alone in my journey. I have thoughts racing through my head and you are all asleep! NOT FAIR! Of course, I could call you all...then I would really be alone! I would lose all my friends for waking them up....No, I know I could call...just teasing.

So today was an interesting day. Lots of stuff happening. Currently, my hair is beginning to come out. Scalp started itching like crazy and for my hairdresser friends, yes, I am using lotion on my head! It's kind of weird rubbing it in when you still have a little hair, buzz cut that is, but still weird. It helps though. It really isn't bothering me that it is coming out. Although I will say I think I would have freaked if I hadn't taken the initiative and buzz cut it before it started dropping. In my mind, this is a sign that the chemo is working on my body...so no hair...no care (I have a hat coming that says that)! Dr. Patel and I had a great talk today. My cancer has been re-staged since it was found in two lymph nodes. It is now considered a Stage 3A. But that is okay. Those bad boys are being bombarded with chemo and will come out during surgery. Also, I will be doing targeted radiation after surgery to nuke anything that is left. All of this just increases my survival rate.

My nurses are loving my fun surgical masks. Today I wore one of my shark masks. Yes, I have shark mask (4 different ones), a sea turtle snout mask, a mask with a zipper (everyone says it doesn't work to keep my lips zipper), a mask with a smiley face, a mask with a mustache, a mask with panda nose (I crave bamboo).

Then a friend of mine made an applique of the Rolling Stone lips for my disposable masks. The masks, except for the sea turtle mask, are all silk screened. They make my nurses laugh, my students smile and everyone at the stores I visit take a second look. If I can't have fun with this...what good is it????

Speaking of my students...they came up with an idea for silicone bracelets with #Hyderstrong on them to sell at school. The money is going to Relay for Life in my honor. How cool is that. I've ordered some and will have them in the next week if anyone is interested.

Back to Dr. Patel...I love my doctor. He is on the cutting edge of all new things happening with TNBC. We had a great talk today about new treatments when they are being used and why he chose my treatment. He also does NOT want me to experience any nausea. I currently have 4 antinausea meds and he told me today to call if I experience anything and we will move forward with several other possibilities to use.

The only thing they cannot treat is the fatigue. I told him and Dr. Amin that if they can help me not get sick, I can handle fatigue.

The treatment I had today consisted of the Taxol and the Carboplatin. Last time I had the Carboplatin I was nauseated from Friday until Tuesday and dropped 9 pounds in one week. The Carboplatin is aggressive but that is also what is shrinking the 3.3 tumor in my body. So, I am using it. I want this cancer in remission prior to surgery! This week my numbers were good, so we did the treatment. I did drop 3 pounds and I can't figure it out because I pigged out this week and ate everything that tasted good.

Go figure.

After next week's treatment (keeping my fingers crossed that I can have a treatment) I will be driving to Columbus, GA to speak at this year's Georgia Science Teachers Conference. My workshop application was chosen way back before I even knew I had cancer and I am NOT about to miss a chance to encourage science teachers in the area of Science and Literacy! Other news, I have to admit I was kind of bummed about all the things I'm missing...I can't go with the band and chorus to Universal in two weeks, I can't go to Guatemala this summer, I can't do the 50th Peachtree Road Race, and I was scheduled to direct the summer production at my community theatre. The other stuff I can do next summer, but not directing a show, I had given to the script committee for consideration, the entire guild had voted, and I had been given the go ahead to direct and not I can't really hurt. My theatre guild Executive Committee knew how much it meant to me and I like to think they know that I pull together great shows, decided to move my production to 2020. HOW COOL IS THAT? Jonny May, the VP of Production, brought it before the board, they approved and announced it at Tuesday night's guild...everyone applauded. I don't think I could every convey to them how much gratitude I felt. SO STOKED to be able to do the comedy, The Crazy Ladies in the House on the Corner. Oh my, I've written a chapter in a book! Still not sleepy, but think I will give it another chance. If you have read this far...you are a true friend. And let me share one more bit of news!

I am 25% finished with treatments. I have had 4 out of 16! I can see light at the end of the tunnel. At the end of this second round, I will have another mammogram and ultrasound to check out how well the cancer is being treated. Then, after Red Devil (google it...it is kind of scary), then I will have a PET scan before surgery to see how everything looks.

1/4 of the way through! I can do this! I am WOMAN, I AM STRONG!

Cried All the Way Home.
February 11, 2019

So today I went to work. Your prayers really helped this weekend. No nausea. My nausea meds seemed to work and that's awesome because I hate that feeling as most of you do. But one other side effect of the chemo...I don't want anything to eat when I have the carboplatin. I mean nothing. Nothing tastes good and nothing looks good. So this morning I got up and tried to go to work. I did have a piece of toast and drank an Ensure with 30 grams of protein, but that wasn't enough. I had left plans for the day; in case I couldn't be there. I didn't feel the best, but I pulled up my big girl pants and went to work. I lasted until 10:30 AM. I just could not do it. I found myself teaching from my chair, which I NEVER do. I called the front office and my sub was called. Thank goodness for Denyel Davis, who is on call pretty much when I need her. She came in and I went over the rest of the day with her and then I headed to the car...and cried on the way home. I cried because I have cancer, I cried because I was going home and couldn't be with my students, I cried because I couldn't eat, I cried because I was angry with myself for not being strong enough. I cried just to cry...and if you are not a woman; you will NOT understand that! I am so tired of being tired. I am frustrated. I am miserable.... Okay, so pity party over. I'm not giving up. On these bad days when I feel like screaming how unfair this all seems, I can't quit. I am stronger than this. I can do this. And every now and then, it's okay to cry. It's okay to let go of my emotions. Perhaps I should take up boxing so I can punch things when this happens. A punching bag with the word cancer would be ideal! Someone out there, work on that for me!

Thanks for listening. Please continue your positive thoughts and prayers for me. This road is long and I'm doing the best I can but sometimes I don't feel that is good enough.

TNBC
February 16, 2019

Recently I joined a TNBC Facebook group. Most of the women I come in contact out and about with are estrogen positive. My cancer is different, and my journey is different.
A lot of women that are estrogen positive had four treatments and are doing an estrogen blocker. I am doing 16 treatments, bilateral mastectomy, and will finish with 15 rounds of radiation. I decided I wanted to hear from other women who are going through the same thing I am and boy, have I and have I had my eyes opened!
First, I'm amazed at how many women are not getting Benadryl to ward off allergic reactions and many do not get lidocaine for their ports. Wow! I have got a great team of doctors!
Second, they are at different places in their journeys. Some are just starting chemo, some are as far along as I am, others are nearing completion. The ones who are in the same place in their journey, really understand what I am going through.
Third, we are bound together by this thing called TNBC. We are celebrating each other in so many different ways. I love being a part of this support group. I can tell them how I feel and they truly understand. These women are from all over the world and I love getting to know them. My horizons are expanding!
This past week kicked my butt! Carboplatin is hard, but I only have two more of those treatments left! I opted for this and that is what I continually remind myself of when I feel overwhelmed. I want to be aggressive with this cancer because it is being aggressive with me. The Carboplatin basically is attacking my DNA in my cells. I get fatigued because the DNA is trying to fight back. So it's a constant battle in my body.

I was not able to get a treatment Thursday due to low blood counts, so Thursday and Friday I had my friendly bone marrow booster shot. The nurse suggested I eat liver...to which I replied, "Would you eat liver?" and got a resounding "NO!" Well, guess what I'm not eating liver!!!!!
Dr. Patel has come up with a new plan which I really like. Next Carboplatin treatment, I will go in on Friday, Monday, and Tuesday (after treatment) and get boosters, so I should be able to go ahead and get treatments the following Thursday. He knows that I want this part of my journey over with sooner than later.

I was able to speak at the Georgia Science Teachers Conference on Thursday, which is an organization near and dear to my heart. I also drove down on Friday after my booster and was able to sit in on some great sessions. Everyone was shocked to see me. I am NOT going to let Cancer RULE my life! Several have told me lately that I'm an inspiration, I'm amazing, I'm a role model. I'm really uncomfortable with those words. I'm just being me. I'm not going to let Cancer DEFINE me. My doctor has told me to stay as active as I can and that's what I'm doing. It's hard not doing 5K's, but I know I just can't right now. My body says nope, not happening. That's okay. I'll be out there again soon enough. I'm just doing what I believe is what I'm supposed to do. I have enough sick leave to be out the rest of the year, but I'm NOT going to let CANCER WIN! No, that is not an option. I'm in a fight for my life. I've made some hard decisions about what I'm going to do surgically, but I've heard too many nightmares about women who did not opt for a mastectomy, only to regret that decision later. I have a great team of doctors, who are with me on this journey. They have told me to call if I have questions and that they plan to get me through this. I'm not amazing, I have an amazing team. I'm not incredible, I have incredible doctors. I'm not an inspiration, I'm just being me. I have TNBC but TNBC does NOT have me!

STEROIDS...UGH! But it's soapbox time!
February 22, 2019

So, it's 2:00 AM on Friday morning and yep...steroids are helping me NOT sleep. I usually get about 4 hours of sleep on the nights I get a treatment then I'm wide awake for a few hours. Thankfully, I don't have to work tomorrow or today rather, so I can sleep in...HA! Like that is going to happen. Since I'm up I figured, I would start pushing fluids. I don't want chemo drugs sitting in my kidneys causing more problems! Got to flush the system...so there goes my night's sleep.

It's been a good week. I would have rather had a treatment last week because then I would have been halfway through the Taxol/Carbo cycle. But that is okay because next week it will happen. Even though I didn't get a treatment last week, on Valentine's Day, I wanted to treat my nurses. The office staff, the nurses for the doctors, and the infusion nurses have all been great. I took them a little special treat, flowers, and chocolate, and they were so appreciative. So many times, I think people overlook the job they do and it's a tough job. They get close to their patients and sometimes their patients don't make it. I do not know how oncology staff/nurses and hospice staff/nurses do their jobs, I couldn't. Every time I get a chance to show them how much I appreciate them, I do it.

My support group has been awesome this week. Yeah, I'm talking about you all. The texts, the emails, the cards in the mail keep me going. I got some bamboo utensils in the mail from Lori Chen, which really helps with the metallic taste. Silverware makes that worse, so bamboo utensils are perfect. Carla Rapp sent me a cool hat and a gift card for when I'm feeling like eating. I am truly humbled by my support.

There are still people I haven't heard from since my diagnosis. I understand, cancer makes people uncomfortable. It seems some days it surrounds me. The shows I watch...cancer...the news...cancer...Facebook...someone else dealing with cancer. It can be overwhelming at times. Even for me!

I remember that several years ago, someone asked me if I was scared, I would get cancer. Mom and Dad both had cancer and my pedigree chart for my family has a ton of cancer aunts, uncles, cousins. My reply was "No" I don't really think about it. I don't think we need to dwell on something that may or may not happen. My new Facebook group of TNBC ladies came up with a gene just for those of us that are BRAC negative and have no genetic link...it's the S*** Out of Luck gene. Okay, you may or may not appreciate the humor, but I laughed. You must keep a sense of humor through this stuff.

We have no clue what caused our cancer, and a lot of people fall into that category. Inherited breast cancers for BRAC1 and BRAC2 fall within 5 - 10% of all breast cancers. Think about that for a minute! However, the average woman in the U.S. has a 1 in 8 chance of developing breast cancer! We hear a lot about the genetic component with the BRAC tests but there are other genes that they believe can be responsible and other risk factors. Most people who develop breast cancer did not inherit a genetic mutation linked to breast cancer and have no family history of the disease! I've had over 40+

genes checked and nada. Testing is continuing to change and as it changes, my DNA will continue to be tested to see if there is any genetic component. I have a family history and it's possible that I had an aunt who was triple negative because her cancer took her within 6 months of her diagnosis...but no genetics showed up in my testing. I was seeing my doctor every six months for a screening. My point here is ladies get tested. If there is anything in your family, I would strongly suggest genetic screening. Women who are in the high-risk group are being encouraged to have Breast MRI's. That's how my cancer was discovered. If my doctor hadn't of ordered it and I hadn't of gone...by the time I had my mammogram scheduled for this month, it would have been bad. More lymph nodes involved and possibly cancer somewhere else in my body. I was in the high-risk group, even with genetics. My mom had ovarian cancer, my dad's sisters had breast cancer, I have dense breast tissue, never had a child (couldn't think of a name I liked, HA! HA) and had atypical hyperplasia in my left breast several years ago. The cancer showed up in the right breast!

I see part of my journey right now to educate. I guess part of that comes from being a teacher, but I'm still amazed by how many women are NOT being screened. This is serious business. I know when my friends, Vic Bedford (hope you don't mind me sharing, and if you do Vic...oh well, I apologize) and Jane Morgan (same thing Jane, sorry but not sorry) were found to have colon cancer, that spurred me into action to get screened, something I had put off. Those two ladies sharing their journey helped me to see that I didn't need to wait any longer. I know, screenings are uncomfortable...believe me I know. But so is being stuck every time you turn around, so is chemo, so is the surgery to come and the radiation that will follow. Early detection is important. It matters and determines your course of treatment. Okay, I know I'm on my soapbox here, but I want to spare you what I am going through. If I can change just one attitude and cause someone out there to get a screening that they have been putting off...then I have achieved my goal. Breast cancer is scary. TNBC is the scariest of all due to its aggressive nature. That's why I have chosen the most aggressive route I can take on this journey. Aggressive chemotherapy, bilateral mastectomy, and radiation. My journey will be long and I won't lie...I'm impatient to get this over with but it is a step by step process. It's wrecked my plans and caused me to rethink priorities. But I will get through this and come out the other side.

Thank you, those of you, who take the time to read my ramblings. Thank you to those who have called, texted and sent emails. Thank you to those who have sent me little gifts along the way. Thank you to those who bought t-shirts and bracelets. Thank you to those who have sent cards of encouragement. You have ministered to me in awesome ways and you will never know how much your thoughts keep me going! I'm staying strong because strong is the only option.

A Frustrating Week
March 3, 2019

It has been a frustrating week. It seems that I have been on edge all week which hasn't really helped. Thursday, I went to get chemo and when my blood work came back, it was too low. Dr. Patel even stated that my blood work was not my normal and had the tests repeated, but still came back low. One of the receptionists made the comment that I was the only patient upset when I DIDN'T get chemo. I expect setbacks like this but it is my irrational mind at work. I just envision the cancer growing inside on the weeks I don't have chemo. I know, that is totally irrational, but it happens, and I just can't control the thought. I want this gone...out...removed but I think I'm being taught patience. Then yesterday, I look out and the grass (or weeds) look awful, and the gutters are overflowing. I posted on Facebook about my frustration. It wasn't really a cry for help but a cry of frustration. I love mowing the lawn (I know I'm strange that way) but I love it. Right now, I can't do it. Cindy Owens saw my post and told Craig they were coming to help me out. I know they changed their Saturday afternoon plans. Today the grass looks awesome (although very wet at this time) and the gutters are doing their job with no debris! I love having friends who help out and they both helped lift my spirits tremendously.

It's hard though. I'm used to being active. I've been walking 5K's and 10K's and now a simple walk to the mailbox leaves me panting like a wild dog. I'm tired of being tired. I know in my mind it will get better and I'll once again be out there on pace, but for now it is hard and frustrating.
On top of all of that, I'm about to lose my mind with one of my classes continuously talking, not only with the sub but with me in class. I told them Thursday I'm done. That's it. I'll just start piling on the work because I don't have time to waste. I have a sense of urgency to get things done when I'm

at school. Right now, the Carboplatin is hard and I have two more treatments with it. Then after all 12 Taxol and Carbo treatments, I start AC. I don't know how I will handle that treatment. It could be easier, the same as now or worse. I may have to miss more work and I need to get the kiddos ready but I NEED their cooperation.

I'm not having a pity party, it's a frustration party. Frustrated with anything and everything. I know it will get better, I know I'll get over feeling tired eventually, I know that I'll be out walking once again, but for now it's frustrating. There is a downhill side to cancer...I'm climbing up and want to get to the top of the mountain so we can start down toward the finish.

A Work in Progress
March 17, 2019

I haven't updated lately. Lots of thoughts running through my bald head! But I think it's time, so here we go. Had a call from a friend of mine, who isn't facing cancer, but is facing a serious surgery. She wanted to know how I do it. How do I stay positive and not let negative thoughts get me down? I wasn't really sure how to answer. In honesty, I think writing for me has been cathartic. Even if I'm not putting my thoughts down in my blog, I'm continuously thinking about what I'm going to say. I write in my head before putting it on paper or out for anyone to read.

Music has been a big plus. I love to sing, and I love to listen to music. I think my chemo play list is the best ever! All the songs are awesome and positive from Kelly Clarkson to Bob Marley.

There are days I would love to stay in bed. Days I would love to feel sorry for me, but that just isn't me. I just can't do it. I get up, go to work, or go to WW, or go to church. It makes me feel better, makes me feel human on days I may not feel human. My triple negative sisters on Facebook have been a source of inspiration. We are going through something that we all understand. We all share our fears, our frustrations, our concerns. We all share the horrible stories that people just seem to want to tell us about how so and so cancer and they had died! Not stories we want to hear but we understand the word "cancer" is so uncomfortable that they are trying in some way to relate. Or even the horrible stories of how someone just knows how we got cancer. Really, our own doctors don't know the reason!

I know people mean well. People just don't know how to talk to someone with the big "C". We also mourn the women who lose the fight. I'm a work in progress, is what I told my friend. There are days I want to cry, days I want to laugh, days I want to scream and ask why me? But there are more good days than bad. More positive days than negative. I'm working with what I have, and it is all based on hope. This past Thursday, I finished chemo 7. Taxol and Carboplatin and only have 1 more Carboplatin to go through. Then I will have a couple of weeks off and start AC for four rounds. My doctor (who is awesome) has decided that after my treatments we are going to go ahead and do shots to boost my bone marrow, so we can stay the course and get this done. Some days I feel like a human pin cushion. Had a shot on Friday and will head back tomorrow for another booster and then one more on Tuesday.

I have a wonderful support system. Texts keep coming, cards keep coming, phone calls keep coming, and unexpected gifts from unexpected places. I cherish each contact. I tell people they can call, and they don't have to talk about the cancer, although if there are questions, I will be happy to answer them, after all I am an educator! Talking on the phone to someone is a great source of happiness.

This was never my plan when I thought about retirement. I had hoped to be a little healthier and to be able to enjoy it. But my retirement will start with finishing chemo, surgery, and radiation. Then who knows, it may be followed by jury duty! My doctor said I would be ready for that November 1st! Like I said, I'm a work in progress.

Now, I need to ask something from each of you who is reading this blog. One week from Tuesday, March 26th is a BIG day! I'm going for a mammogram and an ultrasound to see how the tumor has responded to chemo. I would love to know that each one of you are praying and sending positive thoughts that it will have reduced in size and is responding. I will admit, I'm a bit nervous because I really want to see progress. To know that what my body has been through with chemo and to see positive progress would be huge!

I promise I won't wait so long to update. Until then...this work in progress just keeps on going...

Infusion Center
March 21, 2019

Today was a big day. Not only were my blood counts normal, but I received my 8th treatment! Halfway to the goal!

But I must admit, it was a scary day in the infusion center. There were 8 of us in the center getting infusion today when I started. Three were newbies to the process and one lady wanted to pick my brain about Taxol and all the possible side effects. We had an awesome conversation and I showed her and her daughter how to remove the plugs from the infusion pump to make her mobile so she could go to the bathroom. Then about 11:00 I think the full moon showed up. A small petite lady came in with her husband. She wasn't there to do chemo, but to get an iron infusion. My fellow sister, who is also Triple Negative, was getting her first infusion of Red Devil. She promised to let me know how her week goes. Now back to the infusion lady. She was shaking and looked scared to death. One of the nurses tried to find a vein but decided to hand it over to the older nurse, who has more experience. So, she goes for a vein in the ladies right arm. Immediately, the woman begins to cry, then proceeds to scream. I mean full on scream! Woke my Triple Negative sister up along with everyone in the infusion center. Then she jerked and the vein blew. So, the nurse had to remove the IV needle and yep, you guessed it, she screamed again, prolonged, and loud. Almost blew out my hearing aids! Now, I have been stuck, prodded, and stuck again, but have never screamed.

Those of you who know me know that I will be the first to admit, I have to work on compassion. I wanted to say "Suck it up Buttercup" and go with the flow. You are getting iron and the rest of us in here are getting drugs that are toxic to our system. No sooner had I had that thought, everyone rushed to one of the gentlemen who started his chemo today. He was having a reaction. I have NEVER seen anyone shake so hard. The doctors rushed in, they stopped his IV, begin pushing Steroids and Benadryl to try to stop the reaction. That's the first time I've seen that happen and it scared me. Okay, and I will admit, I wanted to go to the little petite woman and say, "wanna trade". That was it, I absolutely had no patience with her at that point and I wasn't even a nurse! I don't see how they do it.

All of this made me realize, we never know what may happen. The reaction scared me so much that I just wanted to cry when I got in the car. I'm hoping he is okay. I don't know what happens if he can't get his chemo. I assume they will try something else. I feel bad too for the little screamer, because she may realize that there were patients in there much more serious than she and I hope she does.

I'm still a work in progress and compassion is one area I have to keep working on. I'm sorry the lady hates needles so much, but she has got to keep the screaming under control. I'm praying for the man who had such an adverse reaction and his wife who was scared to death. I'm thankful for the nurses and the doctors who rushed to his aid and started doing everything they could to help him. I'm thankful for life and I hope I can continue to grow and learn more through this journey. Thank you for being a part of it.

Cancer is tough...But God and I are tougher!
March 26, 2019

I am so excited. Did I mention I was excited? I'm so excited...oh I guess I need to update you so you can be excited. Went today for my mammogram and ultrasound and I'm so excited!!!

Okay, enough already. Mammogram looked much better than last time, but it was the ultrasound that cinched it. The tumor that originally measured 3.3 centimeters now measures 2.1 centimeters!!!! The two smaller tumors close to that tumor have DISAPPEARED! Completely gone!!!! The tech couldn't even find them! I was so excited I was ready for chemo right then and there! IT'S WORKING! The chemo is working!

I cannot even begin to tell you how much that means. All the nausea, fatigue, weight loss is worth it. Bring on the next 8 treatments! God's got this and I'm just along for the ride! In all seriousness it is hard to put into words how I feel. Chemo is tough and I wouldn't wish it on my worst enemy on my worst day. Today was like seeing a light at the end of the tunnel. I've got 8 treatments left and I'm hoping that this is completely in remission by the time of my surgery! That would just be icing on the cake.

Thank you, my followers, for all your kind words, your positive thoughts and most of all your prayers. They are working! Please continue to keep me in your thoughts. I'm thinking I may be doing a happy dance Thursday going into my infusion! Wouldn't that be a treat for the nurses!
By the way, one last thought! I'M SO EXCITED! AND I JUST CAN"T HIDE IT!

Chemo Day Thoughts
March 28, 2019

Today was chemo number 9! 3 more of Taxol and next week is the last Carboplatin! Then a week or two off and I will finish with AC - 4 treatments every other week. Another reaction in the infusion center today. This time is was a 25 year old female with breast cancer. Her reaction was a crushing feeling on her chest, so it wasn't nearly as scary as last week, but scary, nonetheless.

Ladies, I cannot tell you how serious it is to schedule your mammograms. The young lady was 25 and fighting breast cancer. It respects no one, no age, no race, no one. You need to get checked. You need to do your exams every month. One of eight will have this disease. From day 1 when you are diagnosed, you are considered a survivor, because you are surviving the treatment and believe me, that is exceptionally hard.

Now on to other thoughts...fatigue is a curse of chemo. But this fatigue is different. It's not something you can rest from and feel better just resting. I could go to bed at 5 in the afternoon and sleep 12 hours and still feel fatigued. It is so hard to explain.

Yesterday, we took my cousin to Ponce City Market. We walked up a flight of stairs and I was completely exhausted. Those of you who know me, now that I was in the best shape ever, when I received this diagnosis. Now walking upstairs wears me out. That's fatigue.

I appreciate all the concern and you all telling me I need to rest, but Dr. Patel told me to be as active as I feel I can be. That's why I'm working. It keeps my mind occupied, doesn't allow me to feel sorry for myself, and believe it or not, it takes my mind off fatigue.

Now a question for you: Why does everyone want to rub a pregnant belly OR SEE MY BALD HEAD? That's right, it's completely bald now. I shaved it because it was growing and starting to hurt again. It's going to fall out anyway with AC, so I'm just looking at what I will look like for about 8 weeks. I'm a little sensitive about my hair and you won't see me without a cap and I have a liner for my head to cover between my skin and hat. So, you can ask, but you won't see, and I probably won't be taking pictures anytime soon. Please realize that this is something personal and I am sensitive about it.

The other thing I have learned through this process, is everyone's cancer is different. I talked to the Physician's Assistant today about the differences. My doctor has the best plan of action for me and I've had a lot of people recommend supplements, etc. I won't take anything without running it by him first. A lot of things can counteract the chemo. I can't even take vitamins at this point because anything anti-inflammatory can counteract chemo! I appreciate all the comments and suggestions but understand I'm following my doctors' orders and obviously the chemo is working, I know I will live with this the rest of my life. Even with a successful chemo regimen, surgery and radiation, there will always be that thought in the back of my mind with every pain...is that the cancer returning. I've been doing a lot of reading about how cancer changes you...forever. I can see how that happens. I'm different today than I was in November. It all goes back to my diagnosis. I'm not giving up, just being realistic. Cancer is now a part of my life. When it is gone, it will still be a part of my life. I will have scars and those scars will define me and I will carry them with me the rest of my life. I will be seeing my oncologist the rest of my life. I've worked on my playlist for chemo. I don't listen to it in the infusion center all the time, but on my way and on my way home. I think I have some good songs. If you are looking for positive songs to boost your spirit I would recommend these:

Stronger (What Doesn't Kill You) by Kelly Clarkson
Another One Bites the Dust by Queen
Fight Song by Rachel Patten
Eye of the Tiger by Survivor
Don't Stop Believin' by Journey
Don't Stop by Fleetwood Mac
I will Survive by Gloria Gaynor
Gonna Fly Now by Bill Conti
Three Little Bird by Bob Marley & the Wailers (LOVE BOB MARLEY)
Happy by Pharrell Williams
Beat It by Michael Jackson
Roar by Katy Perry
Girl on Fire by Alicia Keys
I Run for Life by Melissa Etheridge (I want to sing this song, so powerful)
I'm Gonna Love You Through It by Martina McBride
Make it Go Away (Radiation Song) by Sheryl Crow
Fight Like a Girl by Anita Cochran
Scar by Carly Simon
Survivor by Destiny's Child
Invincible by Kelly Clarkson
One Day You Will by Lady Antebellum

So that's my list. If you have any suggestions, please send them to me! I only have 1 hour and 20 minutes' worth of music!

This are my ramblings on chemo day. I hope I haven't come across as mean spirited because I don't mean to be. I'm just being honest about my feelings. By the way, the screamer was back in the infusion center today...she didn't scream though, I was glaring at her the whole time just waiting for it...Yep, I pulled out the teacher's glare...some of you have seen it...it's a serious stare, don't make me use it!

Melting Away
April 7, 2019

Was so excited to see Dr. Patel this past Thursday and hear the words...it will continue to melt away. I hope that by the time I have surgery, that the tumor will have completely
melted away. I have a little bit more of an idea of what is going to happen now. I will have two more Taxol treatments followed by the pick me up shots. Then Dr. Patel will give me a couple of weeks off before we start AC (Adriamycin/Doxorubicin), which is nicknamed red devil. This will be a little more difficult. I hope I can work as much as possible during this time since it will be close to the end of the school year.

After chemo finishes, we will wait about 3 weeks and redo the PET scan to see how things look. Then that will be followed by surgery. I'm getting closer to the finish line and can see the light at the end of the tunnel. It's been a long tunnel! Started on January 10th and it seems forever ago. I've been feeling rough this weekend and have spent a lot of time sleeping. This was my last Carboplatin treatment and it is always rough. Even though I'm coming off of spring break, I'm taking tomorrow off due to the fact that I still won't be 100%. Carbo kills my wanting anything to eat. So, I haven't eaten a tremendous amount this weekend. Mainly I've nibbled at whatever I thought tasted or sounded good. Please continue to keep me in your prayers. I'm hoping that AC won't be as bad as I've heard. I really want to try and finish the year on a high note since this is my last year.

Thank you again for all your support, your texts, your calls, your cards. I love each one of you! Here's to melting away!!!

A Change in Treatment
April 20, 2019

Here I am at LaGrange Toyota waiting for my 30,000-mile service. Cancer doesn't stop ordinary life from happening! It's been a roller coaster ride for the past two weeks and to be honest I just haven't had the energy to update my blog. Even though my blood counts are still low I have a little more energy, so I thought I would give everyone an update.

Two weeks ago, when I went for treatment, my blood counts were too low, especially my platelet count which was about 79,000. This meant I had to have a blood transfusion. A week ago I was at Piedmont Fayette and received two units of blood. I went in this week expecting my red blood cell counts and my platelet counts to be way up. Boy, was I surprised! Platelets had dropped to 34,000. Dr. Patel told me not to worry, although he was surprised and ran the blood work again. He ordered more tests on my blood and told me that he believes the last Carboplatin treatment really hit my bone marrow hard.

The good news...no more Carboplatin! Those treatments are all finished. We are also forgoing the last two Taxol treatments. He is afraid these will total deplete my platelets and do more harm than good. He also doesn't want to keep pushing my surgery and rads out. So here is the plan now. I am having bone marrow booster shots...one was Thursday, Friday and I go back Monday for my next. I am also taking a steroid that boosts platelet counts...5 pills for 4 days. All five pills are taken in the morning. Then we are moving on to AC, nicknamed Red Devil, for its color and potential side affects. I will have four treatments of this, every other week.

I will also have the Neulasta OnPro that you may have seen advertised on TV. This will keep me from going back daily for shots and it is the equivalent of 12 shots. Hopefully, I will be able to stay on track and finish by the first week in June. He is also going to reduce the amount I get the first week, so my bone marrow doesn't take another hit. Worst case scenario...my platelets don't come up...he will order a bone marrow biopsy. That scares me.

So, I need my prayer warriors and positive thinkers to help me this week. Please pray that my counts come up so we can start AC. Please pray that my body will handle AC as well as I have handled the Taxol and Carboplatin. This chemo, I must be honest, scares me a lot. Please pray that counts are up and I do NOT need a biopsy. I truly don't know how I will handle it if they find something else. Please keep me in your prayers and positive thoughts. Cancer is a scary journey and I'm thankful I have such a great support team. Your cards, texts, comments on Facebook and this blog are what helps me daily. It helps me through the tears and laughter. I have dark days just like anyone else and I am doing my best to focus on the positive. Thank you again!

Staying Strong...
April 27, 2019

It's kind of tough to stay strong with setbacks, but I am hanging in there. This past week saw my platelets double. They were 30,000 and now with the shots, steroids and your prayers and thoughts they shot up to 70,000! We are on the right track. I'm currently getting shots for three days and steroids for 4. Hopefully by Thursday, the counts will be strong enough to start AC.

I told Dr. Patel that there is this irrational fear I have...not discounting faith, medicine or prayers, but just a fear that when I don't get chemo, the cancer is growing. I love my doctor. He knew I was worried and could see that in my face. So what did he do? He told me he was pulling strings and sending me right down for an ultrasound. I got my shot and headed down.

The news was good...nothing is bigger and in fact most have seen a further reduction in size. I think I held my breath for all 64 pictures she took! I'm so thankful that God has provided me a doctor who truly listens and cares. My plan from here on out is as follows.

Keeping prayers, positive thoughts and fingers crossed, platelets will be strong enough on Thursday for AC. He is reducing my dose by 30% to make it easier on my bone marrow. This is the chemo I dread. It has a nickname, "Red Devil". It's pretty red color, but it is harsh. If it gets on my skin, it will burn me...yet, they are putting this in my veins. Please keep me in your thoughts. This one scares me. I only have 4 treatments of it, but some women have ended up in the hospital with fevers due to this treatment. I have currently switched over my allergy med to Claritin because believe it or not, this helps with bone pain from the Neulasta OnPro that I will also have. It will deliver the equivalent of 12 shots at one time to boost my bone marrow and hopefully keep the AC treatments on schedule.

I've got 20 days left with my students and I really want to be able to finish with them. They deserve it and I want to leave feeling that despite cancer, I was able to finish my career strong. It is important to me to do that. I know I have to take time for myself, but I so want this.

Please continue to think of me. I love the cards I've been getting in the mail, the texts, and the responses on FB and on this blog. You do not know how much it means to me and how when the days are dark, you pick me up. I'm singing tomorrow at church and I'm singing a special song that has been on my heart lately. If you haven't heard it, you need to listen to it. "I'll Praise You Through This Storm" by Casting Crowns is an incredibly special song. This is a storm I'm going through and at times I cry myself through it...usually when I'm home alone...because I'm really not usually a crier, but there are times I just want this done, I'm sad about what I'm losing, what I'm missing, the friends I no longer hear from, my students who deserved the best and haven't gotten my best...life in general. I don't know why I have cancer...it's not genetic and there is nothing that TNBC can be contributed to, but it's my walk, my storm, my path and I'm going to make the best of it. Thank you for being there.

Two down...two more to go!
May 18, 2019

Sorry it's been a couple of weeks, but with the end of school madness I've come home and crashed most days. Here is the latest. I had another AC treatment this past Thursday. I was scheduled to have a blood transfusion after because my hemoglobin continued to plummet. However, when Dr. Patel came in and asked me when I had the transfusion, I told him I

Was scheduled at 1 after chemo. He told me whatever I did the week before to continue because my hemoglobin came up on its own...NO BLOOD TRANSFUSION needed! I was surprised and happy! I believe it is a direct result of prayers and positive thoughts from all of you! There is no other way to explain it. Don't get me wrong, I'm not opposed to a blood transfusion at all, it's just I want my body to show it can recover from all of this and give me a greater hope.

Dr. Patel and I then had a heart to heart, and I asked him point blank not to pull any punches about my prognosis. TNBC is different than other breast cancers that have a high cure rate of 90+%. In February of last year, there was no sign on my mammogram and in August at my exam nothing was felt. It is extremely aggressive. Basically, it boils down to this...how well the AC continues to shrink the tumors if surgery is successful and they can get the lymph node that causes me the most concern near my chest wall, and radiation. If there is active cancer at the point of surgery, there is an oral chemo I can do for a year. If I can make it 5 years without a reoccurrence, then my percentage that it will come back goes down.

I have been re-staged with my cancer and now I'm a Stage 3 C. I'm okay with that and I took the news in stride after all we all never know if we are promised tomorrow or not. I'm not morbid in the least and it hasn't changed my attitude. I just plan to do everything I can to continue my fight.

So, what can you do? Well, I need some more prayer and positive thinking...First, continue to pray that my body tolerates the AC. I still have not received a full dosage yet, that is planned for May 30th (my retirement banquet). Also, with this at days 6-7, there is a possibility that when my blood counts drop, I could begin running a fever. If it gets to 100, I must go to the ER. I really don't want this tovhappen, because this could delay treatment. Pray for no fevers!

Second, I am having an ultrasound before treatment on the 30th. Pray for a further shrinkage of the tumors to show that AC is working, and that the cancer is still reducing in size.

Third, pray that the insurance company will agree to the PET scan. Dr. Patel wants to make sure the cancer has not metastasized to another part of my body and they are currently denying the scan. He has written a letter explaining why this needs to be done and if all else fails my surgeon will request the scan. Surgery is tentatively scheduled for around July 11th. This will depend on my AC treatments and if they stay on track and Dr. Powell's schedule.

I've made the decision to not do any type of reconstruction. It wasn't a hard decision but easy. I'm comfortable with it and really haven't heard but one person question my decision. But that's just it, my decision. No one else's. I'm done with something trying to kill me, why would I want to be reminded and that's how I feel. Some of you may be uncomfortable reading all these thoughts and these aren't my deepest, but one thing I have heard over and over is how honest people appreciate me being in my posts.

Cancer is real and it sucks. BIG TIME! My 60th birthday is coming up and everyone asks me what I want. The one thing I really want, no one can give me, except God in heaven and that is to be Cancer free. Wow has my perspective changed. Usually I would have a list, but I don't. Life has happened and I have been dealt a stack of cards that suck. So as the famous Pat Summit would say "Suck it up, buttercup." That's my new motto. And as she also said, "Left foot, right foot, breathe." And that's what I'm doing, there is no other option.

Brutal Honesty
May 26, 2019

Yes, It's 4 AM and guess who can't sleep. So many thoughts running through my brain and I cannot blame steroids for this wide-awake hour. When this happens, I find that writing my blog is very soothing and it helps get my mind clear.

First, I want to say that I am writing this, not to receive any comments or compliments, but to let you know how I feel. When I started this blog one of my main goals was to put what I feel down in writing so that next year when all of this is over, I can reflect on what I was thinking, etc. I also wanted to share with those of you who wanted to follow my journey in a different way. This morning's entry is titled Brutal Honesty for a reason, so be warned. Stop reading now if you don't want to really know what I'm thinking. This isn't a pity party blog or even a sappy blog, just a brutal honesty blog. And before anyone gets the wrong idea; I'm NOT FEELING SORRY FOR MYSELF. This is a journey I've been given and I am trying to make the most of it! Here goes...

I'm tired. I mean really tired. In just a few days I will have been doing chemo for 6 months. I'm tired of being tired. I just want this over. I'm tired of my food tasting funny, water tasting funny, hating the taste of hot coffee (which really bothers me), and tired of trying to find anything I want to eat. I'm tired of my mouth being sore, my tongue feeling weird, my hands feeling like they have been burned. The nurses asked me at the doctor's office on Thursday if I felt more tired than usual and I told them honestly, I don't remember normal any more...I'm always tired. I'm staying as active as I can because Dr. Patel told me that it would help. It has helped and some days I have more energy than others. On those days I do a little more. I walk a little more in my driveway. I take the weed eater and whack some weeds. I garden as much as I possibly can. BUT I'M REALLY TIRED OF BEING TIRED! Boy, that felt good!

Second, when I look in the mirror, I don't see me anymore. I look funny to me. No eyebrows, no eyelashes and WHAT IS GOING ON WITH THIS FUZZ? IT'S LOOKING GREY! I wasn't completely grey before chemo...is my hair going to come back grey???? Not that I mind grey hair, but I really wanted my brown hair a little longer. I know my hair and lashes will eventually come back, but I really do miss them.

I have never been beautiful, and I've never considered myself even cute or attractive. When I look in the mirror now, well, let's just say I try to avoid mirrors. It really bothers me, not because of vanity. I don't consider myself a vain person but I look so different. This is the outward sign of the inward battle. I don't like attention drawn to me. At a party, I'm usually the watcher somewhere in a corner people watching. I know that many of you reading this will find this hard to believe, but growing up I was so painfully shy that I would actually hide behind my mom or dad if anyone spoke to me. It took years for me to come out of my shell and to not be so painfully shy. Some of you may be wishing I would go back in my shell! LOL! But now, the whole world knows the inward battle and I don't like it. Yes, I could wear a wig, but prosthetic eyebrows???? Nah, I don't think so.

I have to wear a mask in public because of my low counts. Dr. Patel told me it was the only way I could even continue to work and I have tried to make if fun with funny masks. That has probably drawn more attention to me than I wanted and most people have assumed it was due to high pollen counts. Every now and then people ask if I'm on chemo and I respond yes and then we have a nice conversation...but I don't look like me...I'm trying really hard not to lose who I am.

Sometime in July, my body is going to undergo surgery. I will bear scars that no woman wants to have to bear. Many women have already been there, and I will soon join that club. The club that no one wants to be a card-carrying member. I will have drains for about 2 weeks that will limit my mobility as my body adjusts to its new normal. Phantom pain will become a part of my new normal. Am I scared, you bet. Am I rethinking reconstruction? No way.

I'm changing through all of this. I've never been a "touchy feely" person. That's just not my personality. In the color personality test, I'm a green, solid green. Logical, analytical, get things done kind of person. I find myself becoming more and more green as the days go by...no filter, no time for drama. I'm not becoming bitter, giving up or anything like that. Just more aware of time...there are so many things I still want to do. I'm a work in progress and I want to come out the other side a better person. Yes, I'm going to be physically different, mentally different, emotionally different...just different. I can't change this journey I'm on and I wouldn't wish this journey on anyone...it's tough and not fun...and there are days you think you won't make it. Days that even two more treatments seem just to long...but when you have no other option...you take the road and make the best of it...praying that the end is in sight and that this too shall pass.

Thank you for traveling with me. As always, I appreciate the ones who read, pray, and comment. Please continue to send prayers and positive thoughts for the last 2 AC treatments, the ultrasound on Thursday (pray that AC is working) and for blood counts to come up so I can get this done. You all ROCK!

Good News!
May 30, 2019

I was prepared today to tell Dr. Patel that if the ultrasound did not show any signs of reduction in the size of the tumors, I was wanting to forgo the last two AC's and get on to surgery. Guess what!?! Tumors are still shrinking...or melting away as he says! He is incredibly pleased with the response to chemo, so I had my 3rd treatment today. ONLY ONE MORE TO GO!

My blood work came up on its own and that was awesome! Next Thursday, I will go in for more blood work and then on Friday as a precaution get one unit of blood at Piedmont Fayette. This is just to put me in a good place for my last chemo in two weeks. He also put me on 1,000 milligrams of an antibiotic to keep this cold from turning into something much worse like sinusitis or bronchitis which is where my colds usually end up heading. I love that he is proactive, and he told me better safe than sorry!

If all continues as expected surgery will be sometime around July 11th or the week after. We must coordinate with Dr. Powell and arrange everything. Speaking of arranging, the insurance company's third party that looks at everything BEFORE sending it to insurance has yet to approve the PET scan. Even with a peer to peer and letter written by my doctor. He wants to make sure that my cancer has not metastasized to my bones or lungs (not often but can happen).

Many of you ask me how to pray and I believe in praying specifically for things so here goes:

1.) Pray that my body tolerates these last two chemo treatments and that side effects are minimal. NO FEVER wanted or needed!
2.) Pray that my counts remain up.
3.) Pray that the PET scan will be approved so it can be done prior to surgery.

4.) Continue to pray for my doctors: Dr. Patel, my oncologist and Dr. Powell, my surgeon.

I see light at the end of this long tunnel. As of June 10th, I will have been in chemo for 6 months.
I can't believe it. It seems like so much longer on some days when I'm tired. I'm trying to stay as active as possible, since Dr. Patel believes it really helps me recover. Some
days it's a chore to walk to the mailbox, but I do it believing that my body will stay stronger.

It's been a crazy week with a 60th birthday/retirement celebration at West Point Lake, a retirement reception at school yesterday and tonight is the county retirement banquet. I've enjoyed every moment. I have loved teaching, but it is time to move to other things.

Watch Facebook! I hope to have something exciting to share soon! Again, thank you for following my journey. I read every comment you post on my blog and it makes me feel so loved and cared for on this journey. You will NEVER know how much your positive thoughts, comments, texts, cards, and prayers are appreciated. I love each one of you and reading your comments keep me on the path!

Finish Line in sight...but...
June 9, 2019

This coming Thursday, my last chemo is scheduled. It has been a grueling 6-month journey...14 treatments and I'm exhausted. The finish line is in sight but...Why is it every show I seem to watch lately someone is dealing with cancer. I mean, literally every show. I try to find things that don't deal with the subject, but it gets harder. I'm not trying to run away from my diagnosis but it even TV seems to keep it at the forefront. And don't get me started on the commercials.

Thirty-five years ago, when I first started teaching, if I had asked my students if they knew someone with cancer, hardly anyone would raise their hand. This year, prior to my diagnosis, when we talked about how cancer is basically a cell gone crazy in mitosis, every student in my classes raised their hand. What are we doing wrong?

My cancer did not come from estrogen or progesterone or even HER2. My cancer is probably related to something environmental. So, what caused it? We will probably never know.

All of this makes me think. I really want to be NED at time of surgery. Will I? Who knows...I really don't want a reoccurrence. Will I have one? No one knows. Do I want to have to do chemo again? I can't answer that at this point. My sister and I even talked about no chemo after we saw what our Dad went through, but I had no other option. Without chemo followed by surgery and radiation; I wouldn't have lasted a year. Have I thought about my own mortality? You bet. There are still so many things I want to do, things I want to see, stuff I want to accomplish.

Will I win this battle? I don't know, no one knows, but I'm giving it my best shot. So many unanswered questions...so many questions period. My thoughts run rampant at times, mostly in the positive, but every now and then I just must stop and wonder why. Why did I end up with cancer? Why did I end up with an aggressive form of cancer? Why at the end of my teaching career? Why? Just plain, why?

It's frustrating not to know the cause. It's frustrating to know that 1 out of 8 women will deal with some form of breast cancer in their lifetime. Cancer is more than just wearing a pink ribbon. It's more than hair loss, it's more than chemo, it's more than surgery. It's just downright frustrating. At every turn I'm hearing of someone else with a diagnosis. One of the ladies I've been in chemo with did not have a positive response to chemo.

16 treatments and her tumors are still the same size. She is only in her 30's. Why did I respond and she didn't?

Does the future scare me? Well, duh...yeah. When the PET scan is approved, do you know why it is being done? To make sure this hasn't traveled somewhere else in my body. Yeah, cancer can travel even when you are doing chemo.

My thoughts are many and I may be rambling, but they are my thoughts. I come to you my support, my readers and ask you the send prayers and positive thoughts for the following things. Your prayers and positive thoughts have helped me through this journey, and I need your support more than ever. 1. Pray that my last chemo goes well, and I can tolerate it once again. I've done Okay with the full dosage. Everything does taste funny, so not much of an appetite and my hands and feet are peeling like crazy!
2. Pray the PET scan gets approved (still hasn't been) and that it shows the cancer HAS NOT traveled.
3. Pray as I meet in the next few weeks with my surgical team.
4. Continue to pray that I continue to stay positive and work through this nightmare that I would not wish on anyone. Thank you so much for listening. I hope I haven't been Debbie Downer. I just had to get my thoughts down. Thank you for caring. Thank you for loving me despite my weaknesses.

I have CANCER, not the PLAGUE!
June 12, 2019

It's 2:30 AM and I have rampant thoughts running through my head. I know my insomnia will not let me sleep until I get this off my mind. This blog has helped me through so many sleepless nights now that I'm not sure what I would do if I didn't have the opportunity to write. Before you read any further you need to understand that this post is full of hurt and anger. You might want to stop reading.

I've addressed this before but tonight, or rather this morning, I'm hurt, I'm angry, I'm frustrated, and I feel alone. I am beginning to understand why other cancer patients avoid social situations and why many call this a lonely journey.

I went somewhere, we will leave it at that, and felt alone. More alone than I have ever felt, and I was surrounded by people I consider friends and family. It was like I had the plague. People avoided me. I realize that everyone isn't comfortable around me, but this was ridiculous. I felt like I had the plague, that I was contagious. I know I've excused it before with "well, they don't know what to say...", etc. But it really bothered me this time.

I don't know how many tears of frustration and hurt I have cried over situations like this in the past 6 months. Those of you who know me, know that I am not a crier. But this hurts. It hurts worse than chemo. At least with chemo I know it will pass. I'm not sure the emotional and mental scars will ever pass. I won't be the same person when all of this is finished because there will be too many of those emotional and mental scars. To have people I consider friends so uncomfortable around me because of cancer makes me want to not be in social situations and to avoid them (the situations) at all costs.

I'm angry. Angry that people don't know what to say or what to do. How about a hug? I know I've not been much of a hugger in the past, but lately, I'll take any and all that I can get to help me through the day. I'm angry that I even have to deal with cancer. I'm angry.

After my last post, I had a friend call to check on me. She will NEVER know how much her call meant. And I know if we had been closer (she lives an hour away) that she would have grabbed me and hugged me. She picked up on my frustration and picked up the phone. That's what I needed.

We've been talking about the Samaritan woman at church the past two Sundays. Our theme right now is "Look. Talk. Act. Pray. Respond Like Jesus." If you know anything about the story, you know that she went to the well to avoid her neighbors and others of her village. I've felt recently like the Samaritan woman, a social outcast. Thank you, cancer, for yet another thing I now have to deal with as if fighting you weren't enough.

Is this post full of hurt? Yes, I've cried all the way through writing, and I apologize for any typos or grammar errors there may be. Is this post full of anger? Yes, because when I'm hurt, I get angry. Angry at myself for letting myself get hurt, yet once again, angry at the ones who are pushing me away but once my treatment is done will act as though nothing happened, and angry that cancer has put me in this position.

Is this post full of frustration? Yes, I'm so frustrated that now I don't want to be in social settings where I make people uncomfortable. I don't know what to say to make it better when I'm in the situation. Nothing I say seems to make it any better. It's awkward and I hate awkward. It's uncomfortable and I don't like to feel uncomfortable. Will I be avoiding certain situations? Yeah, probably. I just have enough on my plate right now and don't need the added stress. And yes, it is stressing me out. Stressing me to the point that I'm up at 2:48 now writing a blog that I will probably regret a few hours from now.

If I make you uncomfortable, I'm sorry. Cancer makes me uncomfortable, but I have to deal with it. I have a feeling that those who follow me on this blog are not uncomfortable around me.
Maybe we all need to just pull up our big girl (or guy) panties and love people like Jesus loved. He even touched the leper. Wouldn't we be better off?

Last Chemo
June 14, 2019

Yep, it was the last chemo today. And yes, it's 3:30 AM because I had steroids! Just love the no sleep with steroids and I will not miss that at all! My infusion center doesn't do the bell ringing at the end of chemo. There are people in the infusion center in stage 4 cancers who will never get the opportunity to ring the bell. That's one of the reasons I love Piedmont Cancer Institute. They think about everyone. Given the opportunity, I wouldn't have rung the bell out of respect for those who can't and won't get that chance.

My greatest excitement was looking at my appointment list and seeing that I don't see Dr. Patel again until August 2nd, which will be after surgery. I love my doctor but seeing that appointment confirmed to me that the chemo phase is over.

We talked about that appointment. At that time, he will go over the pathology report from surgery with me. If there are any active cancer cells left at surgery time, I will go on Xeloda to kill off any remaining cells after I finish targeted radiation on the two lymph nodes that showed cancer activity. This could be a yearlong chemo, but it is in pill form and doesn't have as bad of side effects as what I have already been through. My hope is that all the cancer cells are dead!

Surgery won't be for at least 4 - 5 weeks. Dr. Patel assured me that this last chemo will be continuing to work due to the half-life of the drugs I have been given. And having had a month off from chemo back in March - April, I know that is truth. That's when I told him I was worried, and he scheduled another ultrasound and it showed that the tumors were still reducing in size... and one was completely gone! I will have a blood transfusion on Wednesday of next week. This is primarily surgery prep. Dr. Patel wants me hemoglobin to be up by the time of surgery. I have my last

Neulasta on my arm and that will boost my white counts. Then with 3 - 4 weeks off, my bone marrow, with all these boosters, should be almost back to normal for surgery and that's important.

Emotionally, I'm better. I've had so many hugs, phone calls, wonderful texts, and responses to my last post. You know, it's not just about the hugging, but just saying hello, how are you. I promise my pat response is I'm fine...and I won't bore you with details. I save those for the people who ask questions. This has been a learning experience for me and for some of my friends. Curiosity is a great thing and I have always encouraged my students to ask questions. I don't mind questions...there isn't one thing you could ask me that would embarrass me or make me think less of you as a person. I'm a teacher, a retired teacher, but a teacher still at heart and if I can use this awful disease to continue to teach, then I'm all in and up to the task. One of the greatest ways to learn is to ask questions. I have always taught my students to ask and sometimes it got me in trouble because I answered honestly!

Thank you so much for following my journey and being my support system. I truly do not know what I would do without all of you. You make me feel so much better by listening and reading my blog. You will NEVER know the impact you are making on my life. You, my reader are a Godsend!

If you are wondering specific things to pray for and send up positive thoughts, I do have a few and I believe prayer is getting me through the hurdles. 1.) Pray that I tolerate this last chemo as well as the others. This was a "full load" and minimal side effects would be awesome.
2.) Pray that the PET scan is finally approved. My surgeon will now be ordering it hoping he can get it approved since Dr. Patel believes he is on the most turned now oncologist on the insurance hit list (lol).
3.) Pray that my blood transfusion on Wednesday boosts my hemoglobin.

4.) Pray that surgery is scheduled quickly.

So Tired...and random thoughts...
June 22, 2019

This last chemo was rough. My fingertips feel like they have been scalded in water, appetite is non-existent, and I have been sooooo tired. Red Devil is not a joke. I'm so glad it is done because frankly I don't think I could go one more dose.

I have an appointment with my surgeon on Monday and will know then the date of my surgery and some other details. I've been working on my list of questions. Every time I think of something I want to ask I put them in phone notes, so I have them handy when I have my appointments. I've got quite a few questions for Dr. Powell.

Thanks to Meta Thompson I have the BEST team ever who are a part of M.D. Anderson, who is doing some of the latest, greatest research in cancer treatment.

I've rested this week because frankly I haven't had the energy to do anything. Just taking a shower has winded me each day. I've binged watched some shows but mostly I've watched hummingbirds. I've got two hummingbird feeders right beside the window where my end of the sectional is located. The funny thing is this year the hummingbirds aren't paying as much attention to the bird feeders as they are the lantana. They love the lantana and I see them several times a day flitting from bloom to bloom. It's relaxing to watch them work and takes my mind off how exhausted I feel.

My mom always hung out several hummingbird feeders and I loved it when I would go home and sit out on the carport and listen to their wings as they flew from feeder to feeder. I think at one time I counted six that were giving her feeders a workout.

I hope that in all my exhaustion that the Red Devil is eating away at the tumors that are still around. They have shrunk considerably but I want them gone before surgery. My oncologist will see me on the 2nd of August and go over the pathology and all the results. I'm not hoping for a good report but I'm hoping for a GREAT report. That would make this all so much easier to swallow.

I'll update more Monday after I meet with my surgeon. Please continue to keep me in your thoughts and prayers. Like I said, this past week has been one of the roughest weeks ever. I've lost weight due to no appetite and just so tired. Which I think I've mentioned several times in this post. I hope this passes soon and I can turn the corner. Thank you for sharing in my journey.

Surgery is Scheduled!
June 24, 2019

Met with Dr. Powell today and discussed several things. Surgery has been scheduled for July 16th. He is also going to see if he can get the PET scan approved, since Dr. Patel has now been denied 3 times. This scan is especially important. I have an inter mammary lymph node that cannot be removed because it is in my chest. No one can remove it and we need to see if if is still showing active cancer cells. Also, Dr. Santiago needs to know the exact location so it can be hit with radiation.

On the 16th, I will report first for a dye injection that will show the location of the sentinel lymph nodes. This will be about a 2-hour procedure. We don't have a time for this yet. Then I will report for pre-op followed by surgery. I hope to know more about the timeline in a couple of days.

I will only be in the hospital for a 24-hour period unless there are some sort of complications. The only thing at this point I am concerned about is bleeding since I have had trouble with my counts being low. This may surprise you but at the age of 60 I have never spent a night in the hospital as a patient. This will be a new experience!

Because cancer showed up in two lymph nodes, I am considered to have metastatic breast cancer. I don't like that term; I don't like it Sam I am. It sounds so serious. I'm trying to keep things positive but when you see that on your paperwork it is a little disconcerting.

As far as lymph node removal, Dr. Powell is doing what is called a sentinel lymph node procedure which will only take 5 - 7 lymph nodes are opposed to removing many more or all.

So that's the update. Specific prayer requests:

1) Pray that Dr. Powell can get the PET scan approved. Three doctors are requesting it

and the company hired by my insurance company to screen everything is saying it isn't medically necessary. Hello? Three doctors think it is!

2) Pray that when the PET scan is approved that it will show no active lymph nodes.

Thanks for hanging with me through this journey. I'll post more as I have more information.

Struggling
June 27, 2019

I've been struggling the last few days. It's been a very emotional time. One thing I have learned about cancer is your emotions run the gamut. Mine have been very raw since I met with the surgeon on Monday.

I looked at myself in the mirror yesterday and burst into tears. I hate my bald head. I hate not having hair. I think it makes me look funny and sick. I just hate it. I'm doing everything I can to promote hair growth.

Knowing that I have a lymph node that cannot be removed and may not have responded to chemo makes it harder for me to think I will get over this. Radiation will target it but even that isn't assured that the cancer will be contained. My surgeon told me there is no one who can remove that node. That was a real downer and upsetting. I want all of this gone.

Seeing the term metastatic was devastating. It means the cancer is elsewhere, including the lymph nodes, and that term, frankly, scares me. Finally, surgery will forever change the way I look. I've opted for no reconstruction by choice. Does surgery still scare me...yes. My counts have been so low that I have an added risk for bleeding. I'm losing a part of my body. Even though they don't define who I am, I'm basically having an amputation of a body part. That's scary. I'm nervous about seeing the surgery site for the first time and how it will look. I trust my surgeon implicitly. Still it is daunting.

I'm trying to work through all of this in my mind. It's an up and down roller coaster of emotions. Sometimes my emotions are more raw than other days. It's scary to say the least.

One Day at a Time
July 7, 2019

After much fuss and delay, my PET scan was finally approved. My oncologist told me that my surgeon could request the PET scan and it would probably be approved. Dr. Powell requested and it was immediately approved after being denied three times by the company who screens everything for the insurance company. Amazing! Dr. Patel claims he is on the insurance most wanted list because his scans are denied so frequently.

I'm feeling pretty good. My appetite has come back and I'm actually hungry at times. I don't want any of the foods I ate while I was doing chemo. I was told this would happen and it has, so I'm glad I didn't eat any of my favorites the past six months!

My fingers are peeling something horrible. AC made them feel burned during treatment and now they look like I've had them in water for hours and peeling. Some of the side effects of chemo are so unexpected.

A week from Wednesday I go for surgery. Trying to prepare myself emotionally, mentally and physically. It will be a long day starting at 7:15 that morning. In one way I'm dreading the day and in another way I'm ready to get this done. One step at a time, one day at a time.

I have stubble growing on my head. Just enough to itch but not enough to determine what color, texture or if it will be curly. Will have to wait on the final determination for a few more weeks.

I've found out that because United Healthcare has what is called coinsurance, I have to pay 20% of all bills and according to my policy there is no cap limit. The hospital called and told me my portion is $4000. This does not include any of the doctor's fees.

That is a little frustrating. As a teacher we used to have

Great insurance...not any longer.

Please pray for the following this week:

1.) The PET scan will show the cancer is inactive and has not traveled anywhere else in my body.

2.) For me to be at peace with surgery coming up.

3.) God will provide the $$ needed to meet my financial obligations.

As always, thank you for standing with me in my journey and for your continued prayers.

Surgery Recovery
July 22, 2019

Surgery went extremely well. Nuclear testing finished with me early, so I actually went into surgery 30 minutes earlier than scheduled. The whole procedure took about 3 hours. I slept the entire time! (LOL). I asked for pain meds after I work up but I'm pleased to say I haven't had pain meds since then!

I met with my surgeon today and he is amazed about the no meds. He said it's two things...the health condition I was in (excellent health) and my attitude. Oh, I've had a few twinges but nothing to warrant pain medication. I attribute this to what he said and all the prayers that have been lifted up on my behalf.

I came home on Thursday around 2:00 PM. Dr. Powell told me I could opt for another night in the hospital to which I said, no way. I wanted to come home and sleep and I slept the whole night. It was awesome!

One drain was removed today and the other two will hopefully be removed Wednesday. I have to go back then and meet with the Physician's assistant for drain removal. Then I will go back Friday to meet with Dr. Powell. I don't know if he will remove my staples then, but we are hoping the pathology on the tissue will be back so we can discuss it. He told me today he didn't see anything that looked like cancer but stuff that looked like scar tissue where the tumors had been. It won't be until it is under a microscope that we know if there are any active cancer cells.

My next appointment with my oncologist is August 2nd. I will heal for a while after my staples are removed and then do radiation. I don't know yet how many rads I will have but since I showed two active lymph nodes on my first PET scan, I will do radiation on those two sites to be sure the cancer is eradicated.

The only bad news...I haven't been able to drive for 5 days and I have another 5 days that I can't drive. Tonight, we are making spaghetti...it's what sounds really good! Please pray for the following these next few days:
1) That I continue to be pain free.
2) The pathology comes back clear.
Thank you for all who have followed my journey and continue to follow me!

Meeting with Dr. Patel
August 2, 2019

Today I met with Dr. Patel, my oncologist and he used the following words: "cancer free". "You are in remission from your cancer." I am stoked, but this isn't the end of my journey. Because the cancer showed up in two lymph nodes on the first PET scan, I will meet with my radiation oncologist on August 14th and schedule anywhere from 15 - 20 rads.

I had a little 4 mm tumor that showed up in the pathology report. Dr. Patel told me that anything under 1 cm will not show on a PET scan. He gave me a choice today. I can do radiation and be done OR I can do radiation and start Xeloda a month later. This would be a pill form of chemotherapy with a few side effects that can occur. The schedule would be two weeks on, one week off. It would continue for 6 months. In studies done, this adds a 5% chance that cancer will not reoccur. In my mind, this is a no brainer, but I asked his opinion. He told me that if I were a family member, he would recommend it. And I told him, consider me a family member!

5% may not sound like a lot, but when you add in everything else I have done...5% really boosts my chances of not having a reoccurrence and I would rather be proactive than reactive.

Surgery went great. I had pain meds one time after coming out of anesthesia. Haven't had a pain pill since. My surgeon stated in his doctor's notes: "No pain pills since surgery. Amazing." Haven't needed one. The nurse ractitioner told me she had never seen such a great looking incision. No redness, no swelling...

All my drains are out. Half of my staples are out, and I return to Dr. Powell's office on Monday for the removal of more staples.

I told Dr. Patel today that chemo was not the only thing that helped. I told him I had a lot of people praying for me. And he agreed that was a huge part of my journey. So that's my news. I feel great. My blood work showed that my counts are almost back to normal. Thank you all for your prayers, your cards, your texts, you phone calls and most of all your love. I love you all to the moon and back!

Radiation Plan
August 14, 2019

Today I went to see my radiation oncologist. Dr. Santiago was not there today, so I met with her partner. I will see her next week when I get my tattoo that will mark my radiation site. I will have 30 rads. Five weeks of rads will be on the right side to target the lymph node and areas where the tumors were located. I will also have the site of the intramammary lymph node showed activity in the first PET scan. The sixth week will only target that site.

We went over the possible side effects from radiation. The main one is skin reddening or darkening and of course there could be peeling at the site. Lymphedema is also a possibility. When lymph nodes are removed swelling can occur in the arm. To help with this possible side effect, I was measured today for a compression sleeve. My lymphedema therapist has already recommended it for physical activity and air travel. I decided to have fun and ordered two sleeves...one is a sleeve with flames shooting up the arm and the other is a watercolor sleeve. I didn't want to be boring! The RN who measured my arm today loved both of my choices and said she wished other people who go for the fun stuff!

I have been back at Charlie Elliott this week, both Monday and Tuesday and plan to go back tomorrow. No, I haven't been released by my surgeon, but Kim won't let me lift anything and my job right now is simply working on the computer, so I'm good. I'm heading back over tomorrow. Have I told you lately that I LOVE my new job?

I will see Dr. Powell Tuesday morning before heading down to see Dr. Santiago. My incisions look great and I've started using scar cream to help with the scarring. Still haven't had any pain which is awesome. I know that is a direct result of all the prayers offered up on my behalf. That's my update for now. Thank you again for being with me on this journey. I pray that none of you ever must fight this battle. I would not wish it on anyone, including my worst enemy.

Minor Set Back
August 27, 2019

Last Tuesday I went to my surgeon's office to meet with Marlo. Monday night I had bent over to pick up my shoes and after that had trouble catching a deep breath. I thought I had pulled a muscle, so when Marlo asked how I was, I explained what was going on. Immediately she sent me for a CT scan and the scan revealed several small PE's in my right lung.

Dr. Powell's office called immediately, and my instructions were to get to the emergency room because I was being admitted to the hospital. I spent from Tuesday to Thursday in the hospital receiving two Heparin drips. I left the hospital with a prescription for Lovenox which I will be taking for 6 weeks followed by an oral blood thinner for six months. Oh, did I mention that Lovenox is an injection? Yep, I'm giving myself shots every 12 hours!

I am so glad I mentioned to Marlo what was going on...and more importantly, I'm glad she listened! My team rocks! Dr. Patel climbed 7 flights of steps (elevator was out) to come see me and explain everything in detail. I had an electrocardiogram which showed no damage to my heart from chemo and the blood clots did not originate from there. I also had Doppler on my legs and it showed great blood flow and the blood clots did not originate from there. My blood clots most likely came from my surgery site which is interesting since I was 5 weeks out from surgery.

I was supposed to meet with my radiation oncologist the day I was admitted to the hospital. I'm going today to meet with her and find out my radiation schedule. This of course was pushed back due to the hospitalization. I'm hoping we can start next week at the latest so I can get this next phase over.

The blood thinners will not interfere with radiation or Xeloda, which was the first question I asked Dr. Patel. He assured me that there will not be any issue. Dr. Patel told me that the only thing I cannot do at this point is play contact sports to which I replied "There goes my football career, but at least pole dancing is still available!" He laughed and told me he loves my sense of humor. I'm not sure Dr. Powell, my surgeon, knows how to take me though. He just shakes his head.

This has been a minor setback, which I'm thankful was caught before it became a major setback! As always, thank you for your thoughts and prayers. I'm keeping on and keeping the faith! Love to you all!

Radiation Update
September 17, 2019

Just finished working from home today and wanted to take a minute to update everyone before I must go to treatment.
I am doing well. No side effects from radiation really. Just red and warm after treatment. Doctor let me know yesterday that I may being to see some skin changes beginning next week and some fatigue.

I have completed 7 treatments with 23 left to go. By the end of this week, I'll be a third of the way done. I will head back for a CT scan on October 14th to check the blood clots and, to check some spots that showed up on my left lung.

These have been there for a while and my pulmonologist has been keeping an eye on them. He thinks it is scar tissue from respiratory infections over the past several years.

My Lovenox shots for my blood clots continue. I think I have about two and 1/2 weeks left of giving myself shots. My stomach looks like the solar system! I must be getting better at giving myself shots because the bruising is getting less.

All in all, I'm feeling great. Planning on getting back to walking, but for now that will be indoors due to the heat. I'm not supposed to get hot and I have to stay out of the sun during radiation. The weather here is HOT! 97 today...and it's September. If anyone thinks climate change is a hoax, please send me a private message and I will be happy to explain how it is not and we are experiencing something that has happened before and will probably happen again. Everything has cycles!

I don't see my oncologist again until October 14th after my CT scan. He will probably give me my Xeloda prescription for the following six months.

Hopefully by April of next year, I will have all this stuff behind me...chemo...check...mastectomy...check...radiation...in process...Xeloda...to come. Thank you all for following my journey. I love every one of you!

Close to the end.
October 9, 2019

My 25 regular radiation treatments end tomorrow. Beginning Friday, I will have targeted therapy on the inter-mammary lymph node that showed activity in my original CT scan in January. It did not show any activity on the CT in June. October is Breast Cancer awareness month. Everyone it seems have embraced the pink. I have to admit, I hate the color pink!

Pink, in my mind, is associated with cute little girls, a princess and breast cancer is anything but cute. I hate the motto "Save the tatas". Why save something that is trying to kill you? We need to change that to "save a woman's life". Cancer is not cute in pictures, it is not cute in mottos. It is a killer. 1 in 8 women will be diagnosed with breast cancer.

Cancer treatment sucks...chemo is about toxic chemicals in the body to kill cells and in the process, it kills healthy cells. It's about being nauseated, vomiting, hair loss, feeling fatigued, feeling helpless, feeling hopeless, losing friends, losing family members. There is nothing pretty about it!!!

Any while I am on my soap box, please check before you donate money to a breast cancer organization. Some organizations only donate about 10-20% of total money that they take in from the public. What bothers me...is that breast cancer has become a business. Slap a pink ribbon on something and give 5% of the proceeds to breast cancer. What about the other 95%? Who is that going to?

I've attached two pictures...this is breast cancer. These are pictures from what my skin is enduring throughout the treatments. Thank goodness my skin has not cracked open. Some women have open, weeping wounds when radiation is used. In about 2 weeks my skin will begin to peel. I've had an area where my shirts hit around my neck that caused a blister...and don't even get me started on how bad this itches. Take your worst sunburn and multiple it by 10...then you will get the idea. My right arm is so sore I can hardly move it today.

I'm not complaining, please don't get me wrong. I'm not looking for sympathy. I'm just riled up about how people are capitalizing on women's suffering with this horrific disease.

It has changed me. I have a new normal. I am a different person because of this journey. I have to stay busy to keep my mind off what I will do if I have a reoccurrence. It is always there in the back of my mind, but I cannot dwell on it. I just turned 60 and retired. I wonder if I will see 62, 65, maybe 70. God is in control, but Satan also uses this disease to attack your mind, your mental and emotional state.

There are still days I want to stay in bed and weep. Weep over what I have lost, weep over my scars, I am forever changed. My body does not look the same, my emotions are no longer the same, my mental being is no longer the same. Pink is not a pretty color. It is a devastating color in my book. It is a color of change. It is a color of scars. It is a color of different forever. It is a color of women who have been to hell.

Next Phase
November 6, 2019

I met with my oncologist this past Monday and here is the latest. First of all, we will repeat the CT scan in 6 months because there is a 7mm nodule on the bottom of my right lung. This could be several things: a seroma (pocket of fluid left over from surgery) or even a hematoma from where I had to give myself shots. It could also be scarring from bronchitis in the past. The reason to repeat the CT scan is to make sure it isn't changing. If it were to be growing, that would NOT be what we want.

Second, have I mentioned how much I love my oncologist? He wanted to start me on Xeloda on the 18th of this month after I have education on Thursday of next week. However, in looking at the calendar, he realized that would put me on Xeloda over the Thanksgiving holidays. He wants me to be able to enjoy the holidays, so he backed it up to this coming Monday and moved my education meeting to Tuesday morning.

I told him that this upcoming med has me a little freaked out. I'm not supposed to touch it with my bare hands but I'm supposed to swallow this "toxic" chemical. Not only that...it is super expensive. Right now, since I have met my deductible (several times over) my insurance is covering it and my Equilis. BUT, when my insurance year starts over in January the cost of these two drugs alone, if insurance doesn't pay a good portion will wipe out my pension for every month. He told me not to worry, but he will see what kind of programs I can qualify for to get the cost down.

The side effects are numerous, as is with any chemotherapy. I don't know how much I will be able to work through all of this. I will take the drug for 14 days and then have 7 days off to let my blood cells recoup. In preparation for low counts (which my white cells are still down from rads) I had a flu shot and will be getting the pneumonia series. Please consider getting a flu shot to protect chemo patients, young children, and seniors. It really does help.

Okay, enough PSA...back to the side effects. The three that I am mostly likely to experience are diarrhea (and since I drive an hour and ten minutes to work, this may impact my schedule), hand and foot syndrome (which I had during AC where my feet and hands felt like they were burning and peeled like crazy) and mouth sores (which I had during IV chemo and used salt/baking soda to help). Hand and foot syndrome can be so bad that it impacts your ability to walk and that concerns me because I'm planning on getting back into the 5k cycle beginning with the Turkey Trot on Thanksgiving Day.

Why do you ask am I doing Xeloda? Hopefully to kill any remaining cancer cells that may be floating in my body and looking for a place to land. Even though they got all the cancer tissue (4mm) that was left after IV chemo, there could always be a cell or two left in the body.

I'm doing everything I can to keep this devil from coming back. It's been a tough 2019. I have felt crappy most of the year, lost all my hair, been nauseous, basically had an amputation and had radiation burns. I don't feel tough, I still have trouble looking in the mirror at my scars and I still sometimes just sit and cry. Not because I feel sorry for myself, but because at times I have just felt so overwhelmed and so alone, even surrounded by people. Everyone's cancer journey is different. Everyone has a different support system. But no one can understand how you feel, even a fellow cancer survivor. It's just different for everyone.

I'm still working on me. My hair is growing and looking wavy. I don't know if it will stay wavy or go curly. I still have gray where I had gray before losing my hair. I still have days I just want to sit and not feel anything. I still have days I don't want to get out of bed. I still have days that I'm just not me. I'm a work in progress and I know I will never be the person I was before cancer. Part of me will always be anxious when I feel a twinge, when I watch a show where someone is dealing with cancer (and how many shows is that? It seems like every one of them!) and I just want to cry. I still deal with people who say things like "You don't look sick" or "I had a friend with breast cancer and she died" (and all I hear is...she died for the rest of the conversation) or "You look good, so all must be okay now."

Things will NEVER be the same. I will NEVER be the same. I have to live with the big C for the rest of my life. Physically, my hair is coming back, my appetite is better (most days) and my color is back. Mentally and emotionally, I'm still a wreck...a big one. I'll still smile and tell you I'm fine because honestly no one really wants to know how I really feel, and I don't think I can explain it to you without crying. So please, let me tell you things are fine, hug me, and let's leave it at that. Please keep me in your prayers as I start Xeloda. I'm scared and not afraid to admit it.

Ramblings of Chemo Brain
November 17, 2019

I am finishing my first week of Xeloda. Had my education meeting on Tuesday of this week and learned all about the potential side effects. Will be going for blood work on Wednesday to see how the chemo is affecting my blood counts.

I still have to take precautions, so if I see you out and about and your are coughing or sneezing, please...no hugging or hand shaking. I have to take virtually the same precautions with this chemo as I did with IV chemo, but I'm not going to wear masks. Had enough of those for awhile!

I've had my flu shot and next up is the pneumonia shot series. My doctor wants to protect me from all possible problems. There is even the shingles series in my near future!

Met with my oncology radiologist this past Friday and she is pleased with my healing. I'm no longer red but now have a nice tan in places that have never seen the sun (LOL)! I don't follow up with her for another 6 months and by then the Xeloda will be done.

It's been a rough week. Not for me as far as my cancer treatment goes, but with my pup, Rocky. It's hard watching an animal suffer. I don't want that for any of my animals. We are trying meds and I will say that today he has only chased 4 times and that is way down from the 15 on Wednesday that all occurred after I got home from leaving work. We will see where this leads and I appreciate all of you for your kind words, thoughts, and prayers on Facebook about my Rockstar. He is my baby and a member of our crazy family.

So, I'm not supposed to touch Xeloda and if I do and even if I don't, but handle the bottle, I have to wash my hands several times after. Well, guess what? If you guessed I spilled the bottle, you would be right. That's what happened before I left for church this morning...so I have been hand washing...ALL DAY!

It's a little frightening when you open the package, and it has a hazard warning on it! But you are supposed to swallow these things! If I have any left after I finish, I have been instructed, in my education session, to take them to the doctor and they will dispose of them. Okay...good to know.

I'm feeling better since my last update. It's hard on some days. Some days it just hits me...other days I'm fine. Is my journey over? Not by a long shot. I believe I look pretty good and most days I feel fairly good. Sometimes out of the blue though it hits, and I realize what I've lost, how I've changed, and it hurts. It can be a simple trigger...a picture...a memory...

Recently, I've been listening to Christmas music on my radio (don't judge) and some of the songs have taken me back to when we used to go to my grandparents for Christmas...all the family together...I miss those days...I miss my mom and dad more around the holidays than any other time. I miss them all year, but especially around the times we all gathered as a family.

I've really missed my mom this year with my illness. She always knew the right thing to say and do. I think that's what has made this even harder...not having her here to share my thoughts and my fears. And yes, I miss her potato soup too!

I feel like I'm getting stronger. It is a day-by-day process. Life is still hard at times and 2019 has not been kind. I for one will be glad to see it in my rear-view mirror. The journey isn't over...and won't be until April when I will finally be finished with all the medication.

I covet your friendship and I have appreciated the cards, kind thoughts and prayers through this journey. Please continue to pray. I believe your prayers are helping keep side effects at bay. Thank you all and much love.

A Year Later…
December 26, 2019

Before doing some work today, I thought I would take a moment and update since it has been awhile since my last update.

First, I hope everyone had a wonderful Christmas. I enjoyed my day even though I am currently fighting bronchitis. Seems low blood counts just let your body catch almost everything! But the day was beautiful out at Lake Jackson...great food and wonderful company.

Lots of thoughts this Christmas season...I must be honest with you...a year ago, I didn't know if I would be here to see this Christmas. There was so much uncertainty. I was diagnosed with one of the most aggressive forms of breast cancer and I spent last Christmas quietly wondering if it would be my last Christmas. Chemo was uncertain...would my tumors respond? Surgery...daunting... Radiation...scary... the uncertainty was always there in the back of my mind. Now a year later, I'm still here. IV Chemo is over, surgery has been done and radiation is over...still on chemo…just the pill form...and I survived bilateral pulmonary blood clots.

There are days I almost feel normal...or I should say...my new normal. I'm not sure I will ever get use to the scars and the way this journey has changed me. Today, I have a friend just starting her journey. She has a different type of breast cancer than I had, so her journey is starting with surgery. It is a scary time...when you hear the words cancer. Even though the success stories are out there...I think there is still in the back of our minds...it won't happen to me. Unfortunately, it can happen to any of us at any time. I'm so thankful I went for the breast MRI...without it, I wouldn't have been diagnosed until March of 2019 at the time of my mammogram and at that point it could have spread beyond the four lymph nodes that tested positive.

I'm thankful for all of you who have prayed for me, sent cards, texts and followed my journey. I have an awesome support team and I love each and every one one of you.

Without you, I could not have made it through. My journey continues and will not end until April, when I finish Xeloda. I chose to do more chemo to increase my chances of not having a reoccurrence. My sweet oncologist gave me two weeks off this time because of the side effects I began to experience during my second round…which is probably good since I ended up with bronchitis.

I will be facing more surgery this summer. My gynecologist and my oncologist believes it is in my best interest to have a complete hysterectomy. Breast cancer can often become ovarian cancer and I'm double whammed with losing my mom to ovarian cancer. Surgery will not be scheduled until after I am off Xeloda and Equilis.

The lung nodules that showed up on my CT scan when I had blood clots are resolved. I will probably have another CT scan after finishing Equilis to make sure everything looks normal.

Please continue to think of me. With the new year starting, my insurance goes back to having to meet deductibles…I know the Xeloda is about $2000 a round. Dr. Patel is going to see if I can qualify for a discounted rate on it and the Equilis (close to $550 a round).

Thank you for reading and being awesome friends. I pray that your 2020 is the best year yet.

Update
March 9, 2020

It's been a while since I've sat down and written an update
and I wanted to let everyone know how things are going.
I met with my oncologist today. I am close to finishing up my
Eliquis. When I finish my current bottle, I will have been on
blood thinners for six months and that is the normal
amount of time for blood clots. He also told me today that
after I finish Xeloda this time, I should only have one more
round to do.

I'm so happy that by the end of April this will be over.
I'm tired. My blood counts are still down but should begin to
come up to normal levels once all my treatment is finished. I
still have bad days when it's hard to get up and go and days I
feel depressed. It's hard.

Reoccurrence is always in the back of my mind...with
every pain. There are days I can put it completely out of my
mind and other days I can't. It's still hard to look at my scars.
Breast cancer is not the pink ribbons and beauty. It's ugly,
painful and heartbreaking.

Thank you to those who are continuing to pray for my
journey. It's not over yet. 14 months and counting but I am
seeing the light at the end of the tunnel and I'm grateful
I'm still here and that you my friends still care.

Latest News
March 27, 2020

Met with Dr. Patel today. Piedmont Newnan Hospital's
parking lot looked so empty. Didn't have any trouble finding
a parking space today. This Covid-19 stuff is a bit scary.
My blood work today looked good. My white blood cell
counts are back to normal!

This is the first time in 15 months that has happened! Red blood cell count is still low but he explained that right now my body is producing big red blood cells and the bigger the lower the number...mine is not too low at the moment but is lower than normal ranges.

Other counts are still low but that is due to the Xeloda. Kidney function, liver function results will not be in until tomorrow.

I finished Eliquis this past Wednesday and immediately removed my blood thinner ID bracelet! That part of this journey is over unless I have to go in for more surgery at a later time. If that happens they will probably put me on blood thinners again for a precautionary measure.

The best news yet...Monday I start my last Xeloda regime! I am so excited! For 15 months now I have been fatigued beyond belief...dealt with chemo side effects and the end is almost in sight! I go back April 13th for blood work and then we will probably schedule another CT scan. He wants to view my chest area to make sure we see no activity.

Pray about this. My insurance will likely deny it and we will have to jump through hoops once again. I plan to keep my Caring Bridge site going for a while. You all have been such a tremendous support for me, and I will continue to update as things happen. If there is to be a reoccurrence with this it is most likely to occur within the next 2 - 3 years. Triple Negative tends to reoccur within that time. After 5 years, reoccurrence for Triple Negative drops tremendously.

I want to give a couple of shout-outs...Stephanie, my oncology nurse navigator, has been so positive and such an inspiration to me during the past 15 months. She has been there when I needed to talk and she has helped me schedule appointments, met me at my appointments and answered any questions I've had. THANK YOU, STEPHANIE! Katey Lucas, from Dr. Powell's office, has just kept me going with her smile and her positive attitude...and of course she is a fellow Vol fan! THANK YOU KATEY!

One more shout out...to those who have read my blogs and sent me encouragement in the form of Facebook posts, cards, texts, and phone calls...you have helped me in this journey more than you will ever know. I'm going to keep plugging away and sheltering at home for now. You all stay safe and pray for our medical teams that are on the front lines. They need all the divine intervention they can get.

Haven't Posted in a While...
April 23, 2020

I just finished watching a special on Jane Goodall. She has always been someone I've admired for all her work with chimpanzees. Made me a little sad. She has done so much good for the plight of the chimps and people. She really cares about the people in Tanzania. Her legacy is awesome, and she had made such a huge difference in the world of science and with the people she has meet throughout the world.

It got me thinking...have I made a difference? What will be my legacy? I came up with an idea a couple of weeks ago and I will share with you what I'm up to. I've decided to write a book on my cancer journey. I don't know if anyone will actually read it when I publish but I've been thinking, maybe my cancer journey is something I'm supposed to share with others who may be going through the same thing.

There isn't a lot to read about Triple Negative Breast Cancer and everything I have read mostly gives the facts, treatments, etc. My perspective is from my journey, like my blogs. It will go through my chemo, surgery, radiation, depression, loneliness, fear and stuff like that. Maybe it will help someone. Maybe that is to be my legacy.

My dear friend, Sarah Klein, is my editor. She is reading each chapter and giving me great input to make my writing better. I'm wanting my raw emotion to be in the book like I feel it has been in this blog. If I can help someone else navigate through this horrible disease then my journey will have been worth it.

In case you haven't heard (what you've been under a rock?), my last PET scan showed No Evidence of Disease. I did a happy dance and hopefully when I see Dr. Patel in July I can hug his neck and thank him.

I hope everyone is staying safe in this crazy mess we have right now. My butt is staying home. I love you all and thank you for hanging with me these past months. You have been my lifesavers!

Prayers Please
May 12, 2020

I met yesterday with my plastic surgeon. I have what is commonly referred to as "dog ears" under both arms. The purpose of the revision surgery will be to get rid of the excess skin left from my surgery last July.

I like my surgeon and I have been given all clear from Dr. Patel. I shouldn't need to go back on blood thinners after this surgery. The surgery will be outpatient and will not be as intensive as my first surgery.

Please pray that my insurance will cover this. By law, insurance companies are supposed to cover revision surgery, but you all know the battles I have had this past year with things. When they approve, then the surgery will be scheduled.

My strength is slowly coming back. I did some yard work and took breaks every 10 minutes. I'm hoping to be able to start walking again but I'm trying to be aware of how my body feels and not overdo.

Thank you all so much for your continued prayers and thoughts. Thank you to those who continue to check on me and make sure I've got what I need. I'm staying home until June 12th per the governor and since they have now found a link between low Vitamin D and Covid-19. I'm definitely staying put!

Thank you in advance for lifting my concerns with my insurance company in your
prayers. I'll post an update when I know. I love you all!

September 2, 2020

Haven't updated in a while and wanted to share with those of you interested what is going on. First, my last CT scan showed: "Lungs: Minimal apical predominant centrilobular emphysema." So I googled it first and found out that this is associated with smoking. I have NEVER smoked, so this concerned me. Forgot to ask about it at my last meeting with my oncologist so I sent a message and was told that it is "chronic lung changes that can develop over time." That was from my oncologist's PA.

I will be following up on this at my next appointment later this month. Cancer and chemo continue to give. I left the oral surgeon's office today and I have been stress eating and crying. I have decay under one of the anchor teeth for my bridge. Here are my options:
1) I can have the tooth pulled and let the socket heal for 4 - 5 months while wearing a temporary partial. Then have implants (2 - 3) and a new bridge.
2) I can have a root canal and then have implants for a new bridge.
3.) I can have the tooth pulled and wear a partial.

Sounds like I have several options, however, there was one thing I was not prepared for...Prolia can cause issues with teeth. Yep, the very thing that is supposed to help my bones, causes issues with healing in the bones of the mouth. I just had a Prolia shot in June, so we would have to wait until close to December to remove the tooth to see if it is going to heal.

There is a chance that **Osteonecrosis** can set in if any bacteria remain. That would be death of the bone basically. This means that implants may not work, and a root canal may not work. I could spend $2800 per implant + $1100 for each unit of the bridge and have it all fail due to the Prolia. The oral surgeon said I would need to delay the shot in December and delay shots through the implant procedure and there are no guarantees that the implants would be successful. I could easily spend $10,000 to $15,000 dollars and this is only one side and who knows what will happen in the future. Then again, it could be successful.

As you can see, I'm in a state of frustration and dilemma. I know that as women age osteoporosis is something that happens. There was no evidence prior to chemo and with the last bone density test it reared its ugly head. My oncologist believes the chemo caused it. The other side of all this is that women who have been through chemo and radiation can also have issues with dental work.

I had thought (as my dentist had) that I had escaped the dental problems that follow chemo. I didn't and I am so frustrated. Sometimes I feel like I take one step forward only to slide 10 feet back. I'm just broken frustrated and discouraged. Thank you for allowing me to vent.

Acknowledgements

There are some special people whom I need to thank. Thank you to:

Stephanie Martin-Rohling for being an awesome oncology nurse navigator. For listening to my fears, holding my hand, and answering my questions. You have become a dear friend and helped me to navigate the most difficult journey I have ever experienced. Thank you also for your encouragement to write this book.

Dr. Minesh Patel for being a great doctor. You listened to my concerns and fears, were honest with me, and gave me the best treatment. You worried for me and I will be forever grateful for your decision to enter the world of oncology.

Dr. Sarah Klein for being a wonderful friend and didn't hesitate to say "yes" when I asked her to edit this book! You are a wonderful teacher and friend, and I can't even begin to tell you how much I appreciate you!

My crew…Jeani, Angie, Shannon, Lisa, and Jennifer for walking this journey with me. You were there every step of the way, encouraging and being my strength and support. You are my family!

My friends and students who supported my journey by purchasing #hyderstrong t-shirts, contributed to my GoFundMe account, sent cards, texts, prayers and read and commented on my blog entries. Without your love and words of comfort, I could have never completed this journey.

The doctors nurses and staff at Piedmont Cancer Institute who work day in and day out with cancer patients. You are a source of comfort and inspiration. Thank you for all you do to work with this disease. I cannot begin to imagine how hard it is to stay positive and supportive. Thank you for all your work and dedication. You are a wonderful staff and I love each of you.

To my readers who I will never meet. Thank you for taking time to read my words. I hope they provide a comfort and inspiration to you. Cancer does not have you…you can and will show it who is boss. Stay positive, stay motivated and stay hopeful.

*If you would like to contact me personally to share your story, please feel free to do so at: **rmbpublishing59@gmail.com**. I would love to hear from you.*

A portion of the sales from this book will go to Triple Negative Breast Cancer Research.

www.ingramcontent.com/pod-product-compliance
Lightning Source LLC
Chambersburg PA
CBHW071217240726
48654CB00009B/826